For the Radium Girls and all the lives
and loves they might have had.

And for Ashley Hearn, editor extraordinaire,
storytelling magician, and bookish fairy godmother.
Thank you for helping Kit, Jane, Quinta & Twain
make their ways into the world.

Published by Peachtree Teen
An imprint of PEACHTREE PUBLISHING COMPANY INC.
1700 Chattahoochee Avenue
Atlanta, Georgia 30318-2112
PeachtreeBooks.com

Text © 2022 by Jamie Pacton

Edited by Ashley Hearn
Jacket design by Lisa Marie Pompilio
Design and composition by Adela Pons
Map illustration by Catherine Scully

Printed and bound in September 2022 at Thomson Reuters, Eagan, MN, USA.
10 9 8 7 6 5 4 3 2 1
First Edition
ISBN: 978-1-68263-488-2

Library of Congress Control Number: 2022941159

JAMIE PACTON

THE
VERMILION
EMPORIUM

PEACHTREE
Teen

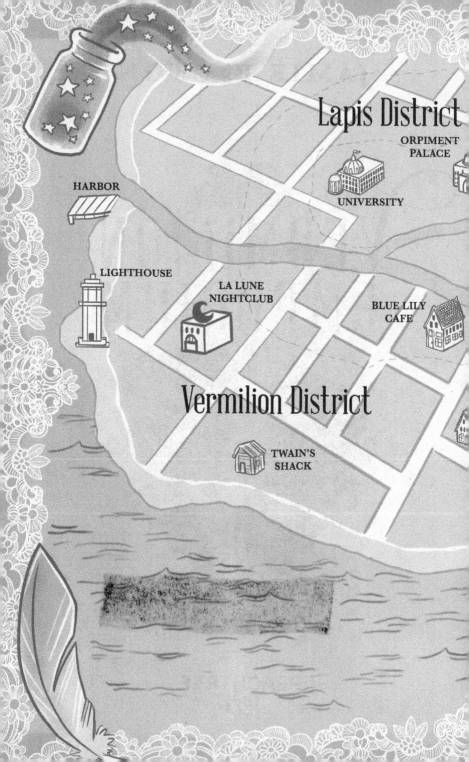

Lapis District

ORPIMENT PALACE

UNIVERSITY

HARBOR

LIGHTHOUSE

LA LUNE NIGHTCLUB

BLUE LILY CAFE

Vermilion District

TWAIN'S SHACK

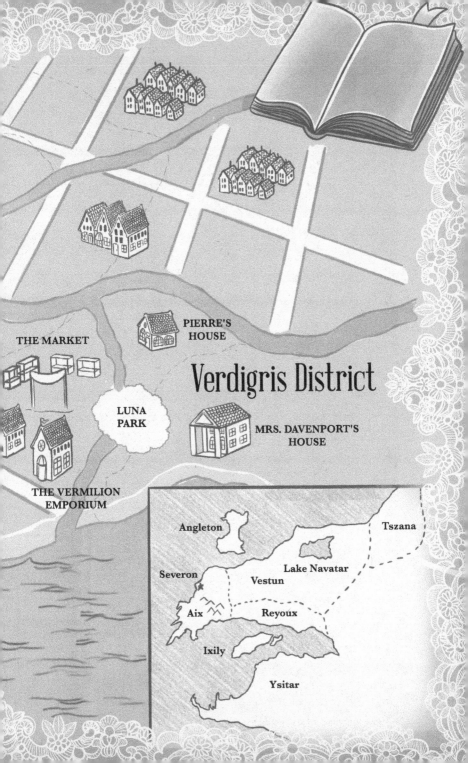

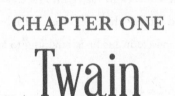

CHAPTER ONE
Twain

It was a day for finding things.

Twain Vernier knew it in his bones. Not that he had time to dwell on the knowledge, since he was currently clinging to a cliff face, half a mile off the coast of Severon, looking much more like a spider than a seventeen-year-old boy. A brusque October wind whipped around him, smelling of salt, snow that would soon arrive, and bird droppings. Relentless, the wind pulled Twain's hair out of the cord he'd tied it back with and cut through his thin shirt.

It was well past midday, and there was fierce music on the air. It howled: *You shouldn't be here, foolish boy. Go back down now, before it's too late.*

Ignoring the wind, Twain jammed his light-brown fingers deeper into the crevice beside his head. His muscles burned from the climb up the tower of stone, and his hands no longer looked like the carefully tended ones of a musician. His knuckles were bruised, his fingertips bloody. Good. Music was for a different time. A different Twain. He would break his fingers on this rock if that was what it took to reach the top and earn a way out of Severon.

Go!

With a shout, he lunged upward, snagging his fingers in a vertical crack a few inches to his right. His toes grazed a narrow ledge and he held himself there, legs trembling, breath catching in his throat, every muscle in his body straining to keep him on that cliff.

That was close. Too close, maybe.

Keep moving.

Twain willed himself not to look down. After three ragged inhales, he couldn't help it. He glanced past the slim shelf where his frozen toes curled around slick rock. Far below, waves pounded the stone tower. It had taken him most of the morning to row out to the rock; and now his rowboat bobbed in the dark water, held in place by an anchor. From where Twain clung to the cliff, the boat looked no bigger than a washbasin.

It was a long way down, and there were knife-sharp rocks beneath the foaming water.

Even this high up, icy spray splashed the edges of Twain's pants, stinging his bare feet. This late in the year, it was too cold to climb without shoes, but it was also impossible to make it to the razorbills' nests any other way. And Twain needed money more than he needed all his toes. If he moved fast enough, he might get to keep both.

Wrenching his eyes away from the gnashing teeth of the sea, Twain measured the distance to the razorbill colony on the ledge above his head. Piles of feathers littered the top of the stone tower. So close. But *close* wasn't there yet. He still had to scramble from below a horizontal shelf of rock and haul himself to the top. As he considered the rock face, the wind gusted, scattering some of the valuable feathers.

"No!" Twain shouted. He reached out to grab a feather as it floated past, but he missed. It was like watching gold fly into the sea.

Get moving now, before the rest of the feathers are swept away.

Ordinarily dull gray, razorbill feathers turned indigo when they dropped from the birds in the wild. None of Severon's Scientifica scholars knew why it happened, and the fierce raptors withered in captivity, their plumage never changing color. Scarce, beautiful, and deadly to retrieve, the indigo feathers were coveted by the richest women in Severon. For hats. Or the collars of velvet gowns. Or, in the rarest of cases, to make cloaks the color of nightshade.

It was said that the Casorina, the leader of Severon, had thirty such cloaks.

With this sort of demand, there used to be more climbers, but one by one they met their ends on the cliffs each season. Finally, only Twain and his younger brother, Zand, were left. Not that Zand was much of a climber—or that Zand was here anymore.

Twain swore as a knife of grief sliced through him. All he wanted was to forget that afternoon three months ago. He wanted to go back to who he was before Zand fell—a protective older brother and charming musician who played the violin in taverns, kissed girls who came to his shows, and climbed cliffs for feathers when he needed extra money. There was simplicity to those roles, and Twain knew how to fill them. He didn't know what do now that everything had changed.

Forget about that life. Ignore it all and move on.

Much as he wanted to, it was impossible to forget the way Zand's body had tumbled down this very rock pillar. Or the way the hungry waves pulled him under before Twain could reach him.

Twain closed his eyes, unable to silence Zand's scream in his head. That was the thing about someone you loved dying—you had to go on without them, even if you didn't want to. So you got out of bed every morning (on the mornings when you could). You put one foot in front of the other. And maybe someday, you'd wake up and it would hurt less. Or you wouldn't think you saw the person you'd lost all around town. Or you wouldn't hear their voice. Or their screams.

Twain let out a long, ragged inhale.

Just hang on. Climb this rock. You can do it.

In the months since Zand's death, Twain had made his way through their meager savings. He couldn't bring himself to play music anymore, and his tavern friends stopped asking about him. Today's desperate climb was his only chance of buying passage out of Severon.

If you can get to the razorbill feathers, you can name your price.

It was a bitter comfort and the only advantage of going out this late in the season.

Twain had failed to save his brother, but that didn't mean he intended to die on this rock. Shoving all thoughts of Zand away, Twain calmed his shaking hands. He shifted slightly, adjusting the canvas bag slung across his chest. Like an engineer, he examined the cracks in the pillar. Much to his scholar parents' chagrin, Twain had been climbing since before he could walk. This particular rock face was merely a puzzle. A labyrinth of lines and fissures for him to solve. The answer was here; he just had to find it.

The horizontal crevice above his head was outside his reach, but it would be quicker than trying to ease his way up the long vertical cleft to his right. It was likely certain death either way. But he'd woken up this morning with the sort of knowing that came to him sometimes: today was a day for finding things. And so, he would leap.

With a deep breath and a prayer to whatever gods or ghosts might be listening, Twain pushed off the cliff, lunging for the crevice. It was too far. Too much of a reach. Twain stretched to the end of his spine, fingers extending, grasping, slipping. Pebbles flew past Twain as he scrambled for a grip, a handhold, anything.

He missed.

His hands flailed, and his body slid down the cliff, stone shredding his shirt, ripping into his skin. There would be nothing of him left to find if he hit the rocks in the wrong place. But then a great gust of wind surged around him. It pinned him to the cliff for a moment, like a giant's hand holding him in place. Clambering, Twain caught himself in the slimmest of cracks. He shouted as pain surged across his shoulder. Then, his shout turned to a laugh. A great, high, golden sound of pure delight.

Twain lived for moments when he held life and death by his fingertips.

Hanging by one hand, halfway up a cliff, above a ravenous sea, he looked like a jewel dangling from a rich woman's ear. Spinning there for the world to admire. But there was no one to see. No one to marvel at how Twain's broad shoulders bunched as he pulled himself up the last few feet and then flopped onto the ledge covered in razorbills' nests.

He'd done it. Barely.

Hauling air into his chest, Twain lay on his back among the feathers. Gulls wheeled above, but there was no sign of the razorbills. If his luck held, they'd stay out at sea until he was long gone.

Slowly, painfully, Twain sat up and stuffed as many feathers as he could into his bag. Adrenaline coursed through him and his hands were shredded from the climb, but he had solid stone beneath him. And that counted for something. Once all the feathers on the top of the rock were securely in his satchel, Twain pulled back the pieces of his shirt and examined his wounds. A few scratches crisscrossed his chest, and one long cut dripped blood down the planes of his stomach. Gingerly, he prodded his ribs. Not broken. And he'd had worse before.

Relief flooded him as he caught his breath. He'd made it. That was something at least. Taking a canteen from his bag, Twain relaxed for a moment.

It was beautiful up here. All around him the sun glittered off the sea. Ships dotted the horizon like ants marching toward Severon. A three-masted ship with red-and-blue striped sails caught Twain's eye, and he watched it glide into the city's main harbor. Perhaps it was full of foreign scholars, sailing into Severon to study the rare Arcana texts in the Great Library. Or perhaps it was stuffed with fur-clad traders from the northern kingdoms, here to see what technological marvels had been crafted in Severon's Scientifica workshops. Or perhaps it held ordinary people eager for a glimpse of Severon's legendary museums and galleries.

Farther down the docks sat *The Lady's Revenge*, a freighter with bright-green sails. Twain's heart surged to see it. Today was October first. The *Revenge* was set to leave Severon on the last day of the month, headed on a voyage of adventure and discovery around the world. Twain was determined to be on it.

Twain stretched, letting the sun warm his frozen toes. *If only my parents could see me now. Ready to strike out around the world and leave Severon behind.*

They wouldn't have been proud, but they would've been relieved he was no longer their problem. It was Zand who would have missed him.

Now, no one will miss you.

The thought delivered another dagger of heartache, this one jagged-edged and twisting. Twain doubled over, surprised again at all the ways sorrow snuck up on him. Every morning he thought he would be fine, but at some point every day, grief brought him to his knees, filling him with regret.

Fuck. He missed Zand. He missed the way his brother's eyes would light up when reading a new tidbit of magical history. He missed the way they would fight over silly things, like who ate the last heel of bread. He missed Zand's loud laugh and the way he brought home stray cats. Twain missed all the tiny nothing things that somehow added up to making a tremendous person.

If he could talk to Zand one more time he'd apologize. Tell him that—

Stop.

Such thoughts do no good. Especially when you're so very alone.

Roughly, Twain swiped his bruised palm across his eyes. It came away wet.

You're not here for feelings. You're here for feathers.

To stop the grief, he would do what his mother taught him: observe, detach. *Scientifica scholars prize logic over emotion*, she would remind him time and time again.

"Too bad I never made it as a scholar," Twain muttered to the sky and sea. "Maybe then this wouldn't hurt so much."

Observe, detach.

It wasn't much by way of loving parental advice, but it was good enough to stop Twain from falling apart on a pillar of rock in the middle of the sea.

Observe.

Twain looked toward Severon, capital of Aix and the great jewel on the coast. From this height, the city looked like an artist's messy paint palate. That dash of yellow in the middle was the Orpiment palace—home of the Casorina. It gleamed in the afternoon sun, its roof winking with golden shingles. Filling the space beside the Orpiment were the dull browns of the university and Great Library. Ringing those buildings was a swath of bright blue marking the Lapis Loop. Aptly named, the museums, galleries, restaurants, and boutiques in Lapis had dazzling cerulean porticos, roofs, and columns. Along the bluffs above the sea stretched the Verdigris District. The oldest, most expensive mansions there were roofed in copper that had turned blue-green—verdigris—through the years.

And then there were the crimson splashes of the Vermilion neighborhoods. Roofed in cheap red clay tiles, they filled in the gaps between Verdigris and Lapis, unfolding all the way to Severon's beaches. Once, there'd been talk of walling up Vermilion, as if that could keep the district from spreading somehow; but, such plans were quickly dismissed because too many rich people liked to slip into its dark lanes, cafés, bookstores, brothels, and shops.

Twain's house, a small shack at the fringe of the Vermilion neighborhoods, was tucked between a dozen other falling-down workers' cottages. From this far out at sea, he couldn't tell which one was his. Along the eastern horizon of Severon rose the mountains that walled off Aix from its larger, fiercer neighbors. When he was small, Twain had spent many nights being quizzed by his Arcana scholar father on how the protection of the mountains had helped Severon grow into the magnificent city it was today.

Not that Twain found much magnificence here now. The thought reminded him of why he was on the pillar of rock. *Time to get going.*

Twain looked around for any feathers he had missed. A large bunch of them were crammed into a crack in the rock, tucked among a pair of nests. Twain shoved his hand inside the opening, pulling out a handful. But that wasn't the only thing that emerged. Something silvery and sleek lay among the deep purple of the feathers.

"It can't be," Twain murmured.

Dropping the razorbill feathers into his bag, he carefully pulled at the silvery thread. It was strung with bits of seaweed, nest, and tiny fluffs.

The silver filament glistened, sparkling like dew-soaked spider's silk. A soft, metallic song emanated from the thread. As Twain closed his eyes, listening to the melody, a series of images whispered with the music, singing to him of a dark-eyed girl, a circus under the stars, and a million wishes.

Gently, he turned the thread over in his hands.

It was starlight.

He had found a thread of starlight.

The thought nearly made him fall off the rock.

Starlight was more coveted than anything else in Severon—maybe more so than anything else in the world. Two centuries ago, the Salon, a small group of Severon's artists, painted with starlight and made lace from it. Twain's father used to tell him stories of magical lace that could shape the future and change the world.

According to the history books, only the Salon members knew where the starlight came from, and they took the secret to their graves. No one had found a sliver of starlight in a very long time, but here was Twain, coiling an entire thread of the stuff around his arm. It glowed there like a priceless bracelet, singing its melancholy song.

Twain let out a shout of triumph, startling a pair of gulls who'd landed on the cliff beside him. If he wasn't so far above the sea, he might dance.

Because the thread of starlight would get him more money than cartloads of razorbill feathers. With it, he'd be able to buy new clothes and passage out of Severon, and he could start a life—a good life—somewhere far across the sea.

He stared over the water, his mind churning with possibilities. With the money from this thread of starlight, he could find the freedom he'd always longed for. He could reinvent himself and travel the world. He could buy a better violin (if he ever started playing again) or a home in Verdigris—something he and Zand had fantasized about on long, cold nights in their shack.

With this strand of starlight, he could do anything.

Well, almost anything.

He certainly couldn't use it to fly off this rock. Which was a more pressing problem than deciding how to spend his hypothetical riches.

Careful not to damage the starlight, Twain began the long trek back down the cliff, confident his life was about to change entirely.

CHAPTER TWO
Quinta

It was a day for finding things.

Quinta Aurore, a sour-faced girl who'd barely managed to survive her seventeen years, knew it in her bones. But she'd been at the photography studio where she worked since dawn, and right now, she had no time for finding anything. It was all she could do not to lose her temper as she adjusted the portrait screen behind Mrs. Davenport, a tall, broad white woman wearing a ridiculous witch's costume. Mrs. Davenport was a wealthy, middle-aged widow, and this was her thirteenth portrait session this month, a fact she considered quite lucky.

"Find your pose, please," instructed Pierre, the photographer who owned the studio. As always, he was dapper in a well-fitting suit and a green silk scarf that set off his golden-brown skin perfectly. He adjusted the bellows on his camera, bringing the image into focus.

"Like this?" Mrs. Davenport warbled, looking over her shoulder and holding out her left arm, as if she were casting a spell. A pointed, spangled hat perched on her head precariously.

"Beguiling," Pierre cooed, still looking through the lens. "Quinta, her cape!"

Quinta scowled as she smoothed out the long piece of cloth that flowed off Mrs. Davenport's shoulders. Fluffing it twice for the "added mystery" Pierre's shop specialized in, Quinta stepped over the chalk line on the floor that marked the photo's space.

"And, hold it!" demanded Pierre.

Mrs. Davenport tried, she really did; but, right as Pierre pushed the glass plate into the camera, she lost her balance, tumbling forward and landing in a mess of cape, stars, spangles, and props. Pierre swore under his breath, and Mrs. Davenport blushed.

"They'll never let me in at this rate," she muttered to herself. "Not even with my pedigree."

"They" were the Severon Witches Society, an elitist group of rich women who cherished nothing more than getting together in their drafty mansions to shuffle decks of tarot cards, read spells out of old books, and get their photos taken in absurd costumes. By all rights, Mrs. Davenport should be part of their ranks, since, like Quinta, she was descended from one of the original magical Salon members. But the SWS members were snooty and didn't quite think Mrs. Davenport was worthy of them yet.

Poor Mrs. Davenport had been trying to join for the last few years, but her photos kept getting rejected, and to date, she'd not provided the SWS with any useful magical information.

Which was really a ridiculous bar for entry since magic had been gone from Severon for nearly two hundred years. Still, that didn't mean Arcana scholars and the richest ladies in the Verdigris District weren't looking for it. Magic was the key to power, prestige, and fashion, the likes of which hadn't been seen in centuries. Mrs. Davenport, and all the women like her, craved it more than anything else.

Quinta knew the feeling well.

As Quinta rushed to help Mrs. Davenport stand up, her eyes darted to the wall where photos of SWS members hung. Thanks to Pierre's techniques, one woman drank tea with a skeleton stylized as Death. In another photo, a young lady rode a broom over the rooftops of Severon. There were dozens of others, all outrageous and so clearly fake.

But those images weren't what held Quinta's gaze. It was the picture of her mother, the Grand Eleina—leading lady and former owner of Severon's once-famous Celestial Circus—she couldn't turn away from. Proudly displayed in the center of all the SWS photos, this one showed a beautiful white woman wearing a flowing dress and sitting on the edge of a fake crescent moon. She hardly looked old enough to have been a mother and, unlike Quinta, her face wasn't permanently scrunched up in dismay.

"You should smile more," her mother used to say. "Otherwise no one will know what a great destiny you have before you."

Quinta's scowl deepened to remember that, and she asked herself the same question she always did as she looked at her mother's portrait: Was she more furious at her mother for dying than sorry she was gone?

Yes? No? Both? She didn't know.

Letting out a frustrated sigh, Quinta touched the small glass bottle hanging from a ribbon around her neck. Her mother had given Quinta the bottle right before she died—instructing her to open it only if she had no other hope. Inside swirled the barest bit of moonshadow. It was bright blue, decidedly magical, and Quinta had no idea what to do with it.

Not that she hadn't tried. But trying had only brought her a long line of failures. There was her botched attempt to become an Arcana scholar and learn more about magic. And the disastrous magical demonstration she'd tried to put on using a spell she'd paid a trader for. And that child she couldn't save from the cold. And that time she—

Stop. Even if you've failed a hundred times, that doesn't mean you stop trying. You are meant for great things.

It was another of her mother's sayings, and Quinta fought hard to remind herself of it. Especially on the dark days.

"She was so talented," the SWS members would say when they looked at Eleina's photo. "We thought for certain she'd be the one to bring magic back to Severon."

Eleina and Quinta had thought that too. Which was why, when she wasn't performing in the circus, Quinta's mother was reading books about starlight magic, always searching for what their ancestor Marali, founder of the Salon, had discovered. But the answer to the origin of starlight was elusive, and Eleina's obsession with finding it grew more intense every day. In exchange for peeks into the SWS members' libraries, she and Quinta would haul all sorts of props, books, and equipment to Verdigris mansions. Together, Quinta and her mother would spin outrageous tales of starlight lace and magic. Eleina always promised the SWS that she was close to discovering where the threads of starlight came from. It had been a great way to earn extra coins, even if it was all a lie.

Until it wasn't.

Until something in the magic Eleina was trying to do killed her.

Even after seven years, Quinta didn't know what had destroyed her mother and she didn't know what to do with the bottle of moonshadow, but she knew she wanted magic. Real magic. Like the kind her ancestors had. The type of magic that would change her life for the better and make her the master of her own fate. The kind that would turn her from a failure into someone actually meant for great things.

"Quinta," Pierre called, interrupting her thoughts. "Can you fetch the skeleton please?"

"Oh yes!" Mrs. Davenport cheered, clapping her hands. "Bring Old Skelly for the next photo!"

Frowning, Quinta let go of the bottle of moonshadow and hauled a rattling bunch of bones out of Pierre's supply closet. She placed the skeleton beside Mrs. Davenport, who beamed at it.

"Enchanting," Mrs. Davenport murmured. "He's so handsome!"

Quinta rolled her eyes and stepped out of the photo's setup. She wasn't here to haul skeletons. She'd taken the job with her mother's former Celestial Circus companion, Pierre, because the SWS members thought she was too poor and untalented to let her into their secret meetings—but they did nothing but gossip when they were getting their photos taken. This was how Quinta tried (unsuccessfully so far) to learn more about her family's magical legacy.

"Do you think these pictures will help you get into the SWS?" Pierre asked Mrs. Davenport, as he set up a giant cauldron beside Skelly for the next photo. An amused smile quirked on his lips. He was happy to take business from the SWS, but Quinta knew he thought all their attempts at magic were fool's errands. He had studied in the Scientifica before turning to photography full time.

"I'm hopeful," Mrs. Davenport said, rather breathlessly. "I have incredibly useful information. I heard yesterday—from a fortune-teller's maid I met in the market—that a shop, which sells magical items, is coming to Severon soon. We've heard whispers of such things before, but to have them really appear here! What a treat! If only I knew where it was going to be."

"A shop that sells magical things?" Quinta asked, her attention wrenched away from her own thoughts.

Quinta's voice was hungry, eager, ravenous. It was so surprising, Pierre stared at her for a moment. Quinta was not usually given over to excitement, and he looked at her like she might be coming down with something. She shot him a small smile.

"That's right," Mrs. Davenport trilled. "The magical shop is supposed to appear tonight, somewhere in the city."

As Mrs. Davenport leaned over the giant cauldron, pretending to stir a witch's brew, Quinta ran her hand over the business card she always carried in her pocket. Her mother had given it to her moments before she died. It was worn smooth from all the worrying Quinta's fingers had done over the years. Despite the card's age, its letters were still bright crimson, and they practically glowed:

"Find this place," her mother had said with her last breaths. "You'll understand what to do with the moonshadow then."

It seemed like an easy-enough task when Quinta first took the card, but her search had only brought more failure. She'd walked the twisted streets of the Vermilion District for years looking for the shop, but there was no such place in Severon. Nor was it in any of the other cities Quinta had visited surreptitiously, using the funds she picked from the purses of women like Mrs. Davenport. The Vermilion Emporium was a nowhere place, a shop that didn't exist. Except on the card in her hand.

Even if you've failed a hundred times, that doesn't mean you stop trying. You are meant for great things.

"Do you remember the name of the shop?" Quinta couldn't keep the hope from her voice.

Mrs. Davenport shrugged. "I don't. But it's supposed to be quite a wonder."

Quinta plopped down on a leopard-skin-covered ottoman. It was a better chance than she'd had in a very long time. Pierre caught her eye and raised one eyebrow expectantly. She gave him the barest of nods.

Tonight.

Everything would change tonight. She just knew it.

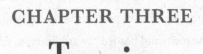

CHAPTER THREE
Twain

Twain made it off the rock tower somehow. Yes, the descent from the razorbills' nests to his boat was a blur of controlled falling. But, importantly, he didn't die on the way down. And he didn't lose any of the feathers or the silver strand of starlight. He'd tied it around his neck like a scarf once he was in the boat, but now he was having a hard time resisting the impulse to wind it around his hands like a child with a bit of string. The music from the starlight had quieted, but the echo of its melody filled his head. Perhaps he would try to play it on his violin tonight?

No. He wouldn't do that. Even if the starlight music was beautiful, he wasn't ready to play again. And his fingers were bleeding anyway.

Just get back to the city. Everything else comes after that.

He raised the small boat's anchor and glanced up at the cliffs again.

Where had the starlight come from? How had the birds found it? Would there be more here if he dared to come back?

"One thing at a time," he whispered to himself, remembering the way Zand used to say it as they were studying together for the Scholar's Exam. "First you have to sell what you found."

Putting his back into it, Twain rowed away from the cliff. The waves fought him, wanting to push him into the wall. Somehow, he made it past the rocks and headed toward Severon, thinking only of the starlight around his neck.

The sea was choppy, but eventually, arms aching, he steered his boat through the surf and into the shallows. Before anyone could see, Twain undid the loop of starlight at his neck and coiled it into a knot in his pocket. Then, he jumped out of the boat. Salt stung the scratches on his calves and feet as he pulled the craft onto the shore.

It had taken Twain most of the afternoon to climb down the cliff and row back to Severon. Already the sun lingered near the western horizon, sending his shadow across the beach like a sentinel. As he settled the boat in the sand, Twain waved to Horst, an old man who sat outside a cottage near the shore.

"Did you find anything?" Horst called as he strolled toward Twain. Tobacco stains yellowed Horst's beard, and his face was lined from spending long hours squinting at the horizon. Raising an eyebrow at Twain's bloody, torn shirt, Horst tossed Twain the boots, socks, and coat Twain had left with him.

"It was a good haul," Twain admitted as he sat down on the sand and brushed off his feet. His socks stuck to his toes as he slipped them on. "Once I sell the feathers, I'll bring some coins back to you."

"You don't need to pay me." Horst waved a hand in the direction of his cottage. "Want to eat supper with us? Martha is making fish stew."

Twain's stomach growled at the invitation, reminding him he hadn't eaten since the bruised apple he'd choked down before leaving his shack at dawn.

"I should get going." He pulled his boots and his coat on quickly. He wanted to stay, but eating with Horst and Martha was not as simple as enjoying a warm meal with kind people.

Two years ago, Twain and Zand's parents had been lost at sea during a nasty storm. They'd been out for a pleasure cruise on their patron's ship, but the squall had come out of nowhere. After their deaths, the patron's widow, a wealthy woman whose husband had supported Twain's family for years, refused to give the newly orphaned boys any more money. In those first lean months, Twain and Zand learned not to trust anyone but themselves and Horst and Martha, a pair of retired musicians Twain had befriended as a child. Before turning fisherman, Horst had been a famous violinist, and he'd taught Twain to play. Twain and Zand had eaten at the old couple's table half a hundred times over the last two years. Or, they had, until Zand passed the Arcana Scholar's Exam earlier that year and gotten a whole new set of fancy friends.

"Are you sure you don't want to eat with us?" Horst pressed. "You're looking mighty thin."

Twain shook his head. "I'd love to, really. But I can't tonight."

Eating at Horst's table meant there might be questions. He and Martha might want to see the feathers Twain had found. They might somehow catch a glimpse of the starlight or hear its song. And Twain wasn't ready to risk that. Or to sit at the table where his brother had once laughed. Where his seat would be achingly empty. Twain hadn't joined Martha and Horst for dinner since Zand died, and he still wasn't ready.

"Next time then," Horst said agreeably. "Thanks for bringing my boat back in one piece."

"Thanks again for letting me use it."

They looked at the boat for a moment. Between them was that day three months ago when Twain and Zand had gone out to sea together, but only Twain had returned. And all the times Twain had taken the boat out after that, searching the water for Zand's body. And how Horst finally had to lock the boat up because Twain wanted to sail farther and farther, on the chance his brother might be somewhere he could reach.

Today had been the first time that Twain had rowed out since then.

"It's good to see you working again." Horst patted Twain on the shoulder roughly. "I think Zand would've wanted you to stay busy."

Horst made a noise in his throat, as if he wanted to say more, but the words got stuck there.

Twain swallowed hard and nodded. "I'll be back before long with coins."

"Forget about all that. You take care of yourself and keep the money. Boat's yours whenever you need it."

Twain turned away before Horst could see the tears in his eyes.

✳

To get from the beach up to the city, Twain had to climb a set of wobbly wooden stairs. Farther on down, near the Verdigris District, stone steps had been carved into the steep bluff that separated the city from the beach, but on this side of town the steps were made from driftwood, broken planks from ships, and whatever else could be shaped into a passable staircase. It wasn't quite as risky as the cliffside ascent Twain made this morning, but still, he held the railing as he climbed.

He was halfway to the top when two young white men came stumbling down the stairs, making the whole structure sway. One wore pinstripe pants and an expensive-looking red vest over a wine-stained shirt. Strands of unkempt blond hair hung beneath his bowler hat. The other was hatless, his brown hair shaved short, his mustache well-waxed and curled extravagantly. He wore glasses, a white shirt, black pants, and a rumpled purple velvet jacket.

"Move," muttered the man with the bowler hat as he shoved past Twain. His voice was rough, and he stank of booze.

Exhausted from his day of climbing and not wanting a fight, Twain bit back a reply and stepped out of the way so the two could pass. He kept his eyes down, though his hands curled into fists at his side.

He knew who these men were: Gustave and Henri, Arcana scholars who'd studied at the university with Zand. They were both from wealthy families and they'd never liked Twain—not when he dragged Zand away from their late-night card games or when he refused to pay Zand's debts after a game went sideways. Twain had been dodging them for months, certain they'd only bring him trouble. But there was no way to avoid them on this very narrow, rickety staircase. He only hoped he could get past without Gustave and Henri recognizing him, which might be possible since he was much thinner and his dark hair was longer than it had been the last time he saw them.

The man with the ridiculous mustache—Gustave—paused in front of Twain. He was long and lean, and his hands were smooth, telling the story of his upbringing in a Verdigris mansion.

"Do I know you?" Gustave peered at Twain, adjusting his smudged glasses. He stepped forward.

Twain shook his head, hurrying up the next step. "Don't think so."

Gustave gripped Twain's arm with surprisingly strong fingers. "I think I do. You're Zand's big brother. The musician. Don't you think it looks like him, eh, Henri?"

"That's him alright." Henri lifted the brim of his hat in a mocking salute. "Where are you coming from? The gambling tables?" He nodded to the rows of ramshackle buildings farther down the beach, closer to the harbor. "Do you share Zand's bad luck?"

"Where I'm coming from is none of your business," Twain said sharply.

"Since your brother is dead, our business is with you." Gustave pushed his fingers deeper into Twain's arm.

"Leave me alone."

"Your brother stole something that belongs to me." Henri's voice held a dangerous edge. "Something valuable that I intend to have back. Maybe you've seen an invitation to the Scholar's Ball lying around your place?"

Twain's heart sped up. He knew what they were talking about because he'd found the silver-and-blue invitation last week. It had been tucked under the floorboards of the shack he'd shared with Zand, wrapped in cloth and hidden away in the farthest corner. Twain's hands had brushed over it while he was looking for the last of the coins they'd saved.

"I don't know what you're talking about," he lied, trying to keep his voice calm.

"Come now." Henri tucked his hands in his vest pockets. "Surely little Zand told you about the Scholar's Ball?"

Of course Twain knew about the Casorina's legendary annual ball. It was a place for Arcana and Scientifica scholars and guests from all over the world to mingle with the richest people in Severon. For some it meant a night of decadent food and entertainment that they could never afford in their normal lives. For others it was a chance to share ideas with like-minded souls. And, for a very few of the most brilliant scholars, it was an opportunity to find a wealthy patron.

Admittance to the ball was by invitation only, and Twain's parents had attended it regularly. Only a select few first-year scholars were invited, and Zand had been one of them.

"I've heard of the ball," Twain said carefully. "Why would you have an invitation? Zand told me you weren't invited."

Gustave leaned forward, his boozy breath washing over Twain. "Did he also tell you he gambled his invitation away?"

Twain knew that too. It had been one of the reasons they'd fought on the morning of Zand's death.

Henri didn't let him answer. "Your thief of a brother lost his invitation fair and square, and then he stole it back from us. We've been trying to find you for the last three months."

"Zand lied about where he came from," Gustave added. "Told us he was from a good family of scholars. One with a wealthy patron. We didn't expect you to be down here with the fishing scum."

Twain wrenched his arm out of Gustave's grip, his anger rising. "I'm not my brother, and his debts aren't mine. I don't have your invitation." He moved up another step, trying to put distance between himself and the two men.

Gustave snatched at Twain's bag. "Even if you don't have the invitation, maybe we'll take what you have here and call it even?"

His hand snaked into the bag and pulled out a razorbill's feather. Twain grabbed for it, but Gustave stepped back, laughing.

"Ooo, now isn't this a pretty thing." He held it above his head, like it was stuck into a hat. "Look at me," he said in a high-pitched, mocking voice. "I'm a fancy Severon lady, ready for a dance at the Casorina's palace."

"That's mine." Twain snatched the feather away from Gustave. He was all too aware of the coil of starlight in his pocket. And what Henri and Gustave would do to get their hands on something like that.

He could still hear the starlight music, but it was fainter now. Drowned out by the rush of his heartbeat. Gustave and Henri didn't seem to hear the melody at all.

Before Twain could move away, Gustave shoved him against the cliff wall and Henri stepped forward, pinning Twain by the shoulders.

"Let me go!" Twain shouted, struggling to break free. He was bigger than both of them and he knew how to fight, but it was two against one on a very precarious staircase. A wrong move could kill them all.

"Not until you tell us where the invitation is," Gustave snarled, throwing a punch.

With the reflexes of someone who'd dodged punches since he was a child, Twain avoided the blow and kicked out at Gustave, hitting him in the groin. Gustave doubled over with a cry, and his glasses tumbled off his face. Henri tightened his grip on Twain's shoulders, but Twain was bigger and faster. Grabbing Henri's lapels, he slammed the top of his head into Henri's forehead. The blow was harder than Twain intended, and, as Twain released him, Henri stumbled, landing against the wobbly staircase railing. There was a splintering sound, then a crash, as the railing shattered beneath Henri's weight. With a surprised cry, Henri lurched backward, falling toward the beach far below.

Henri's scream rent the air, and Twain turned away. It was Zand all over again. He couldn't have stopped it— He hadn't meant to push him— He shouldn't have fought— Fuck. What was he going to do now?

Gustave's eyes widened as Henri screamed again. Then, it was silent on the beach below.

"You killed my friend!" Gustave roared, fumbling to put his glasses back on. "Do you know who his father is? You're dead!" He punched wildly at Twain.

Twain darted away from Gustave's blows. Beneath him the stairs swayed, off balance as more of them shattered.

Get moving. Now!

There was no time for thinking or fighting. Twain raced upward, taking the steps three at a time.

A sickening crack filled the air as more stairs sheared off behind him. Gustave shouted, but Twain didn't look back. He was nearly to the top of the staircase. The gas lamps of the Vermilion District glowed in front of him. With a burst of speed Twain leaped up the last four steps, landing on his injured belly. His breath whooshed out of him and pain lanced up his side. A moment later, the entire staircase crumpled beneath him.

Twain gasped for breath, his hands shaking as he lay in the gravel at the top of the cliff.

It was the second time that day he'd cheated death by seconds. He glanced down at the wreck of the staircase. Pieces of wood, fragments of rope, and two lumpy shapes lay on the beach far below. One of them was moving, but the other—a crumpled figure who was somehow still wearing a bowler hat—didn't move. The broken bodies were too much like Zand's, and Twain had to look away.

What would happen to him if Henri and Gustave were dead? They had powerful parents and rich connections—people who would miss them and make sure to hang the person responsible for their deaths.

Twain swore under his breath. Now more than ever, he needed to get out of Severon.

But first he had to sell the razorbill feathers and the starlight. Then he'd book passage on the *Lady's Revenge* and lie low so no more of his brother's debts or so-called friends could find him.

Hauling himself to his feet, Twain readjusted his bag and pulled up the collar of his coat. His body ached with every step, but he started walking. Soon, he was just another shape moving through the maze of streets in the Vermilion District, lost among the shadows of the coming night.

CHAPTER FOUR
Quinta

Quinta *had* to find the magical shop. Her entire life had been building up to this moment, and she was going to find the store. Even if she had to walk every damn street in Severon. Even if her shoes fell apart and she wore herself thin. She. Was. Going. To. Find. It.

She wasn't going to fail again. She was going to live up to her mother's legacy.

Except Quinta didn't just want her mother's legacy. She was going to be so much more than a circus performer who did parlor tricks for the SWS. She was going to use magic to have real power. People would look up to her and respect her for what she could do. She wouldn't die ordinary and be forgotten. She would be remarkable and successful and remembered.

You are meant for great things.

She was certain of it.

Mostly.

But first she had to find the shop Mrs. Davenport had mentioned. Quinta didn't let herself imagine that the shop wouldn't appear or admit the possibility that it might not be the Vermilion Emporium. Belief was important in these cases, and she had it in spades.

Her heeled boots clicked along the cobblestones as she strode through the city like a bloodhound following a scent. A nearby bell tower chimed five o'clock, and already the light waned, as it did at this time of year. Quinta wasn't sure where she was going, but something urged her through the jumble of Vermilion's streets. It was likely the wind, but it sounded like her mother's voice whispering: *hurry now; keep going; you're almost there.*

"Hey, Quinta," called out a loud male voice from a food stall as she passed.

She spun around, scowling. It was Raif, a handsome redheaded baker she'd once foolishly spent the night with after too many drinks in a pub. She usually avoided his food stall but hadn't realized she was on his street until it was too late.

"What?" she snapped. The smell of pastries on his counter made her stomach rumble, but she ignored it.

Raif shot her a lazy smile. "Where you been? Step on over here so we can catch up."

Impatient, she waved his words away. "Not a chance. I've got somewhere to be."

"Where?"

"Not telling." She didn't bother mentioning she wasn't quite sure where it was she was going. That was her problem.

"Too bad for you," Raif said, waggling an eyebrow. "What will you do without me?" He flexed his bicep, and she rolled her eyes, furious at her former self's terrible judgment. She was not a girl who stayed longer than one night, and she made a point to avoid anyone who might want more than that.

"I'll muddle through," she called over her shoulder.

Raif's laugh followed her into an unfamiliar backstreet. She hurried down it, eyes moving over every new sign and shop window. At the end of the alley, she turned left, slipping into a maze of smaller passageways. Drunks, children in ragged clothing, and sex workers leaned out of the doorways in this part of the city. She leaped over a pile of filth in the street but failed to keep her dress out of a foul-smelling puddle on the other side.

"Dammit," Quinta cursed under her breath as she marched on. At least she wasn't meeting anyone or going anywhere fancy tonight.

Narrow alley after narrow alley opened before her as she snaked through the Vermilion District. At one point she passed a pair of run-down men in green Scientifica robes, who were fiddling with a box of gears.

"Does the lady care to see some of the newest Scientifica technology?" asked one of the men.

"This is going to change the world!" promised the other, holding up a clock with its guts hanging out. "This uses only steam to keep time and is precise to the minute."

"Not interested," Quinta growled, hurrying past them.

At the end of the closest lane was a store she didn't recognize— something with a red-painted sign. Maybe it was the Vermilion Emporium? She hurried toward it, her heart pounding.

But no. The sign above the store said MIDNIGHT MILLINER AND LADY'S ALTERATIONS. The window was full of scandalous-looking gowns, and a pair of well-rouged women stood outside it, arguing loudly over the merits of a low-cut black dress.

Quinta kept walking.

She headed north, where Vermilion butted up against Lapis. Storming into Lapis like a hurricane, she strode past coffee shops filled with students and scholars. Her stomach complained—she ignored it, turning down street after street. Finally, near the Great Library, her stomach yowled so loudly she had to stop.

Fine. Maybe she could spare the time for one cup of coffee. She turned toward a small café near the library steps and froze when someone called her name.

"Quinta? Is that you?" It was a hopeful voice, belonging to a very pretty Black girl nearly hidden behind a pile of books.

For heaven's sake. Apparently Quinta's trek to find the Vermilion Emporium was going to take her past every ex-one-night stand of hers in Severon. Which is why she usually preferred to stay at home, reading books about magic and ignoring everyone.

She turned, a sheepish smile on her face. "Hello, Alice. I hadn't planned on meeting you here."

Alice's face lit up, and she pushed her glasses up her nose. "It's really lovely to see you. I'm busy studying, but could I buy you coffee? We could talk, like old times?"

Alice was a Scientifica scholar. She and Quinta met in the library last year and became friends. One rainy evening, after too much wine, they spent the night together. That tryst had brought forth a torrent of feelings on Alice's part and filled Quinta with regret. She knew Alice liked this coffee shop for studying, and, like Raif's food stall, she usually avoided it.

"Sorry, I can't. Have to be somewhere."

Alice's face fell as Quinta slipped into the crowd. Quinta mentally kicked herself for not being more careful with where she was walking. The heartbroken look on Alice's face was why Quinta didn't stay more than one night. Why she didn't fall in love. She was a disappointment. A failure. Someone who would always let you down. It was best people knew that about her from the beginning, before things got serious.

Which was why she needed magic—so she could remake herself into someone entirely new. That version of Quinta wouldn't disappoint or fail. That Quinta would be someone who mattered and who made a difference in the world.

But she was a long way from being that girl.

Head full of dark, terrible thoughts, Quinta moved away from the well-lit streets of Lapis. A cold breeze blew through the city, making the flames in the gas streetlamps flicker and Quinta pull her jacket close as she marched on.

Back in Vermilion, she hurried through neighborhoods where squat houses overflowed with dirty, screaming children; in Verdigris, she marched past ancient mansions where nannies watched over children in pristine clothing. The city's clocks chimed six, then seven. Quinta walked and walked until the sun was below the horizon. Her stomach rumbled more loudly, insistent and angry.

One more street. Just one more. Then she'd stop for dinner. She turned toward a wide lane, full of tiny shops and junk stores. It was the perfect place for a magical shop to appear. Was that a new store at the end of the lane? It looked possible, and its narrow windows were stuffed with grubby old things.

She hurried toward it, heart in her throat.

But no. OLIVER'S ANTIQUES was all the sign said. And it was closed. Dammit.

Picking up a wine bottle from the gutter, Quinta flung it at the nearest wall with a shout of frustration. The bottle smashed, raining glass onto a pile of crates and startling a pair of alley cats who yowled at her indignantly.

"Sorry, kitties," Quinta murmured, bending down to pet one of the cats. It hissed and hurried away.

She probably deserved that.

Letting out a deep breath, Quinta took herself in hand. She had to accept the truth: she was never going to find the Vermilion Emporium. Severon was an enormous city, full of thousands of stores and even more people. Mrs. Davenport was always making up things to get into the SWS, and this information of hers about the magical shop was probably no good.

Quinta hated that she'd believed it for a moment. That she'd let herself hope. That she'd bumped into Raif and Alice, two people who reminded Quinta of how awful she really could be. She wasn't going to find the Emporium tonight, and there was no sense in walking through the city so she could run into even more people she'd disappointed.

Turning away from the noise of the city, Quinta slipped into Luna Park, a gorgeous, wooded space that marked the boundary between the Vermilion and Verdigris neighborhoods. Quinta knew this place, though it had been a long time since she'd been here.

Leaves crunched under her feet as she cut through avenues of maples, which whispered in the wind. In the shadows of an ancient oak, a pair of men embraced. She scowled at them as she passed. Fools. Thinking anything like love would last.

She plunged deeper into the shadows. Luna Park was dangerous at night—the Casorina's guards didn't patrol the Vermilion section like they did the other districts—but it was also the fastest way back to her apartment above Pierre's studio.

Quinta moved toward a small pond in the middle of the park. This place was so familiar it hurt like a splinter, buried beneath her skin. She stopped beside the pond, taking a deep breath. The air smelled of earth, pond water, and something that Quinta could only describe as memory. It was almost too cold for frogs to be out, but still they sang their melancholy songs. Across the pond stood an enormous cedar that had been brought to Severon many years ago by some ambitious horticulturist.

Oh, that tree.

Who knew a tree could make her heart ache so painfully?

Quinta closed her eyes for a moment, remembering the worst night of her life. Like now, it had been early October. She had been ten and asleep in the small circus trailer she shared with her mother. Quinta had been dreaming of walking through the Great Library when a scream woke her. Knowing something was awfully, terribly wrong, Quinta ran outside, calling for her mother. She found her collapsed beneath the cedar, eyes wide with terror, gasping for breath.

"What can I do? How can I save you?" Quinta had asked, desperate, terrified. Her hands fluttered uselessly along her mother's arms, her face. The Grand Eleina writhed, gritting her teeth against invisible pain. It was agony to watch.

When Eleina could speak, she managed: "There's nothing you can do, my love. I've done this to myself, trying to gather moonshadow. . . ."

She had only been able to give Quinta the moonshadow in the bottle, and the card for the Vermilion Emporium, and convey one last wish before she died.

"Find this place. It will help you understand the purpose of the moonshadow."

You are meant for great things.

Wrenching herself back into the present, Quinta let out a shaky breath.

Dammit. Even if Mrs. Davenport had been lying, she couldn't give up. Not if there was some small chance that the Vermilion Emporium was in Severon. After all, she needed the Emporium to figure out what do with the moonshadow.

Quinta gripped the bottle at her neck, watching the blue substance inside undulate, like a slippery eel in a basket.

Quinta never had the chance to ask her mother more questions about the moonshadow. Every night since her mother's death Quinta had been tempted to open the bottle, but she hadn't yet. It would be such an easy thing, especially tonight, when her hope was running low. All she had to do was pop the cork off and—

No.

She wasn't going to open the moonshadow. She was going to find the Vermilion Emporium and learn more about the magical substance there.

She had to keep looking.

You are meant for great things.

Imagine if the shop she'd been searching for all these years was in the city and here she was standing beside a tree, crying silently, and staring at a tiny glass bottle. What sentimental nonsense.

"Time for a new plan," she said out loud, rallying herself. "I'll search the streets on the far side of the park until midnight. After that, I'll get dinner, go home, and try again tomorrow."

Magic was here somewhere, and Quinta was going to find it.

Energized by her plan, Quinta hurried out of Luna Park. She emerged on a familiar street in Vermilion. It was packed with restaurants, bars, cabarets, and all sorts of businesses that really picked up around this time of night. A bustling market spilled onto the street, and vendors yelled out to passing groups of people. A trio of fresh-faced Ixilian mercenaries in their customary blue-and-red uniforms navigated through the market, their eyes wide. Ixily was a fierce, warlike island to the southeast of Severon, and all its citizens were required to do three years of military service. Many of them went on to be swords or guns for hire after that. These three fighters—two boys and a girl—had knives at their hips and looked like this was their first time in Vermilion at night. Quinta would be willing to wager they'd have empty pockets and bellies full of regret by morning.

A loud group of scholars—two Scientifica in their green jackets and three Arcana in their blue coats—pushed passed the Ixilian mercenaries. The mercenaries shouted something, but the scholars were too absorbed in their arguments about what was more worthy of study—science or the arts—to pay them any heed. Scholars were like rats, and there would be more of them wandering the streets soon enough as the city filled in anticipation of the Scholar's Ball at the end of the month.

Quinta wanted nothing to do with the Scholar's Ball. Not anymore, at least. She'd only taken the Scholar's Exam in the hopes that joining the Arcana would help her learn more about magic. But who needed that path when she could just find the magical shop with all the answers? Not her.

The bells of a nearby church rang eight times, and Quinta scanned the storefronts until something stopped her in the middle of the street. That finding feeling was back. She slipped her hand into her pocket, running her fingers over the business card from her mother.

You are very close, whispered the voice on the wind. *Hurry.*

Quinta couldn't help but listen.

Rather than going right at the edge of the market like she might to get home, Quinta turned left. A salty breeze blew in from that direction, and a gull squawked overhead, as if it was urging Quinta onward.

When she emerged from the alley, Quinta caught her breath. There, on a tucked-away corner, was a shop that looked like it had been in the same spot for a century. Which was ridiculous, because Quinta knew for a fact this shop hadn't been there a few days ago. Its facade was deep ruby, and its mullioned windows were crowded with piles of books, toys, hats, coats, and dozens of small bottles, each of them a different color.

A tall, skinny boy with light-brown skin, shoulder-length dark hair, and a torn shirt stood outside the shop, hands in his pockets, staring at the display window. He was about her age, and when he turned to look at her, Quinta noticed his eyes were sea-glass green and he was beautiful in a way that made her insides ache.

But none of that was what made Quinta gasp. It was the sign hanging above the shop's door that stopped her.

Painted in a flourish of red and gold, the sign boldly declared:

It couldn't be, of course.

But it was.

Here was exactly the nowhere place Quinta had been searching for all these long years.

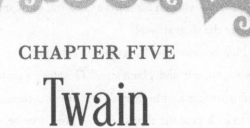

CHAPTER FIVE
Twain

Twain turned away from the shop window he'd been considering when he heard someone gasp. A pale girl with thick eyebrows, dark eyes, and a riot of curly black hair stood marveling at the shop's sign. She wore a black-and-white striped dress with a short red jacket over it, and there was a glass bottle on a ribbon around her neck. He'd never seen her in his life, but something about her was instantly familiar. She was like a song Twain had heard once but couldn't quite remember the notes to.

The girl's hands trembled as she raised them to her lips. She looked like she wanted to shove the gasp back inside her mouth. Her eyes met Twain's, and she scowled.

"What are you doing here?" She sounded shocked to find anyone else in the city with her at that moment.

Twain—a boy who loved challenges, dangerous things, and girls with edges he could cut himself on—liked her immediately.

He grinned at her with his sideways smile, a hint of his old charm flickering to life. "Here, as in on this street, or here, as in present within the city of Severon?"

The girl made an irritated noise. "Here, as in beside this shop. Do you know where it came from? Did you see it arrive?"

"See the shop arrive?"

He'd been looking for a place to eat and trying to put distance between himself and Henri's and Gustave's smashed bodies. He wasn't quite sure how his feet led him here, but something made him stop to look in at the shop's window. And once he started looking, he couldn't tear his eyes away. In one corner of the display was a toy ship that was almost an exact copy of the one his parents had died on. Beside it was a book Twain could've sworn he and Zand owned as children. On the other side of the window, sitting beneath a silver kaleidoscope, was a map that charted a voyage around the world. All these things and many more oddities had held him spellbound until the girl arrived.

"That's what I said," the girl snapped. "Do you *always* repeat every question someone asks you?"

"I do not *always* repeat every question someone asks me." Twain was unable to keep a smile out of his voice. Something about this girl made him want to keep talking to her. Even if he had places to be and death at his back. She was a lovely distraction, and it felt good to forget all the lonely, sad things in his life for a moment.

The girl huffed in annoyance, and a laugh bubbled out of Twain. She glared at him expectantly.

"And, no," he continued. "I didn't see the shop arrive. As far as I know it's been here since forever."

"It hasn't. But, of course, if it moves around, you wouldn't know that it's new." The girl peered into the window. "I can't believe I didn't find it first. Have you been inside?"

Twain shook his head. "I'm on my way to find some dinner and sell some things, not stop inside every shop I pass." Twain shifted his shoulders and showed the girl his bag. He wasn't sure why he did it, but he grabbed one of the razorbill feathers out of it and offered it to her.

"What's this?"

Twain could tell from her face she knew what it was.

"It's a present for you. Beautiful feather for an exquisite girl."

"Don't be absurd. Do you think you'll charm me with feathers?"

Twain shrugged as he smiled. The girl scowled again and tucked the feather into her jacket pocket.

Twain liked that she didn't thank him, but he really did have to see about selling this strand of starlight. And staying hidden in case the Casorina's soldiers came looking for him.

But the lovely girl was already moving past him. For all the surprises Twain had stumbled across today, she seemed the most extraordinary. He couldn't let her disappear.

"I'm Twain, by the way," he called out. "In case anyone asks you about the dashing man who gifted you a razorbill feather."

"I'll be sure to tell them," she said, barely disguising a snort.

"What's your name?"

"None of your concern."

"Ahh, lovely to meet you, 'None of Your Concern.' And why are you so interested in"—Twain looked up to read the sign—"the Vermilion Emporium?"

The girl already had her hands on the shop door, but she paused, sighing again like she was being asked to explain something very obvious to a very annoying child. "My name isn't 'None of Your Concern.' I'm saying that you knowing my name is none of your concern."

"Perfectly clear, None of Your Concern."

The girl gritted her teeth. "You know what, never mind. I'm Quinta. There. Happy?"

"Extremely." Twain grinned. "Hello, Quinta. And why are you so in love with this shop?"

"I'm not in love with the shop."

"Could've fooled me. You're staring at it like it's a long-lost sweetheart."

Quinta made a growling noise in her throat that was truly alarming. "If you must know, I've been looking for this shop nearly half my life. Now I've found it, and I mean to go inside. Alone. Right now. Goodbye forever."

What an odd thing to be looking for, Twain mused, but before the thought could really dig in and become a proper mystery, Quinta pushed the shop door open. Twain—whose curiosity wasn't going to let this lovely, prickly girl explore the strange shop without him—followed her. A smell immediately wafted over both of them, making Quinta stop in the doorway.

It was a remarkable scent: old books, dusty furniture, a thousand different perfumes, rainstorms, and a hint of something else that instantly reminded Twain of the cakes his father used to bring home from a Verdigris bakery.

"It smells like time," Quinta whispered in a voice so soft Twain almost missed it. All her edges were gone, smoothed out for a moment with awe.

And she was right. Somehow the collection of all those scents together smelled like laughing with Zand on a summer day, or like the moment Twain put his bow to his violin's strings, ready to play a new song. It was the smell of things that were gone and would never come back. A razor of grief sliced through Twain.

"It smells like loss," he said, one hand curling around his stomach, as if he could stop the invisible blade from slicing deeper.

"And it smells like memory," Quinta added. Her voice was shaky now, as if memory was exactly the sort of thing she didn't want to smell.

Twain wasn't sure why he did it—perhaps his body knew better than his mind—but his wounded, bruised fingers snaked around Quinta's, lacing their hands together. Instantly, he felt less carved open with his hand in hers.

"What are you doing?" Quinta glared at him. "Do you hold hands with every stranger you meet?"

"Only the pretty ones," he said with a wink, trying again at charm.

She rolled her eyes but didn't let go. Which was perhaps more surprising than anything else.

Hand in hand, they stepped through the doorway of the Vermilion Emporium.

A wide, round room greeted them. Filigreed silver lanterns hung from the ceiling, their panes made of purple and blue glass. Inside the lanterns, candles flickered, sending colored shadows dancing. Thick woven rugs covered the floor, and a mismatched collection of tables and chairs filled the room. Old letters (many still in their envelopes), jewelry of all descriptions, glass bottles with dead insects inside them, children's toys, books, and a thousand other things lay scattered across the furniture.

"Hello?" Quinta called out, dropping Twain's hand. He instantly felt its loss as she wrapped her fingers around the tiny bottle at her neck, her face a mix of anticipation and worry. "Is anyone here?"

A long moment of silence passed between them as they waited.

"None of our concern?" Twain suggested at last, just to fill the silence.

Quinta huffed.

Partly from curiosity and partly to have something to do with his now-empty hand, Twain ran his fingers over the thick dust on the closest table. They brushed across a sketchbook, three miniatures in oval frames, and a silver mirror that had long ago tarnished.

The mirror clattered to the floor, and Quinta shot him a look. "Don't break anything."

"How would anyone know if I did? This place is chaos."

A voice sounded from the back of the room before Quinta could reply.

"There you are!" It wasn't a young voice, but it was one that seemed too light to be buried among the strange items in the shop.

"Who's there?" Twain picked up the silver mirror.

Quinta raised an eyebrow. "Going to kill them with vanity?"

"Something like that. You never know who could . . ."

Before he could say more, an old woman—because of course this grimy, strange shop was run by an old woman—appeared in a doorway between two bookcases. Twain could've sworn there'd not been an opening between those bookcases a moment before.

The woman strode toward them. "There you two are. I've been here hours already and was starting to worry."

The woman didn't move like she was old, but her long white hair was wrapped into a bun, and wrinkles made deep channels in her papery white face. She wore a high-necked blouse, tucked into a pair of trousers. Her gray eyes sparkled as she held out a hand to Quinta, who warily offered her own.

"Very nice to see you, Quinta," said the old woman. When she had given Quinta a firm handshake, she turned to Twain. "And you've brought a friend. Never thought I'd meet you here, Twain, but there we are. Life is strange and friends stranger." The woman's eyes sparkled for a moment with what could've been tears.

Twain was stunned she knew their names. His eyes sought out Quinta's, but she was staring past the woman's shoulder as if she'd seen a ghost.

"Where did you get that?" Quinta asked, gripping the bottle at her neck more tightly. She moved toward a black-and-white photograph hanging beside the bookcase that had just opened up. Twain followed.

The photograph showed a lovely woman holding the hand of a dark-haired girl who looked to be about ten. The woman and the girl stood outside a huge striped tent, and the woman wore a spangly silver dress. A small bottle hung from around her neck. The woman's smile was infectious.

"Is that you?" Twain asked softly. He pointed to the child in the photo. Of course it was Quinta. The scowl on the child's face was identical to the one she wore now.

She nodded, her fingers brushing the photograph. "This was taken not long before my mother died. But, how did it end up here?"

"That's not the only mystery in this shop," the old woman said gleefully, coming up behind them. "Perhaps someday I'll tell you how I knew your mother. But today is a day for finding things. And it's already well past sunset. You better get started."

It occurred to Twain that he might be able to sell the razorbill feathers or the starlight here. But before he had a chance to show the old woman his treasures, Quinta moved through the door between the bookcases. She was peering intently at the row of photographs stretching down a hallway lit only by a single candle in a silver holder, resting on a small table.

"Well, go after her," urged the old woman. "I'll be up here by the front when you find what you're looking for."

The old woman gave Twain a little shove, and he stumbled into the hall after Quinta. The door of the bookcase banged shut behind him.

CHAPTER SIX

Quinta

Quinta jumped.

"What did you do?" she demanded, spinning around.

"Nothing," said Twain quickly. "It was that woman. She shoved me in here and slammed the door. I think she wants us to find something. But she didn't—"

"We can't be stuck in here," Quinta interrupted, a frantic edge to her voice. "There's got to be a way out!"

Pushing past Twain, she ran her fingers along the outline of the door, looking for a handle—a handhold—a doorknob. Something. Anything. But there was nothing. It was smooth wood and stone under her palm. Quinta rammed her shoulder against the wall, but it didn't budge. Her heartbeat fluttered like the candle flame that barely illuminated the narrow passageway.

No. She couldn't be stuck in here. She wouldn't let herself.

Quinta pounded on the door as the walls shrunk around her.

This wasn't a small space, but she hated being trapped anywhere. She had to get out. Now.

Quinta hadn't always been afraid of being trapped, but after her mother died, the Celestial Circus broke up. None of the performers—even those who'd been her mother's friends—offered to take Quinta with them as they scattered. She woke up the morning after her mother's death in their circus trailer and decided she would have to take matters into her own hands. Gathering a few of her things, Quinta left the remains of the circus without a look back. She was a motherless girl of ten, with only a bottle of moonshadow, a few coins, and not a friend in Severon. But she was determined to stay alive. After all, she was meant for great things.

In those early months, she got good at both surviving and stealing. She discovered many of the mansions in Verdigris were mostly empty, and using tricks she learned from the circus performers, she slipped into windows to find warm corners of a house.

Which was all well and good until that night she got wedged in a tight crawl space in one of the Verdigris houses. She'd ended up stuck for two days until she finally wormed her way out. Since then, the feeling of being trapped anywhere overwhelmed her.

Quinta took a deep, ragged breath, pulling herself back into the present. Right. There was a hallway. A candle. A door.

She wasn't trapped. There was a way out of this. She had to push the door open, force her way through, and get out of here before things got any smaller. She pounded on the door again, more insistently.

"Quinta?" Twain grabbed her fists, forcing her to stop hitting the door. "Are you hurt? What's wrong?"

Wrenching away from Twain, Quinta stumbled a few steps down the hallway. She'd forgotten he was still here. She gulped in air.

"Are you okay?" Twain approached her very carefully.

Was she okay? Quinta wasn't sure how to answer that. Why was breathing so difficult? Wasn't her body supposed to know how to pull air into its lungs? Why was a gasping sob coming from her mouth?

A hand rested on her shoulder, bringing her back to herself.

"Breathe in for four counts," Twain said softly. "Then hold it for four. Then breathe out."

Quinta followed his voice, matching her breath to his counts. 1-2-3-4. 1-2-3-4. 1-2-3-4.

When her sobs stopped and her breathing was almost normal again, she gave a nervous laugh. Her eyes found Twain's in the candlelight. His sea-glass eyes were darker now, like a rain-washed ocean.

"Thank you," she said, finding her voice at last. "I don't . . . don't do very well in shadowy, enclosed spaces." It cost her a lot to say that, because it meant letting someone she barely knew learn something tremendous about her.

"We all have rooms too dark to walk in." A shadow moved over Twain's face, and in that space between blinks, Quinta desperately wanted to know what his dark rooms looked like. But there was no time to ask him.

"Which way do we go?" She pushed some of her reckless hair behind her ears. Her hands still shook slightly as she considered the long hallway in front of them. But she would be okay. She was in the shop she'd been looking for most of her life. Time to see what it held.

The smallest of smiles curved Twain's lips. "Well, the door we came through is locked, as you so helpfully discovered. And the old woman said she'd be at the front desk when we 'found what we're looking for.'"

"What does that mean?"

"I have no idea," Twain replied, rather more cheerfully than he had a right to be. "But there's really only one way to find out. We have to explore."

Twain picked up the candle and offered Quinta his hand. Although, with the exception of a few moments ago in the store, Quinta never held hands with boys (that was not how a one-night-only girl worked), she took it. Her fingers slid over his hard calluses, bruises, and many cuts. Where had he gotten them? Perhaps the same place he got the feathers and the wounds across his stomach?

She didn't ask him about it, though, and she tried not to stare at all the photos from the Celestial Circus that lined the walls of the hallway. The candlelight flickered across them, showing Quinta's early life, one black-and-white image at a time.

Which was alarming, to say the least. Why did her mother send her here? What was she supposed to find? Could she ask the old woman about the bottle of moonshadow? Was the answer to where starlight came from hidden behind one of these doors? All she could do was look and hope.

They walked toward the end of the hallway where three open doorways and a set of stairs going downward waited.

"That one?" Twain asked. He pointed to the closest doorway. Music poured out of the room. His fingers tapped out a beat against her palm.

Quinta nodded.

He set the candle on a table beside the doorway and stepped inside.

All words fled Quinta as she followed Twain. Music rushed in to fill the spaces the words had left behind.

The room beyond the door was unbelievable. It was the size of a concert hall and like nothing Quinta had ever seen. Chandeliers were fashioned out of instruments, all of which played the same melancholy song. The walls were strung with harp strings, and thousands of music boxes in all sizes, shapes, colors, and designs rested on the long tables that filled the room. Quinta turned the key of the closest music box, one shaped like a gold and blue star, and as she did so, all the other music stopped. A small door in the middle of the star popped open and seven brightly colored planets emerged. Lilting music rose from the star-box, and the planets hung in the air, twirling around each other until the star song was done.

"Wow," Twain murmured. The word was far too small to cover what had just happened.

"Wow," Quinta echoed, simply because she couldn't think of any other word to hold the wonder of the place.

"Look at this one."

Twain pointed to a dollhouse-sized marble palace with rounded golden domes. He turned a small key set into the front door, and music rose from the palace. It was a melody of waiting and grief; it was a prince's lament upon the death of his great love. The entire room, Quinta and Twain included, seemed to freeze as the notes wove around them. The prince's music was a shroud, holding each of them together for one more moment with the ghosts of beloveds they never knew they missed.

When the dirge stopped, Quinta looked around at seemingly endless rows of music boxes. Tears rolled down Twain's cheeks, and it took every ounce of Quinta's will not to reach up and wipe them away. Which was nonsense, she knew, since she'd only just met this boy. But he was so entirely heartbroken beneath his charming smile. What—or who—had he lost that would make him weep over a melody?

Not her concern. She had questions of her own to answer. Yes, that was exactly it.

You are meant for great things.

"There are so many music boxes," Quinta said. "I bet each one has a different song."

Did one of these hold the key to understanding the moonshadow or starlight magic?

Twain ran his finger lightly over a small brass plaque hanging on the wall beside them. He read out loud: "'These music boxes contain the songs of a thousand people in a thousand towns across a thousand ages. They were collected by the Vermilion Emporium for your listening enjoyment. Browse as you will, but know that to take a song home means the music becomes part of your story as well.'"

Quinta raised an eyebrow. "What does that even mean? A thousand songs from a thousand ages? Is that something clever to make people want to buy a music box?"

"I don't know. Do you want to take one and find the old woman?"

Quinta shook her head, though her fingers lingered over a fingernail-sized box inlaid with jewels the size of dewdrops. "Let's see what's in the other rooms."

It hurt Quinta to walk away from the room full of songs, but maybe she'd have a chance to come back. Then she'd take her time and listen to each song in turn, letting them fill her up with the stories of those who'd lived long ago.

With a glance backward, Twain led the way out of the music room and through the next open door, a green one decorated with silver whorls.

"This is even more incredible than the last room," Quinta whispered as soon as they entered.

And it was. Her mind objectively knew they were still in a small shop in the Vermilion District, but somehow this room opened up like a cathedral. Its ceiling soared above them, buttressed by columns in the shape of giant, humanlike forms. A net of silver threads hung from the ceiling, and the entire expansive room glowed with pale light, like the full moon shining on the ocean. Beneath the glorious ceiling, the rest of the room was in disarray. Broken furniture, dress forms, piles of old clothing, toys, and even a full-sized sailboat with a cracked mast lay scattered without any order at all.

"Can you hear that?" Twain stared up at the silver-threaded ceiling.

Quinta didn't hear anything other than her own breathing, but Twain stood mesmerized, like he was listening to his own private concert.

Another small plaque hung by the door to this room. Quinta read it out loud: "'Beneath celestial threads, you might find what you seek. But be careful, as these things have been taken from those with nothing to lose. Owning such a thing might bring you more trouble than you expect.'"

"Is that cryptic or needlessly dramatic?"

Quinta quirked an eyebrow at his skepticism. "We've been trapped in an impossible shop by a mysterious old woman. And this plaque is what gives you pause?"

Twain grinned at her. "I confess I'm overwhelmed by the absurdity of it all." At that moment, his stomach gave an awful grumbling that sounded so much like a beast awakening that Quinta had to laugh.

Quinta clapped her hand over her mouth. "I'm sorry."

"For laughing?"

Quinta nodded miserably.

"Never be sorry for a laugh like that," Twain said, his eyes holding hers. "I'm sorry for my stomach, but I'm glad it acted up so I could hear you."

Embarrassment flooded Quinta. Now this extraordinary stranger knew three things about her: who her mother was, because he'd seen the photograph; that she was afraid of dark, enclosed places; and that inside her lived a laugh that that could stitch together broken things. All of it was quite enough of herself to share for one evening.

"Let's go," she said, turning away from Twain. "I want to see what's in the third room."

"Just a moment." Over several trips, Twain hauled two spindly chairs and a carved wooden table toward the closest stone column. "I think that's starlight up there. And I could use a whole lot of it. Hold this. And stay close; I don't want to lose you in here."

Twain thrust his bag into her arms. Quinta watched in amazement as he stacked the chairs on the table, and then scampered up them. She'd never seen anyone—or anything besides a squirrel running away from a determined cat—climb so quickly.

Twain was up the furniture and digging his fingers into the stone column before Quinta really had a chance to understand his words: *I don't want to lose you in here.*

I don't want to lose you.

No one had ever said that to her. Quinta was a girl who was good at being lost and at losing people, but here was a boy who didn't want to lose her.

A strange feeling—some combination of hope and sadness—filled her, and she hugged Twain's bag to her chest. Her eyes never left him as he climbed hand over hand, feet digging into the rough stone of the column. His movements were assured, easy, as if he'd been climbing tall, humanlike columns to silver-spangled ceilings all his life. And maybe he had. Quinta had no way of knowing better.

Twain reached the top of the column—a large, outstretched giant's hand that he could stand on—and his fingers moved through the net of silver threads on the ceiling. Was it really starlight? If it was, could they use it for magic?

Quinta's heart sped up at the possibility.

Twain pulled at one of the threads. It didn't move. He pulled harder, and the glow of the ceiling flickered. It was then, as the lights went out and then blinked back on, that Quinta realized it was not so much a net of silver above them. Rather, it was more like an enormous tapestry of lace woven from gossamer threads of starlight.

Her breath whooshed out of her lungs.

But how was that possible?

No one had made starlight lace for centuries.

Questions raced through Quinta's mind as Twain let go of the silver lace and moved back down the stone column.

"So much for that idea," he said, jumping down from the rickety pile of furniture with a bit of a flourish.

"That was starlight, wasn't it?" asked Quinta excitedly. She still held his bag close to her chest, some part of her not ready to let go of it yet.

"It looks like what I've seen."

"Where else have you seen starlight?"

"On display, in the museums," said Twain quickly, in a voice that held a note of reserve.

Of course that's where he'd seen it. Quinta had seen it there too. Old, dusty stuff that still glowed, but not like the ceiling of this room.

"I wish we had some of it." Longing passed over Quinta's face. She had always wanted to hold starlight, ever since her mother first told her about the Salon and how Marali wove lace from celestial threads.

Twain's mouth opened and closed, as if some secret was struggling to get out. But then he shrugged. "I thought I could get one of those threads, but they were woven too closely. We'll have to move on."

A long moment of quiet stretched between them as they looked up at the ceiling. It was a world of possibility, just out of reach.

"Ready to see the next room?" Quinta asked at last. Disappointment filled her voice—what a thing to be so close to magic but not able to take any of it.

"After you," said Twain, reaching out for his bag, which Quinta reluctantly handed over.

The next room lay beyond a purple door, and it was full of books. But it wasn't full in the way a rich person's library is filled with books. No. This room was stuffed with books in a way that some people are full of sadness or some places are full of memories. It stretched far into the distance, and the books were stacked in hundreds of crooked, bulging piles, making them look like stalagmites. Buttery yellow light illuminated the room, emanating from small glass spheres hanging on chains among the books.

"Oh. My." Quinta breathed as she stepped into the room, following a path between the towers of tomes. "Where would we even begin to find something here?"

But she already had a feeling there was something to find and that this room was exactly where she needed to be. Astonishment filled Quinta as she gazed up, trying to read the titles on each book's spine. For a brief moment, she also wondered if people had titles on their spines. If bodies were the books of our lives, what would her spine say?

Perhaps: Here is a disappointing girl who dreamed of unlikely futures.

Or: The mostly true story of a girl who wore a bit of moonshadow but didn't know what to do with it.

These were ridiculous thoughts, of course, and Quinta usually didn't let herself think such things. But something about moving through a labyrinth of stories made her feel welcome to think any strange thing she liked. It made her believe people could have titles on their spines, and that some of their pages were bent at the corners because they wanted to remember the words there.

"What are you looking for?" Twain asked from somewhere to her right. Unlike in the starlight cathedral, where Twain's voice had echoed across the space, here the books seemed to gobble up his words. As if they wanted to preserve them too.

"I don't know. But it's here."

Twain didn't argue with that, and it was all Quinta could do not to turn around and ask him for his story. She longed to see what the title on his spine might be.

But of course she didn't ask him anything. His story was his to tell, and who was she to get to hear it?

In silence they moved through the cavern. Sometimes their shoulders grazed a low-hanging globe, and the light bounced wildly around the piles of books. With every step they took, Quinta thought they'd reached the boundaries of the room, but there were no edges it seemed. There were just more books and the paths between them, stretching on into boundless space. Here and there, the books became deep canyons, and Twain and Quinta navigated the ravines. She didn't let herself think what might happen if one book fell. Or how long it would take to find their bodies beneath the weight of all these words.

Quinta wasn't sure how long they had been walking. Her stomach grumbled and, behind her, Twain's stomach roared, but even that didn't stop her. Her feet moved forward determinedly. She knew the thing she was meant to find was in here somewhere. Whatever it was. She had to walk a little bit farther. Look a bit more intently. Push herself, even though she was feeling very tired.

You are meant for great things.

The answers she needed to fulfill her mother's magical legacy were in this room. She just had to find them.

Quinta walked and walked until she felt Twain's hand on her arm. It was only a gentle touch, but it shocked her.

"What?" she snapped, spinning around. She didn't mean to sound so sharp, but there was something here she needed to find. Something that her life wouldn't be complete without. Something that—

Twain pointed at the floor of the cavern—no, it wasn't a cavern; it was a room in a shop with a red-and-green tiled floor, where one purple razorbill feather lay.

"We're out of feathers." Twain held up his bag. It hung limply from his hands, completely empty.

"Why should that even matter?" asked Quinta, genuinely confused. "Where did they all go?"

Twain looked at her for a moment, as if he were seeing her for the first time. Amusement and something tender and a bit fierce crossed his face. It was quickly replaced by his sideways smile. He nudged her shoulder. "C'mon, None of Your Concern. You really don't know how long we've been walking? Hours? Days? I'm not sure, but I've been dropping feathers to leave us a trail. Otherwise, I'm not sure we'd ever make it out of here."

Quinta let out a breath and looked around. Her feet did hurt. And the door they'd entered through was nowhere to be seen. In fact, Quinta wasn't even sure where they were. Her sense of direction was utterly muddled by the piles of books, and her head was full of questions: Who had collected and arranged all of them? What kept them in their piles? What happened if someone wanted a book from the top of a stack?

"That was a very good idea with the feathers." She took a deep breath, trying to reorient herself. "Should we turn around?"

Twain's stomach grumbled again, as if it was agreeing before he could say otherwise. "I think we have to."

He bent down to pick up the feather he'd dropped, and they retraced their footsteps, following the feather trail and slowly filling Twain's bag back up. On the walk back, Quinta read endless book titles: *Heartbreaks and Other Maladies to Cure with Poetry; 1003 Types of Tree Songs; Witches Worth Watching Out for in Wallington;* and *The Philosopher's Guide to Making Tea.*

Each title raised a question in her mind, but none of them were the book Quinta was looking for. As they walked, a sick, hollow feeling snickered through her. This feeling was a ghost at her back, tauntingly saying, "If you'd only kept walking, you would've found what you were looking for."

How will you ever be great if you give up so easily?

Hurry. Keep going. You're almost there.

But never mind all that. The room was too big, and they were headed back to the entrance. Whatever she was meant to find absolutely wasn't going to be discovered today.

Which was perhaps not worth worrying about. Perhaps there weren't answers about magic here. Perhaps she could give up her quest for magic and her mother's legacy. Perhaps she wouldn't be great. Maybe her mother was wrong, and Quinta could live a normal life, meet someone to love, become a mother herself, and die by the sea someday when she was so old that she no longer remembered the dreams that brought her to the Vermilion Emporium in the first place.

It was almost a relief to imagine a life without the burden of greatness.

Quinta was just making her peace with these thoughts and the long, normal, un-extraordinary life she most certainly was going to have when Twain bent down to pick up another feather.

He had barely straightened when all the lights across the book-filled expanse went out at once.

Darkness so deep it was like being inside the night itself that fell over them.

Quinta couldn't help but scream.

CHAPTER SEVEN

Twain

Quinta's scream rang out in the cavern, and then the hungry books devoured it. Twain reached out in the darkness, praying he didn't knock over a stack and kill them both. Relief filled him when his hand found Quinta's.

"I'm here, None of Your Concern. I see you. You're not alone."

Quinta laughed at that. Her breath came in shaky gasps, like it had done in the hallway. "Liar. You don't see me. But I'm here too."

They held hands in the darkness. Twain's heart clattered like a carriage racing down a cobbled street. He had never realized that darkness could be so rich, so velvety, so entirely without limits.

"What happened to the lights?"

"I don't know," replied Quinta. "But a more important question: How are we going to get back if we can't see anything?"

Twain had no idea. But that wasn't entirely true. The coil of starlight in his pocket hummed softly, as if urging him to take it out.

But if he did that, then Quinta would know his secret. She might think he'd stolen the starlight from the cathedral room. Or maybe she'd try to take it from him, and then he'd never get out of Severon.

You'll never get out of Severon if you die under a pile of darkness and books in a shop that is somehow hopelessly larger than it seems.

He would have to trust her. It was that simple. Even if he wasn't in the habit of trusting people, he'd break his own rule for Quinta. "I have something that might help. I'm going to let go of your hand, but I'm still right here."

Beside him, Quinta stepped closer, pushing her body against his. "I don't want to lose you in the darkness. Is this okay?"

It was more than okay, but Twain didn't say that. He coughed as her thigh pressed against his leg. Something about this nearness was the closest to home he'd felt in a long time. Her warm breath on his neck was more intimate than the kisses he'd shared with other girls. But how could he tell her such a thing?

"It's okay," he said softly. "Stay close."

Then, with her body pressed against his, he withdrew the starlight from his pocket.

Quinta inhaled sharply. The starlight sat between them, a pulsing silver ribbon in the vast darkness. Its music was silent now, as if the starlight too was holding its breath.

"It's starlight," whispered Twain, leaning in so his face was nearly touching Quinta's. His lips accidentally brushed her ear. He didn't mean to be so close, but he didn't want the hungry books to snatch his words away.

"Where did you get it?" Quinta reached out a tentative finger and touched the ribbon of light. The silver glow softened the harsh lines of her face, making her lovelier than anyone Twain had ever seen.

Twain hesitated for only a moment. Could he really trust her? They'd only known each other a short time, but somehow it felt like he and Quinta had been through several days of adventuring already. "I found it in the razorbill nests today. While I was climbing."

"You climb to the razorbill nests?" Quinta asked, her voice full of disbelief. She sounded like she knew exactly what that entailed, but Twain couldn't tell if she was impressed at his daring or thought he was foolish.

He looped the starlight around his fingers. "Only when I'm especially hungry and entirely out of money."

"Well, that explains the state of your hands, but not what you're doing with real, actual starlight."

"I wasn't expecting to find this there, of course. I was just looking for feathers."

Quinta considered the starlight again. "But where did it come from? It looks like the silver lace in the cathedral room. If it's from the Emporium, how could it have gotten into the razorbill nests?" Her eyes were wide, and silver dots of light reflected in them. Twain had the sudden wild urge to weave the ribbon of light through Quinta's curls. He stopped himself.

Twain shook his head. "I don't know. But we can use it to find our way out of here." He held it up, casting a small circle of light onto the path in front of them.

"Brilliant."

Slowly, they navigated through the stacks of books, following the trail of feathers Twain had left. The music of the starlight started up again, humming its song of worry, wonder, and circus tents.

"Do you hear that?" Twain asked, pausing to listen to the music. For the first time in months, his fingers itched to pick up his violin and re-create the starlight's melody.

"Hear what?"

"The music from the starlight?"

Quinta paused, straining her ears in the dark for a long moment. "I only hear our breathing. And your stomach." She nudged her elbow into his side, making him grin. "If hunger is making you hear strange music, we're in more trouble than I thought."

"Hilarious. But I wonder why you can't hear it. There's a song coming from the starlight." Twain bent over and picked up one of the razorbill feathers.

"Can I hold it?" Quinta asked, reaching out a hand for the silver ribbon. "Maybe I can hear the music that way."

Twain hesitated. It was one thing to show the starlight to Quinta—another to hand it over. What if she took off running with it, leaving him in the dark?

That was possible, but he wanted to trust her. For the first time in months, the lonely parts of Twain were full of laughter. He wanted so badly for this girl to be different from all the others.

"Be careful with it," Twain said as he handed Quinta the starlight, curious to see what she would do with it.

"Is this a test?" She ran the starlight through her fingers.

"Maybe. Are you good at tests?"

"I flunked the Arcana Exam twice." Bitterness laced Quinta's voice.

Twain instantly liked her that much more. "I can beat that. I failed it three times."

Quinta snorted. "I'm not sure you should brag about that."

"My parents and brother definitely would've agreed with you. Why did you take the exam? You don't strike me as the scholar type."

"I'm a woman of mystery," Quinta said, holding the light up to a pile of books. "You don't seem like the scholar type either—"

"Thank you very much."

"Why did you take the test in the first— Oh!" Surprise made Quinta's voice loud and strong. "Oh, so there you are!"

Twain thought she was talking to him, but Quinta wasn't looking at him. She stared at an especially tall pile of books. With the starlight coiled around her wrist, she reached toward a bright-blue volume near the top.

"What is it?" Twain glanced upward.

"What I've been looking for. Can you help me?"

The book she wanted was just out of his reach, and Twain couldn't scale one of these piles. From his many years of climbing, he knew as soon as he put a foot on the stack it would tumble to the ground.

"We can reach it if you sit on my shoulders."

Quinta shot him a look. "You want me to sit on your shoulders? In this dress?"

Twain shrugged, a wicked look in his eyes. "You want that book, don't you, None of Your Concern?"

He could tell that she did want the book, and some war between propriety and desire happened within her before she decided. "I very much want that book."

"And you don't want me to sit on your shoulders."

"Decidedly not. You're enormous."

Twain crouched down in front of Quinta, offering his broad shoulders as her sedan chair. "I understand if your delicate sensibilities—"

Quinta barked a most unladylike laugh. "Delicate sensibilities! I was raised in the circus. This is nothing."

In one quick move, Quinta clambered onto Twain's shoulders. She was a tiny thing, all bones and skirts and he stood up easily under her weight.

"Where is it?" he asked, disoriented by the warmth of her thighs so near his cheeks.

Above him, Quinta held the ribbon of starlight aloft, making a silver lantern in all the darkness. "To the right."

Twain stepped forward, pitching slightly.

"Slowly!" squealed Quinta, her legs tightening around his shoulders. "We don't want to run into the stacks."

Ignoring the pounding of his heart, Twain took a few careful steps forward, steadying himself between each step and praying he wouldn't fall over. He stumbled on the last step, but as he'd done that morning on the cliffs, he caught himself in time and they stayed balanced.

"Are you really sure you need this book?" It took all his will not to lean against the stack of books.

"Of course I'm sure!"

"How do you know?" Twain's voice was teasing. He really just wanted her to keep talking to him. "What's the book called? What are you going to do with it?"

"I'll know when I get it. Now, move a little more forward."

Twain took one wobbling step, stopping right before his nose touched the pile of books. Quinta's hands moved so fast, he almost didn't believe she'd gotten what she wanted. But one moment she held only the starlight, and the next she'd somehow grabbed the blue book from the pile without bringing the whole thing down upon them. It really was the most remarkable bit of thieving. There was decidedly more to this girl than it seemed.

"Where did you learn to do that?" Twain asked as Quinta slid down his back. He tried very hard not to feel every space where their bodies pushed together, but that was all but impossible. Her architectures burned trails down him, leaving him breathless by the time her feet hit the ground.

Quinta's breathing was steady and her focus entirely on the book in her hand. Clearly she was not at all fazed by being as close to Twain as he was at being near her. She turned the book over, peering intently at it, brows scrunched together in the silver glow.

Should he let her read, just for a moment? Or should they get going? A noise in the dark room decided it for him. It started out as a rumble but became something more sinister the next second.

"Quinta," Twain said, his voice insistent. "Move!"

She looked up from her book for a moment, really hearing the noise for the first time. "What's that? Your stomach?"

"No!"

"Is it the music of the starlight?"

"The what?"

"The mysterious music that only you can hear?"

Twain shook his head, trying to make sense of her question. "No! That song is all glissando. This is more martelé—"

Quinta looked at him like he was speaking a foreign language, which he technically was on all accounts.

"They're violin terms."

"You play the violin?" A delighted look passed over Quinta's face. "I love violin music!"

Twain filed that information away for later. "I don't play anymore but—"

A loud crash cut off Twain's words.

"Tell me that one was your stomach?"

"Not this time. C'mon! We have to get out of here!"

Side by side they ran through the stacks of books, following the trail of razorbill feathers. As they ran, Twain bent down to grab some of them, but each time he did so, the thunderous noise grew behind them. It pained him to leave anything behind, but what could he do?

In front of them, a yellow rectangle of light shone in the darkness. The door to the hallway! They were almost there when the roar got even louder and a book fell onto Twain's shoulders. Dozens more followed that first one.

"The whole room! It's collapsing," Quinta shouted. She hugged her blue book to her chest while her other hand gripped the starlight. "Hurry!"

In front of Twain, Quinta bounded through the doorway. Behind him the entire room shuddered and books rained down like ink-and-paper hailstones. Twain slipped on the closest pile, landing on his injured belly. A stabbing pain shot through him, but it barely registered because at the next moment the floor tilted, sending him sliding backward.

"Twain!" Quinta yelled from the doorway. A shocked expression crossed her face. "Hang on!"

But there was nothing to hold on to. There were only shifting mounds of books and a floor that had turned into a slope. Books tilted past him, banging him on the head and shoulders. Despite all his years of climbing, Twain had nothing to grip this time. Every book he reached for fell away. The slant of the floor sheered off, and a void opened beneath him. This was it. Like Zand he would fall down, down, down to his death, and there would be nothing left of him to find.

CHAPTER EIGHT
Quinta

Quinta watched in horror as Twain staggered, fell, and then began to slide backward. For a moment, she lost him under the piles of books that tumbled and then rolled away like waves in a stormy sea. She could only see into the darkness of the book room with the light from the hallway and the coil of starlight in her hand, but Twain's eyes met hers for a moment as he emerged from under a cascade of books.

"Help!" he managed to yell, before another surge of books covered him.

Quinta couldn't believe she was watching a boy she'd only just begun to like drown in a flood of words, ideas, and stories. That was ridiculous. Twain couldn't die here. But who was even talking of death? Could one die in a bookish cavern in a shop in the middle of the Vermilion District? Had anyone else in the history of History ever died while book shopping before?

Twain screamed again and Quinta's thoughts reordered. Right. Save the boy. Then consider the dangers of books and shopping.

Tucking the blue book into the pocket of her skirt (what a miracle—skirts with pockets!), Quinta tied the ribbon of starlight around her waist.

"Twain!" she called out, shouting to be heard over the avalanche of books. "Grab this!"

It really shouldn't have worked. It was a strand of starlight, no bigger than a girl's hair ribbon, but somehow, as Quinta threw the starlight, it became a thick silver rope. It was a luminous arrow in the night, a glowing artery into the body of the abyss.

Twain saw it coming and yelled something, but Quinta couldn't hear what it was. She could only hope he caught the rope, and then she could figure out what to do next.

It was a narrow thing, the space between when Twain's hands reached for the rope—he very nearly grabbed it!—and when he missed it entirely. As he tumbled into the hole in the floor, Quinta knew for certain she'd never see him again. In that moment, her heart was a porcelain teacup, dropped and shattered into a hundred pieces.

But do we ever really know anything for certain?

We certainly do not.

There was a great lurch on the other end of the rope, a pull so strong it almost plunged Quinta into the darkness of the book room.

Twain!

"Hang on!" she yelled, grasping the doorframe with both hands.

Digging her fingers into the wood, she planted her heels and peeked quickly into the void.

Somehow, there, at the end of the silver rope, hung Twain. He clung to the cord and grinned up at her. She didn't know how he'd grabbed the rope since she so clearly saw him miss it, but she couldn't stop her own outrageous, contagious, euphoric smile.

It was perhaps then, as Twain dangled above a chasm, tied to her by a magical thread of starlight that shouldn't have existed at all, that Quinta began to fall just the smallest bit in love with him. Or perhaps she didn't fall—because falling hurts—but what's the opposite of fall? Climb? Ascend? Rise? Yes, any of those were better than falling. So, in that moment, as Twain moved hand over hand up the rope of starlight, Quinta's heart rose with him. She climbed the smallest bit into love.

By the time Twain made it to the top of the rope, Quinta's knees were shaking. She collapsed on the ground once Twain could bear his own weight. His breath came in great heaving mouthfuls as he sunk beside Quinta.

They both lay on their backs for a moment, shoulder to shoulder. Her passing fancies about love were gone, and she was merely grateful that he'd made it to the top of the rope and she'd not fallen into the abyss with him. Twain still held the end of the silver cord in his hands. Each of them didn't move for a bit longer than they needed to. Which was fine with Quinta. It occurred to her that she'd never felt so comfortable lying beside someone else.

"That was unexpected," Quinta said at last. And by "unexpected" she absolutely meant the book-filled room falling away into nothing, but also the way she had felt when she thought she'd lost Twain.

Beside her, Twain laughed and rolled onto his side. He propped himself up on one arm and looked at her. Now, his sea-glass eyes were tide pools in the sunshine fringed by long lashes. He was breathtaking, but the look was slightly spoiled by the egg-sized purple bruise rising on his forehead. "That was unexpected, indeed. Thank you for saving me. We have to be friends forever now, since I owe you my life."

Quinta smiled, feeling something in her stitch together at Twain's words. "Thank you for helping me retrieve my book." She wasn't sure about friends forever—even if she wanted to know this boy more, she was a one-night girl—but she could at least say thank you. And maybe buy him some dinner.

Twain leaned forward, and Quinta thought-hoped-imagined that he might kiss her. But no. His fingers just lightly brushed her forehead. He plucked a small feather from her hair and held it out to her. "You found what you were looking for. Now, let's get out of this shop before it tries to kill us again."

Quinta took the razorbill feather and tucked it into her pocket beside her other feather and the book. Later, she could take the book and the feathers out and consider what they meant. But for now, her stomach growled, and she smiled at Twain. "I'll buy dinner. Let's try the bookcase door again. Now that we have the book, maybe it'll open."

"Excellent plan."

Twain helped her to her feet, and she untied the rope at her waist. She offered the length of starlight to him, and it shrank back to ribbon size as he coiled it around his wrist. Once that was done, Quinta slammed the door to the book room shut, but as she did so, three more doorways appeared farther down the hall. The downward staircase was also still there. How big was this shop? Could they keep exploring rooms forever? She spun around, turning back toward the way they came in.

The bookcase door stood open now, inviting them toward Severon and into a world that made sense.

"Sure you don't want to explore any of these other rooms?" Twain glanced between the open door at the end of the hallway and the others that had just appeared. His brow furrowed, conflict written into his features.

Quinta was curious about what lay beyond the new doors, but she was also hungry, tired, and afraid to walk into the unknown again. Plus, the feeling she'd had—the finding feeling—was gone. She'd found both the book and Twain. That was more than enough for now.

"Not a chance. At least not tonight."

"Deal," Twain agreed. "I'm leaving Severon at the end of the month. So, we have plenty more time for this shop to try and kill us before then."

Quinta's eyebrows flew up at the casual way Twain mentioned leaving Severon, but she didn't ask him about it. Maybe she would later, but maybe not. Instead, she laughed as breezily as she could after an evening of avoiding death, and together they walked to the end of the hallway, a bit bruised, but eager to talk about what had happened. Neither of them could figure out how the lights went out or why the books had turned into a death trap, but both were grateful to leave the hallway and emerge into the shop.

Twain gestured that Quinta could go through the bookcase door first, and she shot him a grateful smile. Which hurt her face a bit because she was not a girl given over to smiling, grateful or otherwise. She decided that she absolutely had to make up for all the smiling by telling the old woman who ran the Vermilion Emporium exactly what she thought of her deadly shop and all the weird things there.

"You're back already!" the old woman crowed as they stepped toward a counter near the back of the shop. She had a small black dog in her lap. "I'm so pleased you're not dead!" The dog yipped at them excitedly.

Twain rubbed at the bruise on his head. "Do you often kill your customers?"

The old woman shrugged. "Depends on what they're looking for. Never know what will happen." Then her eyes alighted on the thread of silver starlight around Twain's wrist. She gripped his hand and pulled him closer. "Ahh, this is lovely. But it's not one of mine. You brought this in with you, yes?"

Quinta had no idea how the old woman could've known that, but there was no disguising the extraordinarily pleased look on her face.

He nodded.

"And you hear the music?"

Twain nodded again. "Though it seems like I'm the only one. Do you know why that is?"

"Tremendously exciting!" the old woman said, letting go of Twain's hand and ignoring his question. "I wondered why we'd traveled back to Severon, but now I think I know. Many things are afoot if you've found starlight already."

"What are you talking about?" Quinta asked, stepping up to the counter. "Who did you travel with? What do you mean, 'things are afoot'? Can you tell me about this?" She pointed to the bottle of moonshadow at her neck.

"It's moonshadow."

"I know that," Quinta grumbled. "But what do I *do* with it?"

The woman shrugged again. "That's part of the mystery of it all, my girl. I can't tell you about the moonshadow. I don't know why I'm supposed to be here. Or why Twain found the starlight, but I certainly know it cannot be by chance. We shall have to figure it all out in time. Now, what did you find?"

Quinta would've liked to ask more questions, but she was still digesting the old woman's reply. She pulled the blue book from her pocket and set it on the counter.

Beside her, Twain bent over to peer at the book. The old woman gave a delighted hoot as she read the title.

"You see! He has the starlight, and you have the book. It all makes sense!"

Quinta couldn't quite believe it herself. She read the title out loud, just to make sure she wasn't imagining things: *A Beginner's Guide to Making Lace from Strands of Starlight. Written with an eye toward crafting lace for dreams, dalliances, despairs, damage, and duels.*

Quinta was stunned speechless. Here was a magical lacemaking book, and they just so happened to have the material—starlight—that they needed to begin the process. The old woman was right; that couldn't be a coincidence. Or perhaps magic was nothing more than coincidences piled up together to make something strange and new.

"You found exactly what you needed," the old woman said in a voice full of hearty approval. "I couldn't be more excited for you, and I can't wait to see where this adventure takes us." She scratched the small dog under his chin, and he licked her hand happily.

Quinta shook her head, gripping the bottle of moonshadow at her neck. Perhaps this wasn't the book she was looking for. Perhaps there'd been some mistake. How could she make magical lace? That hadn't been done for centuries, and no one remembered how to do it anymore. Assuredly, every child in Severon knew the stories of the kings and queens who had worn the lace once and how it had shaped empires. But now, all the lace that was left was grimy, drained of power, and in museums. Would this book really teach her how to create it again? Would she become as powerful as her ancestor who founded the Salon?

You are meant for great things.

What if she failed?

"I don't want the book," Quinta said. Which was a lie. She desperately wanted the book, but she didn't have enough money to pay for it. And she certainly didn't need another thing to fail at. Reluctantly, she pushed it across the counter.

The old woman slid the book back toward Quinta. "Nonsense. It was yours to find and you found it. That's how these things work."

"I can't afford it." She had a few coins in her pocket, enough to buy her and Twain some street food, but not enough to purchase anything in this strange shop.

"I can trade you some razorbill feathers." Twain pulled a small handful out of his bag.

The old woman shook her head and took a long sip from the cup of tea beside her. "You don't have to pay me anything. That's not how the Vermilion Emporium works. Take the thing you were meant to find, and then come back to me when you have questions."

"So you just give things away in this shop?" Quinta narrowed her eyes. She knew nearly nothing about business, but even she could see the flaws in this model.

"For some people, yes, but it's more complicated than that," the woman said. "As you'll come to find out. I'll be here for as long as you need me to be. Be sure to return soon. I'd love to show you the costumes room and the clock room. And pay attention to that starlight music, Twain! You'll need it if you want to find more celestial threads!"

And with those strange words, the old woman picked up her cup of tea and turned away, humming a song that sounded a bit like the waves on the shore at night. The dog followed at her heels as a door opened up in the wall behind the counter. The old woman and the dog disappeared through the door without another word.

Quinta and Twain were left standing beside the counter, trying to fully understand what had just happened.

"I guess we're done here," Quinta said, picking up the lacemaking book again. She slipped it back into her pocket. "Though I have about a thousand questions. Starting with what just happened and including where you're going in a month."

Twain put the starlight ribbon into his pocket. "I bet I have more. But let's get some dinner and try to make sense of all this on a full stomach. Does that work for you?"

Since Quinta was in no way ready to say goodbye to Twain yet, and since there was no one else who would be able to understand the very strange evening she'd had, it sounded like a great idea. "That is absolutely fine with me, but I'm warning you, surviving certain death has given me quite an appetite."

"I'm sure that's none of my concern."

Quinta groaned and Twain laughed, a high, golden sound that made Quinta believe she'd been hearing laughter all wrong for her entire life. What troubles could life hold when there were boys who laughed like that in the world?

"It is most certainly your concern," Quinta said. "Now, come on. Let me buy you dinner."

Twain held out his arm, and together they walked out of the Vermilion Emporium, quite a bit more delighted in each other than baffled by what they'd been through.

CHAPTER NINE
Twain

Quinta had exactly enough coins to get them half a scrawny roasted chicken from a grubby food stall in the Vermilion market.

"Absolutely not." Twain eyed the burned chicken and the seller's filthy hands and apron.

"What about two penny pies?" she suggested, nodding toward a stall farther down the street. "Or a ham sandwich from a coffee shop in Lapis?"

"We deserve far more than any of that after today." Twain pulled the remaining razorbill feathers from his bag. "I've only got nine, but that should be enough for a fancy supper."

"I'm supposed to buy you dinner!" Quinta protested. "It's my treat!"

"Next time you can pay," Twain said, certain there would be a next time. He led the way to his favorite trader's shop—a grim-faced building on the edge of Verdigris and Lapis.

Nine feathers weren't nearly enough to buy him passage on the *Lady's Revenge*. Of course, he could try to sell the starlight. But after what he had just been through with Quinta, he wasn't sure if that was a good idea, or if he even still wanted to do that. He didn't owe her anything, but somehow selling the starlight felt like a betrayal of her and the way she'd saved him.

"Here," Quinta said, pulling the two razorbill feathers from her pocket. "At least take these. I know these were gifts, but they're yours to sell. You should get every coin you can for them."

Twain took one of the feathers and pushed the other back toward her. "I'll sell an even ten feathers. Then, you still have part of your gift, and I'll have enough for a few weeks of food."

Twain could see Quinta trying to hide her expression of delight as she tucked the feather back into her pocket. "Want me to come in there with you?" She pointed to the shop.

"I've got it. Wait out here for me, okay? And can you hold this too?"

He pulled the coil of starlight out of his pocket and handed it to her.

"How do you know I won't run off with it?" She slipped it into her own pocket.

Twain shrugged. Trusting this girl he'd just met with the most valuable thing he'd ever found was perhaps the most foolish thing he'd done today, but he couldn't help it. He had trusted Quinta with the starlight and his life in the book room; he had no problem handing her the silver thread a second time.

"I hope you won't run off with it. Because then I can't buy you dinner. And I promise I'm full of interesting conversations."

Quinta scrunched up her nose at him, but a smile lurked beneath the gesture. "Fine, I'll be here. But don't take too long. I'm starving."

Twain promised to be back soon, and he left her standing outside the shop. Luckily, the store wasn't crowded when he went in, and the owner was in a buying mood. He cackled to see the razorbill feathers—"Only wish you had more! Can't keep these things in the shop, what with all those rich ladies in Verdigris wanting dresses from them. If you find more, bring them to me first!"—and he gave Twain five gold coins for them. It was a princely sum for feathers, and Twain wished for a moment that he'd never stopped at the Vermilion Emporium. Then he'd have been able to sell the dozens of feathers he'd found. His pockets would've been heavy with coins and his ticket on the *Lady's Revenge* paid for twice over.

But then he would've never met Quinta, and perhaps knowing her would be worth more than a dozen pockets full of gold.

Twain wasn't sure about any of that, but he did know exactly the restaurant to take Quinta to.

After the feathers were sold, he led Quinta to the museum district in Lapis. They stopped in front of a café with a marble facade and bright-blue awnings above all the windows.

"Blue Lily Café? Are you sure we can afford this?" Quinta peered through the windows, taking in the small tables with candles on them and the outrageous, expensive clothing the diners wore. She glanced toward Twain's torn shirt and brushed at the dust on her own skirt.

"We absolutely can," Twain said. He'd never been in the Blue Lily, but he and Zand had dreamed of going there many times. After nearly dying twice today, he was going to eat there tonight.

Although the hostess scowled at their clothing, after Twain flashed his gold coins she led them to a terrace that overlooked the sea. As they walked through the restaurant, whispers of disapproval followed them. Boys in torn shirts and girls with filthy hemlines didn't usually dine on the terrace in Lapis, but here they were. They ordered everything on the evening's menu: fish in a creamy sauce, gem-bright vegetables, fresh bread, and purple fruit. As they ate, Twain pointed out the cliffs where he'd gathered the razorbill feathers and Quinta told Twain stories about the Celestial Circus. Behind her, the full moon rose and the lights of the city danced off the ocean. Seagulls shouted their accusing, mournful songs into the night, and Quinta wove a world of magic with her words. Twain lost track of how many times he laughed at something she said, and he kept asking her ridiculous questions to keep her talking.

How long had they been at the table?

Twain had no idea, but he was now quite certain he could listen to Quinta talk for many more hours. He liked watching her mouth shape words and the ways her dreams, like herself, were daring and bold. He also liked the way she cut her fruit into pieces, and then forgot to eat it because she was gesturing too wildly with her fork.

Around them, diners came and went. Most of them were Very Respectable Folks, who wore richly woven coats or ropes of pearls that brushed their chairs as they sat. Two artists were positioned at the edge of the terrace, painting the night sky and the harbor for the pleasure of the guests. It was quite a coveted thing, being an artist. And the people of Severon paid highly for the pleasure of seeing them work. They liked to imagine themselves in their shoes.

One woman at the table beside theirs was saying loudly, "Well, you know, I'd like to have been an artist. But there were the children to think of. You can hardly have a mother living in a garret, painting and doing who-knows-what-else until after midnight." The other people at her table laughed, and Quinta shot the woman a poisonous look.

What the artists thought of being ogled, Twain didn't know. But he didn't much think he'd like to be gaped at like a zoo creature while he was making something beautiful. Nor did he think that every beautiful thing needed to be consumed by others. Sometimes it was enough to create something, even if no one else ever saw it.

"Hello there, are you listening?" Quinta asked, breaking into his thoughts. The waiter had just brought them cups of coffee, and she had her hands curved around her china teacup. Which was entirely not the right way to drink coffee in a fancy restaurant, but Quinta didn't seem to care. "You look like you're floating out there somewhere over the sea."

Her voice held a teasing note, and Twain smiled at her. "I was thinking about art and beautiful things."

Maybe he held her gaze for too long, because Quinta blushed at that comment. He started to say that he was really not thinking about her, but there was no reason to do so. Quinta was art herself, a wild, lovely, dream of a girl with the night at her back. A long moment of silence stretched between them.

"Speaking of art," Quinta said finally, in a low voice that only he could hear. "I want to make lace from your starlight. Can we try that?"

Twain wouldn't have been able to say no to Quinta, even if he had anything better to do. He was also terribly curious about how lacemaking was done, and he wanted to spend more time with her.

"We can." Twain took a long sip of his coffee, savoring the bitter flavor. It was his favorite luxury and one that he almost never treated himself to.

"Even if it destroys the starlight? That's possible, you know." Quinta bit her lip, looking worried.

Twain paused for a moment. Even with their extravagant dinner, from the sale of the feathers he had enough money to live on for the next few weeks, but that was it. Without selling the starlight, he'd still have to find a way to pay for his ticket on the *Lady's Revenge*. And if anyone came around to collect Zand's debts, then Twain would be out of money much faster.

But where would they find another strand of starlight? And what if Quinta ended up doing something truly amazing with it?

Also, Zand had studied the history of starlight magic, and ever since they were kids, he'd wanted to find out more about it. Twain couldn't bring his brother back to life or take back the words they'd hurled at each other that last morning, but maybe by helping Quinta, he could complete some of his brother's research. Maybe for once in his life, he could actually help and not hurt.

"I'm willing to risk it. Want to try tonight?"

"Of course," Quinta said, draining her coffee. "Let's go now."

A clock nearby struck eleven, its bells ringing out while Twain paid the bill.

Once they were outside the restaurant, bellies full and the prospect of something tremendously odd and perhaps magical in front of them, Twain got nervous. Quinta was also quiet. They'd just spent hours talking, and now they had nothing to say.

Which is what happens when you meet someone in a heady rush, nearly die together, and then share a meal. For a long moment, they stood outside the Blue Lily as rich people promenaded past and carriages clattered over the cobbled streets. People came to Lapis to see and be seen, and even after dark, the museums and galleries stayed open. Noise from dinners, concerts, and parties spilled onto the street, filling it further.

Twain watched as a pair of scruffy-looking boys put a ladder beneath the gas lamp closest to the restaurant. It had gone out, and the boys were here to relight it. They joked with each other as the tallest boy climbed up the ladder, holding a small candle. He held the flame inside the lamp, and it caught fire immediately. The boy on the ground cheered and the one on the ladder gave an exaggerated bow.

For a painful moment, Twain was reminded of how he and Zand used to dare each other to climb the light poles, and how their mother would scold them for it.

"Your place or mine?" Quinta asked, cutting into his memories.

Before Twain could answer, a tall, broad woman in a long black dress passed by them.

"Quinta?" The woman stopped suddenly and turned around. "Whatever are you doing here?"

Quinta stood a little taller, smoothing her hands over her skirt. "Hello, Mrs. Davenport," she said in a peevish voice. "Do you mean, what am I doing outside the studio? Well, even us drudges have to eat sometimes."

Twain froze when he heard the woman's name.

Mrs. Davenport?

Dr. Davenport had been a businessman and his parents' patron. Was this Mrs. Davenport his widow? The woman who had refused to give Twain and Zand any money? He'd never met her—he and Zand had gone to her house after their parents' deaths, asking for some support, and a rude butler promptly ejected them—but he'd always wondered why she abandoned them. What sort of cruel woman left two children to starve? Not that they were actually her responsibility, but there was an understanding between patrons and the families of those they supported. If Mrs. Davenport had kept that understanding, then he and Zand would've had it easier. Zand wouldn't have had to work twice as hard to get into the Arcana. Twain wouldn't have had to hustle quite so much to feed them, and they wouldn't have been on the cliffs that fateful day.

If Mrs. Davenport had kept her husband's promise, Zand would still be here.

Twain inhaled raggedly, fighting to keep some self-control. He didn't know this was the same person. There could be a hundred Mrs. Davenports in Severon.

Mrs. Davenport laughed and patted Quinta's arm, which made Quinta flinch. "Such a funny little thing you are. Of course I know you need to leave the studio to eat. I'm just surprised to see you here in Lapis. The Blue Lily is almost too expensive for me, even with my late husband's money, bless Dr. Davenport's soul."

So, this really was the Mrs. Davenport who had ruined his life.

Twain took another shaky breath, biting his tongue. He couldn't start a fight with Mrs. Davenport in Lapis because the guards might come. And they might somehow connect him to Gustave and Henri. And then he couldn't help Quinta weave lace. And then—

"Charming, as always," Quinta muttered with a scowl. "It's a pleasure to say goodbye, Mrs. Davenport."

The woman gripped Quinta's arm and tilted her head conspiratorially. "Do you know where I'm going?"

Quinta shook out of her grasp. "No idea."

Twain found himself leaning toward Mrs. Davenport too. She had a sort of air about her, as if she was the keeper of tremendous secrets. He wasn't sure if he wanted to hear this secret or shake her and demand to know why she'd ruined his life. Of course, he knew Zand's death wasn't her fault. But that didn't stop a hot whip of anger from searing through him.

Quinta crossed her arms. "I bet you're going to a meeting of the Severon Witches Society."

"Wrong!" Mrs. Davenport cried. "I'm hosting a Midnight Party for them! Tonight! And would you believe it: they're going to let me in! If—and this is perhaps a big if—I can show them that magical shop I told you about."

"The Vermilion Emporium?" Quinta asked quickly.

"Haven't seen it, have you? That would be just my luck if the photographer's girl found it before I did. Though I suppose if you are your mother's daughter, then there's always a chance. . . ."

Quinta's face changed at the words. Her customary scowl deepened into a fierce look that was part fury and part resolve. "I'm absolutely my mother's daughter, but no, I've not seen it. Now, if you'll excuse us, we have to be going. I hope you and the SWS find what you're looking for. Even if such a shop is utterly, wildly impossible."

Quinta grabbed Twain's arm and marched him away from Mrs. Davenport, who still stood in the middle of the sidewalk, gaping a bit as she tried to work out what Quinta had said.

With one last glance over his shoulder at Mrs. Davenport, Twain quickened his steps to keep up with Quinta. His anger was still there, but another part of his mind—the more rational part, which sounded a bit like Zand—reminded him: the past was the past, and thinking murderous thoughts about rich widows wouldn't do any good. He was here to help Quinta figure out what to do with the starlight. Once he did that, then he'd find a way to buy his ticket out of Severon. "Where are we going?"

"My place." Quinta wore a determined look that was very nearly terrifying. "I'm going to make this magic work. Even if it kills me."

CHAPTER TEN

Quinta

This magic might in fact kill Quinta. After all, her mother had died working with it. And—as she'd told Mrs. Davenport—she was her mother's daughter. As she and Twain walked through Lapis and to the edge of Verdigris, she tried to make sense of how she could weave lace from starlight and not meet the same fate as her mother.

You are meant for great things.

This was her chance. Her ticket to great things. And she'd risk whatever else that might bring along the way. Of course, she didn't even know how she was going to make the lace. But thanks to having to mend costumes for the Celestial Circus as a child, she was decent enough at sewing; maybe that would be helpful.

"That's where I live," Quinta said, pointing to a small building tucked into a row of shops. "Pierre's—my boss's—apartment is above the studio, and I have the entire third floor to myself. It's not much, but it's home."

As they stood outside the studio, Quinta thought about the first time she met Pierre after her mother's death. It had been four years after the circus broke up and she had been living like a ghost in one of the great houses of Verdigris. There were rumors at that time in some parts of society about a spirit who ate a household's food and slept in their beds. Some of the more superstitious houses even took to leaving food out for her. On the day Pierre walked into her life again, she'd been fourteen. He'd been standing outside the mansion where she'd spent the night. He spoke in loud carnival-barker tones to the woman of the house. The noise of his voice woke her, and she rushed to the window.

There he was, wearing a striped shirt and top hat, just as she remembered. He had been Quinta's mother's best friend, and he'd left Severon on the night of the Grand Eleina's death without a backward glance at the daughter she'd left behind.

Quinta had more than a few questions and a bellyful of anger for him. Without thinking about her safety or being discovered in the great house, she'd run down the main stairs, startling the housekeeper and a maid carrying a pile of sheets. Before they could yell at her or drag her into the scullery for questioning, she was out the door.

Pierre stood in the gravel driveway, fiddling with a box camera on a tall wooden tripod. As she approached, he fussed at the family, gesturing at them to scoot over. But his voice left him as Quinta skidded to a stop in front of him. His eyebrows shot up as he took in the sight of her—she was scrawny and dressed in a dirty blue dress she'd stolen from the attic of a house where she'd slept a few months ago.

"Quinta?" he'd gasped. His beard was longer than she remembered, and he blinked a dozen times at her. "How are you still alive?"

"No thanks to you! Why did you leave?"

It sounded like she meant, "why did you leave Severon after my mother died?" but what she really meant was, "why did you leave me?"

"Excuse me," trilled the lady of the house, interrupting their reunion. "We're ready for our portrait now. Please do hurry. I have a lunch engagement in an hour."

Quinta and Pierre both turned. The woman wore a hat as wide as a sink, trimmed in purple feathers. A fur wrap covered her shoulders. Beside her stood a man in a white suit and two children dressed like dolls in a shop.

"Excuse me, Mrs. Davenport," Pierre had replied, bowing low. "My assistant came to tell me of something we forgot at the shop. Hold still; we'll get this shot."

And that was how Quinta started working with Pierre.

Although Pierre let her sleep above the apartment where he lived and was generally kind enough, he had his own life and his own friends. That's why he had abandoned her—because he didn't want the responsibility of raising a child. And that was fine. She wasn't his responsibility in the first place. Quinta knew that. Even if she still got angry at him sometimes for deserting her.

Occasionally, Quinta missed being a ghost in the great houses. It was quiet in her room above Pierre's shop. Warm, but lonely. There was no way she could imagine her family was downstairs, waiting for her. No friends to pretend to meet at the balls—

"Pierre's Photography Palace: photos of all sorts, specializing in the occult and other flights of fancy," Twain said, interrupting her thoughts as he read the sign above the shop. "These are certainly interesting."

He quirked an eyebrow as he pointed to the photos in the shop window, all of them contrived images of fortune-tellers, members of the SWS, and a few ridiculous, over-the-top wedding photos.

"We have a corner on the market. If you can believe that there's actually a market for such things."

"For every door a key, I suppose. Will I get to meet Pierre?"

Quinta had told Twain all about Pierre over dinner, but for some reason she didn't want them to meet each other. Something in her wanted to keep Twain to herself for now.

"He should be out tonight," Quinta said, hurrying into the alley between the studio and the art gallery next door. She led the way to a back entrance, but as soon as she opened the door, a chorus of male voices—all loud and quite drunk—rushed at them, belting out a sea shanty.

"Soon may the Wellerman come . . . ," sang the group enthusiastically through cheers and the clink of glasses.

Quinta closed the door. Pierre was clearly having a party, and by the sounds of it, they'd be going for a long while yet.

She could try to sneak Twain past the group in the living room, but if Pierre and his friends saw them, they'd want introductions. And they might ask all sorts of questions. Pierre would probably wink at Quinta conspiratorially, as if he was somehow delighted that she was taking a boy back to her rooms. It was too messy, and Quinta didn't want to deal with it.

She closed the door. "Not my room. Can we try yours?"

A dark look passed over Twain's face. "My place isn't very nice." His voice was hesitant, carrying a hint of shame. "I haven't really had anyone over in . . . well, a very long time."

"I don't care about nice. We just need a spot away from prying eyes and too many questions."

Twain paused for another moment. "We can try my house. But I can't promise you're going to like it."

What was she getting herself into? Perhaps she shouldn't follow Twain to his home—but she'd survived on the streets for years; she could handle a little mess.

As it turned out, Twain's home was beyond messy.

"This is where you live?" Quinta asked in dismay as she surveyed the small seaside shack Twain had led her to. It was one room, and the only furniture inside it was a table made from a barrel, two rickety chairs, a pile of water-stained books, and a mattress in one corner. A violin case sat out on the table, but there were no cupboards and no stove. "How do you stay warm in the winter?"

The winters in Severon, especially this close to the sea, were wolves in the night. They would find their way into all the cracks in the cottage.

Twain nodded toward the violin case. "Usually I spend the winter playing in taverns. After they closed each night, my brother and I would burn driftwood. When that ran out, we'd huddle under the blankets and think of summer."

"Your brother?" Quinta wasn't sure more than one person could live in this tiny shack.

"Zand. He was an Arcana scholar. He . . . died . . . a few months ago. Out on the cliffs. After he fell, I sold his mattress and clothes. . . ."

"Is this where you grew up? What about your parents?"

Twain shook his head. "Our parents were scholars—Arcana and Scientifica, if you can believe it. They died at sea two years ago. We lost our house and everything in it to my father's debts. We didn't have anywhere else to go, but my violin teacher and his wife own this hut. They let us stay here for free. It isn't much, but it's been home. . . ." Twain's voice trailed off, and he ran his fingers over the violin case.

So much loss. Quinta was both heartbroken for Twain and impressed by his ability to survive in this place for so long. She wanted to go to him, wrap him in her arms, and tell him that since they'd found each other, perhaps they'd never be alone again.

But, of course, that was an incredibly strange thing to do, so she put her hands in her pockets and didn't say anything.

They stood there in silence, the room feeling smaller and smaller the longer they didn't talk.

"Want to get started on the lace?" Quinta asked at the same moment a knock sounded on the door, startling them both. It wasn't a friendly thump. It didn't ask: "Are you home?" It demanded: "You better be home!"

A loud, rough voice yelled: "Open the door, Twain! We know you're in there. We spotted you coming back through the city."

"You can't attack upper-class people and get away with it, Vermilion rat!" added another voice. "We're here for the invitation. You better get it or we're going to see you hanged!"

98

"You expecting someone?" Quinta darted a glance toward the door as more pounding shook it.

"No one good." Twain's face looked like he'd seen a ghost. He flipped over a paper-thin rug, lifted a floorboard, and pulled out a wooden box. Inside the box was a book, and inside that was a silver-and-blue piece of paper. Quinta had time to read, "You're invited to the Scholar's Ball"—(what was Twain doing with an invitation to the Casorina's ball?)—before he dropped it on the mattress. Then he shoved the table against the door. Grabbing his violin case, Twain moved to the window at the back of the cabin. He pushed at the window, trying to force it open. It was swollen from salt spray and didn't budge. Twain grabbed a blanket from the bed, wrapped it around his hand, and smashed the glass. He knocked the broken glass out of the window, and a gust of sea air surged into the shack. "C'mon. We don't want them to find us. I'll help you through."

The thumping on the front door grew louder and another voice called out: "Did you hear that? He's getting away!"

"Get the door open now, Gustave!"

Quinta snatched up the silver-and-blue invitation as someone slammed into the shack's front door. The table surged backward. Somehow the door held together, but it wouldn't last long. With a glance over her shoulder, she moved to where Twain crouched by the now-shattered window. In one quick motion, she stepped on Twain's knee and let him boost her over the windowsill. Since the shack was built on a dune, the drop from the window was higher than Quinta had expected. Another crash sounded behind her, and Twain swore loudly. Quinta looked down at the beach, said a prayer to her mother's ghost, and jumped.

Quinta landed on the sandy slope below Twain's window and skidded down the dune. The invitation flew from her hands as she bumped along the sand, rolling and sliding. On her right, Twain rolled-fell-slid past her and somehow landed on his feet at the bottom of the slope. She stopped beside him a moment later.

"This way," he said, grabbing her hand and helping her up. In his other hand was the violin case.

"But your invitation! I dropped it!"

They both glanced up the sandbank, where the silver-and-blue piece of paper sat, half-hidden by the sand. Two men, one in a bowler hat and the other in a torn velvet jacket, stood at the top of the dune, yelling something.

Twain looked conflicted for only a moment before he shook his head. "Forget it. We have to get out of here."

As one of the men started sliding toward them, Quinta and Twain ran along the beach, kicking up sand beneath their feet, putting distance between themselves and their pursuers.

"Who are those men?" Quinta asked breathlessly.

"Long story. Not a happy one. Tell you when we find a place to hide?"

Quinta nodded, and they hurried up an incline that zigzagged toward the city. Her fancy dinner churned in her stomach, and she wished they had stayed at her place, even with Pierre and his friends there.

The cliffside path ended, depositing them in Vermilion. Quinta glanced behind her as they headed into the city. The two men were nearing the top of the path. The one in the bowler hat had Twain's invitation clutched in his hands.

For one dangerously irrational second, Quinta wanted to snatch the invitation back and do something that would make these men stop chasing Twain for good. But she couldn't fight two people. It's not like she had magic.

Yet.

She patted her pocket, relieved to find her book of lace patterns was still there. Behind Quinta, the two men spotted them, and they yelled out.

Twain pulled on Quinta's hand, and, still running, they turned down another street, this one full of bars and brothels. A loud group of men and women in green Scientifica scholars' jackets surged around them, filling the street. The scholars laughed and called out to one another drunkenly, and Quinta and Twain slipped into the crowd, hoping to be lost among the press of bodies.

"This way," Twain said, pulling Quinta down a side street and into a shadowy doorway beside a brothel. "Don't suppose you know any secret places to camp out for a bit? I don't want to bring this trouble to your doorstep."

Quinta didn't want that either, and she still desperately wanted to see if she could do something with the starlight. Mrs. Davenport's words about the SWS party she was hosting floated to the surface of Quinta's mind.

"I know a place," Quinta said. "This way."

With a glance over their shoulders to make sure the two men weren't behind them, Quinta and Twain headed out of Vermilion and toward Verdigris. Quinta took the long way to her destination, a great stone mansion that overlooked the sea. It was the crown jewel of Verdigris, and servants bustled in and out of the house. A look of recognition crossed Twain's face as he stared at the mansion.

"Remember the woman we met earlier, Mrs. Davenport?"

"I remember. This is her place, right?" His voice was tight and the set of his mouth grim.

Quinta wasn't sure how he knew it was Mrs. Davenport's house, but she nodded. "It is. She's hosting a party tonight for the Severon Witches Society, and I'm sure she won't notice if we borrow a corner of her attic."

Despite the risk of being recognized, Quinta loved the idea of working real magic just a few floors up from all these want-to-be witches.

"How do we get in?" Twain asked, warily eyeing the mansion.

"Just look like you belong. And don't say anything."

Linking her arm through Twain's, she strolled across the street as if they were Verdigris born and bred. Despite their torn, dirty clothing, none of the wealthy SWS women getting out of carriages or standing near the front door looked twice at them, even though Quinta had seen most of them during photography sessions. Mrs. Davenport's voice rose above the hum of the others, and Quinta nearly fell over to see that she greeted her guests in a cape spangled with silver stars and a pointed black hat. Pierre must have loaned them to her after today's photography session. Quinta had to bite her lip to keep from laughing.

"Witchy," Twain murmured. "I appreciate the added mystery."

"This way," Quinta managed through a laugh. She pulled Twain down a path between two enormous hedges.

They threaded along the path and came to the back door of the mansion. Without hesitation, Quinta opened the door and strolled into the kitchen. A delicious smell rose from the stove, and, despite her huge dinner and long run, it was all she could do not to grab one of the tiny iced cakes off a nearby tray. They hurried through the kitchen without anyone fussing at them or really noticing. Quinta had learned in her years of staying alive in other people's houses that if you looked like you were doing something, and the household's servants were busy, they'd leave you alone.

No one stopped them as Quinta and Twain slipped into the servants' stairway and dashed up several flights, moving toward the top of the house.

Quinta paused on the third-floor landing and opened a door.

"Have you been here before?" Twain asked.

A flash of memories moved through Quinta's mind, but she shook her head, refusing to give too many months of hunger and cold a place to take root. All she said was: "I stayed a winter here, a few years after my mother died. I explored the whole house. Now, shh—"

A pair of maids walked past the servants' stairway, and Quinta pulled her head in from where she was peering out the doorway. She held a finger to her lips as the maids moved down the hall. Once they were gone, she turned to Twain.

"The attic is at the end of the hallway. Once we're up there, we'll have all the time in the world to talk. Let's go!"

With a quick motion, Quinta opened the door and slipped through. She was down the hallway in a flash, barely sparing a glance for the open doorways that led to guest bedrooms. Twain's feet pounded behind her, and she almost turned around to shush him, but they were already at the attic door. And not a moment too soon as the maids who'd passed them earlier were now coming out of the bedroom they'd been in, carrying piles of sheets and gossiping loudly.

"Here," Quinta said, pushing on a panel in the wall. A door sprang open, and she stepped through it.

"You're marvelous," Twain muttered as he closed the door and followed Quinta up the stairs. Darkness enclosed them, but Twain pulled out the starlight, which made a silver globe in the gloom.

Quinta couldn't keep a silly, smitten grin off her face. She was feeling rather marvelous, but she'd never had anyone tell her that—especially not a boy like Twain.

CHAPTER ELEVEN
Twain

Twain was still not used to having company. After so many months alone, being near another person—much less someone like Quinta—for this many hours overwhelmed him. Not that he would've left. Not for all the money in Severon. He was here with her for as long as it took to figure out if this book of hers really could teach them to make starlight lace.

His violin case banged against his legs as they walked up the attic stairs. He wasn't sure why he'd brought it, but Quinta said she liked violin music, and his fingers itched to try and play the starlight melody. Plus, the thought of Gustave and Henri taking his violin made Twain cringe.

"Holy furniture graveyard," Twain said with a low whistle when they reached the top of the attic stairs.

He moved the coil of starlight around, illuminating a wild landscape of broken tables, old-fashioned armoires, dusty clothing, old toys, and lots of other things from the house downstairs. It was a bit like the mess in the Vermilion Emporium, but at the Emporium the piles of stuff had an air of anticipation. They were mysteries waiting to be solved. Here, in Mrs. Davenport's attic, there was just a feeling of neglect. These things were cast aside, no longer useful, forgotten. She'd abandoned all of them as she'd abandoned Twain and Zand. How much of this stuff could Mrs. Davenport have given to him and Zand to use or sell? How would their lives have been different with just an ounce of her charity or discarded goods?

Twain pushed those thoughts aside as Quinta threaded her way through the maze confidently, like a Verdigris debutante walking through a ballroom. Thinking of a ballroom made him remember his invitation to the Scholar's Ball, clutched in Henri's hands. Twain wasn't going to go the ball anyway—he wanted nothing to do with scholars and the ball, as he'd made so abundantly clear to his parents time and time again—but that didn't mean Gustave and Henri should—

"Are you coming?" Quinta's voice was impatient. "What are you looking for back there?"

He hurried to catch up with her, skipping over her question because he didn't want to get into his complicated history with Mrs. Davenport at the moment. "You seem to know your way around this attic pretty well."

"I'm a queen in an empire of junk. Now, let's see if my treasure is still here." Quinta plopped down on a yellow velvet sofa that had been shoved beneath a round stained-glass window. Weak streetlight filtered through the glass flowers and peacock design on the window, decorating the floor with gems of light. The sofa had one broken leg and tilted precariously. A cloud of dust rose from it as Quinta dug her hands between the cushions.

"Aha!" she said triumphantly, pulling out a stubby candle and a box of matches. "I hoped these would still be here."

Quinta struck a match, and a ball of golden light joined the silver glow of Twain's starlight, illuminating their corner of the attic. Quinta rested the candle in a dish on a side table and looked up expectantly at Twain. In the candlelight, she was lovely. Twain's heart ached with longing. Sharp edges and all, Quinta was a girl he would very much like to kiss, but she deserved more than just a quick tavern-style dalliance. And Twain wasn't sure he could give her that.

Not that she was asking anyway.

"Are you ready?" Quinta held out the book, forcing his thoughts back to practical matters.

He had so many questions: Would anyone find them up here? Why did Quinta look like she was at home on the broken, dusty sofa? And what would happen if they unleashed something powerful and strange that they couldn't stop, like the book avalanche in the Vermilion Emporium?

But he didn't ask any of those things. Placing his violin case on the table next to the candle, Twain sat down beside Quinta. The tilt of the couch sent Quinta nearly sprawling into his lap, but she didn't even notice.

Eagerly, Quinta pulled the table toward them, positioning the book so they both could read it. "Ready?"

"Ready."

With a sharp inhale, she flipped open the blue cover, revealing creamy-white pages that had large water stains on them.

Nothing happened.

"Huh." Quinta glared at the book. "I'd hoped for a bit more fanfare. That's why I'd not opened it yet." She turned the book over, shaking out its pages, as if that could make magic appear.

Twain nodded, trying to keep a smile off his face. "I expected at least a small dragon to appear when you opened it. Or maybe a magical ship to float past. Or perhaps a whole family of mermaids to greet us."

Quinta made a noise of disbelief. "You're a clown, now? Is that it? Did you ever think of joining the circus?"

"I'm teasing, None of Your Concern. You looked like you were about to cry."

"I was most certainly not about to cry."

"Well, then I'll admit, I expected something a bit weird or wonderful to happen, but it looks like it's paper and ink, dust and stories. So, perhaps we should read it?"

"Magnificent reasoning," Quinta muttered, but a smile twitched at the edge of her mouth. "I'll begin. 'Chapter One. Things you need when weaving starlight. First, have a steady supply of starlight. . . .' Well, of course we would need that, but what do we do with it?" She flipped through the first chapter impatiently.

"Does it say where starlight comes from?" Twain shifted in order to read over Quinta's shoulder.

"No . . . it assumes you'll have a supply. . . ." She flipped through a few more chapters. "This is all background on weaving, a chapter on the advantages of hand weaving over using looms . . ."

"You're not going to read those?" Twain wasn't a patient soul, but when working with magical substances that shouldn't exist, he felt perhaps it was a good idea to go into things prepared.

"Later. What I want to know tonight is how to turn this"— she pointed to the thread of starlight coiled in Twain's hand—"into something we can do magic with."

It started to rain outside, a low thrum against the window. Quinta bent her head over the book, and Twain did the same. Together, they read:

> Making lace from starlight has long been the goal of many dreamers. But, you see, the process itself is far less simple than it might seem. Why make lace, you might ask. What even is to be gained from . . .

"It does go on, doesn't it," Twain said, looking up from the page.

It did. The book, written by some jolly, verbose soul, went on and on at length. Quinta skimmed sections with titles like, "A History of Lace and Its Magical Counterparts"; "Knots for Forget-Me-Nots"; and "Ladies and Lace, Some Considerations." Finally, she stopped at a diagram near the back of the book. It was titled: "A Joyful Beginning: Lace for Healing."

"That looks like a fisherman's net." Twain traced a finger over the lines. "Want to start there?"

With a glance at Twain's cut and bruised hands, Quinta reached for the ribbon of starlight. Right now, it flowed like sand or seawater, but in the book room it had been a rope. How could it become lace?

"Let's try to heal your hands," she said, studying the picture. She started separating the starlight into smaller threads. "It says: 'this pattern is the basic one for all future lace works, especially for healing. Joy is the beginning, and this is meant for steadying a dreamer and pulling their hopes into a shape.'"

Her fingers moved through the strands of starlight as she talked, twisting it and teasing bits apart in some sort of textile alchemy that Twain couldn't even follow.

Over, under, through, around, back, beside, below, and beyond the filaments of starlight went in Quinta's hands. Somehow, she seemed to know exactly what to do. She didn't stop moving the starlight until, abruptly, she did. The whole time, her eyebrows were knitted in concentration as her busy fingers made magic out of mystery.

"How do you know what to do?" Twain asked in an awed whisper.

"Shh! It's nearly there. I just need to figure out this last section."

Abashed, Twain scooted up the couch (he'd been sliding toward the floor) and looked again at the diagram in the book. Somehow, Quinta had moved past the first fisherman's net and was now twisting the starlight into what looked like an elaborate floral pattern.

It was as if she was listening to some music that Twain couldn't hear. Which was interesting since he'd been hearing the starlight's song throughout the day. Now, it seemed to be singing to Quinta. Her hands did a few last acrobatic things, and then stopped.

"What do you think?" Quinta held out the starlight, which was now woven into a rectangle the size of a handkerchief. Somehow she had separated the one thread into three-dozen silver filaments and twisted them into a pattern of flowers, stars, and feathers.

"It's beautiful. May I?"

Quinta passed him the starlight handkerchief.

The moment it touched Twain's hand, something happened inside him. Yes, he'd been holding the starlight ribbon for hours, and it had been a bit warm on his hand and it had brought light. But, somehow, through the transformation into lace, now it felt different. As Twain held the lace, a surge of sunlight went through him. It was the joy of hyacinths peeking through the soil at the first breath of spring. It was a child finding their footing and taking their first steps in the world. It was a puppy seeing its beloved owner return home after a long day apart. It was pure joy, fragile as an eggshell, but holding something precious and necessary inside.

It warmed his shredded hands, soothing them with a faint silver light. As he watched, the torn skin grew back and his cuts healed.

"What do you feel?" Quinta peered at him anxiously and then read from the book. "'This pattern will bring the wearer the most profound joy for a few moments and heal any surface wounds. Done correctly, it can weave pleasure with joy, leaving the receiver of the lace lighter than they've ever been. They will take this joy into their life, and it shall change them, just a little bit.'"

Twain didn't know what to say, but tears streamed down his face. Something in the lace handkerchief reminded him of every time he and Zand had a good day. Of the few times his mother read him to sleep. Of the first time he climbed to the top of a cliff on his own. Of what it felt like to put everything he was feeling into a violin's song. He stood up, hands outstretched, wonder propelling him a few steps away from the couch.

A cushion thumped against his back. "Hey!" Quinta called. "Are you alright? Do I need to throw another cushion? Because if you don't say something soon, I really will start to worry. Maybe I did it wrong? The book says if you make a mistake in the pattern—"

Quinta's words stopped as Twain turned toward her and held out his hands. "Look."

She stood, reaching for his hands and taking them in her own. "Your hands? They're healed?"

He nodded, holding her gaze. Her hands were warm inside his. He'd been surprised to meet Quinta today, but now he knew that it had also been a day of joy. Another tear rolled down his cheek.

Quinta watched it, biting her lip. "But have I also broken you? Why are you crying . . . ?" Her voice trembled, as if some much deeper fear lived beneath the words.

"Sweet Quinta. I'm already broken, but you've given me joy. Thank you."

Quinta exhaled sharply. "Oh, thank goodness. And you're welcome."

She moved a step closer, gently wiping away another tear that trailed over his cheekbone. Twain held his breath at her touch, not sure if he should bridge that small gap between them and kiss her. Her lips parted slightly as her hand lingered on his face, her eyes searing him. Between them, the silver starlight handkerchief glowed.

He was so much taller than she was, but she would fit in his arms perfectly. Letting out a shaky breath, she tilted her head upward. He would just have to bend his head down, meet her lips . . .

But he held back, not wanting to step over the threshold. Quinta deserved more than a casual kiss from a boy who was leaving in a month. And Twain was a boy who broke things. He didn't want to hurt Quinta. Better to keep his distance. Fighting his desire to kiss her, he instead touched the small bottle that hung from her throat.

"What's this?"

Quinta was so near, Twain could count the flecks of honey in her dark eyes. "Moonshadow. My mother gave it to me."

Despite his resolve, the closeness of Quinta was muddling his brain, making him want to hold her now, even if it was only for a short time. Who was to say a month wasn't long enough? Why did he have to make that choice? "What do you do with moonshadow?"

"I have no idea," Quinta admitted. "But I'm going to find out."

Quinta tilted her head thoughtfully then, quirking a small smile. Twain ached to kiss the side of her mouth.

She was so close her knee bumped against his. Her hand still rested on his cheek, small and tender. Surely one kiss wouldn't hurt anything. Surely they could figure out what to do with leaving and staying. Why couldn't they try, just for a night?

113

Twain's arm moved before his brain caught up. It snaked around Quinta, pulling her toward him so their bodies pressed against each other. Her sharp intake of breath made something clench inside him, low in his belly. Unable to help himself, he leaned down, right as Quinta rose up on her toes to press her lips against his.

It was a slow, sweet, summertime kiss, both tentative and hinting at things to come. As Quinta wrapped her arms around his neck, he imagined they were kissing under the stars on the beach in July, not in some dusty attic, made chilly by the October wind and rain. Twain's mouth moved hungrily over Quinta's as they found a new music within their bodies.

Joy. It was joy to kiss her. To have found her, even though he hadn't known he was looking.

"Oh no! I'm sorry," said Quinta, pulling away suddenly.

Reality crashed in, bringing Twain back to the fact that he was kissing someone he met a few hours ago like she was precious to him. Which was silly, of course. But was it really so wrong to find a little joy together? She had kissed him back and, even though he knew Quinta deserved more than he could give, maybe they could enjoy each other for a little bit.

"Don't be sorry. We can do that as much as you'd like. I assure you, I don't mind."

Quinta shook her head. "You don't understand. I always leave the people I sleep with. I'm a one-night girl."

Twain brushed a curl away from Quinta's face. "We're just kissing. I'm not asking you to marry me, None of Your Concern.

Believe it or not, I've done this before. I know a kiss is not a big deal." Twain tried to flash his most charming smile, but it fell short.

Most kisses weren't a big deal. But this one with Quinta had felt like so much more than the other kisses he'd had. He didn't tell her that, of course.

Quinta stepped out of his embrace. "You don't understand. I *always* abandon the people I sleep with, and I usually sleep with the people I kiss. Which means I leave them the next day. And—"

She didn't say it, but Twain felt it too. He didn't want her to leave the next day. Even if they just met and he was leaving in a month.

"We won't kiss again." It cost him to say it, but it was the right choice.

"Promise?"

"I absolutely promise not to kiss you again until you're ready to stay with me forever."

Quinta laughed at that, breaking some of the tension in the room. "Does that line work on the tavern girls? Or is it because of your violin skills?" She nodded toward the violin case.

"You'd be surprised. I can do a lot with a violin." He winked at her, and Quinta rolled her eyes.

"Will you play for me?"

"Not tonight, but sometime. Maybe I'll play you the starlight song." He held up the handkerchief, listening for its song. "It's quiet now, however, since you've woven it into something new."

"Let me see."

Twain handed Quinta the starlight handkerchief. As it left his hands, a confusion of emotions rushed into him. Joy still lingered, but there was also desire, hope, fear, and something that felt bittersweet like loss. He turned to look at her, surprised to see tears on her cheeks.

He wanted to kiss her again, but that was off the table, of course. "Why are you crying?"

"Because I made something, and it worked. And because we found magic. And because this is the only thread of starlight we have."

"Maybe we'll find more."

"Maybe *you'll* find more," Quinta said, a yawn splitting her face. "Apparently, I can't hear the mysterious music of the stars."

"This is why you want to keep me around," Twain agreed, also yawning. He was suddenly aware of how much he'd done today and how many times he'd nearly died. He stretched out on the couch, opening his arms. "I know we're not sleeping together, but want to sleep beside me?"

Quinta looked around the attic. "It's either that or on that old pile of rags."

Twain patted the space on the couch next to him. "Promise I'm comfier than a pile of rags."

"Absolutely no kissing," Quinta warned as she slipped off her jacket and her shoes. She slid into the space beside Twain, yawning again.

"No kissing."

"This is nice, though," Quinta said, lifting up his arm and settling it around her. "Very reasonable considering it's a small couch and you're a huge human."

She nuzzled into the space under Twain's arm. Placing the lace handkerchief on the table, Twain fell asleep, listening to her breathing, more content than he'd been in a very long time.

Outside, the rain picked up, lashing the windows; downstairs, the Severon Witches Society party got louder and wilder. But neither Twain nor Quinta were bothered by these things, because between them was magic and the promise of something more.

CHAPTER TWELVE
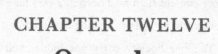
Quinta

A beam of early-morning sunlight woke Quinta. She lay wrapped in the curve of Twain's body, both of them perched precariously on the sloping yellow couch. For a moment, she let herself lie still, feeling his breath on her neck and watching dust motes dance in the gems of light from the stained-glass window. Twain's arm cradled Quinta's waist, and she felt like it belonged there.

That's ridiculous. You met him yesterday—not even a full day ago, in fact—and now you've spent the night with him.

Of course, they hadn't done more than share one kiss and go to sleep together. But this thing with Twain was different. Quinta had the strongest feeling that there was nothing quick or silly about him, nor about what might be growing between them.

It was totally ludicrous to be feeling anything for someone she'd known for less than a day, but that was the way of things sometimes, wasn't it? Some people found their way into your secret self the moment you met them, and they would stay there if you allowed them to.

Or perhaps they'd just disappear. Maybe Twain would wake up and realize what he felt for Quinta was all because of the magical lace and whatever its patterns made him feel. Maybe he would leave the moment he woke, and she would be alone again, having tasted real magic and perhaps a hint of love for a few hours. Maybe she wasn't worth staying for, and she should just focus on the magic.

Yes, that was a good plan.

Snuggling deeper into Twain's embrace, Quinta made a face—*feelings*—such absurd, nonsensical things. She had words to read and patterns to learn. When Twain woke, if he wanted to leave her, she'd shake his hand goodbye and that would be the end of it. But, if he wanted to stay, then she would insist they try to find more starlight, so she could attempt some of the other patterns in the book.

Because, while Twain felt joy when he held the starlight lace, Quinta experienced something else altogether as she twisted the threads. It was like some part of her—a part she hadn't even known existed—was guiding her hands. In some ways, weaving the lace had felt like leaving an impression of her very being on the world, and then sharing it.

Quinta did not usually share parts of herself with anyone, which is why the fact that she liked making the lace, being near Twain, and yearning to do more of both was all so peculiar.

"Well, magic is a strange thing," Quinta murmured as she stretched and grabbed the blue book off the table. Behind her,

Twain shifted slightly, and Quinta held still. He kept sleeping, however, and one arm of his pulled her to his chest. She burrowed there, letting herself be held. Who knew that just sleeping next to someone could be one of the most beautiful experiences of her life?

She closed her eyes, feeling safe and loved. For a moment, she was not a disappointment. She was cherished. Even if it was just all in her own mind.

"Get it together," she whispered to herself. "Focus on the magic."

Quinta started reading.

By the time Twain woke up, there was much more sunlight streaming through the attic window, and Quinta had finished three chapters in the book: "Lace Patterns to Ensnare an Enemy," "Desire and Lace: A Case Study in Three Parts," and "Magical Lace: A Brief History" (which was entirely not brief).

"Good morning, None of Your Concern." Twain flashed her a sleepy smile.

"Morning," she said, suddenly embarrassed to still be curled up on the couch with him. Quinta stood up quickly, running a hand over her wild hair.

Twain yawned and sat up. "Have you been awake for long?" He stretched and his torn shirt flapped open, showing the long cut on his ribs. It was bright red at the edges today.

"I've been up long enough to read a bit more. You should get that cut looked at."

"I'll just put your magical lace on it," he said. "That worked on my hands."

He picked up the handkerchief and placed it on his belly. They both watched, but nothing happened.

"Maybe it only works once?" Quinta suggested.

Twain shrugged. "It'll heal. I have some bandages back at my house." He paused for a moment, thinking. "Though, I'm not sure I can go back there."

Quinta had been meaning to ask him about what had happened at his house last night. "Do you normally get chased out of your home by angry men?"

Twain frowned. "No. Those men are Arcana scholars who were once friends with my brother. They wanted to collect my brother's debts and get that invitation back."

Quickly, he told her about the invitation and how he had met the men on the beachside steps yesterday. The explanation answered some of Quinta's questions, but it also made her feel terrible.

"I'm sorry I lost the invitation." She let out a long sigh. Why hadn't she put it into her pocket? But everything had happened so fast, and she hadn't had time to think as they'd fled Twain's shack.

Twain shook his head. "Don't be sorry. Perhaps now that they have it, they'll leave me alone. Plus, I'm leaving soon enough. At least that's the plan. I still have to find money for my ticket."

A shadow crossed his face, but it was gone before Quinta could ask more about his brother or the two scholars. Instead, she asked about his departure.

"Where are you going when you leave Severon?" Mostly to have something to do with her hands, she opened a steamer trunk that had been piled in a corner.

Twain walked over to her and peered into the trunk, considering its contents. "Around the world. I want to see all the places on the map and maybe a few off it."

"How much is the ticket?"

"A lot. Perhaps I can sell this?" He picked up a woman's hat trimmed in feathers. It was years out of fashion and looked like a molting bird. He plopped it on his head and turned to face Quinta. "What do you think? How much would you pay for this horrible hat?"

A laugh burst out of Quinta. "You couldn't pay me to wear that. But you can sell the starlight handkerchief. Maybe that would give you the money you need."

Twain flung the dusty hat at her. "Are you kidding, None of Your Concern?"

Quinta picked up a stuffed toy bear whose eyeballs were missing and lobbed it at Twain. "Not kidding. The handkerchief is yours to do with what you like. Sell it. Cherish it forever. Pass it on to your grandchildren. I don't care."

That wasn't technically true, but what was she going to do with it? Hold on to the handkerchief as a souvenir of the one time she did magic? Also, the starlight she made it with belonged to Twain. He deserved to keep the handkerchief.

Twain tossed the bear back to her and clutched the handkerchief to his chest. "I would sooner sell my own life. This goes with me always."

He held her gaze for a moment, and she wasn't sure if he was teasing. She had to look away. It was such a big declaration in the small space they'd carved out in the attic. Quinta very nearly kissed Twain again, but she couldn't be sure that's what he wanted, and besides, he had moved away, clutching a slightly dusty button-up shirt from the trunk. Perhaps he was getting ready to say goodbye? She watched the muscles in his back bunch as he traded his old, ripped shirt for the new one, which strained against the breadth of his shoulders.

It was the desperate wish to not part company with him yet that made her say it: "If you can't go back home, perhaps you could spend the day with me? The photo studio is closed." And Pierre wouldn't have noticed or cared that she hadn't come home last night. "But I was hoping we could go back to the Vermilion Emporium to find more starlight. Maybe we can harvest some from the ceiling and use it to make lace, and then—who knows?—maybe you can sell that to buy your ticket. . . ."

Her words left her in a rush, like water running down a mountainside.

"Yes," Twain said, turning toward her. His sea-glass eyes crinkled at the corners as he buttoned up the shirt.

"Yes? To the Emporium? Or making more lace? Or spending the day with me?"

"Yes to it all." Pulling on his boots and coat, he grabbed his violin case and offered her his hand.

The smile on Quinta's face was brighter than all the sunlight filtering into the room.

They slipped out of Mrs. Davenport's house by way of a secret staircase that ran from the attic to the basement. Once there, they clambered through a small window that put them out in the middle of a thicket of rosebushes. A few tore at Twain's new shirt, but it was still an immense improvement over the raggedy one he wore yesterday.

The Vermilion Emporium was closed when they got there, the sign on the door reading "Opening again between noon and nightfall; odds are out when that could be," and so they wandered to Quinta's favorite bakery.

They each had a sweet bun and a coffee and meandered toward the bluffs that overlooked the sea. It was a crisp morning, and red and orange leaves littered the streets.

They found a bench on the promenade and sat down. As is the way with these things sometimes, neither of them talked about what had happened between them the night before. But Quinta found Twain stealing glances at her. When it happened for the fourth time, she snapped at him.

"What are you looking at? Do I have some food on my face?" Hastily, she swiped at her cheek with her sleeve.

Twain had the good grace to look embarrassed. He fiddled with the clasps on the violin case he was carrying and cleared his throat. "You don't have anything on your face."

"Well, then stop staring at me."

"You're very lovely to look at in the morning light."

Quinta wasn't the type of girl to blush—really, who had time for such things?—but this boy had completely undone her sense of what type of girl she was. Perhaps she *was* the type of girl to blush, or find magic, or spend the night not sleeping *with* but sleeping *beside* a strange boy for whom she had woven joy.

It was all too much right after breakfast, and Quinta just shook her head and turned to the sea. Gulls wheeled over them, squawking their demands for some crumbs. At one end of the city, on the edge of a cliff, an enormous steam-powered dirigible—the latest invention from Scientifica—was preparing for launch. Quinta watched as men and women in top hats and goggles ran around it, checking gauges and waving and yelling.

"When do you think the Vermilion Emporium will open?" Quinta blurted, sidestepping Twain's compliment but also noticing (quite giddily) that he too was lovely to look at in the morning light.

Twain shrugged.

"Should we wait outside it?" she pressed.

They could do that, certainly. Quinta didn't have anything better to do today. Pierre's was closed on Sundays, and he didn't keep track of her comings and goings.

"Let's go to the Severon Museum," Twain said, finishing up his bun and coffee. "I saw starlight in the paintings there once—the ones from when the Salon members were working. Perhaps we'll learn something about where those artists got it from."

"That's a wonderful idea," Quinta said with a smile. It was such a perfect thought, she could kiss him for it. But, of course, that was against the rules.

She was not kissing this boy again.

Sadly.

They made their way slowly toward the Lapis District, threading back past the Emporium—still closed and shuttered—until they were outside the Severon Museum of the Arts. Its blue roof was made of glazed ceramic tiles that glittered like a handful of sapphires. The museum opened right as they arrived and was almost empty.

"Two tickets." Twain set his violin case on the counter and pulled out a few coins. A spindly white woman with a roll of gray hair on top of her head looked them over.

"There's a dress code," she said, pointing to the sign above her head.

It read: LADIES MUST BE IN DRESSES; GENTLEMEN MUST WEAR JACKETS AND HATS.

"Well, no problem then," said Quinta quickly, pushing the money in Twain's hand across the counter.

Twain grabbed his violin case and grinned at the woman. "I assure you, we're neither ladies nor gentlemen, and so those rules don't apply to us."

Before the woman could stop them, Quinta and Twain dashed up the wide marble stairs of the museum. They laughed as they ran, surprising a group of rich, elderly matrons who were chatting beneath a marble statue of a naked man. All the women shot Quinta and Twain shocked looks, but the two of them ran on heedless.

"This way," Twain said, taking Quinta's hand and pulling her through the galleries full of paintings of rich people in the sort of stuffy clothing that was in fashion two hundred years ago.

They stopped in a room near the back of the museum. It overlooked the sea through floor-to-ceiling windows. Along the walls hung paintings that looked like they'd been dreamed rather than painted. Blues, greens, red, yellows, and oranges moved across the canvases in wild patterns.

"Look." Quinta pointed at one painting in particular. It depicted a morning by the sea. "There's starlight."

She moved toward the picture, leaning her head in so her nose was nearly touching the canvas. Beneath layers of white, blue, gray, and soft pinks shimmered a vein of silver that let off warmth. Twain stepped up beside her, peering at the painting.

"It's beautiful," he breathed out.

Together, they watched the silver undulate under the paint like a living thing. It was all Quinta could do not to touch it.

A card hanging on the wall next to the painting read:

Starlight on Water, by Marali, 1646.

Curator's Note: As far as we know, this was the last of the paintings created by Marali, the Salon's founder. After its completion, the Salon was disbanded and the secret to starlight artistry lost. When asked why she stopped creating with starlight, Marali only ever said that the cost was too high.

"What cost do you think she was talking about?" Quinta asked. Marali was her great-great-great-great-grandmother, a fact that Quinta had been raised to be proud of. But Quinta's mother had not told her why Marali disbanded the Salon, and they had no surviving letters or diaries from Marali to better help them understand things.

"No idea," Twain said, as his eyes moved from the card back to the painting. He shifted his violin case from one hand to the other. "Do you feel alright after making the handkerchief?"

She felt more than alright. "Better than I have in many years."

"Then perhaps there's not a cost. Or not one that matters? Maybe Marali was tired of creating with starlight, and she made up the idea of a cost?"

"Or maybe it had to do with fame and all the pressures that caused?"

"Maybe. But it's still lovely."

They watched the starlight gleam and wriggle under the paint for a moment longer before moving on to the other paintings in the gallery. In each of them, slivers, spoonfuls, and strands of starlight highlighted parts of the images. Some of the artists had used it to accentuate faces or bodies; others made it look like the moon, glimmering on the water; still others used it as flames in the mouths of dragons. For a breath, Quinta wondered if dragons were as real as the starlight they'd found.

"How did we forget to do this?" Quinta asked, her voice soft with wonder.

Resting his violin case on a bench, Twain glanced around the gallery. After confirming it was still empty of anyone but them—a fact that was rather strange in such a large city, even for a Sunday morning—he pulled his starlight lace handkerchief out of his pocket. "*We* didn't forget."

Quinta still couldn't believe she had created something so beautiful with starlight. That she was like Marali and the artists who'd made Severon famous. Her mother would've been so proud of her.

The thought nearly dropped her. If only her mother was still here to see what she'd done.

You are meant for great things.

Before memories could overwhelm Quinta, a voice trilled behind her. "Oh my stars, children, what have you got there?"

Quinta spun around, her jaw dropping when she saw who was in the gallery with them.

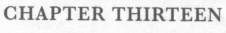

CHAPTER THIRTEEN
Twain

Twain had never seen the Casorina in person. Assuredly, he'd seen her image on coins—she was the closest the country of Aix had to a queen, after all—and paintings of her bedecked in jewels hung all over the city, even in the museum they were in; but seeing her in real life was different. His first thought upon turning around and finding the Casorina's eyes on him and Quinta was that she was much older than her portraits made her look. His second was that he was going to be in trouble if he kept staring. He dropped his eyes right as Quinta sunk into a deep curtsy.

"My lady," Quinta murmured.

"Rise, child." The Casorina's skin was dark brown, and wrinkles touched the edges of her eyes and her forehead. Diamonds threaded through her silver-gray braids, and she wore a magnificent purple gown. A fan of razorbill feathers poked out of her hat.

Twain looked around the gallery. How were they alone with the Casorina? As if she were reading his mind, she smiled gently at him.

"I tour the starlight galleries every Sunday morning. My attendants are outside, but there's not usually anyone else here this early."

"We can go." Quinta moved toward the door.

"Stay," the Casorina insisted. "You must show me what you have."

She held out her hand for the lace handkerchief. Reluctantly, Twain passed it over. Again, as it left his hands, he felt its loss profoundly.

The Casorina inhaled sharply the moment the lace handkerchief touched her palm. Slowly, she traced a finger over the knots and patterns.

"It's magnificent," she murmured. "Where did it come from?"

Twain's eyes met Quinta's. Should they tell the truth? If they did, what would happen to them? If they didn't, would the Casorina think they'd stolen the lace?

They hesitated for a second too long. The Casorina's sharp gaze darted between them.

"You two have a secret. Is that correct?" Her tone was light, but there was iron beneath it. This was not a woman you lied to and got away with it.

Quinta nodded at Twain. They would have to take their chances on telling the Casorina the truth.

"I made that lace," Quinta admitted. "Last night."

"But, how?" The Casorina continued moving her fingers over the handkerchief. "No one has made something like this since my great-great-great-grandmother's time."

"I found a starlight thread," Twain explained. "In the razorbills' nests."

"And I found a book," Quinta added hastily. "One that taught me how to create the lace. I read part of it and just started weaving. It was really much easier than I thought it would be. But that handkerchief is Twain's. I made it for him." Her tone was defiant, as if she was daring the Casorina to take the handkerchief that so clearly belonged to someone else.

Understanding dawned on the Casorina's face. "Ahh. I see. That's why I don't feel anything other than warmth, almost like being beside a fire on a cold night. This magic was not woven for me." She held the lace handkerchief out to Twain, and he took it gratefully. She paused, tapping a finger against her rounded cheekbone. "You two are very interesting people, indeed. I find these days—despite all the scholars I talk to—that I don't meet as many interesting people as I would like to. I must invite you back to my palace so you can make me a starlight dress. Can you do such a thing?"

"We can't—" Twain started to say, but Quinta stepped on his foot.

"You want us to go to the Orpiment with you? To make a dress?" A hungry look passed over her face.

"Do you have other commissions?"

"No," Twain said. "But we're not important. We're just two kids from Vermilion. And I'm leaving in a month."

The Casorina quirked an eyebrow. "You may be 'two kids from Vermilion,' as you say, but you're obviously quite important. And I could very much use some magic in my life. Come back to the Orpiment, stay for the next few weeks as my guests, and weave something from starlight for me. I'll pay you handsomely, and then you may be on your way."

"Do we have a choice?" Twain asked.

"You always have a choice, my dear. But from the looks of both of you, I guess that you don't have many other better options."

She was right about that. Twain knew it, and he was sure Quinta did too. He looked over at her, and she gave him the smallest of nods. Yes, they would do it. They would travel to the Orpiment with the Casorina because now that they had a little magic, anything seemed possible.

"We'll go with you," Quinta said. "And we'll make you the most beautiful dress Severon has ever seen."

It was no more than a whim and a foolish hope, since they didn't have any more starlight. But they'd figure it out.

"I'm counting on it," the Casorina said. "Also, let's keep this between us for now. I want you to make me something wonderful for the Scholar's Ball at the end of October. We can debut your talent to the world then. Come, come, this way!"

And just like that, the Casorina sailed out of the art gallery with a swishing of skirts and the smell of lilacs.

Twain turned to Quinta. "Are you sure you're comfortable going with her? We don't have to."

"What else are we going to do? Run away together? Keep working our jobs and hoping to make enough so we can eat each day? This is a chance. We have to take it. Plus, it means you'll be able to afford your ticket out of Severon."

Twain shot her his sideways smile. "That's all true, though I wanted to keep the magic between us, even if only for a short while longer."

Quinta leaned in toward Twain, standing on tiptoe so her cheek pressed against his and her lips were beside his ear. "There will always be magic between us," she whispered in a voice that made every muscle in Twain's body tense. Then, she pulled away just enough so she could see his face. Her eyes took on a teasing glint. "But you need a shirt that fits, and I would very much like to see the inside of the Orpiment."

Then she did something most unladylike and dropped a kiss onto his nose right there in the middle of the public gallery.

"What happened to no kissing?"

"Doesn't count if it's not on the lips." She twirled away from Twain before he could kiss her again. "Follow me."

Quinta shot Twain such a dazzling smile he felt his bones quiver. This girl would be the making and the undoing of him. He knew it already. There had been yesterday morning, in the time before Quinta. And today, and every day thereafter, there would be the time after Quinta. He only hoped he wouldn't let her down.

Tucking his starlight handkerchief into his pocket and grabbing his violin case, Twain followed Quinta out of the gallery to where the Casorina waited for them.

CHAPTER FOURTEEN

Quinta

H ow were they going to make the Casorina a dress?

They didn't have any more starlight, and Quinta wasn't sure her weaving skills were good enough to make an actual garment. But those were problems for later. For now, as the Casorina's white and gold enameled carriage, which was pulled by a great steam-driven bronze horse, clattered through the streets of Severon, Quinta knew she was moving closer to her dream.

You are meant for great things.

If she could make this dress, she would have power. She would no longer just be a photographer's assistant; she would be sought after, maybe even famous. She wouldn't be a disappointment; she'd be someone people admired and talked about. That was exactly what she wanted.

Mostly.

Because after yesterday's adventures and the look on Twain's face when she kissed him last night, some part of her wanted nothing more than to slip away with him and head back to the Vermilion Emporium. She wanted to forget all her old dreams and make new ones with Twain.

But that was silly. Was she really the type of girl to give up everything she'd wanted for years over one kiss (admittedly a very magical one)? No, she was not.

"Doing okay there?" Twain whispered, bumping Quinta's leg with his thigh.

He sat on the carriage seat next to her, holding his violin case on his knees. Quinta didn't dare whisper any of her doubts to Twain, not with the Casorina in the seat across from them. As they drove, the Casorina prattled on about technology and the division between magic and science in Severon. She was especially keen to talk about how her commitment to the sciences plus her belief in Arcana (in the form of the dress Quinta made her) might be the thing to bridge that divide.

"I'm doing mostly okay," Quinta whispered.

"We'll figure it out," Twain said under his breath. "Don't worry." He gave her knee the tiniest of squeezes, and her heartbeat quickened. Which of course was probably just because she was nervous about making the dress. Not because being this close to Twain made her want to lean her head on his shoulder and snuggle into his embrace.

Absurd.

She didn't have much more time to worry about any of these things, however, because at that moment they arrived in front of the Orpiment.

"Here we are!" The Casorina beamed at the palace through the carriage window. "I never get tired of arriving here. Even after all these years."

The outside of the Orpiment was made to impress. Everything from its pale-green marble facade to the glass dome atop its gilded roof spoke of wealth beyond imagination. Three stories tall, there were rows of windows edged in gold and hung with sumptuous curtains. Carved columns held up a soaring portico, and a wide set of marble steps led to the front door. Marble statues flanked the steps, and guards in blue-and-gold uniforms stood at attention every few steps. All of them bowed as the Casorina ascended the stairs.

Quinta had walked past the Orpiment many, many times, but she'd never been inside. Her heart raced as she and Twain followed the Casorina through the gilded doors.

You are meant for great things.

"Are you nervous?" she asked Twain.

"Entirely."

They stood in a wide hallway. The floor was marble, shaped into an intricate star pattern, and the ceiling was painted with a scene of mermaids, ships, and starlight-lace-wearing maidens. A tremendous gold and crystal chandelier hung down, illuminating the space.

"It's gorgeous," Quinta whispered, trying to make sense of the palace. Everywhere she looked was more gold, velvet, marble, or paintings of the Casorina's relatives.

Twain laced his fingers through hers, which was reassuring and familiar in this strange place.

The Casorina swept into the palace ahead of them, her heels clicking on the marble floor. She spoke quickly to a butler, and then led Quinta and Twain into an atrium larger than most city blocks. Three stories of arched balconies lined the walls, and a glass dome covered the space, letting in creamy midday light. Beneath the dome burbled a tall fountain with mermaid and dragon statues set throughout it. Lemon trees, orange trees, rosebushes, palms, and dozens of other lush plants in glazed ceramic pots filled the space. Clumps of well-dressed people and scholars in their colorful robes milled about the atrium. Some of them studied the paintings along the walls; others listened to a trio of musicians set up near the curving marble staircase that led to the upper levels of the palace; still others wandered the palace in fine gowns or well-cut suits, whispering to each other.

Plucking two small oranges off the nearest tree, the Casorina turned back toward Quinta and Twain. Quinta had only eaten an orange once, when she stole it from a rich person's table one Winter Feast night long after the family had gone to sleep.

"Help yourself to whatever you like," the Casorina said, handing each of them an orange. "My staff will get you settled and see to it that you have everything you need."

"What about our lives out there?" Quinta asked, gesturing toward the city. She didn't think Pierre would have any trouble running the studio without her, but she couldn't just abandon him.

"Send a note to whomever you like," the Casorina said airily. "But I must ask you to keep your activities with the lace a secret. I want to surprise everyone at the ball. Can you do that?"

"We can do that," Twain said. "But only if Quinta wants to."

Oh, her heart. This sweet, broken boy with a laugh like sunlight on water. Quinta would do anything to stay by his side.

"Of course I want to," she said rather peevishly. "I wouldn't leave you here alone." She couldn't help her edges. They were as much a part of her as her unruly hair or her pale skin.

"It's decided then!" The Casorina clapped once, startling Quinta. "Get cleaned up and settled. Figure out what you need, and my people will get it for you."

"Excuse me," interrupted someone from behind the Casorina. It was a tall, redheaded young man who was built like a wrestler. He wore a well-fitting black suit and carried several books under his arm. A smattering of freckles covered his nose, and his blue eyes narrowed when they met Quinta's for a moment, as if he was trying to figure out what she was doing talking to the Casorina.

"Ahh, Damian," the Casorina said warmly. "I was just going to come find you. Is the lecture prepared?"

"It is, my lady," he said with a deep bow.

"Excellent. Damian, I'd like you to meet Quinta and Twain. These two are Arcana scholars from Severon—" She winked broadly at them. "Damian is an Arcana scholar from Ixily whose work on alchemy and celestial alignments is all the rage right now. He's here in Severon to tell us about it and to attend the ball."

Damian now turned to Quinta and Twain and made another small bow. "Pleased to meet you," he said in a soft voice that didn't seem to fit his wide, muscly build. "What do you study?"

Beside Quinta, Twain's fingers pressed into her hand. He opened and closed his mouth, but no sounds came out. What had she learned about lying? Give it some truth, but not too much.

"We're interested in patterns of magical lace," Quinta said quickly.

Damian's eyes lit up. "Indeed? I'd hoped to see some of Severon's famous magical lace while I'm here. Where did you study? Have you read Xaranaz's theorem on the ten uses of celestial—"

The Casorina put a hand gently on Damian's arm. "Now, now, that's enough of all that. There will be time to speak of such things later. Please tell the others the lecture will start soon." She nodded toward a group of scholars standing near the fountain.

Damian bowed to the Casorina, and then flashed Twain and Quinta a warm smile. "Nice to meet you both. Hopefully we'll bump into each other in the Great Library soon."

Quinta returned his smile, as did Twain.

"Are there always other scholars staying in the Orpiment?" Quinta asked as Damian joined the scholars by the fountain. She wasn't sure they could keep up the lie if actual scholars were asking them questions while they worked in the palace.

The Casorina shook her head. "No. A few, like the ones from Tszana, prefer to sleep on their ship. But most of our visiting scholars—including Damian—have taken rooms in the apartments near the university. I like for them to stay near Severon's scholars, so they can exchange ideas and learn from each other."

"But we're staying here? In the palace?" Quinta asked, even though the Casorina had already said as much.

"You are," she confirmed again. "I want to keep you two a secret, which means please don't say anything about your real work to the other scholars. I'll show you my library after you're cleaned up. You can work there. Then, later tonight, after you gather your materials, we can go over some ideas for the dress you're going to make me."

Quinta shot Twain a worried look, but he winked at her.

They would figure it out.

Together.

Before Quinta could ask the Casorina more questions, the elegant old woman moved away, heading toward the gardens near the back of the atrium.

Once she was gone, the butler and two maids walked over, all of them wearing curious looks. The Casorina might have introduced Quinta and Twain as scholars, but their appearance told a different story.

The older of the maids, a woman with a halo of frizzy yellow hair and a ruddy face, spoke first. "Don't know what the Casorina is thinking, bringing two Vermilion vermin into the palace, but if she says we must, I guess we'll get you cleaned up."

"Hush, Margot," the younger maid replied. She was pretty, with light-brown skin and short black hair. "You'll not be calling anyone vermin in this house, no matter where they're from." She turned toward Quinta and Twain. "I'm Penny. I expect you'll both be needing baths. Horace, please find them some new clothes. I'll draw the baths, and Margot, the Casorina said they could use her personal library."

Margot huffed out a breath and stormed away, muttering to herself. Horace, a wraith of a butler with skin like curdled milk, just raised one eyebrow disapprovingly.

"I suspect they will be needing to bathe in separate chambers?" he said archly, echoing Penny's words.

Heat flooded Quinta's cheeks, which was rather silly given what they'd nearly been up to the previous evening.

Penny just rolled her eyes. "Of course, Horace. Find them clothes, and I'll show them to their rooms. Plural."

Horace sniffed. "I'll see what I can rustle up."

Once he was gone, Penny grinned at them broadly. "Not everyone who works here is as awful as those two. You'll see. Come on—this way."

She walked quickly over to the wide marble staircase that curved toward the upper levels of the Orpiment. Still holding each other's hands, Quinta and Twain followed her.

Penny led them down so many corridors, Quinta was well and truly lost before long.

"How will we find our way out again?" she whispered to Twain.

He smiled at her. "We'll manage. This is no trickier than finding our way around the Vermilion District. Or the Emporium."

He had a point there. "Stay close, please."

In reply, Twain just squeezed her hand. "I'm not going anywhere."

Penny stopped when they got to a long hallway that was lined on one side with elegant wooden doors. The other side of the hall overlooked the atrium.

"You'll be here," she said to Quinta, opening one door. "And you'll be over there," she said, pointing to a door a bit farther down the hall for Twain.

"Where do we bathe?" Quinta asked, suddenly quite aware of how disheveled she looked and how bad she smelled.

"There are bathrooms in each of the guest rooms," Penny said. "Soap, towels, and everything you need are already in there. Get cleaned up, and I'll leave fresh clothing on the bed for you. Is there anything else you want?"

Quinta glanced at Twain. He was looking as awestruck as she felt. A bath, clean clothing, and towels? These were the sorts of things that didn't just appear in their worlds.

"I think we're fine," Quinta managed.

"Very good," said Penny. "Be back soon!"

And then she hurried off down the hallway, leaving Quinta and Twain alone for the first time since the Casorina came upon them in the art gallery.

"Can you believe this place?" Twain asked, walking over to the railing that overlooked the atrium.

Quinta joined him, staring down at the fountain and all the plants below. The Casorina and the scholars were nowhere to be found, but maids, official-looking men in suits, and a group of ladies in brightly colored dresses all wandered through the lush foliage.

Quinta watched a stream of water burble from the fountain, sparkling in the sunlight from the glass dome. "I cannot. I always imagined what it might be like inside the Orpiment, but now, having seen it, I can't believe it's real."

You are meant for great things.

They stared a moment longer.

"Do you think we can do what the Casorina wants?" Twain asked. Doubt edged his voice.

"You mean, can we find more starlight and then somehow use it to make not just a handkerchief but a whole magical gown?" A sick feeling filled Quinta just saying the words out loud.

"Exactly that."

Quinta turned away from the view of the atrium to look at Twain. She quirked an eyebrow. "I don't think we have a choice, so we might as well try. We can always run away in the night if it doesn't work."

Putting his violin case down, Twain reached out and rested his hands on her hips. She took a step closer to him, so their bodies were touching.

"You're quite brilliant," Twain said in a low voice. "I believe you can do anything." He leaned down, resting his forehead gently against hers. His hair had come loose from its tie again, and it made a curtain around their faces.

"And you're quite clever," she whispered. "I'm certain you can discover more starlight."

They stood like that for a long moment, breathing each other in.

"I'm not going to kiss you." Twain's voice was strangled. "As much as I'd like to."

Relief and regret chased each other in circles around her heart.

"Good. That's against the rules." Quinta resisted the urge to brush an eyelash off his cheekbone. "As much as I'd like you to."

"Let me know if the rules change."

She couldn't do that to herself or to Twain. Much as she wanted to, she didn't trust herself not to hurt him, and they had to work together. She didn't want—

"Ahem," Penny said, clearing her throat. She held two piles of clothing, and amusement sparkled in her eyes as they darted back and forth between Quinta and Twain. "I have your clean clothes, but don't let Horace catch you standing that close. Believe me, it's not worth the trouble." She winked at them, and Quinta and Twain hastily stepped away from each other.

"We're not—" said Twain at the same moment Quinta said, "Oh no, this isn't—"

"Sure it's not." Penny laughed and walked away.

"I'll see you later," Quinta said to Twain, with one last look over her shoulder as she hurried into her room.

As Quinta sank into a tubful of warm water and lavender-scented bubbles, she could still feel the heat of Twain's mouth near hers and the press of his hands against her hip bones. It was enough to keep any thoughts of starlight lace, magic, or the Casorina far, far away.

CHAPTER FIFTEEN

Twain

How were they going to make the Casorina a dress?

Bathed and dressed in freshly pressed black pants, a gleaming white shirt, and a vest, which hugged him like it was made for his body, Twain stood in the hallway outside Quinta's room, waiting for her and thinking about what they'd promised the Casorina.

The one thread of starlight they had was already woven into the handkerchief that healed his hands. Was he supposed to climb the razorbill nests again, looking for more? That was ludicrous. He'd been to the nests dozens of times over the last few years, and this was the only thread he'd ever found. A nearly certain death wasn't worth the chance of a starlight strand.

But where could he find more? And they had to find more. Twain knew that their success or failure rested on him, and he'd seen the desperate, hopeful look that crossed Quinta's face when they entered the Orpiment. She wanted a home in this glittering world, and her ticket to it was making the Casorina's dress. But that wouldn't happen if he couldn't find more starlight. What if he failed someone he cared about again? Would Quinta ever forgive him? Should he just get out of there now and leave Quinta to this new world?

But, no, he couldn't do that. He had to find more starlight.

The only other place they'd seen starlight was in the cathedral room in the Vermilion Emporium. They'd have to go back there and try to harvest some. Maybe there was a secret to getting it down from the ceiling? Or maybe if they just cut a few threads from the starlight ceiling, the old woman wouldn't notice. Maybe—

"Well, don't you look nice," Quinta said as she opened her door.

Twain nearly stopped breathing when Quinta joined him in the hallway. Somehow, she was even more beautiful than she had been before. Maybe it was the way her skin looked against the emerald gown she wore or the way her hair curled after the bath, but whatever it was, he was having a hard time focusing on the task at hand.

He cleared his throat, stalling for time so he didn't blurt out something embarrassing about how lovely she looked. Or how much he'd like to kiss her again. "You clean up pretty well too, None of Your Concern," Twain finally said, after fiddling with one of the buttons at his cuff for longer than necessary.

"Shall we go?"

He took the arm she offered, and they walked down a long corridor on the second floor of the palace, using the hand-drawn map Penny had given them to find the Casorina's private library.

"So, we're going back to the Vermilion Emporium for starlight, right?" Twain asked, stopping beneath a painting of a bowl of fruit and examining the map. "We'll need loads of it I think, if you're going to be making a gown."

"That was my first thought. Unless you want to wander the city listening for the starlight music? Maybe you could play some of it on your violin and that would attract more?"

Twain shook his head. He'd left his violin back in the room, still not sure why he'd brought it from his house in the first place or what he meant to do with it, but happy to have it anyway. "I don't think that's how it works."

"Let's hear what the Casorina has to say, and then go to the Emporium at the soonest possible opportunity," Quinta said.

"That sounds like a plan."

"But what if we can't make the dress?" Quinta fidgeted with the bottle of moonshadow around her neck. "What if we fail?"

"We'll figure it out. Maybe we'll even discover where starlight comes from. That would make things easier."

"I'm hoping the Casorina's library has an answer," Quinta said, making a left turn. She studied the map again. "Where is that library, anyway? It says here to stop beside the moonlit garden and look for a small notch."

A painting that was taller than either of them hung on the wall. It depicted a moonlit garden path that curved around night-blooming flowers, topiaries, and a fountain that was so beautifully painted, Twain could almost hear the water splashing from it.

"Is that starlight?" Quinta asked, peering at the painting more closely.

Twain leaned in, studying the silver glints of paint that touched the leaves of the painting's topiaries and the water in the fountain. It moved ever so slightly on the canvas.

"It is," a familiar voice said. The Casorina walked down the hallway. She pointed toward the silver spots in the garden. "This is one of Marali's, and it's one of the first paintings to ever use starlight. It's at least two hundred years old, which is why the starlight has faded."

Quinta's forehead scrunched up, and she bit her lip, which meant she was thinking. "Can you weave lace from the starlight in paintings?"

Twain had been wondering the same thing all morning.

"I'm afraid not," said the Casorina. "Many people have tried that over the years, but it never works. And it destroys a beautiful work of art along the way."

"But where did the artists get the starlight originally?" Twain asked. "It had to come from somewhere. I found this strand"—he held up his handkerchief—"and obviously we have more to make your dress. But they couldn't have just been finding the threads one at a time. That's too random and it would've taken ages to find all the starlight they used."

The Casorina nodded, furrowing her brow. "You've hit upon the exact problem that's haunted magical scholars for years. They know what's been done with the starlight; they know when it came into use and how many people used it; they've pulled it out of paintings and taken it apart until it's just a shred; but none of them can figure out its origin. There's talk of a cost to using starlight, but we still don't know what it is. That's the problem with enigmatic, magical things. They want to keep their mysteries close."

The Casorina reached around Quinta and touched the smallest of whorls in the wood paneling beside the painting. The moonlit garden sprung open, as if the path had come to life.

"Please," the Casorina said, gesturing into the room beyond the painting. "Come see my library. This is the work of several generations. None of the Arcana scholars in Severon have access to this collection, and I bet all of them would do unspeakable things to explore it."

Twain's jaw dropped as they stepped inside the library. It wasn't as big as the book cavern in the Vermilion Emporium, but it was the largest library he'd ever seen. Bookshelves lined the marble walls, curving upward and around even the pair of arched windows that overlooked the city. Tall ladders rested against the shelves, and a wide balcony ran around the room, breaking the shelves in half. A pair of tables and two armchairs sat beneath lights carved from green stone. On one wall of the library was a map of Aix and all the countries surrounding it. Twain exhaled sharply, thinking of Zand. His brother would've loved to study in a library like this.

"These are your books about starlight?" Quinta asked in a faint voice. She looked as awed and overwhelmed as she had in the Vermilion Emporium's book room. She was also vaguely greenish, as if she might be sick at any moment. "We have to go through *all* of these?"

The Casorina smiled. "These are all the books about magic— its history, uses, and prospects—that my family has collected over the last few centuries. But fear not, the entire collection isn't about starlight. That section is over here." She led the way toward a shelf closest to the armchairs. It still towered over Quinta and Twain, but it was certainly less intimidating than going through the entire library. "You can go get your supplies today and read whatever you'd like. I'll be back later for a dress consultation."

And before they could ask her any more questions, the Casorina pushed on a panel beside one of the windows. A door sprung out of the wall, and the Casorina disappeared down a long hallway, leaving them in the secret library, deep within the palace. Twain couldn't help but wonder: How many secret doors and passageways did the Orpiment have?

"What do you want to do first?" Quinta asked, interrupting Twain's thoughts. "Want to research the origins of starlight or go to the Vermilion Emporium to hopefully get more?" She moved her fingers across the books. All Twain could think about as she did that was the way her fingers had trailed over his skin last night, as she examined his healed hands.

Focus, he told himself. If they could somehow discover the origin of starlight—and solve the problem that had eluded magical scholars for generations—then forget just one dress. With that knowledge, they could make hundreds of dresses and earn enough money to go anywhere and be anyone they'd like.

"Let's start in the library. I doubt we'll be able to do more than generations of scholars, but we might as well try to discern something. After that, we can go to the Emporium."

"Worth a try." Quinta pulled a book off the shelf.

Twain grabbed the closest book and took it to the table with a sigh. "I'm warning you now, though, I'm not a scholar. My parents couldn't beat a love of books into me, no matter how they tried."

He resisted the urge to run his fingers along the scars on the back of his arms, made from a whip-sharp reed and testaments to his parents' frustration with his reluctance to study.

Quinta opened and closed her mouth at that, as if she wanted to ask him more, but then she just nodded.

"No one is asking you to be a scholar. Just search these books for any hint of where starlight comes from."

The book Twain had picked up had a black cover and was embossed with silver. "*A History of Art and Artistry in Severon, 1721–1789*," he read aloud. "Sounds dreadful."

He flipped open the dusty book, skimming the first pages. It was written in a flowing script that was terribly hard to read. Again, an image of Zand, bent over books like this, his eyes straining to read the impossible scripts, filled Twain's head. He gripped the edge of the book, willing away the tears that had sprung into his eyes.

Putting her first book aside, Quinta stood up. She pulled another book from the shelf. She snorted as she read the title. "This one's called: *Fool's Errands and Errant Fools: The Art Collector's Guide to Starlight Paintings from Severon and Beyond*."

"I think we can skip that."

Quinta shook her head. "What if there's some tidbit of information that will tell us where starlight comes from? We can't take that chance." She grabbed three more books from the shelves and plopped them on the nearest table. "I think we have to pull them all down and see what we find."

"We have a month to make this dress. I don't think we can read every book on starlight by then."

"Do you have a better idea?"

He did not. So he lugged six books off the shelf and brought them over to the table.

Quinta's fingers brushed his hand as she walked past him. "It's not as exciting as the Vermilion Emporium, but we can still discover all sorts of things together."

Twain smiled his sideways smile at her and started reading.

✸

Several hours later, Twain was no longer smiling. A pile of books sat between him and Quinta as well as a tray with their lunch dishes, which Horace had brought up, much to his great chagrin.

"My brain hurts," Twain moaned, letting out a huge sigh. He had read more in the last few hours than he had in months. Part of him liked sitting around reading because it reminded him of long days with Zand as they both studied for the Arcana Exam, but as he always did around books, he felt fidgety. Like his head wasn't big enough to hold all the information it needed to. He was ready to get out of here.

"Listen to this," Quinta said, hoisting a huge book titled *The Impact of Starlight Lace, Some Reflections*. She read from it: "'When the Salon members started making starlight lace, it was all the rage in fashionable circles. Soon, however, it was discovered that different patterns of lace produced different effects. One pattern might heal a wound, for example, which proved very helpful to battlefield surgeons and in hospitals. Another pattern might sway anyone who touched it to do exactly what the wearer wanted. These effects (and many others) had rulers clamoring for magical lace; businesspeople were furious over it as they lost shares of markets; and ordinary people were eager for a glimpse of the magic. Overall, it was more trouble than it was worth, and it is this scholar's opinion that we're better off without the stuff.'"

Twain nodded. "I read a version of that opinion in this book too. It seems like as much as Severon grew to power thanks to the lace, it caused all sorts of conflicts. According to this book"—he held up the one he'd been reading—"spies were sent into Severon, and there were attempts on the Salon members' lives."

"Maybe that's what Marali meant about the cost?"

Twain shrugged. "Not sure. Do you think that sort of danger would've been enough to get them to stop weaving it altogether?"

Quinta gnawed at her bottom lip. "Surely not? Still, I wonder if we're stepping into more trouble than it's worth. . . ."

"It's one dress, None of Your Concern. No one is going to kill us over a dress."

"I hope not. Did you find out anything else on the origins of starlight?"

Twain shook his head. "Not a word. There's lots of speculation— one scholar thinks that a star crashed into the earth and the Salon members scooped up all the pieces, but he was discredited by astronomers almost immediately."

"I didn't find anything either. The only thing I saw was this." Quinta held up a piece of paper, where she'd scrawled a note. "According to Hutchinson, 'only the Salon members knew the origin of starlight. They were sworn to secrecy and all five of them refused to divulge the secret. After four of them succumbed to tragically early deaths in the same year, Marali declared that she would no longer use starlight. She took the secret of its origin to her grave.'"

"So more mysteries, deaths, and dead ends. Perfect." Twain stood up and stretched. "I need air, sunlight, and a walk. Let's go see if the Vermilion Emporium is open. We don't need to find out where starlight comes from if we can harvest a bunch there."

Quinta pinched the bridge of her nose and yawned. "I could use a break," she admitted.

"We can be back in time for dinner if we hurry."

Quinta scrawled a hasty note to the Casorina, leaving it on top of a pile of books.

"Shall we go by the front door or the secret passage?" Twain asked. As if it was even a choice.

"When a secret passage is offered, I find it's best to walk that route."

"Agreed."

The secret passage was lit by gas lamps, which were spaced at long intervals. It took them deep into the Orpiment—they glimpsed bedrooms, sitting rooms, and the atrium through small holes in the wall. Eventually, the paneled hallways of the palace ended at a great wooden door set into a stone wall. A key hung beside the door, and they opened it without hesitation. A long set of stone steps disappeared into darkness.

"Should we venture down there?" Twain asked, holding up his starlight lace handkerchief. It made barely a wink of light in the darkness.

"Of course," Quinta said. "I can smell the sea. This has to lead out to the city."

And taking his hand, she began to descend the stairs.

They walked for a long time through a tunnel that twisted and turned. It smelled damp, but mercifully, the path was dry and clean. Occasionally, they'd pass under a grill set high into the ceiling. Sunlight streamed through these grates, as did the clatter of carriages and clomping of horses' hooves from the streets above them. Finally, when Twain's feet were starting to ache, they came to stairs that went up toward the city.

"Where are we?" Quinta asked as they ascended the stairs. A stone archway with another door set into it waited at the top.

"Somewhere in Vermilion, I'd guess, from how far we walked." Twain pushed at the door, but it didn't budge. "It's locked, though, and there's no key hanging here like there was with the last door."

"Not a problem," said Quinta. She pulled two pins out of her hair and bent down to study the lock. With just a few quick turns of the pins, the door clicked open.

"Where did you learn to do that?" asked Twain.

Quinta grinned at him and stepped back. "Thieves carnival I once attended. I'll tell you about it someday."

"I'll look forward to it," Twain said, inclining his head. "After you."

Quinta ran her hand across his arm as she passed, sending a shiver through him.

They emerged from the tunnel under a stone bridge. A wide river flowed beside them. Boats bobbed along the river, and the sounds of the Vermilion market filled the air. Behind them, many blocks away, the Orpiment gleamed in the late afternoon light. Twain knew exactly where they were, though he'd never noticed this door under the bridge before.

"This must've been built so the Casorina or her relatives could get into Vermilion without being noticed," Twain observed.

Quinta smirked. "How else could they drink, dance, and do every other lovely thing in between?"

"We can use it to get back as well, I hope." Twain smiled and together, they walked up the steps that led from the river to the street. The Vermilion Emporium waited a few yards away. The city street was crowded, but no one lingered near the Emporium. A thrill of anticipation crept through Twain. What would they find next?

They strode to the door, and Quinta paused, looking up at the shop's sign. "I suppose I should be surprised we ended up exactly where we intended, but I don't think anything about this shop surprises me anymore."

"I'm sure there are still a few surprises inside. Let's see if it's open."

This time it was, and when they walked in, the old woman behind the counter clapped her hands in delight. Today, she had on a dazzling blue gown, and a silver thread with a small lace bag attached to it hung around her neck.

"Back so soon? I can't say I wasn't expecting you, but it's lovely that you've arrived! Come this way. I have much to show you." She opened the bookcase door again.

Twain's hand found Quinta's as they followed the old woman down the long hallway, heading deep into the Vermilion Emporium.

CHAPTER SIXTEEN
Quinta

Quinta couldn't believe they were back at the Vermilion Emporium so soon, or that it had been less than twenty-four hours since they were last here. Again, she asked herself, had she really only known Twain for a day? Did she really work for the Casorina? Could she actually weave more starlight lace? Would they find what they needed in this strange shop?

You are meant for great things.

Right. They had to find what they were looking for. There was no choice.

"What brings you back today?" the old woman asked as she led them past dozens of rooms with shut doors. From behind those doors, Quinta heard the whispers of a thousand secret things.

"We need more starlight," Twain said to the old woman. "For a dress the Casorina wants."

"We're hoping to return to the room with all the piled-up furniture and the ceiling of starlight lace," Quinta added. "So we can harvest more starlight. Can you take us there?"

The old woman shook her head gravely. "Oh no. You can't take those threads. They're holding this place together. Each thread was contributed by a former proprietor of the Vermilion Emporium. To take any one of them out would be to unravel all that stands here."

For a moment, Quinta marveled at the fact that there had been so many proprietors before this strange old woman. But the matter at hand won out over her wonderings. "But where do the threads come from? How did the other proprietors 'contribute them'?" If she could figure out the answers to these questions, then perhaps she wouldn't need to unravel the lace ceiling.

"Unfortunately, my dear, that's exactly what I cannot tell you." The old woman patted Quinta's shoulder. "The secret of starlight's origin is one you have to discover on your own, just as the artists before you did as well. Ahh, here we are. In here please."

She turned off the seemingly endless hallway and walked toward a metal staircase that curved like the inside of a shell. It went up into the ceiling, which, of course was impossible, since the Vermilion Emporium was a single-story storefront. But, as Quinta was constantly learning, life is full of mostly impossible things.

The old woman pushed open a jade-green door at the top of the staircase. Beyond it was a long, sunlit room filled with dresses and suits. A wall of windows overlooked all of Severon, the gleaming Orpiment, and the sea.

"How is this possible?" Twain asked, echoing Quinta's thoughts as he gestured to the view. "We must be at least five stories high."

The old woman shrugged. "At the very least. I don't make the rules; the Emporium always becomes what it needs to be. But I rediscovered this room yesterday morning, and I'm so glad it made the trip with us."

Quinta heard what Twain and the old woman were saying, but it was the stunning silver creation on a dress form in front of her that held her attention. It was a dress woven from starlight lace, in a pattern that was far more complex than anything in Quinta's book. Slowly, lovingly, she ran her hand over its threads, knots, and whimsies. The faintest whispers came to her as she did so, speaking of loves lost and found, adventures that were over centuries before she was born, and a dying wish to be remembered. Was this what Twain meant when he said he heard starlight music?

"This dress is magnificent," she said with barely contained reverence. "I never even dreamed such a thing was possible." She could feel Twain's eyes on her as she considered how the dress was woven.

"You'll be able to make something like that," Twain said. "I know you will."

Quinta shot him a grateful look. "I'm not so sure, but we'll see. First we have to get starlight."

"That dress belonged to the greatest artist ever to live in Severon," said the old woman. "Your ancestor, Quinta, Marali the Enchanter, they called her. As you probably know, she was the founder of the Salon. This would have been about two hundred years ago."

"Were you alive to see it back then?" Twain asked at the same moment Quinta said: "Did you know Marali?"

The old woman laughed in a creaking voice. "I'm very, very old, but I'm not quite two hundred. My great-great-great-grandmother Viola was the proprietor of the Vermilion Emporium at the time, and she was one of Marali's lovers. Marali gave Viola this dress before she died, and it's been here ever since."

"It's truly a work of art," Quinta said, reverentially. "How can I ever make something this fine?"

"That is for you to discover," said the old woman.

"Can I take it with me? To pull apart for another dress?" Quinta bit her lip, afraid to hope that all their problems were so easily solved.

The woman shook her head. "If you're going to do magic with it, the starlight must be fresh or at least never woven. The magic also only works for the person its woven for. If you pulled this dress apart, you could make something lovely, but it would be no more magical than my shoe."

Quinta paused to consider the woman's sensible leather boots. Probably a little magic had rubbed off on them with all her steps through the Emporium, but Quinta saw her point.

"Do you have any unwoven starlight we could take with us?"

The old woman turned away from them to riffle through a trunk, pulling out bits of starlight scraps and putting them into an empty teacup on a nearby table. The scraps glowed there, casting a pale silver light on the old woman's face. "I only have the tiniest remnants to give you, but you can come back and study Viola's dress anytime you'd like."

That was something at least. Quinta could work with it for now.

Twain picked up one of the starlight remnants. "What happens if we run out before the Casorina's dress is done?"

The old woman paused. "You heard starlight music when you found that first thread, correct?"

Twain nodded.

"I can't hear it," Quinta said, wishing she could. Then, she could help Twain find more. That would make her feel less useless and more like she was moving closer to the great things she was meant for.

"I'm not surprised," the old woman said. "Only a select few can hear the music of the stars. Now that it's revealed itself, the starlight will sing to you, Twain. And only you. If you want to find more starlight in Severon, you'll have to listen for it."

"What do you mean? Should I go somewhere specific? Is there a certain time it's best to hear it at?"

"You'll see." The old woman just smiled a mysterious smile and wrapped up the small tidbits of starlight in silver-and-blue paper. She handed the package to Quinta. "This isn't much, but it'll get you started. You may stay in the Emporium as long as you like and explore where you will. I'll expect I'll see both of you back here soon."

And with that, the old woman turned and left the room.

"We really need to ask her name next time we're here," Twain said as she walked away. "Somehow she seems to know volumes about us, but we don't even know what to call her."

Quinta knew there would be a next time. "I was thinking the same thing. Want to explore anywhere else on the way out?"

Twain grinned. "I entirely do, but we have to get back to the Orpiment for the Casorina's dress consultation. Shall we come back tomorrow?"

Quinta nodded, and they made their way back toward the front of the shop, passing so many strange and enticing doors. *We could spend years exploring this place*, Quinta thought, as they passed once more through the hallway covered in photographs. It felt like a dangerous thought, but not an unwelcome one, and Quinta knew in a flash that she could be very happy doing just that as long as Twain was at her side.

*

Using the secret passageway again, they got back to the Casorina's library long after sunset.

"Maybe no one noticed we were missing?" Quinta said hopefully. She held the package of starlight scraps in her hands.

But of course that wasn't true.

"Where have you been?" the Casorina demanded as soon as they returned to the secret library. She rose from the armchair she'd been sitting in. Two deep frown lines bracketed her mouth. "I was starting to worry you'd left—"

Her words stopped when she saw what they were carrying. A bit of silver light glowed through the paper.

"But, how?" she managed to say.

Quinta smiled slightly. "That's our secret, and this is just a small sample to get us started. We'll bring the rest for your dress after I design it. Are you ready for your consultation?"

Quinta and Twain had agreed while walking back to the Orpiment that they wouldn't mention the Vermilion Emporium, at least for now. It's not like others in the city wouldn't see it if they walked past—and Quinta knew Mrs. Davenport and the SWS were looking for the shop—but for now it felt like Quinta and Twain's secret, and they wanted to keep it that way.

"We'll be going out at least once a day," Twain said to the Casorina, in a confident tone that sent a thrill of surprise down Quinta's spine. "We're not prisoners here and we'll do the work you ask of us, but we have to do it on our own terms."

Quinta and Twain had also agreed to visit the Emporium every day, just to see what new things they could find.

The Casorina nodded distractedly as she moved over to the table where Quinta had opened the package of starlight scraps. Slowly, she ran her hands through the material. "Whatever you need to do," she said softly. "I trust you. As long as my dress is magical, you may come and go as you please."

And that was that.

The Casorina had dinner sent up to the library, and they spent the rest of the evening talking with her about her life—something that was essential for Quinta to know in order to make the Casorina the right kind of lace dress. They learned the Casorina had had a very grand life and a very sad one. Her greatest love, the man she married despite her family's objections, died mysteriously on the eve of their first anniversary. Her second greatest love was a female violin player who had a tragic accident a year after they met.

"You see," said the Casorina as she took a long sip of her tea. "To love me is to sign your own death warrant a year later."

She was so beautiful and sad and so very old in that moment, Quinta knew immediately the kind of lace she needed to make.

She got started as soon as the Casorina retired for the night.

"'Lace for a broken heart,'" Twain read, peering at the page Quinta had turned to in the book she'd found in the Vermilion Emporium. "'A pattern of armor for the weary one who has to go into the world each day.' Are you sure this is right for the Casorina?"

Quinta studied the elaborate pattern. "It has to be. You heard her story too. What else would we make?"

Twain turned to the chapter list. "Lace for a powerful person to wear as art? Or lace for forgetting? Lace to stay young forever? Lace to heal divisions?"

Quinta shook her head. "None of those get to the essence of her. She told us some of her secrets. Now, we have to make something so beautiful it will wrap her in light and make her forget, if only for an evening."

Quinta wasn't quite sure why that was the goal or how she'd achieve it, but she had a feeling this was the right path.

She rested a hand on Twain's arm. "Let's just try it. Trust me."

"I trust you entirely. But we don't have a lot of extra starlight to experiment with."

Quinta smiled a secret smile and twisted the scraps of starlight between her hands, smoothing them out. As it had last night, the starlight flowed through her fingers like silk. Twain read for a while in the chair beside her, but as the hours passed, he snored softly, head on a pile of books. As he slept, Quinta worked, weaving sadness and stories, heartache and hurt, loss and love in a pattern that began as the one in the book, but eventually became something else altogether. With a start, she considered the span of lace in her hands, realizing she hadn't woven the Casorina's story into it, but rather her own. Was she making herself a dress?

You are meant for great things.

She really shouldn't have done that. Making herself a dress wasn't part of the plan, and what would the Casorina say if Quinta showed up at the Scholar's Ball in a magical outfit?

Her fingers hovered over the lace, but she couldn't bring herself to tear her work apart.

Maybe it was fine for now. She still had a month. Twain would find more starlight, and then she could make herself a dress *and* weave one for the Casorina.

"Done for now," said Quinta when she'd finished.

It was after midnight according to the clock on the mantel, and the library lights were turned down low. Quinta put the last handful of remaining threads and the starlight she'd woven into the trunk the Casorina had sent up, so no prying eyes could see what they were working on. Then, Quinta turned the key to the trunk, slipped it into her pocket, and woke Twain.

"Did you do it?" Twain mumbled sleepily as he stood.

"I started," she said. "But we're going to need a lot more starlight."

Twain ran a hand over his face and yawned. "I'll find us more. Promise."

"I know you will." She handed him a pile of books and they worked in silence for a few minutes, putting things away and tidying up the room.

"What if I don't, though?" Twain paused outside the library door. "What will we do then?"

She slipped her arm through his. "You'll find more. I believe in you."

"That makes one of us."

Quinta leaned her head against his shoulder for a moment, trying to put all her belief and hope into that gesture.

The thick carpets muffled their footsteps, and there was no one in the long hallways as they walked through the palace. No one to ask them what they were doing or what they talked about in low voices.

"Sure you don't want to come in?" Twain asked when they stopped at his room.

"Against the rules," Quinta said through a yawn.

"Rules were made to be broken."

"As were hearts. And I don't want to break yours. I like you too much."

"I like you too." A smile crept over Twain's face and, for a moment, Quinta thought he might lean in and kiss her. "But you're right. We've got things to do and a world to see. No time at all for kissing."

"No time at all. We'll keep looking for starlight tomorrow."

"Sounds like a plan. Good night, None of Your Concern."

"Good night, you impossible boy."

Twain shot her one more sideways smile before closing the door to his room.

Quinta returned to her room full of more feelings than was altogether good for her.

CHAPTER SEVENTEEN
Twain

"How are we ever going to find enough starlight to make this dress?" Twain asked the next day as he paced the library, a half-eaten apple in hand. It was lunchtime. They'd been skimming books about starlight most of the morning. More tales of woe and the ways starlight had affected empires appeared in every book, but they'd not yet stumbled across anything about its origins.

The question of finding more starlight had kept him up half the night—well, that and the questions of whether he would ever kiss Quinta again and if that was a good idea and if they had a future together and if he even wanted that—but he was no closer to answers on any front. Still, he had to figure out the starlight question at least. Because if he didn't find more, then there would be no dress for the Casorina. And that meant no money for him or Quinta. And no way to achieve their dreams, and no—

"Stop pacing and keep reading?" Quinta suggested, interrupting his thoughts.

She looked at him over the rim of her teacup, and his stomach flipped. Today, her curly hair was piled into a messy bun and a pencil was stuck behind her ear. She wore a purple dress that complemented her dark eyes perfectly. She was beautiful, and the dark red of her lips kept distracting him from his research.

"Reading is useless!" he said. "We should be out in the city, looking for starlight threads."

He'd tried that the moment he'd woken up, slipping out of his room at dawn and heading into the city. He'd walked and walked, looking for threads and listening for the starlight music. But he'd returned with nothing more than a few blisters and a deep despair. If he couldn't find more threads, he'd be letting Quinta down, just as he'd done with his parents, Zand, and every other person in his life. But what else could he do? He couldn't magic the threads out of the air. It was time he told her couldn't—

"Perhaps we should try the Great Library?" Quinta gathered her notes into a pile and closed her book. "The Casorina said we could browse there as we liked."

Twain hated the Great Library. It was his parents' favorite place and Zand's second home once he'd gotten into the Arcana. To Twain, it was an enormous symbol of all the ways he'd failed to live up to his parents' expectations. But he wanted to help Quinta make the Casorina's dress, and he wanted to earn enough money to get out of Severon. If a trip to the Great Library was what it took, so be it.

"I don't think it could hurt," Twain said, trying to keep his voice neutral. "And we can stop at the Vermilion Emporium on the way back. Maybe there's more starlight there and we just have to find it." Or maybe he'd hear more starlight music while they were in the city.

"Perfect," Quinta agreed.

✳

The Great Library was bustling with scholars when they got there. Some of them were dressed in the blue and green jackets of Severon's university. Others wore robes in rich reds and yellows that indicated they were visiting. It was like a rainbow of learning, with the occasional spots of black and gray in the forms of wealthy men and women. The clerk by the entrance hall didn't give Twain and Quinta a second glance as they walked through the doors in their new, expensive clothing.

"We would've never gotten in here two days ago," Quinta murmured as they passed into a wide reading room.

Twain squeezed her arm. "But we're here now. That's what matters."

"Are you okay? You look a little green."

"Long story for a different day. Scholars aren't my favorite."

"Good thing we're starlight finders and magical lace weavers, not scholars."

A flash of gratitude filled Twain. He wasn't much of a starlight finder at the moment, but her belief in him helped. "Excellent point."

Quinta smiled at him. "Where do we begin, though? Have you ever seen so many books?"

Twain had not. Even the Casorina's collection looked meager compared to the Great Library. The reading room they stood in was filled with long tables. People of all races and ages—most of them in scholar's robes—sat at the tables, hunched over books and talking with one another in hushed tones. Bookshelves lined the walls of this space, which was nearly as large as the atrium at the Orpiment. Archways appeared every few feet, leading to other rooms full of more books.

There was a faint music coming from somewhere, but Twain couldn't place it. Sweet and delicate, it sounded like birdsong, but it was more familiar. He paused for a moment, listening.

"Are you alright?" Quinta shot him a sideways glance. "You froze there for a moment."

The music was gone. He must be hearing things. Or perhaps one of the Scientifica scholars was fiddling around with a music-making machine.

"It's nothing. Let's go that way." Twain pointed toward the closest room. "If we get lost, we'll be able to ask someone for directions."

"It can't be bigger than the Vermilion Emporium. And I'd wager death isn't waiting for us around every corner."

"Where's the fun in that?"

Quinta laughed loudly enough to make a few hunched Scientifica scholars look up in surprise. She scowled at them, and they made noises of disapproval.

They strolled into a room dedicated to the study of ships. Thousands of volumes filled the shelves, and Quinta ran her fingers along their spines absentmindedly.

"You know it's impossible to learn everything," she mused. "But I wonder how much you could cram into your mind."

Twain had often considered the same thing. "There must be a limit. I certainly couldn't fit all I needed for the Arcana Exam into my head."

Quinta paused. "Why did you take the Scholar's Exam? It doesn't quite seem like you'd be at home here." She gestured to the library.

Twain let out a small sigh. "It's what my family did. As I mentioned before, both my parents were scholars—but my mother worked in the Scientifica and my father was part of the Arcana. Her parents weren't scientifically minded, she told me, and my mother quarreled with her mother, because she believed science was the way forward. Somehow, despite their differences, my Arcana-loving father found a way into her heart. They were young, reckless, and a terrible match. How they managed to stay together seventeen years was beyond any of us. Mostly they fought or ignored each other. The one thing that united them was how much they hated me."

Quinta placed a hand on his arm. "I'm sure they didn't hate you."

"They named me Twain because I'm what split them apart," Twain deadpanned. "My birth divided them, broke them."

"That's not your fault. No one can blame you for being born."

"My parents did," Twain whispered, his voice on the edge of breaking. It hurt so much to remember this, which is why he had locked memories of his parents behind a wall in his mind. "My birth was just the first in a long series of disappointments to them. Me failing the Scholar's Exam confirmed that belief."

They were quiet for a long moment. Quinta squeezed his arm lightly. "What about your brother? Did they feel the same way about him?"

"Zand was a year younger than me and wildly clever. He'd always been more into books than I was, and he got into the Arcana this January. My parents weren't around to see it, but they would've been so proud. I could never understand why someone would sit inside reading books when there was a huge world to explore."

"But books contain worlds," Quinta said.

They strolled out of the room of maritime books and walked up a staircase. It opened into a long hallway with even more book-filled rooms branching off in either direction.

"That's exactly what Zand used to tell me," Twain said softly. "You would've liked him."

Quinta leaned her head on Twain's shoulder. "I like you. And I'm sorry I won't get a chance to meet him. And that your parents were awful."

"I'm sorry for all that too."

Before Twain could say more, a loud group of voices sounded at the bottom of the staircase. Two of those voices rose above the group, terribly familiar. Gustave and Henri.

He froze, swearing under his breath.

"What's wrong?" Quinta asked, turning toward him.

"It's those men, Gustave and Henri—the ones from two nights ago at my house. They must work here."

"The scholars who were friends with your brother?"

Twain nodded, looking around for a place to hide before the group of scholars reached them. "The same."

"I want to run into them," said Quinta with a fierce look in her eyes. "So I can punch their faces and tell them to leave you alone."

Twain smiled at her protective tone. "I'd love that too, but if they see us here, they'll tell everyone else we're not scholars. And then we'll have to explain why we're staying with the Casorina and where we got the new clothes, and we might get kicked out of the library."

Or they'd weaponize their privilege and have him hauled off to prison for hurting them. Maybe the Casorina could get him out, but he didn't want to take that chance.

"Why would they care what you're doing now?" asked Quinta. "They have the invitation."

Twain pulled her farther down the hall toward a wide set of double doors. He hoped it led to another exit. "Despite their Verdigris upbringings, they're grasping and they're gamblers. My brother owed them money, and I'm sure if they see I've come up in the world, they'll want to drag me back down. . . ."

He trailed off as the group reached the top of the stairs. Gustave's and Henri's backs were to them, and they took turns pointing out things to the group of visiting scholars they were showing around the library.

Gustave gestured toward a room down the left hallway. "Over here, you'll find all the books on the history of magic that have been written by Severon's scholars."

A small pang of satisfaction went through Twain when he saw Gustave's arm was in a sling. He was also giddy to know that these, in fact, weren't all the books of magic written by Severon's scholars. The Casorina's collection would've made these scholars weep in ecstasy, but only Twain and Quinta had access to them.

"And there's an auditorium at the end of the hall," Henri said, pointing in the direction of the double doors where Twain and Quinta lurked. "One of our top scholars is currently giving a lecture on magic in the lands of Tszana and—"

Twain didn't wait to hear the rest of Henri's sentence. He grabbed Quinta's hand and opened the lecture hall door. They disappeared into the room right as the group of scholars turned their way.

Inside the auditorium, rows of seats were arranged in a half circle around a stage. Tiers of balconies reminded Twain instantly of the theater where he saw an opera with his parents once, a very long time ago. On the stage stood a tall, thin man in blue-and-gray scholar's robes. He had brown skin and white hair, and wore a pair of round glasses. His voice was rich and warm as it filled the room.

"I can't believe there are so many people here," whispered Quinta as they moved down a staircase to a pair of open seats at the end of a nearby row. They'd come in near the top of the lecture hall, and good thing too since the upper balcony was the only one with seats left open.

Twain shrugged. "Perhaps it's because of all the people in town for the Scholar's Ball. Zand told me that some lectures could go on for hours, and if a famous scholar was speaking you'd have to arrive—"

"Shhh!" hissed a voice behind them.

They turned to face the glare of a red-faced white man with heavy jowls and short gray hair. He held a finger to his lips and scowled at them. Smothering a laugh, Quinta and Twain hurried toward the empty seats. The scholars in the row they'd joined were all scribbling notes, and none of them looked up as Quinta and Twain sat down.

From the stage at the center of the room, the scholar who was giving the lecture went on: "It's said that in Tszana magic runs down maternal lines and is primarily held by women, the so-called Monstrous Daughters of legend. Whether this is true or not, we're not sure, and good luck asking a Tszanaian scholar for any clues. Visitors are not allowed into their country, though I am hopeful that events like the Casorina's ball can bring us closer together." This statement was met with a hearty chuckle from around the room.

Quinta turned to Twain and raised one eyebrow. Not getting the joke either, he shrugged. "Scholar humor?"

She grinned at him. On stage, the scholar continued: "It is also speculated that magic in Tszana is lunar, as has been the case in many other . . ."

A huge yawn escaped Twain's lips as the lecture droned on. Beside him, Quinta leaned on his shoulder.

"I wouldn't fall asleep if I were you," said an accented voice behind them.

Quinta's head popped up, and they turned to see a freckled, redheaded young man smiling at them. Even his dark-blue scholar's robes couldn't hide his broad frame. It was the scholar the Casorina had introduced them to yesterday. Twain racked his brain for the man's name.

"I'm Damian," the young man whispered, putting down his pen. "We met yesterday."

"We know who you are," Quinta replied haughtily. "And we weren't sleeping."

Damian's grin broadened at that. "Sure you weren't. But you will be soon if you stay much longer. I've already had three naps since I got here two hours ago." He held up his notebook, showing them how the notes he'd taken had turned into long downward squiggles as he drifted off. "Is there any chance you two know where I can get some ice cream? I'll pay for it if you show me your favorite place in Severon."

That sounded far better than staying in the Great Library any longer than necessary.

Twain leaned over to Quinta and brushed a curl behind her ear. "What do you think? Okay if we get out of here and take him for ice cream?"

She shivered slightly at his touch, which stirred something deep in Twain. "Yes. Free ice cream is always good, and maybe we can learn something from him about magic, since he's an actual scholar."

The three of them hurried out of the lecture hall, earning no small measure of dirty looks from the other scholars who were still taking notes.

"It's good to be out in the sunshine," Damian said as they walked from the ice cream cart in Lapis toward a boardwalk beside the ocean.

Twain looked over right as Damian took a huge lick of his strawberry cone. He looked like a little kid in that moment, not a serious scholar.

"It is," Quinta agreed. She took a small bite of her lemon and lavender ice cream. "Is this your first time in Severon?"

Damian shook his head. "This is my third year attending the Scholar's Ball. I've been hoping to learn something new every year, but mostly it's just the same old theories being hashed and rehashed over and over. I'm trying to see more of the city this trip."

"What sort of things do you study?" Twain had ordered a chocolate and toffee ice cream and most of it was already gone.

They all settled on a bench that overlooked the sea. Damian's eyes took on a faraway look as he stared across the water.

"I study the history of magic," he said softly. "I'm not sure how much you know about my nation, but Ixily is a place that's always been on the wrong end of it."

"That's why you train so many soldiers, right?" Twain asked, remembering one of his father's history lessons.

Damian nodded. "Correct. We'd love to have a fighting chance, but we're so small that we just end up fighting."

Quinta furrowed her brow. "But why study magic? Why not warfare or strategy?"

Damian laughed. "I ask myself that question every day, especially when I'm in the middle of another lecture hall listening to wild speculation. Many people study warfare and strategy—and I know much about both subjects myself—but I study magic because it's hope for my people, for myself, and for the woman I love." Just as he went to take another lick, a gull swooped in and stole his ice cream cone. He stood up, waving his hands at the gulls.

"I'll be back," he said with a sigh. "Does anyone else want more ice cream?"

Quinta and Twain shook their heads, and Damian headed toward the ice cream cart. Once he was gone, Quinta moved a little bit closer to Twain, her thigh pushing against his. His breath caught in his throat at her nearness.

"It's lovely, isn't it?" she said softly, eyes on the sea and sky.

"Yes," he murmured. As he stared out to sea, his eyes fell on the pillar of rock where he'd gathered the starlight. Had it only been three days since he was out there, climbing for his life? How had he ended up here, on this bench in Lapis, wearing an expensive suit, and eating ice cream with a scholar from a distant island and a lovely, prickly girl he was falling for hard?

Life was very strange, and who knew what the next moment could bring. He was no scholar, but perhaps there was some magic in knowing that at least.

Right as he thought that, a melody, playful as water burbling in a mountain stream, filled the air. Twain looked around for the source.

"Do you hear that?" he asked Quinta.

"Hear what?"

He turned his head this way and that, listening for it again, but the music was gone. Had that been the starlight song? Had he missed it?

"Nothing. I'm sure it was just music from the city somewhere."

"Was it the starlight melody?"

"No."

It might have been? He didn't know. It sounded different from the song he heard yesterday. Which meant it was probably nothing at all.

Quinta bumped his ankle with her own. "Then, don't pay it any mind. We'll find more starlight soon. I'm sure of it."

He could've kissed her now, just for the reassurance. They *would* find more. He would hear the music again. He had to.

Damian arrived at that moment, carrying another ice cream cone.

"What were we talking about?" he asked, taking a seat next to Quinta.

"How magic might help with the woman you love," she said, scooting even closer to Twain.

"I can't say much more about magic or love," said Damian. "Not without revealing more than I'm at liberty to say. But I will tell you I love someone whom I can never be with. Not without the miracle of magic. If I were to learn something here, I might be able to change my own path and that of my country."

"I hope you find what you're looking for," said Quinta softly. She took another bite of her cone.

"So do I," said Damian. "Though I'm fairly certain this year will be like every other year, and I'll leave empty-handed."

Twain patted him on the back. "You never know," he said bracingly. "So much can change in a day. Now, who wants a cup of coffee? I need one if I'm going to make it through any more studying."

Both Quinta and Damian agreed to that, and they set off to get the strongest cup of coffee they could find. As they walked, Quinta slipped her hand into Twain's. He smiled, at peace for a moment. They might not have answers about where to find starlight, but at least they had each other.

CHAPTER EIGHTEEN
Quinta

Much later that night, Quinta woke to an insistent, soft knocking on her bedroom door. Three times and then three more. Groggily, she crawled out of bed and opened the door. Twain stood in the hallway, wearing only a shirt, trousers, his coat, and an excited expression on his face. His boots were in his hands, a bag was slung across his chest, and he kept looking over his shoulder.

"What is it?" she said, yawning. "Are you going somewhere?"

"I heard it!" He bounced on his toes excitedly.

"Heard what?"

"The starlight music!"

She blinked at him for a moment, as her brain caught up. "Are you certain?"

"Yes! It's the same song as before, and it's getting louder."

"Sure you didn't just have too much coffee?"

"Let's go," said Twain, rolling his eyes. "Come on. This is a night for finding things. I can feel it."

It was outrageous to think that the stars sang to Twain, but if the last few days had taught Quinta anything, it was that the world was stranger than she'd believed and that there was far more to Twain than it seemed.

They needed starlight, and maybe this is how they'd find some. It was worth a try.

"Give me ten minutes," she said.

"Make it five. We've got to get moving."

"Done." Quinta closed the door and hurried to get dressed.

Twain

Twain had heard the strange music again as they walked home from the coffee shop that afternoon. It had been a light melody, like a song playing in a different room. After that, he'd picked up snatches of it throughout the city, but he dismissed it, thinking it was music from somewhere in town.

But the noise grew louder when he got back to the Orpiment, ringing in his ears over dinner and demanding attention as he and Quinta worked in the library. By the time he went to bed, it was a whole orchestra, playing the starlight song. As he tried to sleep, notes swelled, almost as if the starlight itself was impatient at Twain for taking so long to find it.

Still, he tried to sleep, not wanting to head into the city for more disappointment. After a few hours of tossing and turning, he couldn't help getting out of bed. He had to find the source of the music.

"Ready?" said Quinta, a few minutes after Twain had knocked. She wore a gray dress with a long coat over it.

"Ready."

Together, they headed down the palace steps, avoiding night watchmen and servants who dozed at their posts.

"Which way?" asked Quinta as they slipped into the garden.

The moon was still mostly full, its silver light bathing the city. It reminded Twain of the starlight painting that disguised the door to the Casorina's library.

Twain paused, listening. "The music, it's everywhere, but I think it's loudest over there."

He nodded toward an enormous stone folly at the end of the palace garden. It was in the shape of a monster's head. Stairs led into the monster's mouth and vines tangled around its face, creating a nest of foliage. Water tinkled in a fountain as they passed, and an owl screeched in the night.

"Not creepy at all," muttered Quinta as they walked through the moonlit garden.

"I'll be right back," said Twain when they reached the stone monster.

The starlight music soared as Twain moved toward the side of the folly. It was coming from above the statue. Gripping one of the thick vines that fell down the side of the monster's head, he began to climb. A silver glow emanated from deep in the orange-leafed tangles of ivy, near the middle of the folly.

Twain crawled toward the starlight. His knees sunk into pits of vegetation, and thorns bit into his legs. But that didn't matter, because there it was: a silver thread among the inky shadows at the top of the folly. As Twain curled his hands around the strand of starlight, the music surged, all triumph.

Relief flooded him. He'd done it. He'd found more starlight. He sagged into the vines for a moment, hands shaking. Maybe he wasn't such a disappointment after all.

"Did you find something?" Quinta called out from below.

"Yes!"

Quinta cheered, which made Twain grin. Wrapping the starlight around his neck, he made his way back to her.

"You found more!" She flung her arms around him as soon as his feet were back on the ground.

For a moment, he lost himself in Quinta's lavender scent and the feel of her hair on his skin. Without thinking, he bent down and lightly planted a kiss on the place where her neck met the curve of her shoulder.

She gasped, pulling away from him, her dark eyes silvered by the glow of the starlight.

Touching the spot where his lips had brushed her skin, she whispered, "No kissing."

"No kissing," he said. "I'm sorry."

If he was being honest, he wasn't sorry at all. Rather, he was only sorry that he couldn't kiss her again.

A look of indecision passed over Quinta's face before she let out a long sigh. "I'm saying that for myself as well. I got caught up in the moment too. Can I see the starlight?"

Twain handed her the thread, and she twirled it around her fingers. This thread was wider and longer than the first one he'd found.

"We can make so much lace with this," Quinta said. "Is the music quiet now?"

Before Twain could reply, more starlight music surged around them, filling the city with its song. "Not even a little bit. Come on. There's more finding to be done tonight."

Quinta put the first starlight thread into Twain's bag, and they headed into the city. Music came at Twain from every direction as they walked, and he kept stumbling over cobblestones.

"You listen." Quinta took his arm. "I'll make sure you don't fall."

It was a strange feeling, letting her keep him on track as he listened to the song of the city, but Twain liked it. He liked being held up and feeling less alone.

They found two more silver strands of starlight stuffed into a streetlamp. They also climbed the twisting stairs to a lighthouse on the edge of the coast and found six silver threads tangled into its railing; they found another strand in a wooden crate, curled around a sleeping kitten.

"This should be more than enough to make the Casorina's dress," Twain said as they walked back to the palace. It was long after midnight, and his feet ached. Quinta still had her arm looped through his.

"Do you hear any more music?"

He shook his head. The night was full of noise from bars, dockworkers, and people out and about, but the starlight song was quiet.

Until it wasn't.

As they crossed through Vermilion, Twain caught the faintest snatch of song. They followed it toward a district of cabarets and nightclubs that were wild with life at this time of night.

In the center of the street sat La Lune, a nightclub famous for its beautiful dancers and busy gambling tables. A line of carriages waited outside its door, the drivers smoking pipes and chatting with one another while their fares visited the club. An enormous silver crescent moon sat on top of La Lune's roof, lit up by steam-powered lights, and beckoning patrons with its silvery glow.

"Up there," Twain said, pointing at the moon on top of the club. The starlight music was so loud now, it nearly drowned out all the other city noises. "There's starlight up there. I can hear it."

"How are you going to get on the roof?" Quinta eyed the burly men at the entrance of La Lune, and the many people loitering around it, drinking and laughing with dancers and sex workers.

"Quickly." Twain adjusted the bag around his shoulders. "Be back soon."

Quinta grabbed him before he could go and plopped a kiss on his cheek.

His eyebrows shot up.

"For luck," she said. "And as revenge for earlier. One kiss cancels out the other, so we're back to no kissing again."

Twain grinned at her logic. "Be back soon, None of Your Concern."

"You better."

He hurried off toward an alley beside the club. There was a gutter there, which he made quick work of. The roof was unwatched and full of empty wooden crates. From up here, it was much easier to see the clump of starlight tangled around the bottom curve of the crescent moon. Twain snatched it up and shoved it into his bag. He grinned as he slid back down the gutter toward the street. He had done it. He had proven both useful and clever, and now they could actually deliver a dress to the Casorina. It was a marvelous feeling.

Quinta

Quinta never imagined they'd find so much starlight. It was near dawn, and they were back in the palace, dirty, footsore, and safely ensconced in the Casorina's library. As she watched, Twain pulled more and more silver strands out of his bag.

"There was a huge cache at La Lune," Twain said as he untwisted the threads, laying them out on the table in front of Quinta.

She ran her hands through the silvery ribbons, her fingers already twitching to be at work. This was more than enough to make the Casorina's dress and finish her own. "This last bunch brings our total up to sixty-three threads, which is incredible. You truly are the starlight finder."

Twain gave an exaggerated bow. "At your service."

"Do you hear the music anymore?"

Twain shook his head. "It's silent. Almost as if the starlight is satisfied."

Quinta sighed. She was not naturally musical, but she did love to listen. "I would've loved to hear it. Can you describe what it sounded like?"

Twain looked at her for a long moment. The silver starlight reflected in his sea-glass eyes, dancing there like fireflies on a summer night. Her heart thudded in her chest. He was so beautiful, so achingly close. She would only just have to reach out and pull him toward her. She wanted desperately to do exactly that, but she held still, willing herself and her heart to stay calm.

"I can do better than describe it." He picked up the violin case he'd brought in earlier that day. "I've not played in many months, but I'll try to bring you the starlight song."

With some quick tuning, he began weaving a song of love, loss, heartache, and beautiful dreams around Quinta. It was a song that she knew, like one she'd heard long ago. It was silver spangles and the murmur of a crowd filling the circus stands. It was her mother's laughter and the long twilights of her childhood somehow made into song.

Twain played on and on, presenting a starlight symphony just for Quinta. The music poured out from under his fingers, wrapping her in love, even if it was only for a few moments. Even if he was leaving at the end of the month. Even if everything between them was most certainly in her imagination. As Twain played the starlight song, she knew she was climbing even higher into love with him. And that she would do nothing about it.

CHAPTER NINETEEN

Quinta

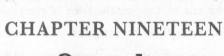

A week later, Twain was reading out loud from a book of old stories about starlight while Quinta took measurements of the Casorina. She was no seamstress, but she was going to do her best with this dress.

"Listen to this," Twain said, holding up the book. He read aloud another story of starlight lace causing a war between Severon and a country on its border.

Quinta let out a long sigh as she finished up measurements and turned to the book of lace patterns. This was the latest in a long series of stories they'd found about the dangers of starlight lace. There was the war between Aix and a neighboring kingdom over who owned a lace dress that was rumored to show the future to the wearer. There were the lacemakers who were hunted in the streets of Severon. There were stories of a kind woman who'd turned to murder as she tried to collect more and more starlight. As much as Quinta wanted to make the dress for the Casorina, she was beginning to wonder if they were dabbling with forces they didn't understand.

"Something the matter, child?" the Casorina asked as she stirred some sugar into her tea.

Twain was also looking at Quinta, his expression worried, one of his fingers resting inside the enormous book he was slogging through.

"What do you think is the point of magic?" Quinta's fingers moved along a strand of starlight, but they kept tangling as she tried to make an intricate knot pattern. For most of her life, Quinta had thought that the point of magic was freedom and power, but now that she had a little bit at hand, the wielding of magic seemed as complicated as the knots she was attempting. After all, magic had killed her mother. What if that was her fate as well? Was death really worth it to be admired by all the fancy people in Severon? Or if not death, what if magic led her astray?

The Casorina took a deep breath, pausing with her tea halfway to her lips. She waited so long to reply, Quinta wasn't sure she'd heard the question.

Before Quinta could ask again, the Casorina took a long sip and said, "I'm not entirely sure what the point of magic is, and everyone will give you their own answer. Some people want magic for power, others for wealth. Some want magic to take away pain, while others want to use it to cause misery. Still others would create or destroy with it. Think of the earliest alchemists, trying to turn metals into gold. They were looking for the spark that would make that happen, but if they had found the spark, what do you think they would've done?"

Quinta paused to think. "Probably whatever they wanted."

"Exactly." The Casorina nodded slowly. "Magic is dangerous because it gives people the means to dream boldly. Which is not always a terrible thing, but some dreams should never be realized. I think the point of magic is to make the world more beautiful, and that's what I love about your lace. Of course, the desire for magic can cause all sorts of pain and destruction. But, used rightly, magic dulls the edges of the real world and makes life more beautiful."

"But," Quinta protested. "What if we could do great things with magic? What if we could save lives or end disease? What if there were never any more hungry children?"

This question haunted her dreams.

For three years, until she was thirteen, Quinta stayed alive by hiding in the great houses, libraries, and museums of Severon. It was a lonely life—she didn't dare make friends for fear that she would get caught, and she avoided the university with its overly curious scholars.

She never took anyone else into the great houses with her. Except for one night when it was freezing and she found a small girl huddled in a doorway. The girl was shoeless, clutching a bundle of rags. Quinta wasn't sure if the girl was trying to sell them or use them to keep warm.

"Come with me," Quinta had whispered.

The girl didn't move. Quinta tried to lift her, but she couldn't. Slipping the girl's arm around her shoulder, Quinta picked the lock of a house nearby. It was a tall townhouse, blazing with light. A dinner party was going on in the main dining room, but no one saw Quinta and the girl slip in. They huddled in the shadows of an upstairs room. Heat and laughter rose from the rooms below, but no one disturbed them. The girl shivered through the night, and Quinta heaped blankets on top of her. Her eyes never opened, and Quinta didn't dare leave the girl long enough to tiptoe downstairs and find something to eat.

The people of the house eventually went to bed, but Quinta stayed up—wary, worried that someone would find them. Eventually, she dozed off. When the sun rose, the little girl was dead, her lips purple, her hands cold.

Quinta left the girl there, tucked beneath the pile of covers in the upstairs room, for the people of the house to find and worry over and wonder about. *How could such an urchin get in?* they would say.

After that Quinta never tried to help another person again. Because she hadn't been able to save her mother. Or the girl. And so she focused on looking after herself. But magic could've kept that little girl warm and fed, and then she wouldn't have died unmourned except by Quinta in a stranger's house. Surely, they should be thinking about using magic for good.

The Casorina smiled a small, sad smile. "Although I see your point, I think the world has moved past the need for magic as a whole, child. For good or ill, it is science that will take us into the next century. That's why I allow all these scholars into Severon, to bring their new ideas and experiments. Some of them will build technologies we've never dreamed of—things even the lace magicians couldn't have imagined."

"If you feel that way, then why are we here?" Quinta asked, gesturing toward Twain and herself. "Why do you want a dress made of magical lace?"

The Casorina's sharp eyes held Quinta's. "Because I can't help myself," she said with a small laugh. "As much as I believe science is the future, I love beauty, and I've never seen anything more exquisite than the lace you make. And because I'm old enough to want my story woven into the fabric of the world. When I die, my son will be the new leader of Severon. He is a man of science, through and through. He has no time for old tales and stories told in lace. I have no doubt he'll help Severon grow and make incredible discoveries, but before I die, I want to wear the lace that gave our ancestors power. I want to walk in beauty for an evening, and then I'll burn it the next day."

"You would really burn your magical lace?" Twain sounded startled.

The Casorina nodded. "I would. As the story you just read illustrates, this much power in the wrong hands could be deadly. We cannot afford to have magical lace make monsters of us, beautiful though it is. At the ball, I'll present you both to the guests, then you can stay long enough to enjoy the party. After that, pack your things, take the money you've earned, and do as you will."

Quinta had started weaving again, something in her settling from the conversation. Her fingers no longer snared in the starlight. Their futures were as simple and elegant as the pattern she wove: They would make something beautiful, and then Twain would disappear into the world. Quinta would stay in Severon, her reputation as a lacemaker helping her rise through the ranks of society, just as she'd planned.

You are meant for great things.

She would miss Twain, but not too much. Her dreams of success and power would be enough. Or at least that's what she was telling herself.

"Thank you for giving us a chance to weave your story," Twain said, coming over to Quinta and standing behind her. He rested a hand on her shoulder, and she couldn't help leaning her head against his stomach. Who was she kidding when she said that her dreams of power would be enough? But what else could she do? She'd wanted to be important in Severon for so long, how could she change her mind now? But what happened when someone like Twain came along, a person who was a dream in and of themselves?

Quinta pushed those thoughts away. She would deal with them later. They still had a few weeks together. Plenty of time to think about the future.

The Casorina beamed at them and finished her tea. "Thank you for bringing an old woman some beauty and some love. I've not been around two young people so smitten with each other in a very long time. It's more refreshing than spring air off the ocean."

Quinta flushed at that—were they so obvious?—but she didn't move her body away from Twain's touch. "We're not smitten with each other."

The Casorina flashed a mischievous smile as she stood up. "Don't stay up too late," she called over her shoulder as she left the library. "And don't forget to have a little fun."

Her laugh filled the room as the door closed.

"Want to get out of here?" Twain asked. "I hear there's a band of performers in Vermilion tonight who have come from across the mountains. We could eat sweet buns and dance until our legs ache."

He glanced toward the secret passage doorway. Quinta had been feeling drowsy, but the thought of being out in the city at night with Twain invigorated her.

"I wouldn't miss it for the world," she said. "Though I don't know how to dance."

"It's easy. Let me show you." Twain offered a hand.

"No kissing?"

"None," Twain promised, pulling her to her feet. Quinta put her hands on his shoulders, and his hands settled on her hips.

"You could come with me, you know," he said softly, brushing one of her curls behind her ear.

Twain's touch sent her heart racing, like a wild animal navigating an unknown forest.

"Where? Into the city tonight?"

Twain shook his head, twirling her gently. "No. When I leave Severon. You could come with me on the *Lady's Revenge.*"

"I can't do that," Quinta whispered. It was a half-truth, but the only one she was allowing herself to tell.

Twain paused their dance.

"I know you've gotten everything you wanted—" He nodded at the grand library and Quinta's expensive dress. "But . . . I don't know, None of Your Concern. I've grown to like adventuring with you."

"I—" She pulled away from him, and they stood still in the middle of the library, looking at each other. How could she say this in a way that wouldn't hurt him?

Sheepishly, Twain ran a hand through his hair. "I'm sorry. I shouldn't have brought it up."

"It's not that I don't want to. It's just . . . I'm finally making something of myself."

Her mother's promise echoed in her head: *You are meant for great things.*

She was, wasn't she? Walking away from this life in the palace would end all her chances of greatness. Wouldn't it?

But was doing great things worth losing Twain? She didn't know. Not yet, at least.

Twain let out a long breath. "I know that, of course. But who knows who you could be—who *we* could be—out there in the world. We could see so many different things, become so many different people."

"That's your adventure, Twain. Not mine." Quinta's voice was tender, its edges frayed with regret.

His face fell. "But you'll be alone."

"I was alone before. And besides, we're here, together, now. That's all that matters."

Twain let out a long sigh and began their dance again. "Of course." Disappointment laced his voice, breaking Quinta's heart.

Maybe being someone who was meant for great things wasn't worth losing Twain. She had a few weeks to figure that out.

"But you can ask me again, one more time. On the night before the Scholar's Ball, okay?" She moved closer to him, resting her cheek on his chest.

Twain secured his arm around her waist and dipped her backward. "I absolutely will, None of Your Concern. You can count on that."

The hope on his face made Quinta wish she already had a clearer answer for him, but instead, she laughed, and their dance continued.

CHAPTER TWENTY

Twain

Now that Twain had found more starlight, both his and Quinta's minds eased and October raced by, each day a bit of the same and wholly different. It had been twenty-nine days since Twain and Quinta met. He was now fully, entirely, hopelessly, and completely in love with her; and he was mostly sure she loved him back.

Not that she said anything about it.

He didn't ask her to leave Severon with him again, though he wanted to every day. He would wait, as he'd promised, until the night before the ball.

They spent their mornings reading about starlight magic, walking through the streets of Severon, and exploring the Orpiment. In the afternoons, Quinta wove lace. They had discovered that Twain was no lacemaker. He had tried, but only ended up with tangled threads or torn fragments. As far as they knew, only Quinta could weave the lace. They also learned that Quinta had to start with one of the patterns in the book, and then she could make something new from there. They both had so many questions about how the magic worked and where starlight originated from, but neither of them could find the answers in the Casorina's books or in the Great Library.

While Quinta wove the lace, Twain sat near her reading or telling her news of the world he'd picked up from around the palace. He also spent many hours in front of the map that hung on the library wall, telling her stories about the countries that surrounded Severon and where he planned on traveling.

"Have you ever noticed that our part of the world looks like a snarling wolf?" Twain said one day.

Quinta looked up from her lace work to snort, but he took her hand, bringing her over to the map.

"I'm serious. Look, Severon and Aix are the upper jaw and teeth; Reyoux makes up the muzzle, and Vestun is the wolf's head. Lake Navatar is its eye, and Tszana is an ear. To the south, Ysitar is one part of the lower jaw."

"Where does that leave poor Ixily?" asked Quinta, pointing to the narrow island between Aix in the north and Ysitar in the south.

"Trapped like a piece of food between the wolf's jaws, is what my father used to say. Which, of course, is why they're so intent on making their people the fiercest fighters in the world."

"You couldn't pay me to visit Ixily," Quinta said with a laugh. "And I wouldn't tell Damian that metaphor."

They'd bumped into Damian, the scholar from Ixily, a few more times, and they'd taken him around the city to see the night market and the grand museums. Something held them back from showing him the Vermilion Emporium—perhaps it was the scholar's intensity as he asked them questions about their work (which they deflected) or perhaps it was just that they still wanted to keep the Emporium a secret. Damian was friendly enough, but he was a passing ship in their lives. Neither of them would miss him too much when he returned to Ixily after the Scholar's Ball.

"I promise I'll never tell Damian his country looks like a morsel of food in a wolf's mouth," Twain said.

Quinta had laughed her sunlight-on-water laugh, which made Twain want to tell her of the adventures they might have together. But that would mean him telling her he wanted a future where they were together. And he didn't want to pressure her about that. Even if he now knew he wanted that future. Whatever it looked like.

When their lacework in the Casorina's library was done each day, they visited a new room in the Vermilion Emporium in the evening.

They saw so many wonders in the Emporium.

There was a room made of time and full of clocks.

There was a room woven entirely from threads of shadow, where, according to the plaque by the door, one could get lost in darkness and take half a century to return.

There was a room specifically for hats that was far more enchanting than it had a right to be.

There was a photo room that was somehow filled with hundreds of photographs from both of their lives. Twain found pictures of his mother as a child, ones of he and Zand as babies, and some of the whole family together on trips. There was a whole wall full of photos from the summer they spent on the shores of Lake Navatar. And a gallery from the year his parents studied at the renowned university in Ysitar. Who had taken them and how they'd ended up in the Emporium, Twain didn't know.

There was a room full of needles and thread for stitching together broken promises. A room full of rainbow-colored sea glass that showed a different part of the world with each piece you looked through. There was even a room full of bottled dreams. They walked through that one very, very carefully.

In each room, they learned something new about themselves, each other, and the Vermilion Emporium.

The old woman—whose name they found out was Sorchia— seemed to have lived a hundred lives in her many years. Each time they visited, she told them about a different place she'd been to in the Emporium. Twain was entirely unsure of the mechanics of it all, but it seemed that the shop traveled through space, going where magic was about to be found or where it was needed. Sorchia never had any idea how long she'd stay in a place nor how long she'd be there. But she was anchored to the Emporium until her death, when she would pass the proprietorship on to someone else.

"But does that mean you can't ever leave the shop?" Quinta asked her, wrinkling her brow.

It was the day before the Scholar's Ball, and Twain, Quinta, and Sorchia were having tea in a room that Sorchia called the fortune-teller's suite. It was a small, round room, decorated with purple-and-blue wallpaper. Exactly one hundred round glass globes hung from the ceiling, each of them flickering with a different future. Today was unseasonably warm, and the windows were flung open. A fresh, salty breeze blew in from the sea.

Sorchia looked up from her tea and laughed. "Of course I can leave the Emporium, child. How else do you think I get food or walk beside the sea in the moonlight?"

She made it sound like the most ridiculous of questions, but Twain thought it was quite a good one. He lifted his own teacup—a paper-thin one painted green and gold and decorated with butterflies—and took a sip. Nearly a month in the Casorina's palace had given him a taste for luxuries like fine tea, and both he and Quinta looked healthier. They wore expensive clothes, and their skin didn't cling to their bones quite so desperately these days. Twain stole a glance at Quinta only to find her looking back at him. Their eyes met, and she smiled at him, sharing some secret joke.

His heart surged at that smile. Tonight. After so many weeks of waiting, he would finally ask her again to leave Severon with him.

"It's a good question." Twain returned Quinta's smile. "Could the Emporium leave without you? What would happen if you were to die suddenly out in the world?"

Sorchia shrugged. "I'm not sure. I don't think that would happen, but you never know. Usually the proprietorship passes down a family line, at least until it runs out. But I lost track of my daughter and her family long ago, so I'm not sure what will happen when I'm gone."

"Which of course won't be for a very long time," Quinta said quickly.

"Exactly," Sorchia said. "Now, tell me, how goes the Casorina's dress? Are you finished?"

Twain took another sip of tea while Quinta bit her lip.

"I'm done with it," said Quinta. "And I've made myself a dress too. Which I'm wearing to the ball tomorrow."

"You made yourself a dress?" Twain asked, dropping his teacup with a clatter. "How? When?"

"I did." Quinta smirked.

"Can I see it?"

"On the night of the ball, yes."

Twain wanted to ask her more, but he could wait a day.

"What does the Casorina think about you having a starlight dress?" Sorchia asked.

Twain had been wondering the same thing.

"She doesn't know." Quinta tried for a laugh, but it came out more like the noise a rusty gate makes upon opening.

"That's quite a gamble," Sorchia murmured. "Powerful people don't like to be upstaged."

"What can she do to me when she finds out? Banish me? Tear it off me in a crowd?" Quinta's hand shook as she lifted her cup for another sip of tea. Hot liquid sloshed onto the tablecloth.

"I'm sure she'll love it," Twain said. "And I'm sure I'll love it too."

Quinta shot him a grateful look.

"Now, since I leave right after the ball, this will be our last visit to the Vermilion Emporium," Twain said, turning to Sorchia. "What room do you recommend we explore?"

"I'm not sure," Sorchia said, peering into her teacup. "About whether this will be your last visit or what room you should peek into today. Have you been to the perfume market?"

They had. It was a labyrinth of empty stalls, each of them selling a different perfume that captured the essence of every person in the world. They'd found their own stalls and spent hours drinking in each other's scents.

"We did that a week ago," Quinta said. "It was beyond anything I've ever seen or smelled."

"What about the paper circus?" Sorchia asked.

That was one of Twain's favorites. An entire life-sized circus tent filled with paper performers, acrobats, horses, and people. They rustled like newspapers in the wind as they flew through the air, and to sit too long among them made Quinta and Twain feel entirely too substantial for this world.

"We loved that one," Twain said.

Sorchia put her teacup down on her saucer and pulled a key out of her pocket. "I was saving this one, but I think it's time. Find the door this key opens, and you'll be where you're meant to."

Twain took the key, and he and Quinta hugged Sorchia goodbye.

"Where do you think this new door is?" Quinta asked as they walked along the now-familiar hallway in the Emporium. Today the walls were hung with maps.

The Emporium's doors changed all the time too, and where the book room once had been, there was now a room full of pillows of all shapes and sizes. The downward staircase remained in the same place, however. They'd not been brave—or foolish—enough to investigate what lay at its end yet. But perhaps today was the day.

"I think we go down there." Twain pointed to the stairs. The key in his hand had twitched a bit as they walked past.

Beside him, Quinta tilted her head, considering. "I think you're right. But I don't want to. Something about that door feels too strange. Even for this place."

"I won't leave your side," promised Twain gently. "Whatever is in there, we'll face it together."

Quinta slipped her hand in his, and they went down the stairs. At the bottom of half a hundred marble steps sat a red and gold doorway carved with runes. There was a keyhole in the middle of the door.

Quinta nodded at Twain as he took the key from his pocket.

Twain turned the key in the lock, and there was a great creaking as the door swung inward.

They stepped into darkness that stretched in every direction. A cool breeze blew through the chamber, smelling of spices and faraway places. In the distance, something glowed faintly silver and golden, like a lantern many miles away. Twain took his lace handkerchief out of his pocket. It cast a glow around them, revealing the stone floor and a pile of boulders to their right. From what he could tell, they were in a vast underground cavern, and water trickled somewhere in the distance.

"Why we never bring a lantern with us on these adventures, I'll never know," Quinta muttered as the room's door closed. Carefully, they moved through the cavern, headed in the direction of the silver and gold speck in the distance. They walked for a long time, but when they finally arrived at it, Twain forgot how to speak for a moment.

It was no lantern, but rather a towering mountain of interwoven silver and gold threads. It looked like cotton candy and glowed like a hundred candles, lighting up their faces.

"It's incredible," Twain managed, finding his voice.

Quinta nodded, moving around the mountain. "This is starlight," she said, picking up a silver thread. It was faded and sat in her hand like dull pewter tableware. "What are the golden threads, I wonder?"

"I'm not sure." Twain ran a finger along one of them.

"Maybe we'll find out someday."

A staircase curled around the mountain of threads, and Quinta and Twain climbed until they were on top of the pile. Enormous bones, emerald-green and bigger even than the whales' bones that washed up on Severon's beaches, waited for them there. The skull was from some great beast with a mouthful of teeth and a long, curved snout.

Twain swore softly in disbelief.

"Have you ever seen anything like this?" Quinta asked, eyes wide. "What is it?"

"I think it's a dragon," Twain said, running a finger over a tooth longer than his arm.

"That's impossible."

But of course it wasn't. Dragons were as equally plausible as anything else Quinta and Twain had discovered in the Vermilion Emporium thus far. The air around the dragon skeleton pulsed with magic, like a heartbeat.

"This must be its hoard," Quinta said, gesturing to the pile of silver and gold threads under the bones. Carefully, she put down the starlight she'd picked up earlier.

"You can take that," Twain said. "I don't think this dragon is going anywhere."

Quinta shook her head. "It doesn't feel right. These are its things, and I'll leave them."

After spending several long minutes debating what the dragon skeleton was doing under the Emporium and why Sorchia had given them the key—was there something she wanted them to find? Or something they were meant to find?—they made their way down the curving steps.

When his feet touched the cavern floor, a feeling of finality settled over Twain. "Is that it then? Our last adventure in the Vermilion Emporium?" An aching, empty feeling snickered through him at the thought.

Quinta pushed some of her hair behind her ears and gazed up at him. "I suppose so. I can't believe you're really sailing away from Severon after the ball."

"I can't believe you're staying," Twain said. He wanted to ask her to come with him now, but he was afraid to cross that line—afraid to push her and be rejected. He would wait a few more hours.

They were silent for a long moment.

"I'm going to miss you," Quinta said at last.

"I'll miss you too."

They stood in silence for a moment, looking around the vast cave, the air full of all the things they weren't saying to each other.

Finally, Quinta spoke. "I don't want to venture deeper into this darkness. Do you?"

Twain shook his head. "I think we've seen enough wonders for a lifetime. Let's get back to the Orpiment and pack."

"And I want to see Pierre," Quinta said. She hadn't been back to the photo studio since she left, and she had told Twain she felt she owed Pierre a thank-you.

"I'll say goodbye to Horst as well," Twain said. He had introduced Quinta to the old violinist and his wife a few weeks ago.

Heads and hearts fully stuffed with curiosities, Twain and Quinta made their way out of the Vermilion Emporium for what they thought was the last time.

CHAPTER TWENTY-ONE
Quinta

Later that night, Quinta sat at her dressing table, scowling at her reflection in the gilded mirror as she brushed out her long, tangled hair. Her feelings were more snarled than her hair, and she was doing her best to sort through them as well.

Quinta was going to miss Twain. A lot. She told him that in the Emporium this afternoon, but she didn't really say what she wanted. Which was somewhere between *don't go* and *take me with you*.

What did she want?

Tomorrow was the ball. Tomorrow, she would wear her starlight dress and be revealed as the lacemaker.

But was it enough?

You were meant for great things.

Why wasn't it enough?

Would Twain keep his promise and ask her to go with him again? And if he did, what would she say?

A knock—three times and then three more—sounded on Quinta's door, reminding her of the night so many weeks ago when she and Twain went into the city, looking for threads of starlight.

"Quinta," Twain called through the keyhole. "Are you asleep?"

She swiped at her tears—when had she started crying?—and stood. "No."

She opened the door.

Twain stood awkwardly in the doorway, his large frame filling the space. "Umm . . . hi."

"Hello?"

"I just wanted to see you. One more time. Before the big day . . ."

Silence stretched between them, filled with the question Twain wasn't asking. Quinta's heart sped up. Maybe he'd forgotten. Maybe he was so ready to leave he wouldn't bother asking her again.

You are meant for great things.

"Well, you see me. I'm here." She didn't mean to sound so sharp, but her feelings were ants under her skin, making her a prickly creature.

Twain laughed at that, his eyes crinkling at the edges, his face softening. "You are here indeed."

"What do you want?"

Twain exhaled slowly, his fingers drumming the wall. "I—"

Quinta held her breath. Hoping—not hoping; not daring to hope—that he might have decided to stay. Or that he would ask her to go. Which one did she want more? And why couldn't she decide? Her mind told her to stay in Severon and enjoy the new fame she would find after the Scholar's Ball. But her heart. Oh, her heart was singing a different song entirely.

You are meant for great things.

Twain pushed on, his words coming out in a rush. "It's the night before the ball. . . ."

"And?"

Quinta was going to make him say it. Make him ask her to go with him. She was a one-night girl. Someone carelessly brushed aside. She didn't want Twain to forget her, but she wasn't going to make this easy for him.

He stepped forward, engulfing her small hands in his large ones. "Quinta, you know what I'm going to ask."

"Then ask it."

"Will you come with me? On the *Lady's Revenge*. Please."

You are meant for great things. You are meant for great things. You are meant for great things!

"No!" She pulled away from Twain and paced over to her dressing table, staring in the mirror, trying to get her mother's words out of her head.

"No?" Twain's voice broke on the word. His eyes met Quinta's in the mirror.

"I'm not talking to you." She scowled more fiercely at her reflection and looked away from Twain's gaze.

You are meant for great things.

But what if she wasn't?

"Who were you talking to, then?" Twain asked, looking around the room.

The ghost of my dead mother.

She couldn't say that of course.

You are meant for great things.

214

She didn't want to stay in Severon. She didn't want to say goodbye to Twain. But could she really give up a life of wealth and power? For a chance at love?

She picked up her hairbrush and put it down again. Picked up a small bottle of perfume and put it down again. Picked up the bottle of moonshadow around her neck and put it down again. "It doesn't matter."

"It doesn't matter?" Twain repeated. "Please, Quinta. Tell me it does. Tell me you'll come with me. Or, even if you won't, ask me to stay and I will. For you. For us." He strode over to her, stopping behind her at the dressing table. His hands rested lightly on her arms and his eyes found hers again in the mirror. *"Please."*

That's when she made up her mind. She would take a chance. She would leap. She would leave all her old dreams behind and see the world with this mystery of a boy. And if she ended up alone? Well, she'd been there before. And the chance of happiness and being together was worth the risk of being hurt.

But she couldn't tell Twain all that in the next few seconds. So, instead, she turned around.

"What are—?" Twain's voice was thick with held-back tears.

Slowly, she traced a line along his jaw, and then ran a finger along his bottom lip. His eyes closed at the touch.

"Quinta." He murmured her name, a whisper of longing, sadness, hope, and reverence.

She leaned forward, rising to her tiptoes. "Can I kiss you?"

Twain's eyes flew open. "I thought you only kissed people you sleep with."

"And I always leave the people I sleep with."

"Are you going to leave me, Quinta?"

She shook her head. "I'm going to leave *with* you, you impossible boy."

Twain's eyes lit with something fierce and hopeful. He pulled her toward him, making her gasp at his strength. "I'm warning you, None of Your Concern, you're not going to be able to get rid of me."

"That's my plan."

"Then, yes, you may kiss me."

Quinta felt Twain's smile against her own mouth as he said the words she'd been longing to hear.

One of Twain's enormous hands skimmed her face, his calluses rough against her cheek. He tangled his hand in her hair. She leaned against his hand, closing her eyes as she pushed her lips to his. This felt right. This was where she wanted to be.

Twain made a low, growling sound, and he deepened the kiss. Quinta melted against him, her heart racing. It wasn't the first time they'd kissed, but it was the first time it felt real.

"You're very good at that, None of Your Concern," Twain said breathlessly, a few moments later. His voice was husky, hungry.

"I'm good at a lot of things."

"Show me?"

A wicked smile curved Quinta's lips as she closed her bedroom door before anyone in the palace could see them.

CHAPTER TWENTY-TWO
Quinta

The following evening, Quinta was ready for the ball. Half her hair was piled on her head in an elaborate knot, and the rest of her curls tumbled around her face. The Casorina had been so delighted with her own starlight dress, she'd gifted Quinta a set of hair combs that dripped diamonds. They were tucked into Quinta's curls, looking like moonlight against the dark blanket of the night.

But even the diamonds didn't shine as brightly as what Quinta had created for herself. She'd labored over it in secret all month, weaving bits of lace when Twain was asleep or when he'd slipped away from the Orpiment on some business of his own. Over a sheath of light-gray silk, Quinta wore a gossamer dress, silver like morning dew, and full of the patterns of her life. There, in her bodice, was her time in the Celestial Circus. Across her collarbones, woven close and fearful, were the years she spent on her own, surviving on other people's scraps. Those parts were lace, yes, but they felt heavy on her shoulders. Her skirt was the story of the last month, since she'd met Twain and discovered how to twist starlight into stories. The lace there was frothy and surged out from her waist like seafoam. It laughed and danced as it kissed the floor. The silver light from the dress emanated softly around Quinta, illuminating her like one of the paper lanterns that had been lit for the party.

Would the Casorina punish her for making a dress for herself? Perhaps. But Quinta had woven so many types of magic into the dress, she wasn't entirely sure what it would do. It contained hope for the future, a spell for beauty, and a surge of joy. Surely the Casorina wouldn't begrudge her those things?

Quinta looked again in her mirror, wildly satisfied with her own art and her own self for the first time in her life.

She had done it. She had surpassed even her mother and woven starlight into lace. She would have the eye of every powerful person in the room, and they would all want to know her.

Part of her—the part that had been craving magic for so long—yearned to stay in Severon. To be sought after and talked about. To be remembered. But what was the good in being remembered if she lost Twain? Would anyone care that she could weave starlight lace if she didn't have any more starlight? Would she care if her heart was halfway around the world?

There was a knock at her door, three times and then three more.

"Hello," she said as she opened the door.

Twain's eyes widened as he took in Quinta in her silver dress. "You . . . you're . . ." His mouth opened and closed as he struggled to find the words.

She was reminded of the all the sweet things he'd whispered to her last night, as they lay curled around each other in her bed.

"I'm what?" she asked playfully. She toyed with the bottle of blue moonshadow around her neck.

"You're more lovely than the stars themselves," Twain replied in a low voice. He almost looked stricken. He stepped toward her, cupping her cheek. His lips trailed a slow line of kisses along her neck, and she closed her eyes, enjoying the feeling of being adored. The heat between them flared, and it was all she could do not to pull him back into her room and skip the ball entirely.

"You're looking quite gorgeous yourself," said Quinta, stepping away from his embrace. She reached out and straightened his gray silk tie, which complemented his dark suit and white silk shirt perfectly. His starlight lace handkerchief peeked out of his jacket pocket. Wealth suited Twain in ways Quinta would've never imagined when they first met.

He offered her his arm, and together, they headed toward the atrium.

"I'll save all my dances for you," Quinta whispered as they neared the marble staircase. They'd been dancing every night since that first time in the library, and they were now quite good at the three dances Twain had taught Quinta.

"Please do," said Twain.

Quinta leaned against him for a moment as they reached the top of the stairs. The atrium was already full, and guests mingled around the fountain below. Candles in glass globes had been strung into the larger trees, and the room glowed like it was full of fireflies.

The Casorina had invited everyone who was anyone in Severon, along with guests from all over the world. Among them, scholars in their rainbow of robes filled the room.

A few hours earlier, Quinta had been putting the last touches on the Casorina's dress in the library while Twain put books away. "Tonight is our night to shine, quite literally," the Casorina had said as she twirled in her starlight dress.

Power emanated off her, and thanks to Quinta's magic, it would be impossible for anyone to say no to the Casorina tonight. Despite her insistence on only wanting magical lace for its beauty, Quinta wondered if she had invited so many people from all over the world to ensnare them in schemes that would profit Severon.

"We're going to miss you," Quinta had said, as she pinned up one last section of the Casorina's dress.

"Are you sure you must go?" the Casorina asked, considering them both.

"We are," Twain said, casting Quinta a look that sent heat through her. They'd talked it over many times, and as much as it would be nice to stay in all this comfort, as soon as the secret about them being the lacemakers was out, everything would change. Besides, there was a world to see.

"Very well then." The Casorina had cast each of them a sad smile. "This is for you."

She'd given them each a purse filled with gold coins. Quinta secured hers in her traveling bag, which contained her new clothes and the lace-weaving book. Twain also had a bagful of clothes and his violin. Those bags waited for them in the Casorina's library, which felt like a thousand miles away as they moved down the stairs that led into the packed atrium. One more curve and they'd be visible to the whole room.

Quinta was ready for this. Ready for all the eyes in Severon to be on her and Twain. She had to be.

There was a collective intake of breath as Quinta and Twain stepped into view. Damian stood at the bottom of the stairs with the other scholars. His look of surprise quickly disappeared as he met Quinta's eye. He inclined his head slightly. Quinta nodded back. The Casorina frowned as she took in Quinta's dress.

A sick feeling curled in Quinta's stomach. She'd made a terrible mistake. What was she thinking making a dress that would outshine the Casorina?

"I think we should go now," she whispered to Twain.

"We'll be fine." He squeezed her hand and led her toward the Casorina. The crowds parted before them.

Why was everyone in the room staring? Was it because they'd never seen so much starlight lace in one place? Or was it because of how Quinta glowed, radiant in her own creation? Or was it because Twain was so handsome at her side?

"Who are they?" someone in the crowd asked, and the question was taken up by all.

The Casorina walked toward them, and Quinta clutched Twain's hand more tightly. If she was going to be punished for her dress, it would happen now. She held her breath. What would the Casorina do? Send her to prison? Humiliate her in front of everyone at the ball?

The Casorina raised her voice over the whispering crowd. "May I please present: Quinta and Twain. The artists who have made my dress—and apparently, Quinta's—out of starlight. Quinta is our lacemaker, and Twain finds starlight for her." She stopped beside them, reaching out a hand to lightly touch the lace on Quinta's shoulder.

"I like your dress," she murmured to Quinta with a wink. "The more beauty the better, yes?"

Quinta let out an audible sigh of relief and returned the Casorina's smile. "Thank you." She sunk into a low curtsy.

All around them, the crowd buzzed.

"It's impossible," a scholar near the staircase cried. "No one has done such a thing for centuries!"

The other people in the atrium agreed—despite the evidence before their eyes. Their questions and conversations grew like a wave, and Quinta gripped Twain's arm. "I feel like I'm venturing into shark-infested waters."

"I won't let them eat you." Twain slipped a hand around her waist protectively.

The Casorina gestured for everyone to give Quinta and Twain some space, and she ordered the orchestra to start playing.

The next few hours were a blur of music, handshaking, fielding questions, and drinking champagne. At one point, Pierre made his way through the crowd of admirers, and he beamed at Quinta.

"I always knew you had it in you," he said. "Your mother would be so proud."

Quinta hugged him tightly. "I will miss you, old friend," she said. But before she could say more, she was pulled away from Pierre by Mrs. Davenport and the other members of the Severon Witches Society, all of whom wanted to ask her a hundred questions and get a closer look at her dress.

Luckily, before the SWS could tear into her, Quinta felt a familiar hand on her waist.

"It's getting late," Twain said close to her ear. "We should have our dance and then get out of here. Want to find someplace less crowded?"

"I'd like nothing better," Quinta whispered, turning to face him.

People had been trying to touch her dress all night, and she felt increasingly violated with each outstretched hand. It was one thing to wear her story on her body; it was another entirely to have others reach for it hungrily. The chance to slip away from the party with Twain for a few moments of privacy was a delicious thing.

They made their way to a long, marble-floored hallway off the atrium. Its entrance was surrounded by massive potted plants and trees, which allowed them a measure of seclusion from prying eyes and dampened the noise from the party. Candles burned in silver holders along the hallway, their reflections dancing in the mirrors hung along the walls. Quinta glowed as well, illuminating the shadowy space.

Twain offered Quinta his hand, and, with a bow and a curtsy, they began one of the dances he'd taught her.

"This is wonderful." Quinta nestled her head against Twain's chest. What she really wanted to say was, "I love you." It was the perfect time, the perfect place. But it took courage to declare such a thing so boldly.

He kissed her forehead as they moved together, slightly off beat but beautifully coordinated.

"I have something to tell you," Quinta continued. Her lips were right beside his ear. She was brave enough to do this.

"And what's that, None of Your Concern?" He planted a light kiss on her neck.

"It's a very important thing. Something I've not told anyone else in years."

He smiled against her cheek. "Take all the time you need."

She inhaled, and his hands tightened on her waist as they turned. "I—"

Before she could finish her declaration, Twain jerked to a stop, releasing her. She stumbled backward.

Twain's arm snaked out to catch her, but another hand was already there.

"Care if we cut in?" said a voice behind Quinta.

Rough fingernails dug into her arm. In front of her, Twain stood very still, a furious look on his face. Behind him lurked Gustave, one of the scholars who'd chased them down the beach weeks ago and who they'd avoided in the Great Library. Tonight he wore blue scholar's robes. As he gestured for them to walk toward the shadow of a potted lemon tree, Quinta saw the silver glint of the knife he held to Twain's back.

"What are you doing here, Gustave?" Twain hissed. He inhaled sharply as Gustave twisted his arm.

"We were invited," Gustave said. "Thank you for that invitation." He waggled his eyebrows at Quinta in a way that he probably thought was dashing. It made her want to throw up. This was all her fault. If she'd not lost the invitation while sliding down the dune, Gustave and Henri wouldn't be here.

"We could ask you both the same thing," Henri said from his position behind Quinta. "But then, we have our answer. You're the Casorina's pets. Not sure how you two did it, but we're going to learn how to make this starlight lace." He ran a hand across Quinta's shoulders, his coarse fingers brushing over the lace.

"Don't touch me." Quinta brought her heel down hard on Henri's foot. He cursed and let go of her. She moved to Twain's side, but Gustave twisted Twain's arm harder, making Twain wince as the knife at his back pushed through his jacket. Quinta looked around in despair, cursing their decision to leave the crowded party and seek seclusion.

She opened her mouth to call out for help, but before she did so, Henri grabbed her wrist. "You make a sound and Gustave will kill the boy." His voice was low and menacing. "We don't need him, and we owe him a beating."

"Tell us how you made this lace," Gustave demanded. "Or I'll gut Twain right here."

His knife pushed deeper into Twain.

"Stop!" Quinta begged. "Let him go!"

"Don't tell them anything," Twain called out.

She shook her head. What did it matter if they knew how to make the lace? Keeping Twain alive was more important than any magic.

"There's a book," Quinta said desperately. "A book of patterns. We'll give it to you if you let us go."

Gustave's eyes lit up. "If we have that book, we'll be the envy of every scholar in Severon. They'll pay us whatever we ask for our knowledge."

"Get it," Henri said. He nodded toward Twain and Gustave. "You two go. We'll wait here for you."

Quinta's eyes met Twain's. He was trying to tell her something with his fevered, distressed gaze, but she couldn't read it.

"Let me go with them," she pleaded.

"No," Henri said. "You're too noticeable. You'll stay down here, looking pretty. When they come back with the book, we'll let you both go."

Henri gripped her arm harder, and a small whimper escaped her lips. Twain looked murderous, but he could do nothing as Gustave marched him toward the staircase in the middle of the atrium. Gustave's knife still pressed into Twain's back, hidden from public view by his scholar's robes.

Before they disappeared, Twain called over his shoulder to Quinta: "Meet me at the palace docks!"

His voice rose above the murmurs of conversation and the music that filled the atrium. Groups of scholars and guests looked around for the source of the commotion.

"Quiet!" Gustave growled, shoving Twain toward the staircase.

Beside Quinta, Henri swore at the unwanted attention. But Quinta just smiled. Because she knew what Twain meant. He would escape using the tunnel they'd found the first day. All she had to do was find a way to shake off Henri and get to the docks. From there, Twain would meet her, and they'd be free.

Turning to Henri, she said: "If you let me go, I'll introduce you to the Casorina. I'm sure she'd be most interested in your scholarly pursuits, especially if I put in a good word for you."

Henri's eyes narrowed for a moment, as if he was looking for a trap, but he couldn't resist the chance to speak with the Casorina.

He dropped Quinta's arm and followed her across the atrium to where the Casorina held court.

CHAPTER TWENTY-THREE
Twain

Twain walked up the marble stairs of the Orpiment, mind racing. Behind him, Gustave shadowed his every step, close enough to keep the knife's edge pressed against Twain's back without anyone seeing it. A hot pain sliced down Twain's side, where the knife had already bitten into him. He turned when they were halfway up the stairs, watching Quinta walk across the atrium with Henri. She moved toward the Casorina with purpose, a glowing silver light among the other guests.

"It's this way," he said to Gustave when they reached the top of the stairs. A pair of maids passed him, including Penny, who shot him a look.

"You doing well, Twain?" she asked, eyeing Gustave suspiciously.

"Fine enough," he managed to say. "Just giving my friend here a tour of the Casorina's library."

Penny's mouth flew open. "You know you can't—" but Twain nodded toward Gustave's hand at his back. Penny stopped talking. Understanding lit her eyes.

"Could you send Horace to fetch us soon?" Twain asked, hoping his message was coming through. "We don't want to miss the whole party."

There was no way Twain would ever ask Horace for anything. The butler would be overjoyed to catch Twain doing something wrong, like giving a scholar a tour of the Casorina's private library. Hopefully, Horace would throw Gustave out of the Orpiment. What he did with Twain wouldn't matter because he'd be long gone.

"Will do," Penny said. "Be safe. We'll miss you and Quinta around here."

Twain smiled at her, and then hurried down the hall with Gustave at his heels.

They walked through the twists and turns of the palace hallways, leaving the atrium and the party like forgotten dreams.

"You sure you know where you're going?" Gustave asked as they turned down yet another carpeted corridor. His hold on Twain's arm wasn't quite as strong as it had been, but his knife was still out.

"Of course I do," Twain said coolly. "I'm the one who lived here for the last month."

"You're trash," Gustave spit out. "Just like your brother was. He told us about that time you—"

Twain didn't wait to hear what Gustave was going to say. He didn't want to know. He had done many things—some of them unspeakable in polite company—to keep himself and Zand alive after their parents died. He always shielded Zand from the worst of it, but they would've starved that first year without Twain's resourcefulness. Now that Zand was gone, he'd be damned if his brother's good name was going to be slandered by this bag of bones who called himself a scholar and Zand's friend.

Twain drove his elbow backward, slamming it into Gustave's gut. Gustave grunted in surprise and slashed out. His knife raked across Twain's ribs. But Twain didn't think of the pain burning up his side; he just kicked out again. His strike dropped Gustave to his knees, and the knife went clattering away.

Twain didn't look back as he ran away from Gustave and toward the Casorina's library. The scholar was right on his heels, calling out as they twisted through hallways and past guest rooms. Twain's heart lurched as they crossed the spot where he and Quinta had kissed just yesterday. But he couldn't think of that now. He had to get out of here, so he could meet her.

Skidding to a halt in front of the painting with the starlight garden, Twain pushed on the whorl in the wood. Gustave was far enough down the hall that he didn't see how Twain opened the door, but his feet pounded after Twain, getting closer.

Twain stepped inside, eyes scanning the library. There were his and Quinta's bags, exactly where they'd left them a few hours ago. Before he could grab them, Gustave charged into the room.

"I'm going to kill you!" he roared, swinging wildly at Twain.

Side aching, Twain grabbed a book off the nearest table and flung it at Gustave.

Gustave dodged the book, but the motion seemed to snap him out of his murderous rage. His eyes widened as he took in the soaring bookshelves and marble walls.

"What is this place?" Gustave's jaw hung slack, and he gawked at all the books.

"The Casorina's library. I'd not let her catch you here."

"If you're here, I'm damn well good enough to be here too," Gustave snapped, as his gaze moved hungrily over the bookshelves. "You're not even a scholar, and I've been studying half my life."

Twain rolled his eyes. Severon's scholars could be so elitist. "It's not what you know that makes you a good person," he said, stepping backward and picking up his and Quinta's bags. The entrance to the secret tunnel was just a few feet away. "It's how you act when things get hard that determines who you are."

Gustave made a dismissive noise. "Tell that to me after I've learned to make starlight lace and I'm the richest man in Severon. Where's the book your girl was talking about?"

Twain took one more step backward, so his shoulders pressed against the bookcase door. "Let me get it," he said, reaching into Quinta's bag slowly.

A shape in the doorway caught his attention. Horace stood there, along with a pair of the bulkiest guards in the Casorina's employ.

"What are you two doing in here?" Horace drawled with undisguised loathing. He had never forgiven Twain and Quinta for holding the Casorina's favor, but he tolerated them. An unauthorized scholar in the Casorina's library, however? That was another thing altogether.

"I'm here to collect my and Quinta's things," said Twain, holding up the bags. "This scholar followed me and has been threatening to steal something from the Casorina's library."

That's all it took for Horace and the two guards to pounce on Gustave. He made a noise of protest as they grabbed him.

"I'll find you, Twain!" he shouted, his voice all menace. "We're not done here!"

Twain had the pleasure of seeing Horace twist Gustave's ear as he marched him out of the library. Then, Twain pushed his fingers into the panel on the wall and the door to the secret passage opened. Twain slipped through the opening and shut the door silently behind him. By the time the other men remembered Twain was still in the library, he was already gone.

CHAPTER TWENTY-FOUR

Quinta

Quinta and Henri were halfway across the atrium, moving toward the Casorina, when a flock of SWS members surrounded them.

"Quinta!" Mrs. Davenport exclaimed. "You slippery little thing. Finally, we can have a chance to talk. We love your dress and simply cannot believe you're the Casorina's lacemaker! How is such a thing possible? Why did she ever keep you a secret? Do you have any extra bits of lace?" Mrs. Davenport reached out a hand and touched Quinta's glowing skirt.

Quinta pulled away.

Mrs. Davenport plowed on. "I was just telling my friends here how well you and I know each other and how much you'd love to come to one of our meetings."

A pair of other SWS members, both in delightfully outdated pointy black hats and wearing more diamonds than even the Casorina, peered at her expectantly. One of the women had actually painted a wart on the end of her nose, and the other carried a hand-bag with a small black kitten peeking out of it. Quinta made a note to tell Twain about the cat in the bag later.

"Ahh, Mrs. Davenport," Quinta said, forcing away any thoughts of Twain. She and Mrs. Davenport most certainly didn't know each other well, and there was no way Quinta would ever go to one of the SWS meetings. "I'd be honored, but I'm leaving Severon tonight. Perhaps you'd like to talk to another scholar about this? This is Henri. He's brilliant—" She nearly choked on the words, but she got them out somehow. "I'm sure he'd love to tell you about his theories on magical lace!" She shoved Henri toward Mrs. Davenport, and he was so surprised, he stumbled into her enormous, feather-covered bosom.

Before Henri had a chance to argue, the SWS members swarmed him, asking him questions about magic and his knowledge of the occult. The woman with the kitten even pulled the poor thing out of her bag and thrust it into his arms. Henri cast Quinta an angry glance as she slipped away.

Free of Henri's clutches, Quinta hurried across the crowded atrium. Her thoughts flew to Twain. Had he escaped Gustave? Was he hurt? Would he really be able to make it to their ship?

The *Lady's Revenge* was departing at midnight, and they had to be on it if they wanted to leave Severon tonight. Which they most certainly did. This city had brought them together and brought them magic, but it was also a place of loneliness, despair, and loss. Now that she'd decided to leave, Quinta couldn't wait to put it behind her.

Dodging the crowd, Quinta glanced at the clock hanging in the center of the atrium. It was already 10:30, and they'd stayed at the ball far longer than she expected. The evening had been such a blur, but still, they would meet at the palace docks.

For a moment, she considered strolling out the front door, but that would gain her unwanted attention. Who knew if there were other Henris and Gustaves waiting around? She was entirely done with the machinations of scholars and was ready to see Twain again and get out of Severon. Checking over her shoulder to make sure no was looking, Quinta slipped behind a group of potted orange trees and headed for a side door. It opened onto a terrace above the Orpiment gardens.

Quinta shivered as she stepped from the warmth of the crowded atrium and into the night. The moon was out, and a cool breeze blew off the sea. She hurried down the marble terrace steps and into the garden. Gravel crunched under her heels as she moved along dark paths, wishing she didn't stand out quite so much in her glowing silver dress and that she'd thought to grab a shawl or a coat. She and Twain had been strolling in this garden just this morning, but at night, alone, it felt much more dangerous indeed.

Quinta was almost at the end of the main path, close to the monster-headed folly where Twain had found the strand of starlight, when a voice rose from a thick clump of darkened shrubbery.

"Such a gorgeous girl, in such an exquisite dress." It sounded vaguely familiar, but still Quinta's heart jumped as a broad man in scholar's robes stepped into her path. Dammit. More scholars. Who would be out here, hiding in the shrubbery? And why did they want to talk with her?

She feared she knew the answer.

The man moved forward, and moonlight shone on his red hair. His freckles were a constellation across his nose.

Quinta blew out a relieved breath as she recognized Damian.

"Oh, Damian, it's just you. What are you doing out here? You startled me."

Damian gave a small bow. "My apologies. I couldn't help but notice you, Quinta. Why did you and Twain not tell me about the starlight lace?"

He strode even closer, blocking the exit to the street. Quinta stepped backward, suddenly ill at ease with this man who'd been so friendly while they were touring the city. He now loomed large and menacing on this shadowy garden path.

"It wasn't our secret to tell." She took another step backward. Her heel caught in between two flagstones, and she tugged at it.

"I'd like to know all your secrets." Damian lunged toward her so fast that Quinta didn't have a chance to slip off her shoes and flee back to the Orpiment like her brain was screaming at her to do.

Damian's hand caught her elbow, and he caressed the lace patterns on her arm gently. Quinta wrenched away.

"Stop being a creep and help me," she snapped.

What was it with men grabbing her arm tonight without her permission?

Twain was the only man she wanted to touch her, and she had no idea where he was or if he'd gotten out of the Orpiment. She glanced toward the atrium again, hoping to see him. But there was no one on the terrace.

Damian released Quinta's arm at the same moment she freed her heel from between the stones. She stumbled, and then took another step away from Damian.

"It's been lovely to see you," Quinta lied as she moved away. "Now, I'll be going. I've got to meet Twain."

"I'm afraid you'll be coming with me." Damian sounded both eager and a bit apologetic. "My country needs you. You're an artist. We've not seen a talent such as yours in a long time. Do you know how we respect artists in my country?"

Entirely sure Damian intended nothing good, Quinta glanced toward the garden gate. The street was only a few feet away, and light from a streetlamp cast a warm yellow glow at the end of the path. She calculated the distance, slipping out of her heels so she could run. "I have no interest in your country or the artists there."

Quinta surged forward, racing for the street, but Damian snagged her waist and pulled her back roughly. She landed hard on the gravel path.

"I *said*, you'll be coming with me." Damian wrenched her upward. Sharp stones dug into her stockinged feet.

"I will *not*." Quinta struggled to loosen his hold. "Let go of me."

She started to scream, but Damian clapped a handkerchief over her face. It smelled sweet and sickly, like apples left out in the sun too long. Before Quinta could break free or think anything else, she tumbled into darkness.

CHAPTER TWENTY-FIVE

Twain

Twain waited beside the palace docks, watching the marble steps and the street for Quinta. After he'd left the Casorina's library, he'd run through the secret tunnel, emerging in Lapis, near the Orpiment. That part of the plan had gone beautifully, but he wished they'd never been separated. He cursed Gustave and Henri again as he scanned the street, looking for Quinta.

Dark water lapped at the dock insistently, singing a song that seemed to be shouting: *Hurry! Your ship will leave without you.*

Where was Quinta?

Doubts crept into Twain's mind. Perhaps she wasn't coming. Perhaps she'd decided to stay with the Casorina and live a life of luxury, weaving starlight lace for all the richest people. Despite their kisses and promises last night, she didn't really need him. And what did the life he could give her have to offer? Friendship, laughter, adventure, love? Yes. But would those be enough?

She did tell him from the beginning that she left the people she kissed.

The thought dropped him, and Twain sat down heavily on the closest step. He plopped the two cloth bags he'd been carrying beside his feet.

From the top of a nearby building, a clock's chimes rang out eleven times. Twain stood up and began to pace. Their ship was leaving in an hour, but they weren't on it yet. Should he go to it and hope Quinta would meet him there? Or should he head back into the party and search for her? What if she was on the ship already and had misunderstood their plans?

Twain paced for a few minutes longer, but time was racing by. He had to make a decision.

He wasn't going without Quinta. That much he knew. Grabbing their bags, Twain sprinted up the palace steps.

Quinta wasn't in the atrium. He tried to talk with the Casorina, but she was laughing in the middle of a circle of diplomats and scholars, all of whom were complimenting her dress. Twain tried to run up the stairs to see if Quinta might have returned to their rooms, but he was stopped by the butler, Horace.

"You're supposed to be gone," Horace said witheringly. He frowned down at him.

Twain scowled, wondering if Gustave had been thrown out of the party or if he and Henri were in the atrium somewhere. "I'm leaving now. Have you seen Quinta?"

Horace shrugged. "She was at the party not long ago."

"I saw her through a window," said Margot, the surly blonde maid they'd met on their first day in the palace. "She was out in

239

the garden on the arm of some gentleman. She was stumbling like she'd had too much to drink too."

Impossible. Quinta wouldn't leave without him. And she most certainly wouldn't leave with another man.

Margot saw his face and barked a cruel laugh. "Doesn't it sting when love wanders off without you? She was leaning on his shoulder and everything."

Twain's guts churned.

She was gone. Maybe another, better, wealthier man had come along, and he'd been able to offer her a life far nicer than what Twain could give her. She looked like a queen, after all, in her starlight gown.

Even as he had the thought, Twain hoped it wasn't true. He remembered the way Quinta had whispered his name this morning, as they lay together in her bed. The way she looked at him as he played the violin for her. The dreams they had spun of seeing the world together.

"Something isn't right." He could feel it in his bones. "She wouldn't leave with someone else. At least not of her own free will."

"Suit yourself," Margot said with a shrug. "Because she sure looked well suited to me."

Twain clenched his fists, so he didn't do something he'd regret. "If you see her, please, *please* tell her to meet me by the ship. She'll know what that means."

Then, without another word to Horace or Margot, Twain left the palace. He would check the docks, the streets, the entire damn city if he had to. He would find Quinta, even if it took him the rest of his life.

✳

Twain raced through Severon, heading first to the docks. His and Quinta's bags banged against his legs as he ran. Their ship, the *Lady's Revenge*, was harbored on the edge of Vermilion, tucked among dozens of other frigates and freighters. A ship with red-and-blue striped sails was leaving the docks as Twain reached the *Lady's Revenge* and bounded up the wooden ramp to its deck.

"Tickets, please." A burly man twice as tall as Twain stood at the top of the ramp. He wore an unbuttoned blue coat, ripped pants, and a striped shirt.

"I've booked passage on this ship," Twain said rather breathlessly. "But I'm looking for my companion. She's a girl about my age, curly dark hair, wearing a silver dress."

The sailor glared at him. "Ain't my job to keep track of every girl in Severon. It's my job to check passengers' papers to make sure they're on the right ship."

"If you could just see—"

"Do you have a ticket for this ship or not, boy? We're pulling out soon. I don't have time to stand here bickering with you."

Hastily, Twain pulled out his ticket. He realized then that he still had Quinta's ticket as well. Which meant there was no way she was already on the *Lady's Revenge*. Maybe he'd missed her down on the docks, or maybe she'd stopped to get something to eat (a rather farfetched theory since people rarely ate at the falling-down, filthy taverns by the docks unless they had no other options, plus there had been food at the party).

Before the sailor could snatch the ticket away, Twain tucked it back into his pocket. "I'll be back as soon as possible. Don't leave without us!" he called over his shoulder.

"Ship leaves soon, boy! Whether you're on it or not," the sailor bellowed.

Twain ran faster than he'd ever done, back down the ramp and toward the closest tavern.

It was called the Ugly Oyster, and it truly lived up to its name. A dingy den, the Ugly Oyster smelled of fish, spilled beer, and the creeping desperation that takes up residence in many waterfront pubs. Twain didn't have to look past the drunks hunched over their ales or the two women sharing a bottle of gin to know Quinta wasn't here. She was a starlight girl, and a place like this wouldn't be able to hide her.

Twain tried every pub on that stretch of the waterfront—the Jealous Seagull, the Broken Mast, the Sailor's Folly (that was the worst of them, and Twain was out the door mere moments after he stepped inside). There was no sign of Quinta, and Twain grew increasingly frantic with each passing minute. The *Lady's Revenge* pulled away from the docks, but Twain didn't care. He only wanted to find Quinta.

But she was nowhere. She had vanished.

Twain stepped into the last pub, hoping against all reason, that this one, the Mermaid and the Whaler, might be the one. For starters, it was bigger than the others and more well lit. It wasn't entirely unreasonable to think that Quinta might be waiting in a place like this. As Twain stepped inside, everyone in the room turned to look at him. Including Henri and Gustave. He swore as his eyes met theirs. What were they doing here? Gustave had a black eye, and Henri was taking a long swig from a pint.

"We've been waiting for you," Gustave snarled, stepping forward. "Tried the palace docks but couldn't find you. Figured you might turn up here eventually if we searched all the ships. What you got in here?"

Gustave pulled Twain's bag toward himself. Twain snatched it back. There was no way these two were getting the Casorina's coins or Quinta's book.

"Get out of my way." Twain moved toward the door. The two men loomed on either side of him, and Gustave's knife was back in his hand.

"Oh, we're just getting started," Gustave said. "Let's take this outside."

Before Twain could protest, Gustave shoved him out the tavern's door.

CHAPTER TWENTY-SIX

Quinta

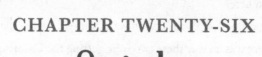

Quinta woke up in a moving room. Well, the room wasn't moving so much as the entire vessel she was on bobbed up and down. The air smelled musty, like wood left outside for too long.

"Where am I?" She sat up slowly. Her head ached like someone had bashed her with a brick. Locks of hair hung in her eyes, and a quick pat of her hair told her that no one had hit her on the head, but the diamond combs she'd been wearing were gone. She looked down. Her toes poked through her ripped stockings, and her heeled shoes lay on the bed next to her. She still wore the starlight dress, but the lace of her skirt had a large hole in it. It was the part that told the story of her and Twain's love, and now it was ripped apart.

For half a heartbeat she hoped that she'd somehow made it onto the *Lady's Revenge*. Maybe Twain was waiting for her, and running into Damian had all been a bad dream.

But it hadn't been a dream. Quinta knew in her bones that something had gone horribly, terribly wrong.

"Oh, Twain," she murmured.

Would he be waiting for her? Wondering where she was? Would he think she'd abandoned him? Or, worse yet, that she didn't want to start a new life with him?

The thought made her breath catch. They'd worked so hard to trust each other, and now what would he think? And, more importantly, what could she do?

"First, figure out where you are," she said to herself. "Then, you can figure out how to get to where you want to be."

Quinta stood up slowly, her head spinning as the cabin pitched to the right. It was far too small a space, and she fought her creeping sense of panic as the walls seemed to close in around her. For a moment, she focused on one of the lace patterns in her skirt. It was a delicately woven thing that showed two hands clasped together—hers and Twain's, holding each other against whatever life might throw at them. As she stared at the pattern, Twain's breathing technique from that first day in the Vermilion Emporium came back to Quinta.

"One, two, three, four," she whispered, counting her breaths as she inhaled slowly.

After exactly forty-eight breaths, she was calm enough to slip her shoes back on and make her way to the door. Cautiously, she opened it, revealing a narrow hallway that ended in a set of wooden stairs. Two lanterns hung along the corridor, swaying with the pitch of the ship, sending yellow light chaotically across the hold. Gripping the wall to steady herself, Quinta climbed the stairs. She'd been on boats before, and she usually enjoyed being on the water. But there was nothing good about being on an unfamiliar boat, rolling across churning seas. When Quinta made it to the top deck, a cold splash of salt water slapped her face, soaking her starlight dress. She stumbled against a pile of lashed-together barrels, clinging to them as the ship rode tall waves. It was the darkest part of the night, and the moon slipped toward the western horizon. Endless sea stretched on all sides, dark beyond the small circle of light cast by the ship's lanterns.

Sailors ran back and forth on the deck, goggling at Quinta and her shining dress. Quinta glanced, up, watching as gusts of wind filled the red-and-blue striped sails.

Letting go of the barrels, Quinta lurched across the deck, looking for anything familiar.

There. Standing by the railing on the opposite side of the ship was Damian. He still wore his scholar's robes, and he was looking out over the dark water.

I could shove him overboard, Quinta thought desperately as she made her way toward him, one tottering step at a time.

But what would happen to her then? Would she ever find her way back to Severon or Twain?

Right as she was near enough to touch Damian's shoulder, the boat shifted. Quinta let out a cry as she flew toward the railing.

"Ahh, you're awake," Damian said, turning and smoothly catching her in his arms. "I wondered if you'd sleep the entire journey." His mouth was set in a grim line.

"Let go!" Quinta wrenched herself free of his embrace, all too aware that if it weren't for him, she'd likely be in the sea at this moment. Though, of course, if it weren't for him, she also wouldn't be on this boat in the first place. She'd be on another ship, with Twain. "Where are you taking me?"

"You'll see. We'll be there tomorrow morning if this wind keeps up."

"You've kidnapped me, and you won't tell me anything?"

"I've not kidnapped you. I'm presenting you with a better opportunity. Trust me, Queen Mathilde can offer you so much more than that Casorina of yours."

"Queen Mathilde?" Quinta said incredulously. "*The* Queen Mathilde of Ixily?"

Damian's face took on a wistful expression. "Yes. She's going to be so happy to see you. And me, I hope."

A few pieces clicked together in Quinta's foggy brain. "You said you loved someone who you couldn't marry. Is it Queen Mathilde? Do you seriously think kidnapping me is going to make her want to marry you? Is that your brilliant, grand plan?" Jagged laughter burst out of her.

Damian glared at Quinta. "You wouldn't understand. Things aren't as easy in my country as they are in Severon. Mathilde and I have loved each other since we were twelve. But I'm the youngest son of a disgraced noble family. I have no money and no connections to help her reign. I'm good enough to be Mathilde's consort but never her partner, because she needs to make a strategic political marriage. If your starlight lace gives her the power she needs to keep Ixily safe, though, then she won't have to marry for an alliance."

"I thought you were a scholar," Quinta spat out.

Damian shrugged. "I am. Or I was, but I'm Ixilian. Which means I've also been trained in the military. I'm a scholar, I'm a soldier, and I'm Mathilde's closest friend, lover, and advisor. My scholarly pursuits aligned with our hope for magic, and that's why I go to Severon every year. This year, I happened to find what we've been looking for."

"Me?"

"Yes. And your magic." Damian sounded entirely certain his plan would work.

Quinta let out a long breath. "Just take me back to Severon. Please. I'll give you the dress, and you can return to your queen."

"No, I need you to *make* her a dress of her own. Like you did for the Casorina and yourself."

Quinta could've cried. "I can't make her a dress! I don't even know where the starlight comes from!"

Damian raised one eyebrow. "I have my doubts about that."

"It's the truth!"

"For your sake, you best hope it's not."

He turned back to the sea, and Quinta fought her urge to punch him. Sighing wearily as her stomach growled, Quinta made her way back to her cabin.

Once there, she tried to remember everything she knew about Queen Mathilde. All she could come up with were fragments from what she'd overheard growing up, and what Twain had told her about the warrior queen who was surrounded by enemies on all sides and whose deepest ambition was to find a way to secure Ixily and help it prosper.

There was no way Quinta's lacemaking was going to make that happen, no matter how much Damian wished it.

Lying down on her bed, Quinta let silent tears fall on her pillow until the rocking of the ship finally lulled her back to sleep.

CHAPTER TWENTY-SEVEN

Twain

Twain had hoped to never see Henri and Gustave again, but now he was getting very well acquainted with their fists.

Even though there were two of them, Twain fought back. The month of good food and rest in the Casorina's house had made him stronger. And there was no way they were getting his or Quinta's bags.

"How much did my brother owe you?" Twain asked, ducking under Gustave's fists as he swung a wide blow. He wore brass rings on his knuckles.

"Doesn't matter anymore," Gustave grunted. "Now our quarrel is with you. I was banned from the Scholar's Ball for life! How will I ever find a patron?"

Twain danced away from Gustave's fist and landed a blow of his own. As he did so, Henri tripped him and grabbed the bags.

"NO!" Twain shouted, falling backward as Henri ripped open Quinta's bag.

"There it is." Henri plucked Quinta's lacemaking book from among the piles of clothing. "Wasn't he supposed to give this to you back at the palace, Gustave?"

"Leave that alone!" Rising quickly, Twain reached for the book.

Those words earned him a punch in the stomach from Gustave. As the brass knuckles hit, landing a few inches below his knife wound from earlier, air whooshed out of Twain's lungs. He doubled over for a moment, but he didn't linger like that. He had to get the book. Gasping to catch his breath, Twain flung himself toward Gustave. He was clumsy from pain, however, and too slow. Gustave cracked another blow across Twain's jaw, knocking him to the cobblestones. Henri rushed forward, aiming a kick at Twain's kidneys.

Every time he tried to rise, Gustave and Henri knocked him down. As their blows landed, he curled in on himself, trying to protect his body.

In the midst of the beating, Henri dropped Quinta's book. Twain managed to reach his hand out and grab it before the book rolled into a puddle of filth on the street.

Gustave stepped on Twain's fingers, crushing them. "I'll take this," he said, snatching the book away. He tucked it into his pocket.

"Quinta," Twain said in a wretched voice as Henri and Gustave took out their rage and frustration on his body. Twice, Twain tried to fight back, struggling to his feet, but Henri and Gustave kept at it until Twain couldn't get up again.

They eventually stopped kicking him, grabbed the coins that had spilled out of his bags, and walked away laughing. Several other pairs of feet moved past him, but no one offered to help. Twain lay in the street with blood running into his eyes. Every part of him hurt, but somehow his heart was the sorest. Quinta was gone. He'd lost the money that was going to get them out of Severon. He'd lost her book. And he had no place to go.

Stumbling, Twain got to his feet. Slowly, with one hand clutching his bruised, slashed ribs, he gathered up what Henri and Gustave had left behind. There were Quinta's dresses, now soaked with mud and filth. A few of his shirts and pairs of pants. His smashed violin, and his starlight handkerchief, which had somehow stayed in his jacket pocket.

But he had no money and no lacemaking book and no Quinta.

Clutching their bags to his broken body, Twain moved down the street with halting steps, desperate to get away from the docks and disappear into the city.

He wasn't sure where he was going, and the night felt unfamiliar around him. Had he really gotten so used to living in the Orpiment that he no longer felt at home in the Vermilion District? Were people staring at him because he looked like he didn't belong here in his fancy clothes? Or was it the blood streaming from the gashes on his forehead and ribs? Could he make it to Horst's cottage, or would he bleed to death in the street before he got there?

The city spun, a haze of lights and sounds, as Twain emerged from an alley.

He nearly wept when he saw what was in front of him: the Vermilion Emporium glowed in the night like a beacon. Somehow he'd found his way back to it. There was no one outside the shop, and for the briefest moment, Twain wondered if it ever had other customers. That thought was quickly followed by a delirious feeling of relief as he pushed on the door and it swung open.

"Oh my boy," Sorchia said, rushing over to him. Concern knitted her brows. "I've been expecting you, but I didn't think it would be this bad."

"I'm not really hurt," Twain slurred as he rested his hand on a table covered in watches. As soon as he said it, his hand slipped and he plummeted toward the ground. The world was spinning: there was a colorful carpet, Sorchia's shoes, his starlight handkerchief, a pile of pocket watches beside his head, and then everything went dark.

Twain awoke to something licking his face.

"Get off," he mumbled, brushing away a small, black dog. It resembled a poufy pillow and gave him one final lick before walking away.

Twain tried to sit up, but his ribs screamed in protest as he did so. He turned his head slightly, taking in his surroundings through his one eye that wasn't swollen shut. He was in a four-poster bed that had a velvet canopy over the top. Each of the bedposts was carved to look like a different kind of tree, and thick curtains hung between the posts. A lantern sat on a small table beside the bed, illuminating a picture of a girl who looked very much like Twain's mother. Beyond the circle of light, Twain made out a small bedroom with portraits on every wall. He couldn't see the details of the paintings, however, and he was in no shape to get out of bed to investigate. From the end of the bed, the small dog yipped, and Twain craned his head to see it.

"That's enough now, Muffin," Sorchia said. She entered the room, carrying a tray set with two teacups. She put the tray on the bedside table and then rested a hand lightly on Twain's forehead. "How are you?"

Her hand was cool, but Twain winced as she moved it lightly over his cheeks, as if she was checking that he was still put together correctly.

"I've been better," he admitted. "Where am I?"

"This is one of my personal rooms in the Vermilion Emporium. I told you my family has lived here for generations, and we have our own apartments. This is my guest bedroom. You've been sleeping in a bed that once belonged to a king."

"Which one?" Twain struggled to sit up. Sorchia helped him, and then handed him a cup of tea.

"Which king?"

Twain nodded.

"I'm not sure. My mother found the bed here one day with a note saying the king no longer required it, and we were welcome to have it." Sorchia played with the long silver string around her neck, twirling it in her fingers before tucking it back under her sweater.

Twain waited a moment longer, to see if there was more of the story coming, but Sorchia just shrugged and picked up her own teacup.

"That's how it goes around here. Things come and go, and you're always surprised. My apartments are anchored in place, though. That way I can always find them, and they stay mostly the same."

It was a lot for Twain to take in, and he still had so many questions—like, who was the girl in the bedside photograph—however, other, more pressing questions pushed those out of the way. "How long have I been asleep?"

"All of last night and most of today. I've been treating your cuts, but the internal wounds are still healing. Want to tell me what happened?"

Twain shook his head and set his cup on the table. "The short story is I got robbed by some scholars, but that doesn't even matter now. I've got to find Quinta."

He pushed the blankets away and swung his legs over the side of the bed. Pain shot through his ribs as he found his footing. He took one shaky step, and then his legs gave out on him. He crumpled to the floor like a discarded scarf.

"You need to rest," Sorchia said gently as she helped him get back into bed.

"But Quinta is out there, somewhere, possibly lost!" Frustration sharpened his voice. "She'll be wondering where I am!"

Would she, though?

Had she run off without him? Was she safe and preparing for a better life? Or was she in danger? Part of Twain—a small, terrible part, and one he hated—hoped she was in danger because that meant she still cared. That she hadn't left him.

But then, he didn't want her to actually be in danger. He wanted her here, beside him. Which might not be what *she* wanted . . .

His head hurt thinking about it and guilt curdled his stomach. He groaned.

"Wherever she is, you'll do her no good in this shape," Sorchia said firmly. "Rest, heal, and then you can seek her out. In the meantime, I'll see if I can find out anything."

Twain wanted to protest, but he was already sinking back into the pillows. Sleep overtook him, and he was soon lost in dreams where he called out across the city, looking for the sour-faced girl who had his heart.

CHAPTER TWENTY-EIGHT

Quinta

Queen Mathilde's castle ran right up to the edge of the Middle Sea, as if it could keep the water itself at bay with its might. Quinta had never been to Ixily—the country didn't admit many visitors and the Celestial Circus only traveled around Aix when she had been small—and she'd never seen a palace as beautiful or intimidating. Once a fortress built by ancient kings, it was made of grayish-blue stone and had walls as thick as city streets. Beside Queen Mathilde's palace, the Casorina's glittering Orpiment was a fragile thing: a butterfly beside a warhorse.

Quinta's hopes plummeted as their ship pulled into the harbor. Any thoughts she had of an easy escape back to Severon and Twain were pushed out of her mind by the sheer heft of Mathilde's walls.

"When will I be able to return home?" Quinta asked Damian as the crew steered the ship into its berth. Quinta dug her fingers into the wooden railing, trying not to scream or fling herself into the ocean and venture to swim home. Although they'd been three days at sea, her dress still glimmered with starlight, radiant despite the salt spray that covered her skin.

Damian just shrugged. "Perhaps Ixily is your new home. I will show you to Mathilde and see what she wants to do with you."

Quinta scowled at him. "It's generally not good foreign policy for ambassadors to kidnap people from other countries—especially when they're guests of that country's leader."

Damian laughed. His laugh was full of shadows and teeth, nothing like Twain's golden one. "My girl, in fact that is the heart of diplomacy sometimes. Your Casorina had something my queen wants. It's my job to get it for her."

Quinta crossed her arms. "And what if I refuse to help your queen? Will you take me home then?"

"Oh, lovely girl, no. You will not refuse to help her. Trust me."

A chill went through Quinta, both at Damian's tone and at what he would expect her to be able to do. How could she make lace from starlight here? The blue book from the Vermilion Emporium was packed in her bags, which Twain had probably taken from the Casorina's house. The only starlight she had was in the threads from her own dress, and she wasn't even sure she could work the starlight magic without Twain around. What if it wasn't something she could do on her own? What if it was something she and Twain had to do together?

Also, she was never going to find more starlight without Twain's ability to hear its song.

Gripping the small bottle of moonshadow that hung around her neck, Quinta tried to calm her racing thoughts. She'd been in tough situations before. She could figure this one out.

But there was no time really even to think because as soon as the Ixilian ship docked, Damian hustled Quinta into a carriage and they drove to the palace. He kept the carriage curtains closed, so she couldn't see any of the city. Once inside the palace, she barely had time to take in the sweeping blue marble columns, the silver chandeliers, and the rows of hard-eyed soldiers that filled the corridors as Damian brought her straight to Queen Mathilde's private chambers.

The queen was a thin, blonde woman who couldn't have been more than thirty. Her face was narrow and her nose crooked. She wasn't pretty, but she filled a room with her presence. A leather breastplate covered her simple red dress, and there was a sword strapped to her hip. Quinta knew that the queen always led her own armies into battle, and before she became queen, she went through the same military training her soldiers did. For a moment Mathilde's face lit up to see Damian, but then, just as quickly, her expression shuttered.

She wrinkled her nose as Quinta walked in, shooting Damian a suspicious look. "What have you brought me, Damian? She smells wretched."

"Curtsy," Damian hissed behind Quinta, poking her in the shoulder.

Quinta had no interest in bowing to her captor, but she also wanted to stay alive. She sunk to the floor in an elaborate curtsy, something that she'd learned during her stay at the Orpiment. "I am grateful to be welcomed into your home, my lady," she said to the queen.

Queen Mathilde's eyebrows shot up. "She has lovely manners, at least. Why is she here, Damian?"

"Surely Your Majesty can see for yourself," Damian replied smoothly. "Her dress is made of starlight."

The starlight dress was grimy now, but it still gleamed silver.

"It can't be. Rise, child." The queen put a pair of eyeglasses on and offered Quinta a hand. Feeling entirely unsure of herself, Quinta took it. The queen's hand was calloused and covered in small scars, reminders of all the battles Mathilde had fought.

As Quinta rose, the queen reached out and ran a finger along the lace at her shoulder.

"It's remarkable," the queen said. "And so new. All the starlight pieces I have are heirlooms. Pretty to look at but faded and containing no magic. Where did this dress come from?"

"She made it," Damian said smugly. "That's why I've brought her to you."

"Impossible." The queen gasped, wrenching her eyes up to meet Damian's gaze. "The ways have been lost."

Quinta crossed her arms, defiant and proud of her work. "I found them."

"You can do this again?" Queen Mathilde's voice was eager, but her eyes were hard.

Quinta wasn't sure she could. But she wasn't going to tell the queen that. She'd tried to tell Damian, and he'd threatened her. She had to lie now. "Yes. Absolutely."

"You will make me one of these then," the queen said decisively. "I want a dress like yours by the morning of the third day. If you can do that, I'll give you a workshop of seamstresses to help you make starlight garments. My entire army could have shirts made of starlight. Imagine, Damian! If we can cloak ourselves in the power of the stars, then we can manipulate leaders and win wars. With magic we can be the strongest country in the world."

He moved to her side. "And then you wouldn't have to marry another for the political alliance," he said softly.

The queen rested a hand on his shoulder for one moment, tender and intimate. Quinta had to look away from their reunion. Her own ache for Twain was bigger than the sea outside the window.

"And what if I can't make the dress?" Quinta asked in a very small voice.

The queen's mouth was a thin line as she raised one eyebrow the slightest bit. "Then you die." She shrugged, as if it were the simplest thing. "I have no use for frivolous girls who can't contribute to Ixily."

Because she had no choice, Quinta smiled weakly at the queen. "You'll have your dress in three days."

Damian dragged Quinta to a guest room off the queen's chambers. He released her arm as soon as he opened the door and shoved her inside. She landed hard on the floor, looking around. There was a bed, a screen for dressing, and a table for sewing. A small window was open at the back of the room, letting a warm, salty breeze into the space.

"Stay here," Damian barked. "This way you're close enough for fittings with the queen. I'll be back to check on you every morning. There will be a guard outside the door."

"What about food?" Quinta scrambled to her feet. Her body ached, and her stomach rumbled. She'd not been able to keep much down while at sea, and she was ravenously hungry all of a sudden.

"Someone will bring you dinner at sunset."

"But I don't know how to make another dress—"

"Figure it out." Damian slammed the door, turning the key in the lock.

Quinta ran to the door, kicking at it until she stubbed her toe. But no one came.

Shit. She was alone, trapped in a country whose queen was known for her cruelty, and she was supposed to make a dress with a material she didn't have.

Well. That wasn't entirely true. She had starlight enough in her own dress. Maybe she could work with that.

Slowly, she ran her hands along her starlight dress, moving over the lace at her belly and along her hips.

"I don't want to rip you apart to make the queen's dress," said Quinta softly. "You're my heart. My story. My last piece of Severon and Twain." The words stuck in her throat, trapped behind a sob.

The dress seemed to rustle in reply. There was a great tear in its skirt, exactly where Quinta had woven her whispered "I love you" to Twain. They were the words she didn't get to say. But she would.

Someday. It was that thought that made her take a deep breath, forcing her sadness away. She could do this.

Twain was somewhere out there. Maybe on the *Lady's Revenge*, or maybe he was still back in Severon. She was locked in a room in a palace by the sea. The only way she was getting back to him was if she made Queen Mathilde's dress, and then the queen let her go. Or if she escaped. Which was ridiculous. Even if Quinta found something to pick the door's lock with, there was a guard outside. And clever as she was at surviving, she'd never learned to fight. Plus, even if she escaped one guard, how was she going to get past the rest?

Forget that plan.

Still thinking, she ran a finger over the frayed threads of her skirt. Would it really be so awful to rip apart her own creation? Wouldn't that be better than turning up empty-handed when the queen summoned her next?

But without the blue book of lace patterns and Twain's ability to hear the starlight music, Quinta was merely guessing at what to do. Plus, the queen hadn't given Quinta a story, so she couldn't weave her heartbreaks and hopes into lace. The queen just wanted a dress to make her enemies give her whatever she wanted, which was a tall order on the best of days. Add to all that the enormous problem of not having any fresh starlight, and Quinta was well and truly stuck on what to do.

Sorchia's words came back to Quinta from when they were examining the dress Marali had made for her lover Viola.

"If you're going to do magic with it, the starlight must be fresh or at least never woven. The magic also only works for the person it's woven for. If you pulled this dress apart, you could make something lovely, but it would be no more magical than my shoe." So that was that.

Another warm gust blew in through the open window. The lace at her sleeve ruffled in the breeze, reminding Quinta of the way Twain's hair lifted in the wind.

Maybe she wouldn't have to go through the door.

Mind still churning, Quinta moved to the window and stared down at the sea. There was a narrow ledge of seawall below, but it was still a long, sheer drop from her window to the water. She wasn't even sure she'd survive such a leap. She sighed, missing Twain and all the mornings they'd spent by the sea. What was he doing right now? Did he think she'd abandoned him?

And thinking of him reminded her of the silver rope of starlight she and Twain had used in the Vermilion Emporium. Perhaps she could use the threads of her dress to escape the palace?

Yes! That was what she would do.

Decision made and heart soaring with the possibility of escape, Quinta went to work pulling apart the lace of her life. Stories, sleepless nights, goodbyes, and greetings shredded under her fingers. It hurt to destroy it all, but she did it. She turned the threads, twisting them and rewriting her story. This was a tale of bravery and escape. Of hope over heartbreak. It was strength and secrets.

Quinta worked on, even after her fingers started bleeding and her stomach rumbled, reminding her she'd not eaten since breakfast on the ship.

As the afternoon waned, Quinta had turned her lovely starlight dress into a thick heft of rope. If she was lucky, no one would come check on her before they brought dinner. This was her chance to escape, and she didn't let herself think over much about what would happen once she was out of the palace—though some part of her worried she would need money for sailing back to Severon, and another part desperately hoped she didn't just fall into the sea.

"This is my best chance," Quinta murmured. "I'll see you soon, Twain."

Quinta lugged her bed toward the window. It wasn't fancy, but it had a sturdy brass headboard that she hoped would hold her weight. With a few quick twists, she secured the silver rope of starlight to it. She was really doing this: climbing out the palace window and saving herself from whatever Queen Mathilde and Damian had in mind.

With a deep breath for courage, Quinta gripped the rope and then lowered herself out the window with her back to the sea. Her heeled shoes weren't meant for climbing, however, and her feet slid down the wall. Biting back a scream, she scrambled for a foothold, and her fingers dug into the rope. She stopped her fall, though her arms trembled as she held herself.

She took a great, gulping breath and tried to remember what Twain had told her about climbing. Right. He always did it barefoot. In one quick motion, Quinta kicked off her shoes. They tumbled down to the ground, bounced off the seawall, and disappeared into the waves that pounded against the rocks below. Quinta hoped she wouldn't go the same way as her shoes.

Barefoot now, she pushed her feet against the warm stone of the palace wall, curling her toes around the edges of the closest rock and willing herself not to look down at the crashing waves or the narrow ledge below. How did Twain do this without any ropes?

She would ask him that the next time she saw him.

And it was the thought of seeing Twain again that gave her the courage to go on.

Slowly, one hand over the other, one step at a time, Quinta lowered herself down the silver rope.

She was halfway down the palace wall when her hands slipped. She couldn't get a grip, and a scream ripped from her mouth.

Too late, she reached for the rope, which slid through her fingers. Too late, she looked up to see Damian at the window of her room. Too late did she realize he had sawed through the rope, and she was now tumbling toward the sea.

Quinta fell fast, cursing under her breath. If she was lucky, she'd drop into the water and somehow manage to avoid being pulped by the churning waves. If she wasn't lucky, she'd slam against the ledge of the seawall the wrong way and be smashed like an egg.

She landed somewhere between the two options. As her fall took her right past the edge of the seawall, her hands managed to grasp the narrow stone ledge. Something cracked as she stopped the momentum of her body's fall with her fingers. White-hot pain shot through her shoulder.

She screamed. The silver rope—her starlight story—raced past her, and she was too slow and too injured to grab it. Plus, doing so would've likely dumped her into the sea as well.

Fingers digging into the ledge, Quinta watched the silver rope and all her hopes sink beneath the waves.

"Stay there," Damian called out from the window. "I'll come get you."

Quinta shouted a curse at him, but it was taken by the wind as Damian disappeared from view above her. Quinta didn't want him to come get her, but with her injured shoulder, she couldn't pull herself up from the ledge. Though she was going to try. Painfully, she moved along the narrow strip of stone. Each small movement was torture, and there was so much more wall to go. As a surge of agony washed over Quinta, she imagined letting go and falling into the sea. This thought was quickly chased by the thought of Twain never knowing what had happened to her. Quinta dug her fingers into the wall more desperately. She would make it to the end of the ledge before Damian came down. She would get out of this city. She would find Twain again. She could do this. She kept moving, one excruciating inch at a time.

She was nearly at the edge of the palace seawall when Damian showed up. He was with a troop of guards, and he had a coil of rope in his hands.

With an anguished groan, Quinta started moving her hands slowly in the other direction, as if she could escape that way. But now, in addition to her dislocated shoulder, her hands had cuts and blisters on them. The salt spray kept getting into those wounds, making them burn.

She hung there, caught between bad options.

She was going to die here. She knew it all at once. If she didn't let Damian pull her to safety, that would be the end of her story.

Quinta wasn't going to let that happen. Not today.

"Throw me the rope," she yelled to Damian. Her voice was hoarse from the screaming and from the sobs of pain that racked through her.

"Good girl," he said, tossing it her way.

Quinta scowled at him. That's how you spoke to dogs and children. Not lacemakers who could wield magic. As she wrapped the rope around her good arm and let herself be pulled to safety, Quinta made a vow to herself: she would escape Queen Mathilde's castle. Maybe not today. Probably not tomorrow. But soon.

CHAPTER TWENTY-NINE
Twain

Three days after Quinta disappeared and Gustave and Henri beat him within an inch of his life, Twain woke, shivering, still in the king's bed in the Vermilion Emporium.

Where was Quinta?

The thought made him sit up abruptly.

The good news was his head no longer spun and his ribs felt like they had a better chance of holding his body together. But he still couldn't believe Quinta was gone. Again, questions and doubts tumbled through his mind. Maybe she had left Severon without him? Maybe he was a fool to think he had anything to offer her? *This is what happens when you trust people*, whispered one part of his mind.

Or she could be in danger, whispered another. *And you're doing nothing other than moping about, feeling rejected.*

A headache bloomed behind his eyes, and he touched his face gingerly. A quick glance in the mirror showed him a face nearly unrecognizable. Purple bruises marked the space under each eye, and a greenish-yellow bruise stood out on his cheekbone. His lip was split, and his hair was a tangled mess.

"One step at a time," he said bracingly as he swung his legs over the bed.

Once he'd bathed and dressed in the clothes Sorchia had put out, Twain made his way down the stairs. More photographs of the girl who looked like his mother lined the walls, and at the very bottom of the stairs was a picture of two boys playing on the beach. Their backs were to the camera, but Twain could've sworn the boys in the photo looked like him and Zand as children.

But that was a mystery for another day, one to dig into once he found Quinta. There was a small door in the wall at the base of the stairs, and Twain pushed it open.

It opened behind the counter of the Vermilion Emporium. Sorchia sat a few feet away, talking to a customer in a tall hat.

"Ahh, there's my assistant," Sorchia said, gesturing to Twain. She shot him a small smile. "He's been unwell, but he's here to help."

Twain walked over to the counter. It took everything in him not to rush out the door and begin his search for Quinta, but he owed Sorchia a thank-you, at least.

The woman on the other side of the counter winced as she took in his battered face. "Goodness, what happened to you?"

It was Mrs. Davenport, and she didn't appear to recognize him from the Casorina's ball. Twain's hands clenched involuntarily. He would not let anger at his parents' patron's widow get in the way of finding Quinta. Not today.

"I fell down some steps," he said through gritted teeth.

"Must be careful," she clucked, turning away from him to peer at the items in the glass display case under the counter. "Now, as I was saying, I need something that will truly help the Severon Witches Society learn more about the arcane arts. Perhaps some fortune-telling cards? You see they've put me in charge of entertainment and education, and I can't disappoint them. We're having some scholars come talk with us at my house, and we'd like to know more before that meeting."

"Yes, of course," Sorchia said. "I have just the thing."

Twain's mind clicked away, thinking back to the last time he'd seen Mrs. Davenport. She had been at the Scholar's Ball, trying to talk to Quinta. Perhaps she had a clue to Quinta's whereabouts. Twain's heart raced at the possibility.

"Have you seen her?" blurted out Twain. He stared intently at Mrs. Davenport.

"Seen who, dear?" Mrs. Davenport stopped looking at the pack of tarot cards Sorchia had handed her and tilted her head to the side. With the plume of razorbill feathers on her hat, she looked exactly like a large bird.

"Quinta," Twain said. "She was the photographer's assistant and the Casorina's lacemaker." Twain pulled his own starlight lace handkerchief from his pocket and placed it on the counter. "Surely you remember her? We were at the ball together." His voice was low and urgent.

Understanding dawned on Mrs. Davenport's face. "Oh yes. The lace girl. Everyone is looking for her, you know. The Casorina— who burned all her starlight lace, by the way, can you believe it!— keeps telling people that the lace girl went off on a great adventure with the starlight-finder boy who was with her at the ball, but that's not true, is it? Because you're the starlight finder and you're here. Do you really have no idea where she is?"

Twain closed his eyes for a long moment. Of course the Casorina would think he and Quinta had left Severon, just as they'd planned. "Yes, that's right." He clutched the lace handkerchief. "I'm here, and she's missing."

Mrs. Davenport made a sympathetic noise. "Well, I'm sorry you've lost her. Is this one of her creations? Is it for sale? I've been yearning for some genuine starlight lace since the ball. How much do you want for it?"

She reached a finger toward the handkerchief, but Twain snatched it back. "This isn't for sale."

"Well, surely it is," Mrs. Davenport said with a high trill of a laugh. "It's in this shop of curiosities, and what could be more curious than such a lovely piece of starlight lace? Now, come on, tell me how much you want for it." She pulled out her handbag and tossed some gold coins on the counter.

"It's not for sale," Twain repeated through clenched teeth. "This is mine. Quinta made it for me."

Mrs. Davenport held a finger to her lips and widened her eyes, making her look like a freshly caught fish. "Not even for a secret? Would you trade it for a bit of information about Quinta?"

Twain paused, staring at her. "What do you know?"

"Give me the handkerchief and I'll tell you." A small smile played at the edges of Mrs. Davenport's lips, like she knew she had a very good hand of cards.

Miserable woman. What a choice this was. Giving away the

handkerchief Quinta had made him hurt Twain almost as much as losing her. But how could he find her without information? And something was better than the nothing he had right now.

Twain slid the handkerchief toward Mrs. Davenport. "Fine, it's a deal. What do you know?"

Mrs. Davenport pulled the lace handkerchief to herself greedily. "I heard that Quinta was seen on a ship with red-and-blue striped sails on the night of the Casorina's party. It left the harbor shortly thereafter."

Something niggled in the back of Twain's mind. A ship with red-and-blue sails? Had he seen that at the harbor? He couldn't be sure, and he was hazy on the details of that night because of the beating. But it was a place to start.

"I hope that helps," Mrs. Davenport said. "And when you do find Quinta, please have her come see me. I'll be wanting much more of this."

She folded Twain's starlight lace handkerchief into a neat square.

He ached to see it in her hand. "Be careful with that. It's . . . it's very special."

"It does feel warm and sweet, almost like eating a cake, doesn't it, dear? I can't wait to see the looks on the other Severon Witches Society members' faces when they see this. They'll be so jealous!"

Mrs. Davenport turned away, heading out of the store with her new prize.

Twain didn't know how to tell her that the lace actually was joy and heartache, and there were the first hints of love woven into its patterns. It was all he could do not to run after Mrs. Davenport and seize the handkerchief back.

Once Mrs. Davenport was out the door, Sorchia put a hand on his arm. "You traded it," she said in a voice that was all warning. "There's no having it back now unless she gives it to you."

"Or I could steal it."

"That's also a possibility," Sorchia agreed. "But not until you're feeling better."

Sorchia was right. Twain would've run after Mrs. Davenport, but he was really only up for collapsing into a chair behind the counter.

"Help me with the customers today," Sorchia said. "Word about the shop has gotten around, and we'll be busy. After that, we can search for your red-and-blue-sailed ship."

At the mention of it, more doubts razored through Twain. Why had Quinta been on a ship with red-and-blue sails? Was Margot, the maid from the Orpiment, right about Quinta leaving with another man? Had she abandoned Twain or was she in danger?

Both options were terrible. Despite all they'd shared, the old feeling of not being good enough swept through him. It was poison, churning his stomach, making him want to sink to the floor and curl in on himself. But instead, he gripped the shop counter, his fingernails digging into the wood. This hollowed-out, not-good-enough feeling was exactly what had spurred him to fight with Zand on that last day.

It had been a blistering-hot morning in late July, the day after Zand's sixteenth birthday. It was nearly noon, and Zand was barely awake. He'd gotten home long after midnight, drunk, his pockets empty of the food money he'd stolen from their savings. He'd also forgotten all about the plans he'd made to celebrate his birthday with Twain.

Twain had been furious. "You're just another useless scholar," he'd yelled. "Another copy of Father, studying long-gone magic and burning through our money."

Zand's eyes flashed. "And you're exactly what Mother always said, a fool who will never achieve anything."

"You wouldn't last a day, doing what I do." Twain dug his nails into his palms so he didn't punch Zand.

"What's so hard about climbing a rock? Even animals can do that."

"Fine," snapped Twain, turning before Zand could see the hurt in his eyes. "Come with me. We'll see how you do away from the library." He grabbed his climbing bag and marched toward the beach, where Horst's boat awaited him. Zand followed, still a little drunk, but determined to show Twain he could climb rocks too.

A few hours later, Zand was dead and Twain was left with the heavy ache of grief and guilt.

He'd lost Zand, but he wouldn't lose Quinta. At least not without a fight.

But since he had no real idea how to *un*-lose her, staying with Sorchia seemed like the best plan.

At that moment, the bell over the shop door tinkled and two women entered the Vermilion Emporium.

"Oh my word!" one of the women said delightedly. "It's precisely as we heard it would be. Take a look at this, Willametta!"

The women barely glanced at Twain and Sorchia as they moved through the main room, picking up small boxes, books, and brooches and cooing happily over all of them.

"Do you show anyone else the rooms down the hallway?" Twain asked Sorchia. He gestured to the door that had led him and Quinta on so many different adventures.

Sorchia shook her head. "Absolutely not. Most people think this is an odds, ends, and novelties shop. Customers get to browse this main room only. Of course, it gets a bit more expansive every day we stay in the same place, and I don't even need to restock it. Things just have a way of arriving here, announcing their own prices, and arranging themselves as they see fit."

"Why do you need me then?" Twain asked.

"I don't. But I think *you* need me and the Vermilion Emporium. Somewhere in here there will be something to help you find Quinta. I'm sure of it."

Twain was not so sure of it, but he was willing to spend his life looking if that's what it took.

One of the women came up to the counter then, holding a magnifying glass with a mother-of-pearl handle.

"How much for this?" she asked.

"Twain, why don't you take care of this customer?" Sorchia patted his hand reassuringly. "I'll see about her friend."

And with that, Sorchia moved away from the counter, leaving Twain to puzzle out the price of the magnifying glass.

And so his days passed. He spent mornings when the shop was open helping Sorchia with customers. She was right; more people had gotten wind of the Vermilion Emporium, and someone—

probably Mrs. Davenport—had let it slip that it was where she'd acquired the starlight lace handkerchief. There were so many customers that sometimes it was nearly impossible to move around the shop.

"No, we don't sell anything made of starlight," Twain would have to say at least a half dozen times every day. The customers would insist that they'd heard it was sold here, but Twain would maintain that they had nothing of the sort and then direct them to a beautiful new display of palaces in glass bottles that had appeared on the shelves that morning.

＊

If his mornings were quotidian, his evenings were something else entirely. Each night that first week, Twain ventured deeper and deeper into the halls and rooms of the Vermilion Emporium, looking for something—a clue, a hint, a whisper of he knew not what. He had gone back to the Severon docks daily, looking for the ship with the red-and-blue striped sails, but no one could tell him anything, and he didn't linger, worried that Gustave and Henri might find him again.

As he explored the Vermilion Emporium, Twain kept coming back to the cavernous room with the silver and gold threads and the dragon bones—partially because it was the last place he'd visited with Quinta, and he could still feel her presence in the wide, dark room. But he also liked to visit it because it was the only room that didn't change every time he returned.

Tonight, as he did every night, Twain started his journey through the Emporium's wonders by paying tribute to the bones of the beast.

His feet pounded down the marble steps, and his heart raced as he slipped the key into the lock. Every time, he expected a different room to be behind the door. But as it had been the first time, the cavern was empty of magical items except for the glowing pile of threads in the middle of the room. Twain had gotten better at exploring, and his steps were sure on the path. The lantern he'd brought helped break up the gloom.

But as he reached the platform on top of the glowing mountain of threads, he noticed something different about the emerald-green dragon bones tonight. Had they always been laid out like that, with the skull and the tail facing in the same way? Or had someone or something moved them?

Or was Twain just not remembering their order correctly?

Lifting his lantern, Twain peered around the cavern. It was still too dark to make out anything beyond the circle of light from the glowing mountain of threads, but he didn't like the thought of something or someone else being down here too. He knew he was being ridiculous, but he couldn't help but feel he was being watched.

"You're being ridiculous," said a voice nearby.

Twain yelped as the lantern in his hand crashed to the floor of the cavern and an enormous shadow emerged from the darkness.

CHAPTER THIRTY
Quinta

After her escape attempt, Quinta was hauled by Damian to the tallest tower of the palace. Her dislocated shoulder ached with every stumbling step she took, and blood covered her torn-apart hands.

"When can I get out of here?" Quinta called out as Damian shoved her into the tower.

"You're just lucky we don't kill you. Is it too much to ask that you make the damn dress already?" He sounded frayed.

"You just sliced up the last piece of my starlight lace!" Quinta cried. "Thanks to you, it's at the bottom of the sea."

She still couldn't figure out why he'd cut the line. It was malicious but also impractical. If she was dead, she couldn't make the lace. Maybe he just wanted to punish her. Or maybe he wasn't thinking clearly. Whatever the reason, she was trapped again, with no lace and a furious Damian.

"That's your problem, not mine," Damian snarled. "Find more starlight."

Quinta glared at him. "If you'd take me back to Severon, I could get you some. Twain is the one who finds starlight, not me."

"I'm not taking you anywhere. You have a few more days before the queen's deadline. Make her a dress."

He slammed the door, leaving Quinta in the gloomy tower. Light shone through narrow slits in the stone, illuminating a staircase that curved upward. She reached out, her torn, bloody palm fumbling along the wall. Stinging pain lanced through her at the touch.

"I will make it out of here," she muttered through gritted teeth.

Damian hadn't said anything about food or having someone heal her. Despair threatened to overwhelm Quinta as she stood there, locked in a tower with an impossible task in front of her. She took a long, steadying breath. No one was coming to help her. If she wanted to get back to Severon, she had to find a way. Not even magic could save her now.

"First, I take care of this," she said, cradling her dislocated shoulder. Her voice shook as she said it. Bracing herself, she gripped the wrist of her injured arm and pulled forward as hard as she could. With a sickening noise, her shoulder popped back into the socket and Quinta promptly fainted from the pain, landing in a heap on the first step.

When she came back to her senses, she looked up, trying to remember where she was. The light filtering in through the slits in the wall was weaker and tinged with pink at the edges, meaning it must be nearly sunset. No one had come to bring her dinner, and her shoulder throbbed. Right. She was a prisoner in a tower in Queen Mathilde's castle. Which was awful, but at least she wasn't dead.

Slowly, painfully, Quinta moved up the curving stairs. All of her hurt, and she hoped against hope that there would be more than a bare space at the top of the stairs. It took her a very long time to climb the tower staircase, and she crawled up the last few steps. At the top was a small door. Quinta pushed it open and made a small noise of happiness to see a straw bed with a thin blanket on it. She stumbled past the window, which overlooked the ocean from very far up. She didn't notice the way the sunset painted the sky peach and purple. She didn't think of making a starlight dress. She didn't even remember the way Twain's arms curved around her as they slept together. She just fell into the makeshift bed, hurting, still wet from the seawater that had soaked her as she hung from the ledge, and utterly exhausted.

"Get up," someone said, throwing water in Quinta's face.

She sat up, sputtering. Damian stood above her, holding a tray of food and a half-empty water pitcher. He looked even worse than yesterday, and his red hair stood up in every direction. He'd replaced his scholar's robes with a red-and-blue striped military uniform, which Quinta thought made him look a bit like a circus clown.

"Oh! You brought me breakfast," she said, finding her wits faster than she thought possible given how badly her body hurt. "How charming. I'd almost think you liked me." She examined the two slices of bread, the bowl of fruit, and the pitcher of water eagerly.

Damian made a face as he dropped the tray on Quinta's lap. "You're definitely not my type. And I'm only bringing you breakfast so I don't have to explain to Queen Mathilde why you flung yourself into the sea."

"I wasn't 'flinging myself into the sea.' I was trying to escape." Suddenly ravenous, she picked up a piece of bread and took a huge bite.

"How'd that work for you? Still think you can swim back to Severon and the love of your life?"

His tone was bitter, and it scalded Quinta like hot water. Damian the scholar had never really been her and Twain's friend, she knew that now, but they'd been friendly enough with him. This man in front of her was a stranger. Where was the kind scholar who'd toured Severon with her and Twain? Or the young man who licked strawberry ice cream off his fingers when it dripped out of his cone? Where was the heartbroken soul who told her and Twain in halting sentences about the woman he loved? Had that all been a lie? Or was he different now that he knew Quinta was standing between him and his heart's desire?

This was how magic could ruin a person, Quinta thought, remembering her conversation with the Casorina. How many other ways could magic eat someone up from the inside?

Quinta took a slow sip of water and returned Damian's scowl. "Don't talk about Twain. You know nothing about us."

Damian scoffed. "I know love is suffering and hardship. And that you and Twain had no idea what you were doing."

"I hate you," Quinta said through another mouthful of bread. "And your queen."

"I don't care. What I care about is the queen staying happy. Since I'm the one who brought you here, I'm the one who'll be blamed if you fail."

"Your queen sounds like a just and wise ruler to me," Quinta said as witheringly as she could manage while chewing. "I thought she was the love of your life. Is she going to kill you if I fail? Even I can see the flaws in that relationship."

"She is a queen. And her whims are my everything," said Damian in a broken voice. "We have . . . different ideas on what do with the starlight lace—and what it means for our future."

If he hadn't kidnapped her, nearly flung her into the sea, and then locked her in a tower, Quinta might have felt the smallest bit sorry for Damian. "What do you want?"

"I want you to finish the dress! I've told the queen that we moved you to the tower because you needed space to work." Damian paced across the small expanse of the room, his agitation apparent in the snap of his steps.

Quinta finished the bread and took a long sip of water. "I can't make a dress. I don't have any starlight." Surely they could see how absurd it was to ask her to make something with no material. "Maybe you can bring me some of the queen's heirloom lace? Perhaps I could use that?"

Damian stopped pacing and shook his head. "Mathilde wants a dress made of new starlight. I don't care what you have to do, but you have to make it. Please." His voice had a desperate edge now.

Quinta barked a laugh. "Where am I supposed to find starlight if I'm locked in this tower?" She shoved her breakfast tray aside and stood up painfully. "What if I don't find any?"

"I don't think you'll like what happens then." Damian stepped so close to Quinta, she could smell the wine on his breath. If he was drinking this early, he really was worried. "Find it or die." His words were knives, slicing into Quinta as he turned and walked out of the room. "You have until tomorrow."

"You know that's impossible, right?" Quinta yelled down the stairs.

Then she burst into tears.

"I can't do it," she whispered as she stumbled over to the window. She sat down on the wide stone lip and wiped her face. "I can't make a dress without starlight." She gripped the small bottle of moonshadow around her neck. "What would you do, Mother?"

Her mother's words about the moonshadow came back to her: "Wear it always, but open it only if you have no other hope."

Quinta stared out the window at the sea a moment longer. There was no hope on the horizon, but perhaps there was a bit here, in her hand.

Untying the string around her neck, Quinta held the small vial of moonshadow. She'd never opened it. Not in all the years since her mother's death. What would happen if she did now? Some part of her suspected it might be full of ink or coal dust suspended in oil. Perhaps it was a trick of her mother's to make her daughter feel better. But there was a chance it could be magical.

"Please be magical," she murmured as she ran a fingernail along the wax seal at the top of the bottle. Taking a deep breath—this was a moment when everything could change!—Quinta pried the seal and a small cork out of the bottle.

Nothing happened.

No puff of smoke or magical music arose from it.

Of course nothing happened. Quinta still wasn't sure if her mother had real magic—she'd always thought that was the case, but now that Quinta had been working with starlight and magic of her own, she didn't know how to think of what her mother did. What was it to gather moonshadow? What even was moonshadow? Why had her mother been the one to harvest it?

For a terrible stinging moment, Quinta wondered if that had just been part of her mother's performance. Perhaps the Grand Eleina wasn't scooping up shadows the night she died. Maybe it was something much more normal, and Quinta's memory of the night was clouded by her grief and how young she was when it happened.

Quinta swore in frustration. Of course it was just a trick. Some circus sleight of hand she'd been wearing around her neck for years, convinced it was part of her mother's legacy. This wouldn't help her find more starlight or make a dress or save her life.

Disgusted, Quinta flung the bottle against the wall of the tower. It bounced off the stone but didn't shatter. That at least was odd. Curious, Quinta moved toward it to take a closer look.

The bottle had landed upright, and the moonshadow—or whatever the dark substance inside was—still sat there, undisturbed.

Quinta grabbed the bottle and hit the bottom of it against the wall. Again nothing happened.

"Oh very well then," said Quinta in an irritated tone. "Is this what I'm supposed to do?"

She sat down on the floor and turned the bottle over in her outstretched hand. As soon as she did so, the dark, cloudy contents rushed out and curled like a coin-sized snake in her palm.

Quinta nearly screamed, she was so surprised. She'd expected the substance to be wet like ink or slippery like oil, but it was something else altogether. It felt warm, alive, and very much like strands of starlight. It also reminded Quinta of her mother somehow, and a tear leaked down her cheek as she held it.

She turned her hand around, and the ribbon of moonshadow slid over it, grazing her fingers and moving along the rope burns and cuts on her palm from her escape attempt. The moonshadow rose up for a moment, like a snake about to strike, and then it crashed into her palm. Quinta screamed as a sharp pain ripped through her hand. The length of moonshadow wriggled, digging deeper under her skin.

She snatched at the moonshadow, grabbing onto its tail and yanking. The moonshadow fought back, as if it wanted to burrow into Quinta, but she pulled even harder. They had a brief and vicious tug-of-war, until Quinta gave a wild, desperate jerk.

The moonshadow snake whipped out of the hole in Quinta's hand, but it wasn't alone. Clenched in what were unmistakably its teeth was a thick strand of silver starlight.

Quinta gasped.

It couldn't be. Where had the starlight come from? Was it from inside her?

That was impossible.

Quinta knew this, but there was no other place the starlight could've come from.

"Do I have starlight inside me?" Quinta wondered out loud. "And can I use it to weave the queen's dress?"

The questions hung in the air as Quinta worked the silver thread out of the moonshadow snake's mouth.

She had to know if there was more starlight inside her. Perhaps it was just an aftereffect of making all the starlight lace? Perhaps some of that magic had sunk into her skin? Of course, to test that idea, she'd have to draw starlight from someone else. But that was something she could think on later. For now, she needed to know if there was more where this strand came from.

With a deep breath, Quinta pushed the moonshadow snake back into the hole in her hand.

"Go get more," she said to it, her voice strained by the pain in her hand. "I need enough to dress a queen."

The moonshadow dove into Quinta's hand, as if it hadn't eaten in weeks.

Quinta pulled six strands of starlight from herself that morning. It was more than enough for the queen's dress, and by the time she got the moonshadow back into its bottle, she was beyond spent. She still had no idea how the starlight got inside her or why her mother died harvesting the moonshadow, but Quinta was grateful to have the material she needed.

"First a nap, and then I'll get started," she murmured. Making a pillow of the starlight, she fell asleep immediately.

It was early evening when Quinta awoke. Her stomach rumbled, but she ignored it. She had until tomorrow morning. It was time to start weaving lace.

Hours later, when the sun rose, Quinta's hands were torn, bloody messes, but she'd done it. All the strands of starlight she'd pulled from herself had been twisted into lace for the queen. Quinta had built patterns of peace and kindness into the lace. She put sadness and joy in there too. Quinta would not make Queen Mathilde a dress of power. The queen had enough power already, which she wielded cruelly as far as Quinta could see.

Not long after she finished, the door to the tower clanged open, and Damian marched up the stairs. "Get up! It's time. Did you finally manage—"

His words stopped as he reached the top of the tower steps. Quinta had spread the great length of starlight lace out across the bed. It glowed in the morning light.

She stood beside it, her arms crossed.

"How did you do this?" Damian spluttered, walking over to the lace. He ran a finger over the glowing silver patterns.

"I found starlight in the most unlikely place. Can I get out of this tower and go home now? Your queen can make this into a dress."

"We'll go to Mathilde immediately, but I have a feeling she'll want even more." His voice was light, hopeful. He moved like a man who'd been given a chance at his dreams again.

Quinta cringed as he folded the lace. What would he say if he knew where the starlight had come from? And if the queen wanted more, where was she going to get it? From herself? She wasn't sure she could pull more from herself. At least not right now. She was too exhausted. But she would do what it took to get out of this palace and back to Severon.

"Fine. Take me to the queen," she said as a yawn split her face. "Let's start there."

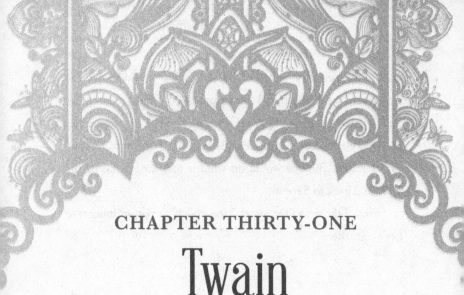

CHAPTER THIRTY-ONE
Twain

The shadow in the dragon-bone cavern loomed over Twain.

"Who are you?" Twain asked, scrambling down the pile of threads.

The shadowy shape stayed just outside the glowing circle of light cast by the golden and silver threads. "I'm the Mapmaker," it said in a voice that sounded faintly amused.

"What does that mean?" Twain stepped backward, moving toward the door he'd come in through.

"It means I make maps. What else could it possibly mean?" Yes. The voice was definitely laughing at him.

Twain scowled. "Why are you down here?"

"Down where?"

Twain gestured at the cavern. "Down here. In the darkness."

"Ahh," said the voice. "I see. I came for some more threads."

"Threads?"

"May I step forward without you driving something through my heart or bashing me in the head? It has been my experience that adventurers tend to bash first and ask for explanations later."

Twain held up his hands. "I promise not to bash you or stab you."

"Or harm me in any way."

"Or harm you in any way," Twain echoed.

"Good enough. I'm pleased to make your acquaintance."

A young man stepped forward. He had dark-brown skin, a shaved head, pale green eyes, and cheekbones like cliff faces. He wore a gray shirt with a red waistcoat over the top, black pants, polished boots, and wire-framed glasses. A bunch of rolled-up maps were tucked under his arm.

The man gave him a small bow. "I'm Marcel, Mapmaker and Navigator."

He held out a hand to shake Twain's, and all his maps dropped to the floor.

Twain pushed his surprise aside and scrambled to help Marcel gather the maps. "I'm Twain. Do you live down here? In the darkness?"

Marcel laughed. "Assuredly, no. Do you live down here?" When Twain shook his head, Marcel continued. "Why would anyone live in this cave? I'm a man of the world, not some mystical creature who survives on scraps of darkness. I live in a city far away from here. I just come down to the Dragon's Den when I need more threads for my maps."

Marcel unrolled one of the pieces of paper and showed Twain a glowing, golden spider's web of lines crisscrossing a continent.

"What is this a map of?" Twain asked. The landmasses were familiar, but the countries on them were unknown to him.

Marcel shrugged. "Mostly dragons. I deal in historical maps, so I need to use the golden threads to map the pathways the beasts have walked."

"But this doesn't look like any country in our world."

Marcel looked at him appraisingly. "Not in our world *at the moment*, you mean. But our world hasn't always looked like it does now." He began to separate one golden thread from the pile. "Once, a very long time ago, there were dragons all over Aix and Reyoux, and most especially in the mountains. These golden threads let me find my way back to those creatures."

"But where do the golden threads come from?" It was a question Twain and Quinta had wondered about every time they visited this part of the Emporium.

"From the bellies of dragons, of course," Marcel said. He pulled another long thread from the pile and coiled it around his hand.

That was absurd, of course. But they were talking about dragons here, so perhaps it was no less strange than should be expected.

Marcel continued: "They're made of sunlight, the same sort of fire a dragon has in its belly. The silver threads are starlight—and the stuff that makes up humans' secret selves."

Understanding danced just out of Twain's reach. "What does that mean? That starlight makes up humans? Do we all have this stuff inside us?"

Marcel's eyes shone. "You'll have to puzzle it out yourself, my friend."

Twain sighed, unsurprised that answers about starlight weren't forthcoming. How many books had he and Quinta read on the same subject only to end up with more questions?

"So, if you use golden threads to trace dragons, could you use silver ones to find a person who has gone missing?" Hope filled Twain's voice.

"If I had some of their starlight, then yes."

Twain wasn't sure if the handkerchief was some of Quinta's starlight, but it was the closest he had. "What about some starlight that the person wove into lace?"

Marcel's eyebrows leaped up his forehead. "Ahh, you've lost a lacemaker?"

"I have." Quickly, Twain told Marcel a bit about Quinta and how she had missed their meeting and about the ship with the red-and-blue sails. "Can you help me find her?"

Marcel nodded as he listened. "Perhaps. A lacemaker leaves a large thread through the world. If you can find something Quinta has woven, especially something she made for someone she loved, then I can find her for you."

It was so slim a chance, but Twain had to take it. "If I get you something she made, how will I find you again?"

Marcel stopped separating gold threads from the pile and pulled a card from the pocket of his vest. "Use my card."

Twain took it, and suddenly the room shifted. In the space between blinks, he was no longer standing beside the pile of golden and silver threads, talking to Marcel. Now, he was back on the other side of the closed door beside the marble steps.

How had he gotten here?

"Marcel?" he called, flinging the door open. But there was only darkness and the faraway glow of the threads. Twain ran toward the pile. There was no sign of a man collecting golden threads and, at the top of the pile, the dragon bones were back in their original order, laid out from head to tail in a line.

Twain slowly made his way out of the cavern again and toward the front of the Vermilion Emporium. He had no idea what happened, but he did have the mysterious man's card. Stopping under a light, Twain looked down at it:

Marcel Montbank
MAPMAKER
Appointments Only

That was it. No address. No further way to contact Marcel. No hints about where he had come from or how Twain could find him again.

But at least now he had a little hope for finding Quinta. He just had to get the lace handkerchief back from Mrs. Davenport.

Which was going to be something of a nightmare since Mrs. Davenport had been in the Vermilion Emporium that morning, talking about the party she was throwing for the SWS to see the handkerchief and the scholars who'd be there to give a lecture on magic.

Somehow, Twain would find a way into that party and he would steal back his handkerchief. It was his only way back to Quinta, and he would move the world to find her if he had to.

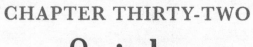

CHAPTER THIRTY-TWO

Quinta

A day after she pulled the starlight from herself using the moon-shadow, Quinta stood in a small, drafty room on the lower level of Queen Mathilde's palace, trying to think of what to say.

Three sets of eyes stared back at her, waiting.

"Um, hello." Quinta fiddled with a pair of scissors on the long wooden table in front of her and looked around the room. It had been a gardener's workshop once, and outside the room's windows the lush palms and flowers of the palace gardens looked like jewels against the sea.

"I guess you're wondering why you're here," Quinta said to the three girls who sat across the table from her.

Queen Mathilde had been so delighted with Quinta's starlight lace that she immediately set Quinta up in a lacemaking workshop.

"Make enough lace and I'll let you go," the queen had promised.

Quinta clung to those words, placing her hope of freedom in them.

To make the lace, the queen had assigned these three girls, all orphans who worked as seamstresses, to help Quinta with the sewing, and she tasked them with making enough starlight lace for an entire wardrobe.

There were two sisters, Anya and Chloe, who both had pale skin and wide gray eyes. But that's where their resemblance ended. Anya had long brown hair, which was pulled back in a neat braid. Her lips were painted berry red, and her blue dress and sewing smock were immaculate. She smiled at Quinta expectantly, and her hands were busy stitching a small, embroidered flower onto a scrap of fabric. To Anya's left sat her twin sister, Chloe, who had short red hair and a fringe of bangs she wore like a helm. Her arms were crossed, and she glowered at Quinta. On the other side of Anya, sitting close enough so that their knees touched in a very intimate, comfortable way, was Ruby—a tall, thin girl with dark-brown skin. Ruby's curly hair was pushed back from her forehead with a ribbon, and she had a small book tucked into the pocket of her apron.

As they all stared at her, Quinta had no idea what to tell them.

Perhaps: *We're going to make lace using the starlight we pull from our bodies.*

No, that would scare them.

Or maybe: *This might hurt a bit, but I can teach you things you've never dreamed.*

No. That wouldn't do either.

What about: *I may not look like much, but, you see, I was kidnapped and brought here to weave magic for the queen, and if I don't do it I think she's going to kill me and perhaps you too. So sorry about getting you involved in all this, but here we are. . . .*

"Well," Chloe said sharply. "What are we supposed to do? Did you bring us here to stare at us?"

"Works for me as long as she pays us," Anya said rather dreamily. "I don't want to go back to sewing for the orphanage just yet."

Quinta didn't know much about them, but Damian had told her that Anya and Chloe worked in a shop that helped support the orphanage they'd been raised in. Ruby also worked in the orphanage shop, but she had once been in the military.

Beside them, Ruby retied the ribbon in her hair, and for a moment, Quinta wanted nothing more than to sit with them over coffee and get to know them better. In a different life, they might've been friends.

But there was no time for friendship, and they had a lot of work ahead of them. Queen Mathilde wanted to wear starlight for every occasion, and she still talked of outfitting her armies in the stuff.

Make enough lace and I'll let you go.

Normally, the thought of armies wearing lace into battle would've made Quinta laugh, but nothing about Ixily was amusing. Despite the nearly constant sunshine and robin's-egg skies, it was a dreary, terrible place where discipline was valued above laughter, and soldiers filled the streets.

Chloe knocked on the table, pulling Quinta's attention back to the other girls. "Well? Where's the fabric? What're we supposed to sew with? Air? Sunshine? Our magical good looks?"

Quinta smiled at her. "Close, but not exactly."

Quinta hadn't told the queen or Damian how she'd gotten the starlight, and she had no idea how much she could draw from herself or if she could pull it from other people. She didn't even know what it was, though she'd been endlessly revisiting everything Twain had told her in their long hours in the Casorina's library, and she had some ideas. She was fairly certain that starlight was part of her, not just some aftereffect of working with the lace. How it got there, what it was doing inside her, and whether it was necessary for keeping her whole were all things Quinta didn't know and couldn't spend much time dwelling on. At least not today.

She pulled a small piece of starlight lace from her pocket and held it up to show the other girls. "This is magical lace. Good for all sorts of things."

Chloe made a noise of disbelief, and Anya stopped sewing. Ruby stood up slowly, her eyes wide.

"Is that real?" she asked.

"It is." Quinta held it out to Ruby, who took the glowing scrap of lace.

"Where's it from?" Chloe scowled. "Did you steal it?" She sounded like she would report Quinta to the queen herself.

"I made it," Quinta said. She smiled a little.

"Impossible," Ruby murmured in a low voice. She turned the piece in her hand, as if she could discover its secrets by studying it more closely. "No one has made starlight lace in centuries."

"That's what I thought too," Quinta admitted. "Until I found a book in Severon that taught me how to weave patterns with the starlight. Pass this bit of lace around and tell me: Does it make you think of anything as you hold it?"

Ruby turned the lace over again. "It reminds me of home," she said, closing her eyes. "Not of the orphanage shop or the military barracks, but my home on the other side of Ixily, where my family used to live. It makes me think of my mother baking a cake and a picnic I had with my brother by the sea when we were children." Her eyes flew open, and a haunted look filled them. Quickly, Ruby passed the lace to Anya.

"It's not a picnic by the sea, for me," Anya said with a frown as she ran her fingers over the lace. "This makes me feel like I'm wearing a silk dress and going to the opera. I'm covered in jewels and everyone's staring at me." Her expression became wistful.

"Let me see that." Chloe grabbed the lace from her sister. As soon as it touched her hand, her mouth dropped open. Tears rose in her eyes.

"What does it remind you of?" Quinta asked.

Chloe shook her head. Beside her, Anya laid a hand on her sister's forearm. "What is it?"

"The shipwreck," Chloe said through tight lips. "And that moment on the beach when I found you again."

Anya pulled her sister into a hug. "That was a long time ago, but I've never been so happy to see you." Chloe hugged her sister back fiercely.

"Were you shipwreck children?" asked Quinta softly. Twain told her that because of the Ixilian distrust of outsiders, children who washed ashore—"Wreckers" as locals called them—weren't eligible for military service. They ended up in orphanages here in the queen's city, working to pay off the indentures of their childhoods.

Chloe nodded. "We were only six when it happened, and our parents were drowned. After we were found on the beach in Ixily, they put us in the orphanage."

"But at least we were together," Anya said.

Chloe handed the lace back to Quinta and swiped quickly at her eyes.

"Can we make lace like that?" Anya asked at the same time Ruby asked, "How does the magic work?"

"I don't know," Quinta replied honestly. She paused, biting her lip. "About either question. I think the way it makes you feel has something to do with your own stories, the pattern I've put into the lace, and what you're feeling at the time. This piece is meant to make you think of your heart's desire. And for each of you that was something unique. For Ruby, I think it was a home full of love; for Anya, perhaps a life of wealth and glamour; and, for you, Chloe—"

"Don't even say it," Chloe grumbled. "We've known you two minutes. I'll thank you not to analyze us through your lace."

Quinta had to laugh at that. "Fair enough. If I'd woven a different pattern, you could've been faced with fear, or hope, or something else altogether. And, as far as whether you can make the lace too: I've only had one other person try to make it, and he couldn't get the designs right."

Quinta closed her eyes for a brief moment, seeing Twain as he struggled to tie knots of starlight together and sew the simplest of patterns. Thinking of Twain—what he might be doing, where he was at, what he thought had happened to her—was still an open wound. She pushed the thoughts down and turned back to the seamstresses. All of them were looking at her with a new level of curiosity.

"I am not an expert seamstress," she said. "But I can teach you what I know about making the lace. Our first lesson will be a pattern for building friendship."

Quinta had done her best to draw a pattern based on what she remembered from her blue book. This simple design was a series of hands holding each other.

From her pockets, Quinta retrieved the four threads she'd pulled from herself that morning. "Each of you will get a thread of starlight," said Quinta. "Separate it into as many smaller threads as you can, like this." She showed them how to pick at the end of the starlight and split it into dozens of other shining, tiny strands.

With some effort and many failed attempts, the girls split the threads and began stitching the pattern Quinta laid out for them. Anya was the best seamstress of them all, and she finished her work fast enough to help Chloe with hers. Ruby had a careful, deliberate hand, and as she worked, she and Anya whispered with each other.

As they pulled and twisted the lace, one of Quinta's questions about the lace was answered. Clearly these three experienced seamstresses could make the lace if she showed them the pattern. But what about the source of the starlight? Could Quinta also pull it from the other girls? Could they pull it from her? Was there anything about Quinta that was innately special when it came to magic? She'd like to think so, but she wasn't sure about anything magic related anymore.

Before she could give these questions more thought, Anya brought over a piece of her lace and they fell into talking about other patterns. Quinta promised herself she'd find answers soon—when they ran out of starlight, perhaps? But in the meantime, there was lace to make and dresses to sew.

And so, the days in the workshop passed. As they made lace, Quinta told the girls bits of her story, and they shared more of themselves with her as well. She learned that Ruby's brother had been killed in action three years ago and that his death sent her into a deep depression. She'd been let go from the military and had returned to the queen's city to find work. None was to be had, and one day, she decided to end it all by jumping off a bridge. Except Anya came along right as Ruby had climbed onto the railing and stopped her. Anya brought Ruby back to the orphanage shop and they'd slowly fallen in love with each other.

Quinta also learned that Anya adored cats and dreamed of having a large family made up of other Wreckers. "I'll adopt at least ten kids," she declared, laughing out loud at the look on Ruby's face when she said that.

Chloe was the least talkative of the seamstresses, but through the noises she made while the others were talking and the small bits of information she let slip, Quinta found out that Chloe hated living in Ixily. She wanted to travel and not spend her life paying off the cost of her childhood. She was a fighter and had long scars up and down her arms from scuffles she'd gotten into at the orphanage.

The days passed quickly, and a fierce protective feeling developed in Quinta toward the other girls. Every night after Anya, Ruby, and Chloe had gone back to the little room off the workshop where they slept, Quinta drew another few threads of starlight from herself.

Doing so drained her of energy, making her joints ache and sending slicing pain through her head. Worrying as all that was, there was really no other way to go on. The queen always wanted one more dress, one more handkerchief, one more scrap of lace to add to her arsenal.

Make enough lace and I'll let you go.

✳

"Are you feeling well?" Ruby asked Quinta one afternoon a few weeks after they'd started making the lace together.

It was mid-November and Quinta sat beside Ruby at a long table, palm on her cheek, eyes closed. She'd taken so much starlight from herself lately that each time she did so, her head spun and she felt like she could sleep for a year. She'd been dozing off, thinking of Twain. It had now been almost a month since she'd been taken from Severon. Did Twain still think of her? Did he still miss her? Would she ever see him again?

"I'm fine," said Quinta, massaging her temples. "Just tired. How did the battle pattern go?"

Queen Mathilde wanted a lace wrap with a pattern of horses, swords, siege engines, and castles. Of course, wars were now fought with guns and cannons, not swords and horses, but the queen loved studying history. She demanded this design as something to wear when meeting with enemies.

Ruby held out a thick line of lace that was intricately decorated.

"That's beautiful," Quinta said. "You're doing wonderful work."

Ruby beamed at the praise, but then her expression turned to concern as a hacking cough racked Quinta's body.

"You don't sound well." Ruby rested a hand on Quinta's back.

"I'll be fine. Just feeling drained lately."

"Is it something we can help with?"

Quinta shook her head. She couldn't tell them how she harvested starlight. She didn't want to scare them, and she didn't want them to suffer. "We just need to keep working."

More coughs ripped through her, making her gasp for breath. Ruby brought her a glass of water.

"Maybe you should rest for a bit?"

"I can't. We need to make enough lace, so the queen will let us go. It's just a lot, retrieving all the starlight...."

They sewed in silence for several minutes before Ruby turned to Quinta again.

"But where does the starlight come from?" A thoughtful expression brought her brows together. "Is that what's making you sick? Are you staying up late to fetch it from somewhere?"

"I—"

"Will you show us?" Ruby pressed. "We all want to know. And maybe if we could help, then you won't have to do so much of whatever you've been doing to get the starlight and you'll feel better."

"I can't tell you." Quinta's voice was pained.

"Why not?"

"It'll—it'll scare you. And I don't want to hurt you."

Ruby touched the new purple bruise that bloomed on Quinta's forearm. It was the result of the moonshadow chomping into her last night. "We don't want to see you hurt more. Please. Let us help."

Quinta paused, searching for a reason to keep resisting. But she was so, so tired. Her strength was waning, and she couldn't keep pulling starlight from herself. But there was still so much more they needed to make. Surely this was the moment to see if the moonshadow would work on other people?

Make enough lace and I'll let you go.

After another vicious round of coughing, Quinta caught her breath. "Fine. Go get the others," she said in a ragged voice. "I'll show you how it's done."

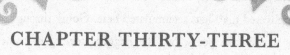

CHAPTER THIRTY-THREE
Twain

The finding feeling was back.

A few weeks had passed since the night of the Scholar's Ball and Quinta had disappeared on the ship with red-and-blue sails. Half of that time Twain had spent recovering from his injuries in Sorchia's apartments, and the rest he'd spent searching the Vermilion Emporium for clues about how to find Quinta. Since meeting Marcel, he had the vaguest bit of hope—though he still wasn't sure how he'd steal back the lace handkerchief he'd given Mrs. Davenport.

But something tingled under his skin today, urging him into the labyrinth of the Emporium. He opened the doors to room after room, only stopping when he came across one full of letters.

Here. There was something in this room for him to find. Eagerly, he stepped across the threshold, his shoes crunching over yellowed envelopes and dusty, handwriting-covered sheets of paper.

Twain read the bronze plaque by the door, running his fingers over its burnished edges. "Love letters of all descriptions await in this room, a hope from the sender, sent across the years."

He looked from the plaque to the mountains of letters stacked on tables, against walls, and in sacks. It looked like centuries' worth of undelivered mail had accumulated here. Going through all the letters would take years, but the nagging feeling of something important being buried here wouldn't leave him.

"The only way forward is through," he said, remembering his father's favorite saying as he slipped off his jacket and rolled up his shirtsleeves.

Two hours and many paper cuts later, Twain sat on top of a bag of letters, surveying the room. Like an arctic explorer navigating tall drifts of snow, he'd carved a path through the piled letters, but after opening hundreds of them, he'd found nothing.

It was preposterous to think there might be something from Quinta in here. But if she'd been able to send him a note or even if she'd thought to write him, maybe it would end up in this room somehow. Stranger things, indeed, lived in the Vermilion Emporium.

All these letters reminded him that he still didn't know how to contact the Mapmaker again.

Perhaps he could write Marcel a letter? But what would it say? And where would Twain send it? Of course, he couldn't send anything until he had the handkerchief in hand.

"Quinta, my love," he said out loud as he pushed another pile of letters aside. "Where are you?"

Even as the words were out of his mouth, he looked down to see a letter in a light-blue envelope by the toe of his right boot.

It couldn't be.

But it was.

Written in silver ink that glowed faintly—like the starlight he'd found on the cliffs so long ago—was one word:

Quinta.

Twain was used to seeing strange, odd, unexpected, and downright weird things after all these weeks in the Vermilion Emporium. But this letter surprised him.

Slowly, he picked it up and opened the envelope. Several thin sheets of paper covered in curling handwriting fell out, and he started to read:

Dearest Quinta,

If you're reading this, I'm already dead. I didn't want you to ever find this letter, but I mailed it to the Vermilion Emporium, in case you needed it someday.

Twain paused for a moment. Should he go on? Was he breaking Quinta's privacy by reading it? But what if it helped him find her? Surely she would understand why he'd read her letter. He kept going.

There is so much I'm sure you won't understand: what I was doing when I died; why collecting the moonshadow matters; what you're meant to do with it; and what the risks are when using it.

Magic has been gone from Severon for a long time, but it is not forgotten. Especially in the Salon families. As you well know, your great-great-great-great-grandmother Marali was the first starlight artist. Many of the paintings in Severon's museums are hers; and she was the first to make lace out of strands of starlight.

But how did she come to find it, you might ask.

This is the story as I know it:

One night, when Marali was walking beside the sea, a coil of moonshadow caught in her hair and burrowed into the place where her ear met her jaw. What it was exactly, Marali didn't know, but she always suspected it might be a Fae creature. Perhaps something from another world, a place where magic was much more common than in our own world. In any event, wherever it came from, she caught the tail end of the moonshadow as it bit her. As she pulled it out of her body, a thread of starlight came with it.

Marali was rightfully stunned to see the celestial threads of starlight and moonshadow dancing together. One was from the world, and one was from inside her. And they were beautiful.

Marali kept the threads of starlight and moonshadow, not sure what to do with them. But she soon pulled a second strand from herself, then a third, then many more.

She used these threads to make her daughter a beautiful lace dress. When the girl went out in the city, glowing like she was a star herself, she caught the attention of everyone. Soon, there was a great demand for starlight, and Marali used the moonshadow to pull it from herself, her daughter, and her friends. It was a grand time! Marali and her loved ones were welcome in every house. The richest people in Severon (and from all over the world) coveted starlight paintings and lace. They paid generously for it, and many of them did utterly ruinous things with it.

Marali made so much money, she was able to buy a circus—the Celestial Circus—and set her daughter and granddaughter up for life within in it.

But, my dearest Quinta, magic always has a price.

Marali found that out the hard way, as she pulled more and more starlight from herself and her family and friends. One day, she couldn't get the moonshadow back out of her daughter, and the poor girl was eaten up from the inside. The other Salon members began to die soon after that, and they were withered husks of themselves, utterly decimated by the moonshadow.

That's when Marali knew they'd gone too far—that there couldn't be any more starlight pulled from anyone, or it would kill them too. She told her granddaughter what had happened, and that girl took the secret to her grave, except for putting it into a letter I found among her papers in the Celestial Circus.

So, why was I harvesting moonshadow, you might ask?

At first I did so because I wanted to see if I could. I needed to know: Did the magical abilities of my ancestors flow in my veins?

The first time I caught some moonshadow I let it pull a thread of starlight out of my arm. (Quinta, dear: If you've opened the bottle of moonshadow I gave you, then you know moonshadow resembles a small, hungry snake. Which should tell you something about it in and of itself.) After that first time, I couldn't stop. Every night, I pulled another silver thread from myself. I kept all the starlight threads in a jar in our circus trailer—maybe you remember it? When you were small, I used to tell you it was a night-light, though I'm never sure you believed me.

Twain paused for a moment, wondering if Quinta did remember that night-light. He desperately hoped he would get the chance to ask her someday.

He kept reading.

> *One day, when you were about seven, we were visiting*
> *my friend Sorchia, who ran a traveling magical shop called*
> *the Vermilion Emporium. I'd brought her the jar of starlight,*
> *wondering if she could teach me what to do with it. While she*
> *and I were having tea at the shop counter, you unscrewed the lid*
> *of the jar and all the strands of starlight raced away, lost in the*
> *chaos of the Emporium. (I imagine if you've found any around*
> *Severon, they belong to me. Which, if I'm being honest, I like*
> *the idea of you finding a small piece of me long after I'm gone.*
> *Though they may not just be floating around Severon. Honestly,*
> *I'm not sure, but I believe they will return on the same day*
> *as the Vermilion Emporium—or at least that's what Sorchia*
> *assures me.) I tried to send my moonshadow after them, but it*
> *escaped my grasp as well.*

Twain paused again, as pieces of a puzzle clicked into place in his mind. So, the strands of starlight he found most likely came from Quinta's mother. It was too much of a coincidence to be anything other than magic. And they hadn't been floating around the city for more than ten years. They'd somehow arrived with the Vermilion Emporium. And Quinta's mother had been friends with Sorchia. . . .

Still marveling at all these connections, Twain turned his attention back to the letter.

After the starlight in the jar was lost, I decided not to harvest any more moonshadow or draw any more starlight from myself. I'd been feeling weak lately, and I'd also found a trunk in the Vermilion Emporium that contained all Marali's papers, including a diary, in which she detailed how she thought the magic worked.

This is what it said:

"Why do we all have starlight in us? Perhaps because the same material that lives in the stars makes us up as well. Whether that's our soul or not, I don't know (I'm not a theologian, nor do I want to be one), but I do know that we can use the starlight to move little bits of the world. It's powerful. When it's made into lace, it can tell stories, change futures, and make things happen. The lace can be even more effective if it's woven from a person's starlight threads and used by them. But—ha!—try getting a queen to weaken herself for the sake of magic. In my experience, the very wealthy will go through an entire city of ordinary people like us before draining their own strength in the slightest."

Marali's diary goes on, of course, but that's most of what you need to know. If you use your own threads of starlight to make lace, you can accomplish almost anything. Same goes with pulling starlight from those in your family or weaving something for people you love. But be wary, my dear, because you will also weaken yourself by doing so, and there are some things I fear you can't come back from.

I learned this lesson the hard way. Last night, I went out to harvest more moonshadow—it had been so long since I'd done it and the Celestial Circus was failing. I thought perhaps to save the circus by pulling some starlight out of myself and selling it.

What a mistake that was. I found some moonshadow, yes. However, as I was bottling the moonshadow, a small sliver of it slipped under my skin, digging in deeply. It was so powerful and so quick, I couldn't pull it back out of myself.

I can feel it now, as I write this, eating away at the threads of starlight inside me.

I don't have much time left, my lovely girl, but I will say this: starlight magic is not worth the price. Don't give your life for it, as I have done. Don't take the chance.

I always said you were meant for great things, but beware the cost. Find something or someone you love, and hold on to it. Greatness be damned.

I love you. Be brave. I will think of you always, no matter where my journey takes me.

Your mother,

Eleina

Twain stopped reading, trying to understand everything. He couldn't believe Quinta's mother had died trying to pull starlight from herself. What if Quinta opened the moonshadow she always wore around her neck? Would it also kill her?

He couldn't wait any longer. He had to find her and warn her.

And to do that, he had to get his handkerchief back from Mrs. Davenport.

CHAPTER THIRTY-FOUR

Quinta

It was time for Quinta to show the other girls how to harvest starlight. Ruby, Anya, and Chloe gathered around Quinta as she overturned the bottle she wore around her neck. The coil of blue moonshadow flowed into her hand.

"Try not to scream," Quinta warned. "You'll want to, believe me."

Then, with a deep breath, she pressed the moonshadow to her palm. It sunk its teeth into her, this time more painful than the last, as she let it wriggle under her flesh. Insatiable and searching, it dug deep within her for threads of starlight. Right when it was almost gone beneath her flesh, Quinta caught it by the tail with practiced fingers—she didn't know what would happen if she didn't catch the moonshadow, but she certainly didn't want to find out.

There was another rush of pain as the moonshadow clamped down on something inside her, somewhere in the region of her ribs. It was all Quinta could do not to cry out and clutch at her sides. When the pain reached a crescendo, she pulled—gently and devastatingly slowly so it didn't snag on anything else—the moonshadow serpent out of her body. It emerged, wriggling, with a thick thread of starlight clutched in its mouth. Quinta placed the starlight on the table in front of her, and then stroked the bit of moonshadow. It arched like a cat under her fingers before she captured it under a bowl.

"Who wants to go next?" she asked, looking at the other girls. She held a cloth to the wound on her hand, which now dripped red pearls of blood.

Silence filled the room as Chloe, Anya, and Ruby gaped at her. A look of disgust crossed Chloe's face as she stared at the bowl that held the whip of moonshadow.

"I can't believe you just let that thing rummage around inside you," Chloe said, finding her voice first. "What if you lose your hold on it?"

Anya made a sign to ward off evil, and Ruby swore softly beside her.

"It's not happened yet. And I'm not going to let it."

"Is there no other way to get starlight?" Anya asked. Even as she said it, her eyebrows pinched together and she made a gagging noise. "Also, disgusting. Are you telling me we've been sewing dresses made out of your insides, Quinta?"

Quinta winced slightly as she shifted in her seat and picked up the starlight thread. "There's no other way to get starlight that I know of, and yes. You've been sewing using my threads."

Anya looked like she was going to throw up.

"Do you think we all have starlight within us?" Ruby asked. She wore a serious expression on her face, like a scholar considering a particularly dense argument.

Quinta shrugged. "I don't know. But there's really only one way to find out. Does anyone want to let me try to pull some starlight out of them?"

There was a long, heavy silence. Panic filled Quinta as the girls stared at her. She needed them to let her pull starlight from themselves. The queen's promise rang through Quinta's head.

Make enough lace and I'll let you go.

How much was enough? If Quinta kept harvesting her own starlight, what would happen to her?

"I'll do it," Ruby said at last. Her voice had a determined edge.

"No." Anya gripped Ruby's arm. "You could get hurt, Rubes! Don't do this." Tears sparkled in her eyes.

"I'll be fine." Ruby squeezed Anya's hand. She brushed a tear off Anya's cheek and turned to Quinta, offering her palm. "I just want to know if the stars live inside me too."

"Thank you," Quinta murmured, her voice full of relief. "Plus, it doesn't really hurt very much. At least not the first few times."

Ruby's eyes widened at that, but before she could change her mind, Quinta flipped over the bowl, caught the writhing moonshadow snake, and pushed its mouth onto the meatiest part of Ruby's outstretched hand.

"Ouch!" Ruby cried as the moonshadow burrowed into her palm. Blood rose under its teeth.

"Maybe it *does* hurt the first time," Chloe said wryly. Beside her, Anya had one hand over her mouth and the other clung to Ruby's arm.

Right before the moonshadow disappeared entirely, Quinta grabbed at it and gave a hard tug on its tail. It fought her for a moment, but then popped out of Ruby's hand gripping a thick thread of starlight.

Ruby gasped, curling her fingers around her injured palm. Anya wrapped an arm around her, and Ruby sagged into Anya's embrace.

Well. That was one of her questions answered: Quinta wasn't the only one with starlight inside her. Which was a relief, since the queen was demanding so much lace, and Quinta didn't feel like her body could give enough starlight to keep up.

"This is yours." Quinta handed the glittering coil to Ruby. "Make it into whatever you'd like. We can always pull out more for the queen's dresses later."

A delighted smile crossed Ruby's face as she took it, and she uncoiled her fingers. "It's so lovely," Ruby breathed.

"Just like you," Quinta said with a smile.

Chloe glared suspiciously from Ruby's starlight thread to the moonshadow curled around Quinta's. "But how does it work? Let me hold that thing." She held out a hand for the moonshadow.

"Be careful," Quinta cautioned, untangling the celestial snake. It wriggled in her grasp, snapping with hungry jaws.

"It's fine." Chloe grabbed the moonshadow from Quinta. Her hands shook, but as soon as the moonshadow touched her palm, it stopped moving.

Anya and Ruby leaned over, looking at the motionless bit of moonshadow. Chloe poked it, but it didn't stir.

"What's wrong with it?" Ruby took the moonshadow, but it remained still, now more ribbon than living thing. The same thing happened when Anya touched it gingerly.

But, when Quinta reached for it, the moonshadow snake jumped to life, snapping upward like a sail in the wind. Quinta shoved it under the bowl again.

"Well, that answers my second question," she said aloud.

"What question?" Anya asked, eyeing the bowl warily.

"Whether I was the only one who could wield the moonshadow. My mother could do it, and so could my many times great-grandmother Marali. Perhaps people in my family have some affinity for the moonshadow that lets us use it to pull starlight from ourselves and others."

"Fascinating," Ruby murmured, rubbing at the wound on her hand.

"Not fascinating. Just weird," Chloe said flatly. "Let's look at what we know: only Quinta can make the moonshadow work, and both she and Ruby have starlight inside them. So obviously the question isn't *can* we do this, but rather it's *should* we do it. Don't you think it's bad to pull out threads from ourselves? If you pull too many threads out of a dress, it falls to pieces; so, what if the same thing happens to people?"

Quinta made a face. "Well, to your first point, Queen Mathilde has ensured it's moot since she's holding our lives hostage for starlight dresses. And to your second point, I think people are far more complex than dresses."

"Of course they are." Chloe crossed her arms. "But you have to admit it's worrisome."

"We'd be fools not to worry, but I've thought about this a lot and I think if we only take a few threads of starlight from ourselves each day, it will be fine. There must be millions more holding us together. It won't even make a difference."

Even as she said it, a stabbing pain in Quinta's knee made her doubt that statement. Did she really have enough starlight left to hold her together? Or was she going to literally fall apart?

Chloe considered her for another moment, and then shrugged. "If you say so. You're the one with the scary shadow snake."

"Who wants to go next?" Quinta asked, ignoring her aching body and picking up the moonshadow again. They had work to do, and the only way she was getting out of here was if Queen Mathilde was satisfied.

Anya started to speak, but Chloe interrupted her. "Do me first," she said quickly. "That way I'll know if it's safe for Anya."

Their eyes met, and Quinta nodded. She pushed the moonshadow into Chloe's hand and, after a few seconds, pulled it out, along with a thin thread of starlight.

"Why is Ruby's bigger?" Chloe asked as she turned her floss-thin starlight over.

"I have no idea," Quinta admitted. "There's so much I don't understand about this."

"Do it again!" Chloe demanded. A cough racked her body for a moment, but when she caught her breath, she said, "Forget the queen. I'm going to make myself something gorgeous."

After Quinta pulled three more threads from Chloe, and eventually some from Anya, they set to work.

✳

In between projects for the queen—who had now made it illegal for anyone besides herself to wear lace of any kind, starlight or otherwise—Quinta worked on her own secret project, just as she had back in Severon. Although the queen had promised to let her go when she had enough lace, Quinta didn't trust her. Mathilde was not the Casorina. She would never burn her lace, and she wasn't interested in science as the way forward. She had complete faith in magic, which made her dangerous.

So Quinta decided to take matters into her own hands. She was going to weave an escape route for herself and the other girls. Starlight lace was undoubtedly magical—she had seen it heal Twain's hands—and so she had to try to make her own path to freedom. And if she died trying? That would be better than wasting away in the queen's castle, each day becoming more and more a ghost of herself.

Her lace escape tapestry was slowly growing larger, but she needed to test it. One morning, while the other girls were busy working on a lace coat for the queen, Quinta pulled out her project from beneath the pile of rags where she was hiding it. It sparkled in the morning light.

Quinta worked on a small section of the lace. In it, she'd made a window that looked just like the one in the palace workshop, and she'd depicted a giant owl landing on the sill. It was the middle of the morning. If she saw an owl anywhere near that window, then she would count the experiment as a success.

"Please work," she whispered as she put in the last stitch.

There was the sound of the wind, blowing off the sea, and the voices of sailors in the harbor, calling out to each other. There was the screech of gulls and the low murmur of Anya and Ruby talking while they sewed.

Quinta stood on shaky, aching legs and moved toward the open workshop window. "Please work," she whispered again, holding the lace and imagining an owl.

The lace grew warm in her hand, and then there was a rustling at the workshop window.

A delighted laugh escaped Quinta's lips as an enormous, confused-looking owl landed on the windowsill.

It hooted once, and the other girls made exclamations of surprise.

"Shoo," Chloe said, rushing over to the owl and waving a piece of lace at it.

The bird hooted one more time, and then flew away.

If she wasn't in so much pain, Quinta would've danced. The experiment had worked. Now she knew, she could create her own escape route and find her way back to Severon and Twain. With that thought in mind, she headed back to her workstation, eager to keep sewing her future.

CHAPTER THIRTY-FIVE

Twain

After reading the letter from Quinta's mother, Twain knew he couldn't fail when he broke into Mrs. Davenport's house. He'd been planning on sneaking in the same way he and Quinta had the last time, but just after breakfast, a less risky option arrived in the form of an invitation.

The party Mrs. Davenport was hosting to show off her starlight lace was tonight, and luckily, since the Vermilion Emporium was her favorite shop, she'd invited Sorchia and Twain via message that morning. They wouldn't be there as guests—not exactly, at least; rather, they were going to deliver some new things for Mrs. Davenport's collection, and she offered to let them attend the party if they didn't mind staying out of the way.

Twain was more than happy to stay out of the way.

Tying a knot in a length of rope, Twain secured the last of Mrs. Davenport's items to a cart—three chairs that had once belonged to an opera singer known for raising ghosts with her voice, a mirror that was rumored to have spent a century at the bottom of the sea, and a trunkful of dresses that most certainly had belonged to a princess who lost her head during last century's troubles. He popped back into the Vermilion Emporium and looked around. It felt emptier these days. Almost like a house that had been packed up for a move. Yes, it was still full of treasures in the main room and all the secret rooms, but something about it reminded Twain of goodbyes.

"Are you almost ready?" he called out to Sorchia when his eyes landed on her standing next to a trayful of feather quills. She selected a purple one and tucked it into the brim of her hat.

"I'm ready now," she said with a broad smile. "You certainly are eager to get these goods delivered."

Twain shrugged. "Just excited to do my job, and I'm hoping perhaps someone at the party might know something about Quinta."

Twain hadn't told Sorchia of his plan to steal back the lace handkerchief because he didn't want to risk her telling Mrs. Davenport. The two women had tea together several times a week and had become something of friends lately. All Sorchia knew was that Twain still searched the Vermilion Emporium's endless rooms for a way back to Quinta. He probably should have also told her about meeting Marcel, but he hadn't for some reason. Perhaps because he liked having a secret among all the many mysteries in the Emporium. Or maybe it was because he didn't think Sorchia needed to know. Not yet, at least.

Sorchia gave him a perceptive look. "We'll find out something tonight about Quinta. I'm sure of it." Sorchia turned a small sign on the Emporium's door, so it now read CLOSED, locked the door, and then took the hand Twain offered her so she could climb up onto the cart.

"Now, remember what we talked about," Sorchia said as the cart's driver made a clicking noise and the horse started forward. "Try to have a bit of fun tonight. I know you're still heartsore over Quinta, but we will find her. I've sent letters to everyone I know to keep their eyes open for a lacemaker. I'm sure we'll hear something."

Twain made a noncommittal noise. If all went as planned, he'd be on his way to finding Quinta this evening.

"Also, this is for you." She handed him a small, brown-paper-wrapped parcel with his name written across the front.

"Who's it from?" Twain asked as he untied the string.

"Me. I have a feeling you might need it soon."

Twain's hands hesitated on the outer wrapping.

"Open it," Sorchia urged.

Twain pulled back the paper to reveal a thick green book with water-stained edges. It was held together with a silver clasp, and stamped on the front in flowing script was *A Book of Very Dangerous Magic.*

"Why is this dangerous?" Twain turned the book over to consider it. There was nothing on the spine, and a large stain blighted the back cover.

"Books like this are traps," Sorchia said. "Quite literally. This one was designed by a tricky magician who lived five hundred years ago. I came across it when I was a bit older than you, opened it, and it pulled me in for nearly six months."

"What do you mean, 'pulled you in'?"

Sorchia quirked one eyebrow. "Exactly that. Open this book and it will suck you in like a ship into a whirlpool. You'll be stuck there until someone else opens it up or it falls off a shelf, like it did in my case."

Twain ran a hand along the silver clasp. "What's it like inside?"

Sorchia shuddered. "Exceedingly dull. It's the story of a woman who runs a notions shop, works hard every day, comes home, eats some fish stew, and then goes to bed. Same story, every day. Over and over and over again."

Twain held back a laugh. "But *you* run a shop now."

"Not like that one," said Sorchia firmly. "The Vermilion Emporium is a galaxy of magic and fancy; the shop in that book was a nightmare of tedium."

"Very well then." Twain slipped the book into his coat pocket. "I won't read it."

"Good boy." Sorchia patted him fondly on the cheek. "Now, let's get to this party."

When they arrived at Mrs. Davenport's house, Sorchia swanned in to help Mrs. Davenport with the party setup and have a cup of tea. They were early, and Twain lurked for a few moments in the front hallway.

"Who are you?" snapped a butler with a walrus mustache as he hurried past Twain to answer the door. It was the same man who had turned Twain and Zand away two years ago. He stopped to sneer at Twain's simple outfit and plainly cut jacket.

Twain's hands tightened into fists as anger flashed through him. Of course, the man who'd ruined his life didn't even recognize him. "I'm here to deliver some furniture."

The butler sneered. "Then go through the staff entrance on the side, *not* the front door."

I could knock him flat with one punch.

It was a tempting option, but if Twain lashed out then his chance to get the handkerchief disappeared.

"Thank you so much for your generous hospitality," Twain said through gritted teeth.

Twain left the house. After untying the cart, he picked up one of the chairs and moved down the small path that ran along the side of the house.

It was the door to the kitchen that made him pause. An image of Quinta, standing beside the door and urging him to hurry, rose in his mind.

He put the chair down and sat on it, letting out a shaky breath.

Missing Quinta didn't hurt any less now than it had a month ago. Every hour of every day of every week, he thought of her. In his mind he heard her laugh and saw her eyes flash with anger as she started to argue with him. He woke up thinking he'd roll over and wrap his arms around her. But she was well and truly gone, and he wasn't sure he'd ever see her again.

Taking a deep, shaking breath, Twain stood. He trudged up the stairs with the chair, placing it where he was directed by the butler. With every piece of furniture he carried in, his eyes darted to the servant's staircase. Yes, he was here to steal the handkerchief, but perhaps he could just take a peek at the attic where they'd spent their first night together.

When he was done unloading the cart and his shirt was thoroughly sweat soaked, he asked a passing pair of maids for the washroom. They giggled at the sight of him but pointed him down the hall.

As soon as they were gone, Twain dashed up the servants' staircase. No one stopped him as he hurried along the upstairs hallway, pausing only long enough to glance over his shoulder when he got to the hidden attic door and make sure the hall was empty. It was, and he pushed the door open, slipping into the dark space. The rough-hewn attic stairs creaked under his feet, and when he reached the top, he paused. Dust motes danced in beams of sunlight, and the lumps of old furniture still filled every space.

"Oh, Quinta," he murmured as he moved toward the round stained-glass window and the tilting yellow couch beneath it. She had been here. Laughing, teasing him, weaving magical things, kissing him . . .

The thought grabbed his heart, squeezing it until his breath came in short gasps. He sank onto the couch cushions, burying his face in his hands. Letting the tears come at last. *Fuck*. He missed her so much. More than Zand, even. She had seen him for exactly who he was and liked him anyway.

"Where are you?" How could he have just lost her?

His eyes drifted over the area near the couch. His and Quinta's footprints still lingered in the dust, and Twain bent down to trace his fingers around the shape of one of Quinta's phantom steps. He hummed the starlight melody under his breath, remembering all the times he heard it. And how he'd played the lilting song on his violin for Quinta.

His voice broke on the first notes, but he pushed on.

As the starlight song filled the attic, a rush of warmth raced into Twain's cracked-open heart. Everywhere Quinta had been missing, it felt like she was back.

As he hummed, he could smell Quinta's hair tumbling through his hands. He could hear her saying his name. He felt her hand in his as they walked along the beach. She was there with him, in that enormous dusty attic.

Twain blinked back tears as he stared into the space in front of him. It wasn't just the song that made him feel like Quinta was there. For a moment, he could actually see her, as if a window had opened up between where he was in the world and where she was. In his vision, Quinta sat at a table that overlooked a garden. Beyond the garden, Twain could hear the sea. Slowly, Quinta got up, moving from her seat to a worktable covered in starlight lace.

But as he looked at her, something wasn't right. She was much thinner than she'd been before; her cheekbones stood out sharply, and her hair hung in limp ringlets. There were bruises up and down her arms, and an angry red cut ran along her jaw. She moved as if each step hurt her.

"Quinta?" he called out, his concerned voice filling the attic.

Startled, she looked up, glancing toward the window. For a moment, her eyes met Twain's and they widened in surprise. "Twain? How are you here?"

"I'm not sure." He took a step closer. "Who hurt you?"

Quinta's eyes lit up for a moment. "I figured it out, Twain! Where starlight comes from. The answer was here all along." She touched the bottle of moonshadow at her neck.

"I know the secret too—but it's dangerous. You're not pulling it from yourself, are you? Tell me you're not!"

Quinta grimaced and shook her head. "I have to."

"You don't! You shouldn't!"

A long cough racked Quinta, and she shuddered. "I think I'm dying, Twain. Come find me. Now. Before it's too late."

"Where are you?" Twain called out frantically.

But before Quinta could say anything else, the image disappeared, leaving Twain alone in Mrs. Davenport's dusty attic, asking himself if the vision had been real or just a product of his fevered, lovesick imagination.

CHAPTER THIRTY-SIX

Quinta

An ocean away, Quinta sat up with a start. She'd been taking a nap at her worktable, but suddenly it felt as if Twain was in the room with her. He'd been standing in Mrs. Davenport's attic, humming the starlight song. She could almost reach out to him, run her hands through his hair, and push her lips softly against his.

When Quinta opened her eyes, Twain was gone.

Slowly, painfully, Quinta stood up. The cut along her jaw throbbed and her bones didn't feel right these days. They were too big for her skin and ached like they were burning away from the inside. Gingerly, she touched the cut with trembling hands. Her legs had given out as soon she got out of bed this morning, and she'd slammed her face into the edge of her bedside table, ripping open a long gash. That wasn't her only wound—her arms, torso, and legs were covered in round bruises and punctures from the bite of the moonshadow snake. A persistent cough racked her every few seconds, bringing up clots of blood with every hacking fit. And then there were the wounds from Damian's and the queen's questioning sessions.

Quinta was falling apart, quite literally, and she had pulled so much starlight from herself that napping every few hours was necessary.

But, mercifully, the pattern on her escape tapestry was almost done. And she would pull as much starlight as she needed to complete it.

Plus, she wasn't the only one feeling the strain. Quinta had been pulling starlight from Ruby, Anya, and Chloe for the last week. All three of them were coughing and covered in wounds. They hobbled around the workshop, complaining of pains in their joints. Anya hadn't even been able to get out of bed this morning.

Quinta hated that she'd done this to them. That she'd pulled so much starlight from them to appease Queen Mathilde, that something in them—something in her—was broken. Would they ever heal? Could starlight grow again inside a person once it had been taken out?

Slowly, Quinta ran a hand over the lacework of her escape tapestry. It was stretched out on her worktable in front of her.

She had to get them out of here while there were still some parts left to save.

Woven into her escape lace was a palace by the sea, full of open doors. The detail in this part was so fine that every door was smaller than Quinta's pinkie nail. There was a boat waiting by the palace.

In the bottom corner of the lace, Quinta had also woven a love knot and a boy standing in front of a shop. It was ridiculous to think that Twain or the Vermilion Emporium would arrive simply because she wanted them to, but that was the nature of wishes, she supposed. They often didn't make any sense, and you couldn't help but keep wanting them.

And Quinta was full of wishes. With an exhausted sigh she picked up her needles again and began weaving.

The door of the workshop creaked as someone turned a key in the lock. Quinta and the other girls had been locked in with their work ever since Queen Mathilde declared the making of starlight lace a state secret. Their meals were brought to them. Once a day they were allowed out to stroll by the sea with armed guards. But they were prisoners in every sense.

As the door swung open, Quinta threw a swatch of blue fabric over her escape tapestry, and then she covered that with a lace piece she was working on for the queen. This lace was intended to keep the queen beautiful for as long as she stayed alive. The details were intricate and exhausting, and Quinta wasn't entirely sure the magic would work, but she just needed it to hold long enough for her and the other girls to escape.

"That's quite lovely," Damian said as he strolled into the room. He glanced around, taking in the slow pace at which Chloe and Ruby worked, and at Anya, who was still asleep. "What's the matter with them?"

"Possibly, they object to being locked in a room in order to make lace," snapped Quinta. Summoning all her strength, she stood up to face Damian on her feet. Her hatred of him and the queen had grown with every day that passed.

"You should take that up with the queen. I'm just following orders."

"Nothing good ever came from that statement," Quinta muttered. "And they're tired. We work through the night in shifts because we have so much to do."

Quinta still hadn't told Queen Mathilde how they were harvesting starlight from themselves. She guessed that as soon as she did so, the queen would start pulling starlight from every poor wretch in the kingdom. There would be no end to it, and Quinta couldn't let that happen. She didn't want all that death on her head.

Not that the queen and Damian hadn't tried to get her to reveal her secrets. She still had bruises from their last "conversation."

Damian ran a hand over his beard. "Tell us how you're doing it, and we'll let all of you go."

"The same way the queen promised to let us go after we created enough lace?"

Damian shrugged. "Once we know your secret, we'll be able to make lace ourselves and won't need you."

"This is *my* secret," Quinta growled. "You can tell the queen we'll take it to our graves." Quinta and the other girls had talked this proposal over at length. Chloe wanted to tell Damian, but the rest of them didn't trust the queen or her ambassador.

"I'm sure that can be arranged," Damian snapped in a frustrated voice. "Keep working. The queen wants her beauty lace soon."

Then he stormed out and slammed the door.

Quinta collapsed from the effort of holding herself upright and landed hard on the stone floor of the workshop.

Ruby rushed to her. "Are you alright?"

Slowly, with Ruby's help, Quinta got to her feet. "I will be. But we can't stay here any longer. Tell the others to pack their things. We're leaving tomorrow."

CHAPTER THIRTY-SEVEN

Twain

Still haunted by what he'd seen of Quinta's declining health, Twain ran down the attic stairs, bursting into the hallway. The pair of maids he'd talked to earlier let out a surprised noise as he hurried past them.

He took the stairs to the main level of the house two at a time. Where was Sorchia? The SWS guests were starting to arrive, and Twain glimpsed Mrs. Davenport standing in front of the locked glass case that held her (well, his) starlight lace handkerchief. He had to get it—now—so he could give it to Marcel and find Quinta. She didn't have much time left.

But how was he going to break through the glass case, especially with all the SWS members hovering around it?

He needed to make it look like an accident. What had Quinta said? Look like you know what you're doing and no one will pay you any attention? Yes. He could do that. He'd look like he was moving furniture, bump into the glass case, shatter it, and then grab the handkerchief.

He ducked into the closest room, a library, scanning it for a chair or heavy metal bust or something that would do the trick, and he froze when he saw a pair of very familiar figures standing in front of a full bookcase with their backs to him. Gustave and Henri. Twain swore under his breath.

"What are you doing here?" Twain demanded. How did he keep running into these damn scholars?

Gustave spun around, nearly sending his top hat flying. Henri turned too and for a moment they just stared at Twain. Apparently, the last month had been good to the scholars. Both of them were in new suits. Their cheeks were round, their hair glossy, and a silver pocket watch on a chain hung from Gustave's vest.

"Twain?" Henri said in an incredulous voice. "You're still alive?"

Gustave stepped forward menacingly. "What're *you* doing here? Don't even think about getting between us and the SWS."

"What are you talking about?" Twain said.

"We've been giving 'lectures' at their meetings for the past month," Henri explained. "Never knew these old birds would pay so well for tidbits of scholarship. It's far more than the allowance my father gives me." Henri winked and held up the blue book of starlight lace patterns they'd taken from Twain by the harbor. "Your starlight girl introduced me to Mrs. Davenport at the Scholar's Ball. Be sure to thank Quinta for me. Or, actually, maybe I'll thank her myself. I'm sure she's tired of you and ready for a man who's moving up in the world now."

Twain pounced before he had time to think. "Don't you say anything about her!" He shoved Henri against a bookshelf.

Henri leered at him. "Oh, mate. You don't want to know the thoughts I've had about her."

An image of Quinta's thin, stooped, tortured frame from his vision in the attic filled Twain's mind. The girl of his heart was suffering, and Henri had the gall to say filthy things about her. It was too much. He punched Henri in the stomach, doubling him over. Quinta's book of lace patterns tumbled from Henri's hands as he clutched his midsection.

A pair of strong arms pulled at Twain's jacket, dragging him away from Henri.

"Enough of that," Gustave said. "You're lucky we don't take you out back again and kill you properly."

Twain shook out of Gustave's grip. He didn't have time for fighting. He needed to steal back the lace handkerchief so he could rescue Quinta. Before he could leave the library, however, Henri noticed the green book poking out of Twain's jacket.

"What's this?" Henri asked, darting forward to grab the book.

Gustave peered at it, adjusting his glasses. "*A Book of Very Dangerous Magic*?" he said, reading the title. "Did you steal this, Twain?"

For a very short moment, Twain considered warning them about the book. But then, a grim smile quirked his lips as he remembered what Sorchia told him: this book was literally a trap.

"I didn't steal it," he said. "But it's a book full of magical secrets. Perfect for a pair of scholars like you two. I've not even cracked it open yet because I didn't think I was ready for its secrets."

He might as well have offered two kids a barrel of candy. Gustave opened the clasp on the green book, and then he and Henri peered inside it, hungry for its magic. As soon as they did, there was a flash of green light and a loud *whooshing* noise as the pages of the book sucked the two scholars out of this world and deposited them between its covers.

Gustave and Henri were gone in the space between two blinks and *A Book of Very Dangerous Magic* fell to the floor with a thump. Twain picked it up, closed the clasp, and stuck it on the dusty top shelf of Mrs. Davenport's library. He doubted anyone would think to open it for a very long time indeed.

Pocketing Quinta's book of lace patterns, Twain grabbed a small bronze statue shaped like a horse and walked out of the library. But he didn't make it far. Mrs. Davenport waited beside the glass case with the handkerchief inside, checking her watch.

"Excuse me, shop boy," she said, recognizing him. "Have you seen two scholars? We're supposed to have them give a little talk about magic, but they've not shown up yet."

Twain smirked as he thought of Gustave and Henri navigating the very ordinary world of the book they were now trapped in. "I haven't seen them," he said with a shrug.

Mrs. Davenport made a frustrated noise and peered into the drawing room, where members of the SWS lingered, talking amongst themselves.

"Well, this is just rude," Mrs. Davenport fumed. "What am I supposed to do? I promised the SWS members a lecture on starlight magic!"

Twain eyed the glass case that held the handkerchief. It was so close. All he had to do was pretend to trip, slam the bronze statue into the case, grab the handkerchief, and flee the house. He just needed to get rid of Mrs. Davenport.

"I can say a few words on magic," Twain offered. "If you'd like to go into the drawing room with the others, I'll be right there."

Or he'd be gone with her handkerchief before she knew what had happened.

"You?" Mrs. Davenport glared at him. "You may have found some threads of starlight, but you're not a scholar."

The words had teeth, and they sunk into Twain's deepest insecurities. His resentment of Mrs. Davenport and the way she had abandoned him and Zand rushed to the surface.

"I know I'm not a scholar," he managed as politely as possible. He meant to stop there, but he couldn't hold back the words that tumbled out next. "But my parents were. Perhaps you remember them? Charlotte and Andre Vernier? Your husband was their patron for almost twenty years, and they died on his ship." His tone was bitter and full of anger.

A flash of recognition lit Mrs. Davenport's eyes. "Ahh, of course I remember Charlotte and Andre! I was so sad to lose them as well as my dear husband. They always brought such energy to a dinner party! So full of questions and theories and always so spirited. Especially with each other. I've never seen a couple argue more in public."

Twain paused as he tried to figure out how to respond. His parents *had* been great fun at parties, and also were always at each other's throats about everything from ideas to how best to raise their children. The one thing they'd agreed on was how disappointed they were in Twain. Which wasn't something he liked to remember. Especially not in front of Mrs. Davenport.

Oblivious to the pain her words had caused, Mrs. Davenport plowed on, her expression shifting to a puzzled one. "But why didn't you come around after their deaths? I would have kept my husband's agreement."

Twain's mouth opened and closed. "My brother, Zand, and I *did* come to your door, but we were turned away by your staff."

Mrs. Davenport's face fell. "Oh no, my child. I'm so sorry. That wasn't on my instructions, and I've been wondering what happened to you these last two years. Where is your brother? Did he go on to be a scholar? I remember the way your parents spoke about him."

"Zand is dead." Twain gripped the bronze horse more tightly.

"I'm even more sorry to hear that." Mrs. Davenport laid a hand across her heart. "I have money set aside for both of you from my husband's will."

"I don't want your money," Twain said, changing tactics. Maybe he wouldn't have to steal the handkerchief. Maybe Mrs. Davenport would give it to him out of guilt for how she'd failed to keep her husband's agreements. "I want that." He pointed to the handkerchief in the glass case.

A few SWS members wandered into the room at that moment, casting curious looks at Twain and Mrs. Davenport.

Mrs. Davenport hesitated, conflict written across her face. She lowered her voice and leaned in toward Twain. "Come now.

Certainly you don't want that scrap. I could give you anything else in the house. Or pay for your education. But that starlight handkerchief is the prize of my collection."

Twain stepped away from Mrs. Davenport, his voice loud, desperate, pleading. "That handkerchief is my only way to find Quinta. I need it. Please. You can make up for all the wrongs of the past and give Quinta a future if you let me have it." He banged a fist against the wooden pedestal that held the glass case, making it shudder.

"What's the matter then?" One of the SWS members, a middle-aged woman with dark-brown skin hurried over to them. She wore a badge that said "SWS President" pinned to her dress.

Mrs. Davenport started to say something, but Twain jumped in first. "Excuse me, Madame President, but my friend Quinta, the Casorina's lacemaker, has been taken. Someone is holding her against her will, and she's hurt. I need Mrs. Davenport's starlight handkerchief to find her."

Quickly, he filled the group of women in about how Quinta had gone missing, how he'd been searching for her, and how he traded his starlight handkerchief to Mrs. Davenport for a tidbit of information. He left out his past with Mrs. Davenport, Marcel the Mapmaker, and the Vermilion Emporium, but he told the women of his vision in the attic and how broken Quinta had looked in it.

"Oh no," said a petite, older white woman with a cat in her handbag. She wiped a tear from her cheek. "You poor boy. I'm sure Annaliese could spare the handkerchief. Couldn't you?"

Mrs. Davenport's eyebrows flew up. "I'm certainly not going to—"

"Oh, but this is for love, Annaliese," said the SWS president. "Surely you want to help these two magicians find each other again."

"And then she can stop lording the handkerchief over the rest of us," a third SWS member indiscreetly murmured.

Frustration and then resolve passed over Mrs. Davenport's face as she looked between Twain and the SWS members. He raised an eyebrow at her, as if daring her to go against the urging of her peers.

After a long moment, a sickly sweet smile crossed Mrs. Davenport's lips. "Of course I'll give the boy the handkerchief." Her voice sounded waspish. "Who am I to stand in the way of love—or the wishes of the SWS?" She took a key out of her pocket and unlocked the glass case.

As she picked up the handkerchief, the other women made noises of satisfaction and walked away. The SWS president patted Twain on the arm. "Good luck," she whispered with a wink.

Once they were gone, Mrs. Davenport turned to him, pocketing the handkerchief.

"What are you doing? You told them I could have the handkerchief."

Mrs. Davenport raised an eyebrow. "I can't just give this to you. I need something in return."

"I don't have anything to give you!"

"You have your story. Tell us how you found the magic and how Quinta made the lace."

"I need to go. Now!"

"And I need someone to entertain my guests. Since those scholars didn't show up, I still need someone to give us a lecture."

Twain wanted to snatch the handkerchief away and run, but if he did that he might get caught and hauled off to jail. And then how could he help Quinta? He wanted to shout at Mrs. Davenport and humiliate her in front of her guests, but that wouldn't bring Quinta back. If a trade was being offered, then that's what he would take. "Fine. It's a deal. But you better keep your word."

"We'll see how good your story is," Mrs. Davenport said archly. "This way."

As he followed Mrs. Davenport into the drawing room, Twain looked around for Sorchia, but she was nowhere to be found. Rather, the room was stuffed with two dozen or so SWS members, sitting in fussy-looking chairs, drinking tea.

Twain swallowed. What did he have to say about magic that they didn't know already?

He closed his eyes, remembering it all. The first day on the cliffs; bumping into Quinta by the Emporium; their first night together; and all those long, wonderful days in the Orpiment. In the end, what did he really have besides his story? Perhaps that was the most magical thing of all.

"Magic is very strange," Twain said as he faced the room. "Some people will spend their whole lives looking for it, and others will find it without even trying. But it doesn't matter how you find it—it's what you do with it when you have it that matters."

He went on, telling the SWS members about a boy hanging above the sea, remembering the ghost of his brother. About a girl who wore moonshadow around her neck. How they wove a dress that changed everything. And about the boy's relentless quest to find the girl, who was now slowly dying from the magic she wrought.

By the time Twain was done, every person in the room had tears rolling down their cheeks.

Mrs. Davenport came up to him at the end of the talk, sniffling. "That was beautiful," she said, wiping a tear away. "I'm sorry about everything, and I've had a change of heart. I fear that in my quest for magic, I've lost my way. Take the starlight handkerchief. Find Quinta. And promise me if you do, you'll both come by someday for tea. I'd like to hear the rest of this story and make up for the wrong I did you and your brother."

Twain promised, folding the handkerchief up and slipping it into his pocket. Mrs. Davenport patted him roughly on the arm, and then turned to talk to another SWS member. Twain spotted Sorchia in the garden and hurried out of the house.

Sorchia was standing near a marble fountain, smelling a rose. "Ahh, hello," she said as Twain ran down the gravel path and stopped beside her. "I see you've got your handkerchief back."

"Yes, though it took some convincing." He pulled Marcel's card from his pocket. "Do you know how I can contact this man?"

"You've met Marcel!" Sorchia said with a delighted clap of her hands. "I'm so pleased to hear that. He doesn't come as often as he used to, and I've not visited the lower levels of the Emporium for some time, so I keep missing him."

"Can you help me contact him, though? He told me if I could find some of the starlight Quinta had made, then we could find her."

"Hence, why you were going to steal back your handkerchief?"

"Exactly. But Mrs. Davenport gave it back to me first."

Sorchia smiled. "Good for her then. See, magic can change people for the better. Now, let's get home so we can contact Marcel and find Quinta."

✦

Once they were back in the Emporium, Sorchia locked the door behind them, leaving the CLOSED sign there. "Draw the curtains," she said. "Then follow me."

Twain did so, and they hurried down the hallway he and Quinta had first ventured through what felt like many years ago. (Had it only been a few weeks since the Scholar's Ball? Twain couldn't believe it.) As they walked, Sorchia told him what she knew of Marcel.

"I met him first a long time ago. I couldn't have been much older than you and Quinta are."

"That's not possible," Twain said. "He looks to be about my age and you're—"

"Old?" Sorchia quirked an eyebrow. "Ancient, withered, doddering?"

"You're none of those things," said Twain hastily. "But you do look a few days past seventeen."

At that, Sorchia gave a hearty cackle. "I'm eighty-three, if you must know. And I did, indeed, meet Marcel more than six decades ago. He has magic that keeps him young. Or perhaps because he maps both time and space, he moves through it differently than we do."

Twain thought on that as they walked down the steps to the door that led to the dragon bones.

"Still have the key to this door?" Sorchia asked. "And Marcel's card?"

Twain pulled the key from around his neck and the card from his pocket and handed them to Sorchia.

"Please let it be the port," she whispered as she turned the key.

The door swung open, and Twain gasped. Rather than the usual dark cavern filled with bones and gold and silver threads, there was now an emerald-green boat waiting for them in a wide, dark river. Golden lights lit up a stone promenade beside the water. Sorchia strolled over to the boat and walked across the gangplank without a second glance. Twain hurried after her, marveling at the boat's design. It was shaped like a dragon's body, its head at the prow, pointing toward the dark river. Long ribs made up the beams of the ship, and the sails looked like wings, raised in the darkness.

"Is it made from the dragon's bones?" Twain asked softly.

Sorchia ran a hand along the boat's railing. "It is. This dragon lived in a time before any of us knew what time was. It shifts from the bones in the cavern to the boat when needed or when it feels like it. Sometimes I can ask it to take me where I want to go."

There were more questions than answers in that statement, but Twain didn't have time to ask them because Sorchia pressed Marcel's card to the dragon's skull.

"Take us to Marcel," Sorchia said. "If you please."

The boat lurched forward and Twain fell backward, landing in a pile of cushions that hadn't been there a moment earlier.

"Hold on!" Sorchia yelled from the front of the boat. Her hair had flown out of its bun, and she gripped the railing. A wide, elated smile split her face and she laughed, a high golden sound that reminded Twain of his mother's laugh. Or his own.

The dragon-bone boat moved along the underground river at unthinkable speed. Twain wasn't able to pull himself to a standing position, so he just gripped the closest bit of boat—a piece that looked distinctly like a claw—and held on as if his life depended on it. Because it most certainly did.

After what felt like several days, but could've only been a few minutes, the dragon-bone boat stopped abruptly. The underground river sloshed against the sides of the vessel, and they docked at a pier just outside a city he'd never seen.

"We're here," Sorchia said, nodding in approval.

"Where's here?" Twain stood up, taking in the view before him. It was evening, and somehow, they were no longer underground. The glowing lights of a large seaside town danced off the water, and the full moon painted everything silver. Buildings with curved domes rose above square-shaped houses, and people filled the streets, eating at outdoor restaurants, buying and selling wares, and strolling along a wide promenade beside the water. A warm breeze lifted Twain's hair, carrying with it the smell of roasting meats and spices. Complex music, woven with a dazzling melody, chased the breeze.

"It's where we're meant to be. Follow me." Sorchia moved down the now-outstretched gangplank and onto the dock, holding Marcel's business card in front of her. As soon as Twain was over the gangplank, Sorchia held out a hand and whispered some words. The dragon-bone boat glowed golden, and then it disappeared entirely.

"Where did it go?"

Sorchia shrugged. "Where it waits when the Emporium is between places. Here, you can hold on to it."

She placed a very small item in Twain's hand. It was a deep-red box, no bigger than a sugar cube.

"Are you telling me *all* the Vermilion Emporium is in this?"

"I am not telling you anything," Sorchia said with a wink. "I'm merely asking you to hold it. Where the Emporium is right now, I'm not sure. Perhaps it's in that box or perhaps it's hiding somewhere else beneath the surface of the world, just below the level we can see. What I do know is it will be back when we need it."

Twain secured the box in his pocket.

"Not like that," Sorchia said gently. "Do you want it to fall out and be left in the street?"

The thought of the Vermilion Emporium disappearing from the world because he dropped it in the street caused Twain physical pain. "How do I keep it safe then?"

Sorchia took a small lace bag on a string from around her neck. It glowed silver.

"Starlight?"

She nodded. "Indeed. So you'll always have a map back to the Emporium if you need it. Ask Marcel about that if you lose me." She put the small cube into the bag and then handed it to Twain. "It also won't come undone or fall apart while you're wearing it."

Twain slipped the string over his neck. The starlight thread was warm and felt reassuringly solid.

"Do you know which way we should go?" Twain asked. The city surged around them—though no one seemed to have noticed the way their boat just disappeared—and Marcel could be anywhere.

Sorchia shrugged and started off down one street. "We'll see where our feet take us."

Twain followed for a few moments and then stopped. He had a feeling—the type of finding feeling he'd learned to trust. "We should go down this street!" he called out, pointing away from the main square and toward a shadowy alley.

"How do you know?"

"I have a feeling. Like when I first found the starlight."

Sorchia considered him for a long moment. "Yes, I suppose it could be happening already," she murmured.

"What could be happening?"

"I'll tell you later. Let's take your path and see what we find."

They walked through the alley, slipping on cobblestones covered in mud and filth. There was no shop or sign of Marcel at the end of the alley or down the next street.

"We need to keep going," Twain urged. They were now deep in a labyrinth of narrow streets that ran past tannery vats and a market that sold live animals.

Sorchia waved a hand, too out of breath to say more, but she followed Twain.

He couldn't have explained how he knew where he was going; he just knew they were almost there. They walked a little farther, now moving into a less crowded part of town.

"There," said Twain. He pointed to a shop front that had a red awning hanging over its windows. Written in curving gold lettering was: MARCEL'S MAPMAKING MARKET.

Sorchia let out a bark of a laugh. "He never was subtle, not unless he wanted to be. I wonder what the neighbors think of him." She pointed to the milliner and a dress boutique on either side of Marcel's shop.

Sorchia didn't wait for Twain to answer as she pushed open the shop door.

CHAPTER THIRTY-EIGHT
Quinta

By the next morning, Quinta was ready to escape; however, she had no idea how to begin. Yes, she had completed the story of their flight on the lace tapestry, but what did that mean in translation? Was she supposed to wear it? Fly it like a flag? Do something else with it? For all that Quinta had been working with the starlight for many weeks, she still hadn't figured out exactly how the magic it produced worked.

It seemed to vary depending on who wore the lace, what they wanted, how it was made, who it was being used on, and possibly hundreds of other factors. All she knew was that today, when she and the other girls went outside for their paltry bit of exercise and fresh air, they'd make their break. If they didn't, Quinta was fairly certain there'd be nothing left of her to bury.

Where the other girls would go after they escaped, Quinta didn't know. But she hoped she could help them find homes away from Queen Mathilde's reach. Anya and Ruby had once talked about setting up a milliner's shop together, and Chloe would follow her sister to the ends of the earth.

"Are you sure you want to do this?" Quinta asked as she wrapped her escape tapestry under her dress. "It could be terribly dangerous."

Chloe nodded. "I'm sure. You look like a ghost, and I feel about the same way. We can't continue—our bodies won't last much longer if we keep pulling starlight from them. Are you sure you can get us out of the palace?"

Quinta was not.

"Yes. We'll make it." Quinta tried to make her voice confident as she helped Chloe sweep the last of the pieces of starlight into a basket.

A key turned in the lock, and all the girls tensed. Ruby and Anya stood up from where they'd been resting at the table. This was it. The last time they'd be in the workshop. Damian would check to see if there was anything he wanted to show the queen, and then he'd let them outside.

"Ahh, good morning, ladies," Damian said. He looked around, nodding to see that everything had been cleaned up. He moved to the worktable and picked up a large swath of lace Ruby and Anya had been working on. "This is beautiful. Queen Mathilde will be most pleased. Come, we'll show it to her now."

"But it's our outdoor time!" Quinta protested. "We need some fresh air. Surely you can see that we're not well enough to have an audience with the queen right now."

Almost as if to punctuate her point, a vicious cough racked her body and she bent over, gasping for breath.

Damian laughed, a terribly thin sound. He took Quinta's elbow, gripping it tightly. "I don't care if you're feeling sick or if you're perfectly well. When I say we're going to see the queen, then that's what we're going to do."

He called for the guards who stood outside the workshop door. Quinta cast a wild look around the room, but she couldn't see anything that would help her shake off Damian or get her out of showing the queen what she could do.

Quinta's eyes met Chloe's, who was now being dragged through the workshop by a guard.

"We'll make it," Quinta mouthed.

She wasn't so sure of that herself, but she touched the escape lace under her jacket, hoping it would work.

Damian and the guards led Quinta and the other girls to Queen Mathilde's private quarters. The queen stood on her terrace, a marble balcony nearly as wide as the workshop. It was a beautiful autumn day, much warmer than Severon at this time of year, reminding Quinta of how far she was from home. Beyond the queen, sunlight sparkled off the water. Despite the warm weather, Quinta shivered and wrapped her arms around herself.

"Ahh, girls," the queen said. She was radiant today in her beauty lace, which Quinta had finished yesterday and Anya had transformed into a breathtaking dress. The silver starlight made Queen Mathilde's face glow, and she looked younger than Quinta and the other girls.

It was then that Quinta realized the magic in the starlight extracted no toll on the ones who wore it. The ones it was drawn from paid the heaviest price. That wasn't fair, nor was it a price worth paying. This disparity between wearer and worn—and the way Quinta's and the other girls' bodies were falling apart—was surely the cost Marali had been talking about and why she broke up the Salon.

"Hello, Your Majesty." Quinta wrenched her thoughts back to the queen. With effort, Quinta shook off Damian's arm and sunk into as low a curtsy as her ruined body would allow. "You look very lovely today."

Queen Mathilde preened. "Yes, I think so. You've done good work, but you see, it's just not enough. I can think of a hundred other frocks I'll need. One for longevity; another three for beauty in case any sauce is spilled on this dress; some for when I'm going to war; a dress for excoriating my enemies in; one to wear just for my lover; the list goes on." She laughed then, as if imagining all the different ways she could show off her power.

The list exhausted Quinta. With effort, she rose from her curtsy. "Those sound like beautiful dresses, Your Majesty, but I'm afraid we can't make them."

"Why ever not? Don't you have food? A place to work and sleep?"

"We don't have enough starlight," Quinta said simply. "We are nearly out of material."

And by that she meant that she wasn't sure how much more she and the other girls could pull out of themselves without falling too ill to stay alive.

The queen laughed. "If you'd just tell us where it comes from, I'm sure we could find you more." Her voice was light, but it carried menace. "Perhaps we need to have another 'conversation'?"

Quinta closed her eyes, remembering the agony of the last conversation session, where Damian attempted to beat the secret of starlight's origins out of her. "I can't tell you," she said. "I'm sorry, but it's not a secret I can give away."

There was a very sharp prickling at her back. She stiffened as the point of Damian's knife pushed between her shoulder blades. Chloe gasped, and Ruby called out: "Don't kill her!"

Queen Mathilde strolled over to Quinta, putting a finger under her chin and lifting it so they were eye to eye. "We won't kill her," she said in a dangerous voice. "We are just going to hurt her very, very badly, until she tells us what we want to know."

The knife sliced into Quinta's back, carving a line between her shoulder blades. If Damian cut her any lower, his knife would bite into the escape lace she'd hidden beneath her dress. Would the magic work if the lace was cut? Or if it was covered in blood?

"I won't tell you," Quinta panted.

"That's what I thought you'd say." Damian cut even deeper into her flesh.

Quinta cried out as agony seared across her back.

"Where. Does. The. Starlight. Come. From?" Damian snarled. The cruel path of his blade punctuated each word, inching ever closer to the lace tapestry. Blood ran in a line between Quinta's shoulder blades.

He couldn't get to the tapestry. If he did, all their hopes of escape disappeared. Grunting, Quinta wrenched herself away from Damian. But she was too hurt. He was too strong. He snatched her arm back, tightening his grip, and ran his knife across her back again. Quinta collapsed in his arms. Damian pulled her upward, holding the blade against her throat.

"Tell me. Or I really will kill you."

"I'll never tell." She spit at his face.

"You will." He pushed the blade against her skin. Quinta gasped as the knife bit into her neck.

The other girls watched her, eyes wide. Damian's fingers dug into her arm. Blood beaded under the knife, and a whimper escaped Quinta's lips.

"This could all be over," he snarled. "You have the power to end it."

Quinta scowled, her anger rising to the surface. "You'll never let us go if you know where it comes from."

Damian grabbed a handful of her hair, wrenching her head backward.

"Stop it! Leave her alone!" Anya shouted. Her voice sounded rusty, like her body could barely make her vocal cords work.

Damian turned toward the other girls. His knife dripped blood. "Perhaps *you'd* like to tell us where the starlight comes from?"

Quinta's eyes met Anya's. She shook her head, but even doing that hurt terribly. Releasing Quinta, Damian stepped toward Anya. His face was a mask of grim determination.

"Tell me where it comes from."

Anya stepped backward, bumping into Chloe. "I can't."

"You can and you will. If I have to carve out every inch of your flesh, we'll have your secret."

He reached for Anya, but Chloe stepped in front of her protectively.

"Promise you'll let us go?" she said.

"We promise," the queen said, in her lilting, lying voice.

"Don't tell them," Quinta croaked, swaying with the effort of standing up. She stumbled over to Chloe, reaching for her hand. "Please."

"I have to," Chloe said, her voice a strangled whisper. "I'm sorry."

She turned from Quinta to Damian and the queen.

"Well?" Damian wiped Quinta's blood from his knife onto his pants.

Chloe exhaled sharply. "It's from our bodies."

"What's that?" Queen Mathilde darted around Quinta like she was no more than furniture.

"It's from our bodies," Chloe repeated. "Quinta pulls it from herself and from us."

The queen furrowed her brow, as if she was trying to make sense of their words, and then understanding dawned. "Ahh, there are scholars who've hypothesized such things! But none of them knew how it was done. Show me."

She gestured Chloe forward.

"I can't do it," Chloe said, holding up her hands. "Quinta is the only one who can."

Quinta's back was a sheet of pain, but a plan had come to her. "I'll show you," she managed to say. "But only if Her Majesty allows me to pull the starlight from *her* body. You want me to make another dress for you? I can do that. But did you know that the magic is stronger if the material comes from your own self?"

Damian stepped forward. "You're not touching the queen. I'll do it. Take some from me." He offered his arm to Quinta.

The queen shook her head. She put a hand on Damian's arm and lowered it gently. "I want lace made from my starlight," she said. "Imagine what we could do with that."

"But it's too dangerous," Damian protested. "Let me do it, Mathilde."

She ignored him and turned back to Quinta. "You may take some from me. What do I do?"

Quinta gestured for the other girls to join her beside the terrace's railing. "Stand close to me," she said in a low voice.

They nodded, looking confused as they arranged themselves around her.

"Hold out your hand, Your Majesty," Quinta said to the queen.

Queen Mathilde did so, and slowly Quinta took the bottle of moonshadow from around her neck. Inside, the blue shadow wriggled in anticipation.

"This will draw the threads from you." Quinta held up the bottle so the queen could see the swirling mass. "Are you ready?"

The queen made an irritated noise. "Just do it already. I don't have all day to stand around. I have a country to run, you know."

"As you say," Quinta answered. She pulled the stopper from the bottle and caught the moonshadow snake as it rose into the air. Unlike the frail wisp it had been a few weeks ago, it was now larger even than the full-grown anaconda Quinta had seen in a traveling circus years ago. The moonshadow had glutted itself on the bits of starlight it had pulled out of the girls, and Quinta struggled to wrestle it into the tiny bottle every time they let it emerge.

Before Queen Mathilde could draw her hand away, Quinta clamped the moonshadow creature's head on the queen's palm. It bit down, and the queen gasped in surprise.

"What are you—"

"This is the only way, Your Majesty." Quinta watched the moonshadow wriggle beneath the queen's skin. She didn't grab its tail as it disappeared inside the queen's hand.

"Very well, then. We'll see how this magic of yours works." A smug look crossed the queen's face. She thought she'd won. Quinta let her believe that. Several long seconds passed, filled only with the sounds of gulls' cries and the wind off the sea.

The queen poked at her hand with one ring-covered finger. "Well? Where is the starlight? How do you get it out? Why is this taking so long?"

Quinta took a step backward, holding up her hands. "You'll see. It just takes a little longer for the moonshadow to find the starlight."

They waited, all eyes on the queen. Suddenly, she cried out, clutching her arm. Beneath the skin, the serpent squirmed ravenously.

"What have you done?" demanded the queen in a strained voice. Her eyes were wide with horror as the moonshadow encircled her upper arm and slithered over her shoulder.

"Only what you asked," Quinta replied. "Shown you where we've been getting the starlight."

"Get it out of me!" the queen shouted. "I can feel it moving through me, eating me up from the insi—"

Her words were lost in an agonized wail.

Quinta hated to see anyone suffer, but she didn't have time for standing still or worrying about the queen. In one quick move, she pulled her lace tapestry out of its hiding place under her dress. It was blood-soaked, but that would have to be okay.

Damian's arms were around Queen Mathilde, holding her as she writhed. He looked up with eyes full of fear and hate, meeting Quinta's gaze. "Someone, stop them!" Damian called out in an agonized voice.

Quinta flung her tapestry over her and the other girls. "Get us out of here," she whispered, begging the magic to work.

For a moment, nothing happened. The guards' footsteps pounded across the terrace as Queen Mathilde's wails grew louder. Then there was a blinding flash of silver light and the world rushed away from Quinta far faster than it had a right to move.

CHAPTER THIRTY-NINE

Twain

Twain followed Sorchia into Marcel's shop, feeling a bit of memory stir as he thought back to the first time he and Quinta walked into the Vermilion Emporium. Except she wasn't here, holding his hand, urging him forward, and this shop was nothing like the Emporium.

Whereas Sorchia's shop was cluttered, dusty, and cozy in a charming way, the Mapmaker's studio was so spotless it practically glittered. Tall cabinets with long, horizontal drawers filled the room. The cabinets were silver and had blue knobs, each with a different design painted on them. Twain longed to open the closest drawer and peek inside. He assumed it was filled with maps, but to where or when? And what were the maps made of if they could move a person through time as Sorchia claimed?

Twain clutched the starlight lace handkerchief, wondering if Marcel could indeed use it to map the way to Quinta.

"Ahh, we meet again," Marcel said, standing up from the table in the middle of the room where he was painting a large map of a continent that Twain didn't recognize. He gave a small bow to Twain, which Twain awkwardly returned.

"It's so good to see you," Sorchia said softly.

Marcel took her hand and planted a slow kiss on it. "My dear Sorchia. Has it really been so long?"

Sorchia beamed at Marcel, looking like she couldn't decide whether to kiss him or weep. "It's been so much longer than I had hoped. How are you looking so young?"

Marcel laughed and winked at her. "The usual ways, my dear. But you are still lovely."

Twain couldn't believe it, but Sorchia blushed pink to the roots of her white hair.

"How can I help you?" Marcel asked.

"We've come because you said you could help me map my way to someone I've lost," Twain said.

"Ahh yes, your lacemaker. Did you bring me something she created?"

"I did, and I can also return this to you." He held out Marcel's business card.

Marcel closed Twain's hand around the card. "You keep that in case you need to find me again. And let me see this lace."

Twain drew both the handkerchief and Quinta's blue book of lacemaking patterns from his pocket. He placed them on the table.

"Aha," Marcel said as he took them. His eyes sparkled. "Sorchia. You rascal. You didn't tell me the Emporium was giving forth its secrets again."

She shrugged. "It does as it will. We were all surprised when Quinta found the book."

"You shouldn't have been." Marcel ran a finger along the lace handkerchief. "She has a deft hand and a very clear signature. And this starlight absolutely belonged to her mother. You can see that in the way the lines of light have responded to her touch."

Twain had no idea how Marcel would know any of these things, but he was much more inclined to accept the mysterious these days than he had been a few months ago.

"That's all very good," Twain said impatiently. "But can you help me find her?"

"Her name is Quinta, yes?" Marcel raised one eyebrow. "And she is the lacemaker. . . ."

Twain confirmed these things.

"Step aside, then," Marcel ordered. "This will take some doing."

Marcel spread Quinta's handkerchief over a blank piece of map paper, studying it. Twain reached out to run a finger over the lace handkerchief, missing Quinta terribly for a moment.

"Don't touch—" Marcel stopped midsentence, then his mouth fell open in surprise.

Twain also cried out in astonishment because where he'd touched the handkerchief, something began to happen. The scent of seawater and the crash of waves filled the room. For a quick moment, Twain caught a glimpse of Quinta on a terrace by the sea. Blood streamed over her shoulders and down her back.

And then the lace began to unravel.

"No!" cried Twain, reaching for the handkerchief, but Marcel gripped his wrist in strong fingers.

"Wait," Marcel said in a low voice.

The lace continued to come apart like it was string being pulled at by a fierce kitten. Twain almost wept to see all of Quinta's delicate work undone. But then something else happened. The untangling threads of starlight began to rearrange themselves, stretching, pulling, and moving until they were aligned on the map in the shape of a wolf's head and jaws. At the center of the map was an island. The starlight there glowed bright blue.

"She's on that island," Marcel said, pointing. "Across the sea, in the capital city of Ixily. But you have to hurry. She doesn't have much time left."

That was all the information Twain needed. He snatched up the map from Marcel's table and pulled the silver bag Sorchia had given him from around his neck. "Take us to Quinta," he whispered to the tiny cube that was both the dragon-bone boat and the Vermilion Emporium.

Nothing happened.

"Why didn't that work?" he asked desperately, shaking the cube.

"Give it to me," Sorchia said, reaching for the cube. Her eyes met Marcel's. "What would you like in exchange for your help?"

He eyed the small cube that Twain had placed in Sorchia's hand. "I suppose it would be too much to ask for a key to the Emporium?"

Sorchia laughed at that, and Twain had the feeling this was a conversation many years in the making. "Too much. But we will owe you a favor, or you may visit any of the Emporium's rooms and take three things from them. Will that be enough?"

"In that case, I will see you again very soon." Marcel kissed her hand again. "Now go; find the lacemaker before it's too late."

Twain didn't need to be told twice. He shook Marcel's hand, and then he and Sorchia hurried back to the river. As they walked, she explained that despite the magicalness of magic, one couldn't expect to sail a dragon-bone boat in the middle of a mapmaking studio in a city. You had to at least get to water.

But just as she said that, she stopped at an empty storefront, tilting her head as she thought. "On second thought, we won't take the boat. We'll take the Emporium," she decided. "Let me show you how to direct it."

Twain had no idea what that meant, but he had the map and he would get to Quinta. Even if he had to swim across the sea to do so.

CHAPTER FORTY
Quinta

Quinta awoke on her belly, in a narrow space surrounded by tall brick walls. Somehow, her bones hurt even worse than they had before. The magic wasn't kind this time; but then, Quinta wasn't sure it ever had been.

Pushing herself onto one elbow, she looked around. It was still daytime, and the sun shone brightly over her head. Something smelled like rotten fish. She was in an alley, next to stinking piles of trash, broken barrels, and wooden milk crates. At the end of the alley, Queen Mathilde's palace loomed.

We have to get out of here.

Chloe, Ruby, and Anya lay beside her, all of them unconscious. The lace escape tapestry was flung across their bodies. What had happened? Her plan had been to use the lace to flee the castle— though she'd been fuzzy on the details of how that would work. But she'd wanted them to somehow end up on a ship. Or at least far away from Ixily and the queen's palace. Maybe the magic hadn't been as specific as she'd hoped because her blood soaked the lace? Or maybe it only took them this far because Quinta was guessing at the patterns to weave in the first place? In any event, the details didn't matter. They were away from Damian and out of the castle. That was a good thing, at least.

Pain blazed across Quinta's shoulders as she sat up. She swore under her breath. The wound on her back was deeper than she'd thought. Maybe the lace could heal it? Slowly, she pulled the lace tapestry toward her and wrapped it around her shoulders.

Please work.

Nothing happened, however, and loud shouts rang across the city, coming from the castle. "The queen is dead! Find her killers!"

Queen Mathilde was dead.

Quinta closed her eyes and let out a long breath. Guilt snaked through her. She had killed the queen.

You are meant for great things.

I never wanted to be a killer.

And yet, she'd known what she was doing when she let the moonshadow curl into the queen. She'd watched it eat her up from the inside.

"I had to do it," she murmured, to reassure herself.

I had to do it. The queen would've had me murder thousands with the moonshadow.

Quinta massaged her temples, overwhelmed by her choices and the strange turn her life had taken. Part of her wanted to lie down next to her friends and just sleep. But she couldn't do that. They had to get out of Ixily before Damian found them.

"Wake up," she said, shaking Ruby lightly on the shoulder.

Ruby made a pained noise as her eyes flickered open. Pulling starlight from her had made her cheeks gaunt, and her skin was no longer the rich, beautiful dark-brown it had been. Now, she looked faded and exhausted. "Quinta? Where are we?"

"Outside the palace," she said. "We have to get moving. They're coming for us."

The brash sound of trumpets split the air.

Ruby made a strangled sound. "That's the war cry."

Loud footsteps pounded down the streets as troops of the queen's soldiers rushed out of the palace.

"Wake Anya and Chloe," Quinta said as she pushed to her feet. A stabbing pain went through her left hip, bringing her down hard on one knee.

"Are you okay?" Ruby said, hurrying over to her.

Stand up. You're not dying in this filthy alley.

"I'm fine." Teeth gritted, Quinta stood. Slowly, she shuffled toward a heap of wooden milk crates. As she picked up a crate, the lace tapestry fell off her shoulders, landing in a puddle.

Fetch it in a minute. First, hide your friends.

Taking two crates in each hand, Quinta piled them in front of the other girls, praying they wouldn't fall over and alert the soldiers. Several trips later, a waist-high pile of crates concealed Ruby and Anya. Chloe was still sprawled outside the barrier, in plain view of anyone who might wander into the alley. But Quinta didn't have any more energy. She slumped to the ground beside her friends, catching her breath.

The sound of footsteps grew louder as the soldiers marched closer to their hiding spot. Anya sat up, wheezing, and Ruby clamped a hand over her mouth. She explained the situation in whispers.

"Chloe, wake up," Quinta said, crawling over to her. The girl didn't move, and Quinta wondered if they'd crossed a threshold. Had she pulled so much starlight from Chloe that she couldn't come back? If that was the case, how much longer did the rest of them have?

Quinta wasn't giving up on her yet.

"Help me hide her," she said to Anya and Ruby. Together, the three of them pulled Chloe behind the pile of wooden crates. Blood seeped down Quinta's back as she dragged the larger girl to the hiding spot. Then they ducked behind the crates, not a moment too soon.

"Oh no!" Anya whispered as she peered through a crack in one of the crates.

Quinta looked, and then swore. Two soldiers stood at the end of the alley. Although the girls were hidden, the starlight escape tapestry was still out there. Even in the bright sunlight, it glowed silver.

"Please don't let them see you," Quinta whispered to the lace itself, hoping it might hear her.

As the soldiers took their first steps into the alley, the starlight winked out, like a candle being extinguished. It now looked like a tattered, blood-soaked piece of grubby lace. Quinta let out a long, slow breath. Beside her, Ruby squeezed her hand.

"Anything down there?" one of the soldiers asked. He was a burly man with deep scars across his cheeks. The red-and-blue Ixilian uniform strained across his midsection.

"Thought I saw something," said the other solider, a short woman who didn't have a button of her uniform out of place.

Ruby gripped one of Quinta's hands and Anya clung to the other, as the woman's eyes darted around the alley. She took a step closer to the girls' hiding spot.

Quinta held her breath, squeezing both Ruby's and Anya's hands.

They would be fine. No one would find them. They would get out of here.

As the woman kicked at the lace with the toe of her boot, Quinta's heart knocked against her ribs, ready to leap outside her chest. Anya trembled at her side. The female soldier took another step toward the pile of crates and then paused.

They won't find us. They won't find us. They won't find us.

With a disgusted noise the woman lifted her boot, examining the stinking fish guts she'd stepped in. "Nothing here but rotten fish. Let's go."

Quinta collapsed against Anya and Ruby, her heart still sprinting. She'd never been so grateful for rotten fish in her life.

The male soldier waved his hand. "Fine with me. Damian said we're looking for four girls. They're sick and injured and can't have gone far."

"Is it really true that the queen is dead? How could four sick, injured girls have killed her?"

The male soldier shrugged. "Don't underestimate anyone. You know they taught us that in training. Those girls could be dangerous."

The female grunted, and the two of them marched out of the alley.

Once they were gone, Quinta darted out from their hiding spot and retrieved the lace. When it touched her hands, it glowed bright silver again.

"I can't believe they think *we're* dangerous," Quinta muttered as she rejoined the others. "When they're the ones with all the weapons and power."

"What are we going to do?" Ruby asked. Beside her, Anya was talking to Chloe, begging her to wake up. "They'll have the whole city out looking for us. Believe me, I know. When I was in the military, we'd stop at nothing to find a fugitive. For the people who killed the queen . . . they'll hunt us until the day we die." She shuddered.

Anya stopped shaking Chloe and leaned her head against Ruby's shoulder. "We'll make it, Rubes. You have to believe we will."

Ruby placed a small, tender kiss on Anya's brow, and Quinta had to look away. Seeing their affection made her miss Twain painfully. The loss of him coupled with the fact that she was probably going to die in the streets of Ixily hurt worse than the wound across her shoulders.

"We have to get moving," Quinta rasped. "If we stay in this alley, so close to the palace, they'll find us eventually. We need to get to a ship."

"But what will we pay with?" Ruby asked. "We have no money."

"We have the starlight." Quinta held up the bloody, torn lace tapestry. "It will have to be enough." Her hand darted toward her neck. The tiny bottle of moonshadow was gone. She'd worn it for so long, it almost felt like a part of her. But she wouldn't miss it; and she certainly would never try to harvest her own moonshadow. In fact, if she made it out of Ixily alive, she never wanted to see starlight or moonshadow again, unless they were safely ensconced in the sky.

A low groan filled the air, and Chloe's eyes fluttered open.

"Chloe!" Anya cried. "Oh, Chlo, I thought you weren't going to wake up." She threw herself on her sister's chest and sobs shook her body.

Chloe reached a hand up and rubbed her sister's back. "I'm alive," she whispered. "But you're smashing me."

"Oh, yes," Anya said, sitting up. She sniffled and gave a watery smile. "Sorry about that."

"Where are we?" Chloe asked. She sat up with a groan and looked around.

Quickly, the other girls filled her in on their escape and what the soldiers had said.

"You killed the queen?" Chloe turned to Quinta. "Everything on the terrace happened so fast. One minute you were offering her the moonshadow, then I remember something being thrown over us, the sound of wings, and waking up here."

"That's what I remember too," Anya added.

"The escape lace got us out of the castle, but I think the blood on it affected the magic. We didn't make it to a ship like I'd hoped," Quinta admitted. "But I killed the queen. Well, technically the moonshadow did it. But it was through my hand."

"I'm glad she's gone," Ruby said. "You did the right thing."

"I hope so."

"Remind me why we're all just sitting here," Chloe asked. "If we're wanted for regicide, we have to get out of Ixily as fast as possible."

"We were just working on that," Quinta said. "Anybody know the way to the docks from here?"

"We do," Anya stood. "All three of us. We came in that way when the queen sent for us."

Quinta got to her feet. "Well, let's get moving then. They can't have sketches of us around the city yet, so if we look like ordinary citizens, we should be fine. Plus, I've found if you look like you know what you're doing, people tend to leave you alone."

Quinta settled the starlight tapestry over her wounded shoulders, and then tore off a wide strip of her skirt hem to cover its brightness.

"Take off your aprons at least," said Ruby. They all did so, leaving them wearing their matching blue dresses. "We might not look quite so strange now in this city of uniforms."

"We can hope." Quinta strode to the front of the alley, with the other girls behind her.

A quick glance in both directions showed tradespeople at booths pushed right up against the castle walls, but no soldiers.

Quinta and the other girls walked down the street and stopped inside a stone doorway of a house whose shutters were closed.

"That's the way to the docks." Chloe pointed toward a wide street perpendicular to the one they were on. It ran right past the front palace gates.

"Is there no other way?" Quinta asked. "We're practically announcing ourselves if we go past the gates."

Anya shook her head. "The other way will take us much longer. And, like you said, there are soldiers patrolling the entire city. If we go this way, we'll be at the docks in ten minutes."

"And we could be on a ship soon after that," Ruby added.

All of them turned to look at Quinta, their faces expectant. How had she become responsible for so many people? What would happen to these brave, beautiful girls if they were caught? Could they somehow go back to normal lives in Ixily after all this was over?

They couldn't. Quinta knew that. Their families were gone, and Damian would never see that it was only Quinta who had killed the queen. He would blame Chloe, Anya, and Ruby too, and they would all suffer. She had to get them out of here. And there was no use staying in the city longer than they had to.

"Okay," Quinta decided. "Let's go the shortest way. Who wants to go first? I would, but I'm not sure where I'm going."

"I'll do it," Ruby said.

"Not alone." Anya stepped up beside her and took her hand.

"We'll all go together," Chloe said. She glanced toward the palace gate, where a troop of soldiers was gathered, checking the faces of all the people going past.

"Look." Quinta pointed to a large crowd of traders with carts and wagons approaching the gates. The traders protested loudly as the soldiers riffled through their wares. Someone threw a cabbage at a soldier's head, and the traders began pushing. All the soldiers' attention was on the crowd, leaving the narrow pathway to the docks open. "Let's go now."

As soon as she said it, all the girls began to hurry forward as quickly as their aching bodies would allow. Quinta's heart raced, and she feared the starlight lace across her shoulders could be seen underneath her makeshift shawl. But they moved past the palace gate, and no one stopped them.

They navigated a maze of alleys and eventually ended up on the edge of a small side street lined with shops. The docks were in front of them, and a passenger ship sat at port. A long line of people with suitcases in hand waited to board it.

They ducked into a narrow alley between shops for a moment.

"Do we take that ship?" Anya asked.

Ruby nodded. "We should try it. But maybe only one of us should go get tickets."

"I'll do it," Quinta said. "That way if I get caught, the rest of you can flee."

"Don't be ridiculous," Chloe grumbled. "You're wounded. We'll all go so we can help each other."

Quinta started to reply, but then someone stepped into the alley, gripped her arm, and pulled her backward. She spun around and gasped. It was Damian. He was alone and blood splattered his white shirt.

"I thought you'd try to find a ship," he snarled. "You're all under arrest for the murder of the queen."

"Run!" Quinta yelled at Chloe, Anya, and Ruby, but they stayed right where they were as if frozen to the spot.

"We won't leave you." Ruby picked up a piece of wood from the ground and brandished it.

"You're not going to hurt us." Anya followed Ruby's lead and grabbed a broken bottle.

Damian snorted at their pathetic weapons and dug his fingers deeper into Quinta's arm.

"Let go of me," Quinta demanded, tugging her arm away. His grip only tightened more.

Damian laughed and pulled something out from behind his back. It was dark blue and coiled like a whip. The moonshadow!

Quinta swore loudly.

With a flick of his wrists, Damian shot the lash of moonshadow outward. It encircled all four girls around the shoulders, corralling them together. Quinta gritted her teeth as her friends' bodies dug into her injured back.

"Where did you get that?" she demanded, pain making her voice jagged. She had hoped it died with the queen.

"I cut it out of Mathilde in an attempt to save her," Damian said, wincing at the memory. "But, unfortunately, I was too late. Now this is mine, and I can harvest starlight from whomever I like."

Quinta made a desperate noise of protest. "You can't. It's not as easy as you think. Only I can do it."

Damian pulled the rope of moonshadow tighter. "You're never leaving Ixily, but before I kill you, you're going to teach me how to use this."

"I'll die first."

"We'll see about that," Damian said. "Let's see how long you hold out when this is loose inside you. Mathilde didn't last more than a few minutes."

He reached down and gripped the mouth of the moonshadow snake. Then he tugged Quinta's hand toward him. Using a dagger he pulled from his belt, Damian slit Quinta's palm open in one quick motion. He grabbed her other hand, placing it on the moonshadow snake. It sprang to life under her touch. She tried to yank her hand away, but Damian kept his grip. Hand over hers, he pushed the moonshadow into Quinta's wound.

"Let go of me!" Quinta tried to grab the moonshadow before it disappeared inside her, but Damian held her other wrist. His eyes gleamed as the blue coil of moonshadow writhed into Quinta.

As the moonshadow clamped down on her bones, wriggling to find the last bits of starlight she had left, Quinta opened her mouth to scream. Only one word—the sound of her sadness, longing, loss, and deepest wish—echoed through the alley and out onto the street.

"Twain!" she cried, her voice racked by sobs as the moonshadow ate into her.

CHAPTER FORTY-ONE
Twain

The Vermilion Emporium landed with a *thunk* on a small city street. Before anyone noticed it, the shop wedged itself between two larger shops, like a cat getting comfy on a sofa. Inside the Emporium, the windows rattled, and Twain caught Sorchia as she tumbled out of the chair she'd been sitting in.

"It's always a little bumpy," she said as she found her footing again. "But that arrival was rougher than usual."

"Do you need help putting everything back?" he asked, looking around the shop. Bottles of perfume and mirrors lay shattered on the floor, books had fallen off shelves, and paintings had dropped from the wall. Chairs were overturned, and a pair of golden dragon statues had somehow ended up tangled in the chandelier.

Before Sorchia could reply, a scream split the air.

"Twain!" It was a voice he'd know anywhere—a voice torn apart with pain, but it was still Quinta.

"She's here!" He ran to the door. "We have to find her."

Sorchia picked up a dagger that had fallen off the wall. It had a key carved into its hilt and the blade gleamed silver. "Take this. I have a feeling you're going to need it."

Twain grabbed the dagger as another scream filled the air.

Sorchia gave him a shove. "Go, go. She's close. I'll be right behind you."

Throwing a thank-you over his shoulder, Twain raced out of the Emporium. It was midmorning by the position of the sun, and he was on a city street by the sea. Uneven cobblestones rose under his feet, and the shops were painted dull grays and browns. The sound of gulls and the whipping of sails in the wind filled the air.

To his right was a dock, where a long line of passengers waited to board a tall ship. Merchants, dockworkers, and shoppers lingered in the street, but among all the other city noise, no one seemed to hear or care about the cry that had just ripped into Twain's soul. He looked around, frantic to find the source.

Quinta had to be here. But where?

A gleam of silver in an alley a few storefronts down caught his eye. Could it be? Yes. He'd know that gleam anywhere. Starlight. He ran toward the silver light, his heart pounding faster than his footsteps.

When he got to the alley, Twain's stomach plummeted. There was Quinta, but she was so much smaller, thinner, and more faded than she had been even since his vision yesterday. A long, gray streak ran through her dark curls, and her posture was stooped. A muscular man with red hair was bent over Quinta, pushing something into her bleeding palm. Three other girls were tied up with her, held together by something that looked like a dark blue snake. It was the same shade as the moonshadow Quinta wore around her neck.

Without thinking, Twain lifted his dagger and slashed it across the man's forearm. "Leave her alone!"

Quinta's head popped up, her mouth falling open in a perfectly surprised O. "Twain?"

He threw her a small smile and winked, but that's all he had time for because the man spun around, bellowing a curse. It was Damian—the scholar from Ixily whom they'd befriended. Twain gasped as the pieces fell into place. Damian had kidnapped Quinta and dragged her back here? How? Why?

"What are you doing here?" Damian roared as he gaped at Twain. Blood rose up from the gash on his arm, and he took a moment to sneer at the dagger in Twain's hand before slashing out with his own knife.

Behind him, Quinta cradled her injured hand to her chest, pulling at the thick snake of moonshadow inside it.

"I could ask you the same," Twain spat out. "I suppose your 'scholarship' includes kidnapping people and trying to kill them?"

Damian darted forward, swinging his knife again, but Twain jumped away from the blade. "I did what I had to. I'm the queen's consort. Or I was. Until *she* killed her." He cast a murderous look at Quinta.

"I don't care who you are," Twain said. "You're going to leave them alone."

He gripped the dagger, planting his feet in a fighting stance. His ribs were still sore from the beating Henri and Gustave had delivered last month, but he hoped he'd be able to buy Quinta and the other girls enough time to get away.

Damian laughed. "So you've come to rescue them? That would be a fine idea if I didn't have all the city guard at my control." He held a finger to his lips and let out an ear-piercing whistle. In the distance, the sound of boots marching on cobblestones echoed through the city.

The tall Black girl who was tied up with Quinta swore loudly. She and the two other girls struggled against their moonshadow bonds.

"Twain, throw me your knife," Quinta called. "We have to get out of here."

Twain started to throw the knife, but Damian charged him. Twain was muscular and tall, but Damian had heft on him. As they crashed to the pavement, Twain's knife flew out of his hands and skidded toward the girls.

Damian stabbed out, but Twain was too fast. He avoided one thrust and then the next. Behind him, Quinta pulled one end of what looked like a huge snake of moonshadow from her hand. The snake gripped a piece of starlight as thick as a line of butcher shop sausages in its teeth.

How did that thing have teeth? Last time Twain had seen it, the moonshadow had been in a bottle around Quinta's neck. Now, it was a monster.

Slipping the rope of starlight into her pocket, Quinta sagged once the snake was out of her body. The moonshadow serpent tightened around the four girls, making Quinta cry out again.

A sharp, biting pain burned into Twain as Damian's knife found his shoulder.

He punched at the larger man, but his eyes were still on Quinta. She and the other girls were walking together as one. A girl with short, red hair managed to reach out and kick his knife back over to him. It skidded across the ground right as Damian raised up to stab him again. In one fluid motion, Twain rolled out of the way. He hopped to his feet and grabbed his knife. He had two choices with his next strike: either try to hit Damian or free Quinta and the other girls.

It was really no choice. Quinta's freedom and her life meant everything to Twain—that's why he was here, after all.

Ducking another of Damian's blows, Twain ran toward the girls.

"Cut us free," Quinta gasped as the moonshadow snake squeezed them more tightly.

Twain slashed out at it, the dagger from the Vermilion Emporium slicing through the thick hunks of shadowy flesh as easily as if it were moving through butter. The moonshadow snake fell into two pieces beside his foot. He picked up one and handed Quinta the other. At the end of the alley, a dozen soldiers massed behind Damian, all of them with pistols, swords, and other weapons drawn.

"We're not going to make it," said a white girl with a long braid hanging past her shoulders. She gripped the hand of the Black girl and tears sparkled in her eyes.

"We will," Twain said. "We just need to get to the Vermilion Emporium. It's a few shop fronts down."

Quinta turned to him, eyes wide. "You came here in the Emporium? But how?"

"We followed a map of your starlight."

Before Quinta could say more, Damian pulled a gun from his belt. "Very fun, these games," he panted, trying to catch his breath. "But let's see how knives and moonshadow fare against bullets and steel."

He raised a hand and yelled, "Fire!"

The soldiers behind him lifted their guns as one and pulled the triggers.

Quinta grabbed Twain's hand, and then lashed the coil of moonshadow in her hand like a whip. Behind them, one of the other girls screamed and there was a shattering noise, as bullets slammed into the brick walls behind them. But Twain, Quinta, and the girls weren't hit because the moonshadow rose up in front of them like a shield.

"That's impossible," Damian said, taking a step forward. "That's just shadow. How can it stop bullets? Fire! Now! Again!"

The soldiers raised their guns, but before they could take a shot, there was a loud crack of gunfire behind them.

As one, Damian and the soldiers turned, leaving a narrow path out of the alley open. That wasn't what froze Twain in place.

What held him motionless was the sight of Sorchia standing behind the soldiers with two pearl-handled pistols pointed in their

384

direction. Her eyes met Twain's and she smiled at him, a sad, halfway smile that told some truth he didn't know yet.

"Go!" she yelled, darting her eyes to the Emporium.

Twain didn't think twice; he grabbed Quinta's hand and ran with her as the shooting started.

CHAPTER FORTY-TWO
Quinta

"We can't leave her!" yelled Quinta as the crack of bullets split the air. They fled the alley, heading into the street. The Emporium was so close, so familiar, Quinta could've wept.

"I think she knows what she's doing," Twain called.

Quinta glanced over her shoulder. Sorchia was indeed holding her own. One of her bullets found Damian and rocked him backward. It was almost happening in slow motion, and Quinta let out a sigh of relief as he fell to the ground. Her kidnapper, her tormenter, the one who would've killed her, had been felled by an old woman's pistols.

"We have to help!" Quinta stopped running and planted her feet on the street. Her hand still bled and her breath came in ragged gasps, but she had the moonshadow and the starlight escape lace. She could do something.

"Get the others to the Emporium," Twain said. "Then come back."

Quinta turned to Ruby, Anya, and Chloe and pointed to the shop. Its facade was now gray, so it fit in with the other buildings in Ixily. *Perhaps it's now the Gray Emporium*, thought Quinta fleetingly. But, no. It would always and forever be the Vermilion Emporium to her.

A bullet whizzed past her head, taking all other thoughts with it. What was she doing thinking of shop names in the middle of a battle?

"Go!" Quinta urged her friends toward the shop. "Get inside, now!"

"Stop them!" Damian yelled from where he'd fallen to the street. Quinta glanced past the passengers huddled on the wharf to where Damian was clawing his way up from the ground.

Ruby, Anya, and Chloe ran past her. They made it to the Emporium and pushed the door open. In front of her, Sorchia fired bullets wildly. Twain cracked his moonshadow snake with one hand, like a lion tamer. In his other hand, he held a dagger.

Following Twain's lead, Quinta lifted her own moonshadow and whipped it using all her strength. The soldiers took a step backward, giving Sorchia space to retreat. Together the three of them edged closer to the Emporium. A movement from the ground caught Quinta's eye. Damian raised his gun, aimed it at Sorchia, and pulled the trigger.

"No!" Quinta yelled as the bullet ripped into Sorchia's side. The brave old woman crumpled, falling beside Twain like wheat at the touch of a scythe.

Quinta was weak beyond measure, but something in her snapped as Sorchia dropped. If it took Quinta giving her life to help the people she loved escape, so be it. Damian had to be stopped. And Quinta was going to do it.

She ran toward Damian as fast as her poor, broken body could take her.

In the back of her mind, she heard Twain yell her name and saw him pulling Sorchia toward the Emporium, but her focus stayed ahead of her. There was only Damian and the moonshadow in her hand. He fired at her as she approached him, but she smashed the bullets out of the air with the moonshadow.

"You! Will! Not! Kill! Us!" Quinta lashed the air with the moonshadow snake, punctuating each word. The starlight escape tapestry glowed on her shoulders. She felt beautiful and terrible in that moment. "You will stop this now, Damian, and let us go."

Damian started to say something, but Quinta had had enough. She flung out her moonshadow snake one more time, and it thrashed toward Damian. As he yelled a curse, the moonshadow slid into his mouth, cutting off his scream. Damian reached for its tail, but the moonshadow slithered in too fast and was gone. Disappearing into him to devour him from the inside. Some of the soldiers rushed toward him, arguing with one another about how to save him. But it was too late.

Quinta felt a hand on her arm, and she turned. Twain. He was here. He was real.

"I'm so happy to see—" Her legs gave out before she could finish, and Quinta collapsed into his arms.

"I've got you," he whispered, lifting her to her feet.

"Where's Sorchia?" She glanced around the street, but the old woman was nowhere to be found.

"I already got her inside."

Twain helped Quinta limp back to the doorstep of the Emporium. As they walked, she held his moonshadow, making a shield out of it to protect them from the other soldiers' bullets. Outside, the townspeople yelled and ran for cover, but for Quinta, there were only Twain's arms and shadow and starlight—each of them flickering on the face of the boy she loved.

"What took you so long?" she murmured as Twain guided her into the Vermilion Emporium.

"I came as fast as I could," he said, laying her on the floor beside Sorchia. "But you're a hard girl to find sometimes."

Quinta met his eyes and smiled, and then her eyes closed. She was so tired. Every part of her hurt, and she wanted to sleep.

"Stay with me," Twain begged.

Quinta opened her eyes again. From somewhere nearby she heard the sound of soldiers, Ruby's voice, and Anya's sobs.

"Lock the door," Sorchia directed. "That will hold them off for a moment."

Ruby ran to the door. "It needs a key! And there's none here."

"Around my neck, Twain." Sorchia sat up slightly, groaning. Blood leaked out of her side.

Quinta turned and held Sorchia's hand as Twain gently lifted the key over Sorchia's head.

"Can you take care of this?" he asked Ruby, holding out the moonshadow.

She shook her head. From somewhere outside, a rattling noise shook the windows.

"Lock it! Now!" Sorchia ordered. Her voice was once again the commanding, confident thing it had been when they first met.

Quinta grabbed the moonshadow as Twain ran to the door. Shoving it into a wine bottle, Quinta looked up as Twain slipped the key Sorchia had given him into the lock. He was beautiful and very much the boy she'd met outside the Emporium—and the piece of her heart she'd never known was missing—but he was also someone different now. More grounded, less likely to scale tall cliffs to reach for unattainable, outrageous things. When Twain turned the lock, there was a great clicking sound that reverberated through the Emporium. Beside Quinta, Sorchia fell back to the floor.

"I knew it," she murmured, so low only Quinta heard.

Outside the Emporium, the Ixilian soldiers pounded on the door and shot at the windows, but the glass and wood held.

"What should we do now?" Twain asked, holding the key.

Sorchia opened her eyes again, sitting up slightly. "Tell it where to go, my boy. You have the key to the Emporium. Find us a place to land."

Twain looked at Quinta, his eyes wide.

"Where should we go?" he asked.

She didn't know where was safe, but she wanted to see her stretch of ocean one more time and walk the streets of Vermilion.

"Back to Severon," she said. "Take us home, Twain."

He held the key and kneeled between Quinta and Sorchia. "Take us back to Severon. Please," he said to the Emporium.

CHAPTER FORTY-THREE

Twain

The key grew warm in Twain's hand. There was a great lurch, like a ship rolling over a wave. Then there was the strangest sense of rushing movement. Outside the windows of the Vermilion Emporium, the world flew by, a blur of sunlight, water, cities, and landmasses, all a rainbow of colors and shapes. After a few moments, the Emporium stopped moving.

"Where are we?" Quinta asked, shaking her head. Somehow, she looked even more drained than she had before. She sat up slowly.

"Severon," Sorchia croaked. "Look out the window and you'll see familiar streets. You brought us back here, Twain. Well done. I knew it was you."

"What do you mean?" Twain asked. He started to give Sorchia the key back, but she pushed his hand away.

"That's for you." Her voice was barely a whisper. "The Emporium is yours now, by birth and by blood. Do you accept?"

Twain's eyes met Quinta's. She was scowling, her brow furrowed as if she was trying to make sense of what was happening. "What do you mean, the Emporium is his?"

"I mean he's my grandson," Sorchia said. "I thought it was the case because he looks just like his mother—my daughter, Charlotte—did when she was his age, but I couldn't be sure. You see, my daughter wanted nothing to do with the Emporium. She wanted to study in the Scientifica. Then she met your father, and the two of them couldn't be separated. We fought terribly when she parted with me, and I never spoke to her again. But I hoped I might meet you. Or your brother. And, of course, you've already met your grandfather."

"My grandfather?" Twain was still processing the fact that they'd found Quinta and fought a battle and that Sorchia had been shot, and now he struggled to understand how he could have had a grandmother this whole time and not known it.

"Marcel," Sorchia said with a small, wistful smile. "I suspect he too knows who you are, though I never told him."

"But Marcel is young and you're . . . not . . ." Twain held a cloth to Sorchia's side, trying to stop the blood that leaked out of her wound.

"Ahh, but we were young together once," Sorchia said, her eyes going misty. "I told you he maps time and space, and he is much older than he looks."

It was a lot to take in, and they didn't have much time. Already, Sorchia looked weaker than she had before, and blood soaked the cloth. Twain traded it for a new one Quinta offered him.

"What am I supposed to do with this key?" he asked softly.

"Whatever you like." Sorchia looked around the room, her eyes crinkling at the edges as she looked up at the statues snarled in the chandelier. "The Emporium is yours if you want it. You may learn its secrets, walk its rooms, and tie your life to it until you can pass it on to someone in your family. If you so choose, of course."

"And if I don't want it?" Twain asked. Beside him, Quinta's fingers dug into his leg.

Sorchia made a pained noise, and a spasm shook her body. She held her hand to the bloody towel, her eyes closed for a long moment. Eventually she opened them again and continued: "If you don't want it, then the Emporium will disappear from this world. You can live an ordinary life, and sometime in the far future, you'll forget that this place and I even existed."

"No!" Quinta burst out beside him. "We can't do that. Twain, *you* can't do that. This place is a gift. It's a mystery and a delight. We can't let it disappear from the world."

Twain held her hand, his beautiful starlight girl who looked like she, too, was not going to be in this world much longer. The other three girls were collapsed on a couch in the middle of the Emporium, asleep with their arms around each other. The magic of the journey back to Severon must have knocked them out.

Could he do this? Tie his life to this strange shop that had countless rooms to explore? What about the adventures he wanted to go on? The places he wanted to visit? The person he wanted to become? Would it be the same if he were bound to the shop? He knew Sorchia could leave the Emporium, but for how long? Could he trade his freedom for a life in the Emporium?

"We can do it together," Quinta said softly. "I'll stay with you in the Emporium if you'd like."

Her eyes held his, and his heart stuttered. They could have a beautiful life here. No, they *would* have a beautiful life—if Quinta didn't die from all the starlight she'd pulled from herself. There had to be a magical way to make her better.

Twain made a decision, letting out a long, slow breath.

"I'll take the Emporium," he said to Sorchia. "If you tell me how to heal Quinta."

Sorchia laughed then, a ghost of her former, joyful self. "I'm so glad you said that. Because I can't stand the thought of not being in the world, but I hate the thought of a world without the Emporium even more." She turned her head toward Quinta. Slowly, she ran one hand over the bloody lace shawl. "You've done so well, my dear. Your name will go down in history as one of the great lacemakers. But now you know the terrible secret of the magic."

"I'm done making lace," Quinta said firmly. "I just want to live."

Twain gripped her hand, as if he could hold on to her in that way.

"You will." Sorchia drew in a ragged breath. "The cure is quite simple: Take any of the starlight you have left and boil it for an hour. It will make a shimmering tea that you can drink. Once you've had a cup of that, share some with your friends. Drink a spoonful of this every day for a month, and the starlight in your body will be restored. But don't draw out any more again or you'll undo all the healing."

"I can do that," Quinta said. "Thank you." She brushed a strand of hair behind Sorchia's head gently.

"Be good to each other, my lovely ones," Sorchia whispered. "Kiss each other every morning, find wonder together, and don't forget to laugh each day. This is how you can share a life together."

"We will," Twain promised.

He looked at Quinta then, and she held his gaze. "We will," she echoed.

"Goodbye." Sorchia's hand lifted, settling gently on Quinta's cheek and then moving to Twain's. "You have both done beautifully, and I'm so glad we met each other." A small, secret smile curved Sorchia's lips, and then she took her last breath.

They waited for a long moment, watching Sorchia to see if she had more to say or would suddenly stand up and laugh at them for worrying. But she didn't move.

"I think she's gone," Quinta said softly. "She saved us, and now she's gone." Her voice hitched as she said it.

Twain wiped a tear from the corner of his eye. "She had a good life, though, I think."

Tenderly, Twain shut Sorchia's eyes, and then he took Quinta's hand and helped her to her feet. Together they walked toward the window and stared out at the streets of Severon. They were back in the Vermilion District, and Twain had no doubt Mrs. Davenport would find her way to the shop eventually. As they stood there, Muffin, Sorchia's black dog, barked from the door behind the counter. Twain had nearly forgotten about him, and he let the dog into the main room. Muffin ran over to Sorchia and nudged her with his head. When she didn't move, Muffin made a low, whining noise that sounded entirely like weeping.

Quinta picked up the dog and cradled him. "Can you believe all this is yours?" she asked Twain, gesturing to the shop and all the many mysteries beyond its hidden doors.

"It's ours," Twain corrected, curving an arm around her waist. "You're as much a part of the Emporium as I am." He ran a hand over Muffin's head, which stopped the dog's crooning. The dog nuzzled deeper into Quinta's arms.

"Where shall we go?" Quinta asked.

"Wherever we dream," Twain said. "I want to explore all the secret places in the world with you."

He started to say more, but Quinta put Muffin down and leaned toward Twain. She cupped his face, her lips finding his. Their kiss was long, slow, and sweet. It spoke of goodbyes they'd not had a chance to say, dreams they would find together, and a life full of possibility.

"I love you," Quinta whispered. "I've been meaning to tell you that for weeks now."

Twain's heart leaped to hear that. He closed his eyes for a long moment, resting his forehead against hers. "I love you too. I'm so glad we found each other again."

"Me too."

They kissed until Ruby, Anya, and Chloe woke up.

"Ahem, Quinta," Anya said, clearing her throat.

Quinta pulled her lips hastily away from Twain and smiled at her friends. "I'm glad you're awake," she said. "This is Twain."

Everyone introduced themselves, and Quinta and Twain explained what had happened to Sorchia and how they'd escaped Ixily.

"She was so brave," said Chloe. Awe filled her voice. "She just ran at those soldiers with her pistols."

"She was magnificent," agreed Quinta. "I wish you'd known her."

Twain covered Sorchia—his grandmother (he was still having a hard time seeing her as that)—with a blue silk shawl and rested her on a settee near the bookshelf door. "We will have to bury her, but I'm not sure where."

Quinta went to him, taking his hand. "We'll figure that out soon. First, let's eat, bandage our wounds, and make some of this starlight tea."

"That sounds like a marvelous plan, my love," Twain said, kissing her once again.

#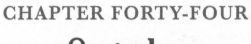

CHAPTER FORTY-FOUR

They buried Sorchia by the sea. They were going to bury her in the city, but Marcel had shown up a few hours after Sorchia's death, wearing a black suit and full of plans for the funeral.

"She would've wanted to look over the water," he said, cradling Sorchia's hand between his. "I know just the spot. It's not far from here." Tenderly, he placed a kiss on the old woman's forehead.

The next afternoon, after they locked the bottled moonshadow in a wardrobe deep in the Emporium and slept for a very long time, Quinta and Twain let Marcel guide them to a spot a few miles outside Severon. It was on a hill high above the water. A tall evergreen tree stood at the crest of the hill, looking out over the coast and the pillars of rock far out to sea. A small horse and cart carried Sorchia's body, wrapped in a starlight lace shroud Quinta had found in the costume room of the Emporium.

Quinta was already feeling better, having had her second cup of starlight tea that morning. Ruby, Anya, and Chloe were also looking better after their own cups of silvery tea. Since they'd not had as much starlight drawn from them as Quinta had, she suspected they'd recover quickly.

The other girls stayed back at the Emporium, watching the shop for Twain and Quinta to give them some time alone with their grief. Anya was entirely smitten with Muffin, and he'd taken to following her everywhere.

"Are you ready?" Twain asked, pulling Quinta out of her thoughts.

He had dug a deep hole beneath the tree and placed Sorchia's body inside it.

"I am," Quinta said.

Walking to the edge of the grave, she said a silent goodbye to Sorchia. "Thank you for bringing us together," she whispered. "And I hope you find another great adventure wherever you are."

Twain took Quinta's hand and together they stood aside as Marcel sang a song in a language Quinta didn't know. It was mournful, sweet, and full of love. Each note burrowed into Quinta's heart, a reminder of how fragile love, life, and time all were.

When they made their way back to the shop, they found the other girls discussing their plans.

"Would any of you like to come with me?" Marcel asked before he left. "Twain? I'm sure your grandmother would've loved it if we spent some time together." He smiled broadly at him, and Quinta laughed at the confused expression on Twain's face. It was a lot to get used to, having a grandfather nearly the same age as yourself.

"I think we're going to stay here for a while," Twain said. "Quinta needs to heal, and then we're going on adventures of our own."

Marcel shrugged. "Suit yourself, my boy. Life is long, and I'm sure we'll run into each other again sometime. You have my card, after all." Marcel turned to the others. "What about you ladies? Anyone want to travel through time and space? I've mapped a new route to a bronze dragon whose scales are supposed to be able to heal any ailment. I'm going to see what I can find."

Ruby and Anya shook their heads at the same time. "We're going to stay here and set up a millinery shop. We want a simple life with work, family, and no more battles."

They held hands and both smiled as their dream was voiced.

Standing to their right, Chloe looked a bit lost and alone. "I'll go with you," she said hesitantly to Marcel. "If we can come back before too long. I always dreamed of a bit more adventure, and the last thing I want to spend my life doing is sewing." She shuddered at the thought.

"I'd be happy to have you on the journey," Marcel said with a smile. "Though your assistance in luring dragons might be needed."

A broad grin split Chloe's face. "I'd like nothing better."

She said a long, tearful goodbye to Anya, promising to come visit whenever she could. She and Ruby also shared a hug, and then she turned to Quinta.

"I don't know if my life is better or worse for knowing you," she said. "But I'm so glad we met."

Quinta hugged her, and Twain handed her a bottle of starlight tea for the journey. Then she and Marcel descended into the room with the dragon bones and disappeared.

Anya and Ruby left not long after that to take Muffin for a walk around Severon. They were looking for a place to live and set up shop, and their pockets were heavy with the gold Twain had found in a drawer behind the Emporium's counter.

Once they were gone, Quinta sank into a couch. Twain brought her another cup of starlight tea. "Tell me about what you did while I was in Ixily," she said.

He told her everything, from how he looked for her on the night of the Casorina's ball, to how Henri and Gustave had nearly beaten him to death, to how he'd met Marcel, to his searches in the Emporium, and his time in Mrs. Davenport's house.

"Oh!" Twain pulled a wrinkled envelope from his pocket. "That reminds me. This is for you."

He handed her the letter, and she gasped when she saw her name in her mother's handwriting across the front.

"How?" she asked, her eyes wide.

"Just read it," Twain urged as he sat down on the sofa next to her.

Quinta shot him a grateful look and began to read.

It was all there: what her mother had been doing when she died, why she wanted the moonshadow, Quinta's family history with the celestial threads, and so much more. As she read, Quinta could hear her mother's voice in her ears. She clutched the letter to her heart when she was done. "Where did you find this?"

"In the Emporium," Twain said. "In a room full of letters."

"I wonder if there are more for us there? Maybe something

from your parents? Or something from Sorchia that will tell you more about the Emporium?"

"I'm not sure," Twain said, standing. His eyes gleamed. "But would you like to go exploring? I bet now that we have the keys to the Emporium, we'll find all sorts of new things. Or are you too tired?"

Quinta smiled up at him, this beautiful, brave boy who had searched the world for her. She finished her starlight tea and got to her feet. "I'm never too tired to explore with you. But this time, we are definitely bringing a lantern and some snacks. Who knows what we'll find and how long we'll be in there."

Twain pulled her in for a kiss. After that, he gathered a bag of snacks and a lantern and offered Quinta his arm.

They walked to the bookcase door and swung it open. The hallway walls were bare, as if the Emporium was waiting for them to fill them with a lifetime of new moments.

"Are you ready?" Twain asked Quinta as they stood on the threshold.

"I've been ready for this my whole life, I think. Let's see what we find."

She stepped into the hallway. Behind them, the bookcase door swung shut, and this time Quinta's heart didn't lurch with fear or panic. She didn't look backward, but rather she stepped forward into an unknown future.

There would be joy and grief; love and loss; laughter and sorrow; but, between them, there would also be magic. So much magic, always.

Quinta squeezed Twain's hand as they reached the first door in the hallway. She'd never seen this particular door. It was dark purple and had small golden butterflies painted all over it.

"Let's try this one."

"After you." An eager, curious look flashed across Twain's face.

Quinta was so glad to have him here beside her.

With a deep breath, Quinta turned the doorknob. As the door swung open, both Quinta and Twain gasped in surprise to see what waited for them on the other side.

Author's Note

Stories, like lives, are strange and take many unexpected turns. For all my planning, this one surprised me many times as it hit the page.

This story has been brewing for years. In part it started on New Year's Eve 2017, when I finished Erin Morgenstern's breathtaking first novel, *The Night Circus*. As I closed the book, I vowed to myself that someday I would write a story that was such a joyful celebration of magic, whimsy, and imagination.

But I didn't know it would be a love story.

Then, a few years later, I read Kate Moore's devastating nonfiction book *The Radium Girls*, about the young female dial painters who used radium to paint luminescent faces of watches. The girls would dip the tips of their paintbrushes in a pot of radium, paint a watch dial, and then lick their brushes to get the tips sharp for the next watch. Over and over they did this, until they started to come down with mysterious ailments. Eventually, many of them died horrific deaths from the radium. My heart broke as I looked at the photos of the Radium Girls in Moore's book, and I longed to write their story. At first, I tried it as a historical YA, but I couldn't get past the fact that all these characters would die in agonizing pain if I stuck to the true story. So, I decided to write a YA fantasy that was a tribute to the Radium Girls, but one that let them stay alive, find love, and see the world. All things the real-life Radium Girls didn't get to do. It wasn't until I started writing that I realized my main female character had to be named Quinta, as a nod to Quinta McDonald, one of the Radium Girls who filed suit against the company who'd let her poison herself day in and day out. Like the real-life Quinta, my Quinta would be brave and bold, and she would glow with beauty, like the Radium Girls did when they went out at night, covered in radium dust.

Since I was writing a tribute to the Radium Girls, I knew the characters would have to make something, and I knew that what they were making had to be deadly to them. But I couldn't figure out what it was for a very long time.

At least, not until I was doing research for another book about Venice, and I stumbled across a fact about how in the sixteenth century, some Venetian lacemakers, most of them young girls, were kidnapped into other countries and courts for their skills. Lace was a sign of prestige and power in those days, and whoever had the best lacemakers would be considered the most powerful people in the world.

405

So, with those crucial pieces in place—this book would be as magical as Erin Morgenstern's books; it would be a romance that paid tribute to the lives of the Radium Girls; and it would also draw on the lives of the kidnapped lacemakers—I knew I had a story.

But what does one call such a book?

I didn't know until I drove past a boutique called the Vermilion Emporium, which was located inside a quaint early-nineteenth-century building, on the edge of a rural, riverside town near my own. This Vermilion Emporium (now defunct) sold women's dresses with lots of sequins on them. But it was such a weird shop name, and one so entirely out of place in this particular town, that I couldn't get it out of my head. Any time I drove past it, I thought: *What if there was a store called the Vermilion Emporium, which sold curiosities and was full of endless rooms that contained magical things?*

And as soon as I thought that, I knew it had to go in the book, which was simply called "The Magical Lacemaker Book" for a long time in my head.

When these four threads of story came together, I knew I had something. Twain started this story stuck on a cliff outside Severon, and I wasn't able to shake him off. Quinta scowled at me across the pages. And as soon as they found each other, the magic really began.

I hope you have found magic in these pages as well.

Acknowledgments

Although *The Vermilion Emporium* was dreamed over many years and it's a story of love and magic, it was forged in tragedy. I wouldn't have made it through 2021 or been able to navigate my overwhelming grief or even have finished this book without the tremendous support of my amazing communities.

Thank you to my brilliant editor and friend, Ashley Hearn. You believed in *The Vermilion Emporium* from the very beginning and your vision helped it become the book I'd only dreamed it could be.

Thank you to my wonderful agent and friend, Kate Testerman. For the good advice, the many brainstorming and check-in emails, and for sending soup when my family needed it.

Thank you to Lisa Marie Pompilio for such a beautiful cover that so perfectly captures the essence of this book.

Thank you to my PitchWars15 family, who showed up in every possible way this last year.

Thank you to my dear friends in the writing world: Lizzy Mason, Jenny Ferguson, M.K. England, Noelle Salazar, Becca Podos, Courtney Gilfillian, Leigh Mar, Kat Hinkel, Cindy Baldwin, Amanda Rawson Hill, Ashley Martin, Heather Murphy Capps, Tracy Gold, Elise Bryant, Grace Li, Amparo Ortiz, and so many others.

Thank you to my dear friends: Cheryl Clearwater and Ashleigh Bunn. Thank you also to Sadie Rogers for making sure E was always deep in an adventure.

Thank you to my sister, Kim Canady, who drove from Tennessee to Wisconsin with her family in a day, just to say hello to us in our darkest time. To Mark Merriman for showing up and keeping us laughing. To my mom who gave me the hug I needed most during those first terrible days in September. To my youngest sister, Margaret Merriman, who loved Twain and Quinta so early on that it made me believe this book was worth writing.

Thank you my Kit Sweetly + Lucky Girl street team. Thank you to Mike Lasagna, Christi Hayes, Aly M, Stephanie Rinaldi, Christine Reed, Stephi Leigh, Rogier Capri, and so many other readers, booksellers, bloggers, bookstagrammers, and other folks who shared the word about my books and helped me celebrate the wins. Thank you also to Vicky Chen for the amazing art.

And, always first in my heart, thank you to my sweet family, Adam, Liam, and Eliot.

Liam: You were brave, kind, funny, and so very sweet. I can't believe you're gone, and I miss you so much. Thank you for your joy and for letting me be your mom. Your story will be one I tell for the rest of my life, and I love you.

Eliot: You are joy. Remember that always. Thank you for that first drawing of Quinta and Twain from 2018, with its reminder to "never give up on your dreams." Your creative spirit, big heart, and sense of humor are a gift, and I love you.

Adam: Thank you for sharing your heart and holding mine so carefully. I'm grateful for it all—the joy, the despair, the darkness, and the light. Thank you for reminding me to breathe, for dancing with me in the kitchen, for getting us outside, and for walking through life with me, no matter what twists and turns it takes. I love you.

About the Author

Jamie Pacton is an award-nominated young adult and middle grade author who writes swoony, funny, magical books across genres. *The Vermilion Emporium* is her YA fantasy debut. When she's not writing, she's teaching college English, obsessively reading obscure history, hiking, baking, or playing video games. *The Life and (Medieval) Times of Kit Sweetly* is her young adult debut, and her sophomore novel, *Lucky Girl*, released from Page Street in May 2021.